1/10/19

Bill + Maurie —

So nice to hear
your voices on the phone!
Hope you enjoy
this narrative.

Blessings,

Ron McCrea
5405 Spyglass Hill Court
BAKERSFIELD, CA
                93309

1-661-397-8945

Ordinary Heroes

Based on a True Story

Ron McCraw

authorHOUSE®

AuthorHouse™
1663 Liberty Drive
Bloomington, IN 47403
www.authorhouse.com
Phone: 1 (800) 839-8640

Published by AuthorHouse   09/30/2017

ISBN: 978-1-4685-9601-4 (sc)
ISBN: 978-1-4685-9602-1 (hc)
ISBN: 978-1-4685-9600-7 (e)

Library of Congress Control Number: 2012907780

Print information available on the last page.

About Ordinary Heroes

ORDINARY HEROES RECREATES the sights, sounds and textures of a world gone by, a world of freedom, innocence and mystery where boys leave home at 6:00 in the morning and return home for dinner: A world of sleep-outs and midnight escapades.

Fourteen-year-old Randy's life begins as a near-death experience. But, cerebral palsy aside, by 1959 he loves Sandra Dee, Sandy Koufax, the Dodgers, Wolfman Jack and a girl named Daisy Clover, in that order.

Things begin to pop when the boys poke around the crumbling old Jefferson place and discover perplexing evidence pointing to something very different than the official version of their neighborhood hero's death: Confusing clues, threatening notes, phone calls and violence. If nineteen-year-old Scotty Jefferson's death is an "open and shut, police slam dunk," why all the fuss?

Ordinary Heroes salutes the goodness of boys everywhere!

Acknowledgements

STARTING A NOVEL is a monumental task. Finishing one is Herculean. This book exists primarily because of the persistent love and support and the hard work of "truth-telling" by a number of folks.

Thanks first to my wife Marti and my kids, Andy and Julie. You guys told me again and again, "Just don't quit" and you put up with my fragile whining and moodiness with grace and patience. Your insights were invaluable.

Thanks to Linda McCarthy for her "butterfly soft" inspiration and for coaxing me into and through Artist's Way. Otherwise, none of this happens. Thanks for being the gentlest cheerleader in my life.

Thanks to all you brave soldiers who read and reviewed chapter-after-chapter through all of my messy fits and starts and who wouldn't quit if I wouldn't: Joyce Aston, Steven Van Metre, Vicki Rathbone, Karl Clark, Sig Fink, Ph.D., Tim Dooley, M.D., and Lew Archer, Ph.D. (Thanks for the Sheriff's badge.) You folks know this book better than I do. Every time we talked, the book got better.

Thanks to Jack Canfield and Steve Harrison at Bradley Communications for publishing insights and inspiration.

Thanks to my daughter Kelsey (1986-2008). You helped me imagine great and perfect things and I miss you every day.

Finally, thanks to all the doctors, nurses and physical therapists who literally straightened me out and taught me not only how to get up but how to fall. I remember each of you.

To my mother and father whose courage and perseverance make everything else pale by comparison. My mother taught me how to care about other people and my father taught me how to work.

To Mark Andrews, Dr. Roger Mitchell, and Larry Barber. I miss you guys every day. You were taken too soon.

To Sandy Koufax and Sandra Dee. You are "such stuff as dreams are made on" (apologies to Shakespeare). I cannot imagine my life without you.

About Language

PROFANITY REFLECTS MORE than a character flaw or a vocabulary deficit. As language, it's an intensifier. Psychologically, it's about power or the lack of it. Folks who feel weak, challenged or incompetent often curse. Verbal aggression sometimes precedes physical violence. People who have enough power, that is, enough money, status, ability, talent or friends—seldom curse. If obviously powerful people, say Marines, curse they are reflecting a need for more power. Think of battlefield language.

The boys in Ordinary Heroes curse a lot. They are battling fear of failure, self-doubt and peer-group comparisons. For them, cursing says, "I am strong enough, I am capable enough, I can do this!" Of course, it is themselves they are trying to convince.

Chapter 1
Cody, Frenchy, and the Field of Dreams

A BRIGHT JULY, late-afternoon breezes slipping through the trees, splotches of light flickering in the shade, I sat comfortably behind the wheel of my Corvette-red, Mazda Miata convertible (muscled-up 2011 model), a monument to my still-fading youth.

What's the line from the old Beatles' song? 'Will you still need me, will you still feed me, when I'm sixty-four?' I'm right there, next October. But, psychologically, youth is always fading. We are always every age we ever were. The fourteen-year-old me is alive and well, right now. The question before the house is simply who's running the show?

I pulled into the lot, settled in a space protected by a massive Sequoia Redwood, opened the passenger door and yelled, "Release."

Cody, my beautiful two-year-old dark-red golden retriever, exploded into the park at full speed, barely touching the ground and getting no attention from the squirrel some thirty yards away. The distance closed to ten yards and the squirrel waited, squirting up the tree at the last second. Cody, a blink too late, skidded—sprawling and spinning to a stop. He smiled his dog smile and looked at me.

I yelled, "Don't look at me! You're supposed to be a bird and water dog, not a tree and squirrel dog."

We stared at each other for a moment.

I said, "Come."

He loped toward me, thumping the green grass and ignoring the boys playing baseball twenty yards to his left. He also ignored birds, squirrels, small children to his right and a billion good smells.

I yelled again, "Good boy!"

As he neared the car, I patted the seat and gave the command, "Jump." Once on the seat, I gave two commands: "Front" and "Dress." Sunlight blinking off his red and gold coat, Cody faced me and waited. I put on his collar, leash and vest. The red vest, trimmed in black, sported a yellow patch with black lettering: "Service Dog Don't Touch."

I labored getting out of the car. A sixty-four-year-old man with Cerebral Palsy who walks with two canes and is forever tangled in hand controls, must labor.

What do those dopey youngsters say? It is what it is? Profound, eh?

I struggled for fifteen minutes. It's not that the car is too small, it's not. It's that I'm too stiff. It's a bit like Chinese handcuffs. It's counter-intuitive. When you want to pull, you've got to push. For me to hurry, I've got to slow down, make my legs think I've forgotten all about them.

It's always been a fragile negotiation.

'Negotiation.' Now, there's a good old Freudian word. Nearly forty years of teaching English and fifteen years of practicing clinical psychology and I still think about that crap. So, here's a news bulletin. Negotiate, horse trade, run a cost/benefit analysis and cut the best deal you can. Bottom line…

Sometimes you eat the bear. Sometimes the bear eats you.

Out of the car, sea legs under me, I closed my door, gave the command, 'jump' followed by 'down/stay.' Cody hit the ground and I closed his door. As it clunked shut, I smacked my hand and my cane flew about five feet and landed in the gutter. So, there I was: able to stand with one cane, but otherwise, utterly stuck.

I said, "Cody."

We made eye contact.

"Release. Come."

Immediately, the big, red, 'chick magnet' came to my side.

I pointed and whispered, "Get it."

In a flash, he picked the cane up by its crooked end. I put out my hand. "Give." He gently dropped the cane in my palm. I gave immediate, effusive praise—many pats and a well-placed kiss or two right between the eyes.

"Good boy! You saved my backside!"

I got doggie acknowledgement: a couple of quick, soft kisses on the hand and a wag or two from that feathery flag of his. Relieved, I wiped the "retriever mouth" off the handle, picked up the leash and headed for the bleachers behind home plate.

Cody earned his money. He kept in step with my halting, erratic gait, maintaining the correct distance without pulling. It's quite a sight, the two of us paying close attention to the other's four legs.

We reached the bleachers behind home plate. Solid aluminum, guaranteed to scorch any clothing on the planet.

I put Cody on a 'Down/Stay' in the shade underneath and decided to stand for an inning or two. Through the netting on the backstop, I studied the scoreboard in left field. Two outs, bases loaded, bottom of the ninth, 1-1 tie. The kid coming to the plate, fifteen-year-old Frenchy Cohen, his once-white uniform now covered in dirt, grimy adhesive tape on his right forearm. He was not big, like his older brothers, but sleek and strong like a race car. He looked good in the uniform, like Shoeless Joe Jackson in *Field of Dreams.*

Field of Dreams triggered childhood memories...

No grass or dirt or uniforms, no wooden bats or hardballs, just an ugly asphalt cul-de-sac and plastic stuff. But, we did play baseball in my neighborhood and I did play—canes and all. Nobody would believe it today. Politically incorrect. Crippled kid gets hurt. Law suit. No risking rejection or ridicule.

What junk...

There was a meeting at the mound, the entire infield.

A guy near-by gave me the game-wide context. Frenchy was 2 for 2 with a walk and a stolen base. His second hit (last inning) was a home run to tie the score. A line drive down the left field line, it was fair by less than a foot and came after the pitcher knocked Frenchy down twice.

In a wider context, I knew the Cohen family well. Frenchy's older twin brothers (Roman and Berlin) were in my English class some years back, good kids. Frenchy's real name? Paris, what else?

As the mound conference broke up, I felt a strong arm around my shoulder. Coming down from the top bleachers, Moshe Cohen stood next to me: Big man, round face, bushy eyebrows and broad smile.

He and I became good friends eight years ago. As the older Cohen twins finished their freshman year in my class, Moshe requested that they continue with me for grades 10, 11 and 12. At the end of the twins' sophomore year, I told their father I was not scheduled for English 11, but I would look forward to seeing them in English 12.

He smiled, shook my hand warmly, thanked me and gave me a dozen assorted doughnuts "Courtesy of the Cohen Bakery."

The following fall, I was surprised to find English 11 on my schedule and the Cohen boys on my first period roll. I learned later that Moshe met with my principal and asked that I be assigned English 11 for one year so that his boys "might have a perfect record."

When asked why this was so important, he said it was a scheduling coincidence for the teacher and "the Will of God" for his boys. The principal laughed, suggested that the will of a motivated father was in there somewhere as well and asked why I was so important. Moshe laughed too and said, "What you say about God's will and a father's will, it is indeed a very Jewish thing to say."

He added that he knew *Merchant of Venice* was eleventh grade reading ("a play with a Jew in it") and that I would be "fair about it." Moshe enjoyed theological discussions, appreciated my seminary training and liked me "because I like anybody who likes my boys!"

****

When I looked up, Moshe's voice welcomed me. He grinned and sounded quintessentially Jewish, whatever that means.

"Ah, my Christian friend! Good to see you! You look good for an older man." He laughed, winked and reached for my hand. "You are late, you know this? It is the ninth inning."

I switched both canes to my left hand and extended my right. We shook hands, hard. I could not see his face. Cloudless, the sun was too bright. What players call a "high sky." Tough to get perspective on a fly ball.

He grinned bigger than life and gently nudged my shoulder. "We end this game, right now, eh?" He paused. "Shall we ask for divine intervention?"

I grinned. "Couldn't hurt."

The big man looked around. "So, where is this beautiful dog of yours? Is it a Christian dog, right?"

I pointed. "Right behind you, down low. And he is whatever I am, plus whatever I say he is."

Moshe laughed. Cody's nose was peeking out. "Smart dog. Outta the heat. Smarter than us, eh?"

"Uh huh," I agreed, "about a lot of things."

Things were heating up on the field. Bases loaded no outs, infield and outfield pulled in. Cut off the run at the plate. Crowd yelling, infield chattering, both benches hanging on dugout railings. Coaches clapping.

Another time out. Pitcher and catcher whispering into gloves.

"So," I asked, "where are Frenchy's big brothers?"

Moshe frowned. "Are you kidding? They are where they should be. At the bakery, working. Frenchy's mother, she is up top. Nobody tells that woman what to do."

He threw up a right thumb like he was calling a third strike. I turned, found the petite Mrs. Cohen and waved. She smiled and waved.

I turned to Moshe and we looked at the field. "You know, I played baseball when I was a kid, thirteen or fourteen, pitcher. I was pretty good, too."

Moshe's eyebrows jumped. He stepped back, his voice high-pitched and awkward. "What?! You play this?"

I put my index finger to my lips, "Shh" and pointed to the field.

Frenchy stepped to the plate, all business: open stance bent slightly at the knees and waist, fingers curled around the end of the bat.

The pitcher, all arms and legs, went into an exaggerated wind up, unfolded in sections and finished in a whiplash. Amazingly, even with all those moving parts, the ball came out smoothly, blazing right under Frenchy's chin.

He leaned back an inch.

"Ball one."

The crowd screamed. The umpire called time and dusted home plate.

"Jesus," I said to Moshe, "how fast is he?"

Moshe spat and coughed, eyes riveted. "Fast enough. Ninety, maybe. Easy enough to hit. It is straight. Problem is, he's got a slider, breaks down and away. Looks just like the fastball, until the last second."

"Curve?"

"No," he scratched his head. "Big, flat. Telegraphs it."

"What did Frenchy hit last time?"

"Curve. He will stay away from it now."

Full wind up again, fastball at his belt buckle, Frenchy jack-knifed and staggered across home plate.

"Ball two."

More screaming in the bleachers, more fidgeting on the field.

The next fastball was right at Frenchy's head. Moshe yelled and stomped. Frenchy collapsed like an accordion.

"Ball three."

Slowly, mayhem in the stands, Frenchy scraped himself together, walked to the on-deck circle, wiped his hands and returned.

That's when I heard it.

Two guttural voices, same twisted mind.

"Hey, kike!"

"Hey, Jew-boy! Let's see you hit it now."

I snapped a quick glance at father and son. Neither had reacted.

The pitcher's eyes were wild, like something trapped. He took the stretch position.

Moshe whispered, "Curve."

Out came a slow sloppy big old hanging rainbow. Flat, right over the middle of the plate. Batting practice. Frenchy's eyes grew as big as Christmas. He swung so hard his helmet came off and he fell to one knee. But, he fouled it straight back, the crowd's gasp rolling in like an ocean wave.

"Strike one!"

I looked around, searching for those ugly voices. I wondered if anybody else was searching. Moshe's eyes never left his boy.

The next pitch looked like a major league fastball. Knee high, right over the outside corner, a perfect pitch. Frenchy was ready and he was right on it. Good, compact swing, another foul straight back.

"Three balls, two strikes!"

Another wave of noise, now subsiding. Frenchy collected himself and refocused.

Suddenly, I heard it again.

"That's two, Jew-boy! Go home now! Don't need yer kind!"

"Take that big honker with you!"

Frenchy called time, stepped out of the batter's box, used the rosin bag on his hands, searched the stands for a moment and looked directly at his father.

Moshe mouthed one word, "Slider."

The frenzied crowd settled and seemed to hold its breath. Frenchy re-entered the box. There was no breeze. The umpire called time and dusted home plate again. The crowd grumbled and shifted, bleachers groaning.

Moshe mumbled, "Shit."

I looked behind me. Cody was asleep.

The skinny baby-faced pitcher released a torrid fastball toward the inside corner and at the last second it broke to the outside. With a flick of the wrist, Frenchy crushed it—a high fly ball to deep right centerfield. The crowd exploded.

Everybody knew it immediately. They heard it before they saw it. A sweet, solid, deep sound. Not a crack or a thump, but the sound of a monster home run. 350 feet and nobody there to catch it. If you ask Frenchy Cohen, he will say, "So smooth, you never even feel it.'

The crowd was schizophrenic. Joy and grief screaming at one another, bleachers rumbling and shaking.

I looked at Moshe.

He grinned, winked, whistled and yelled, "That slider–good pitch."

Frenchy was rounding third, victory mob waiting at home plate.

I yelled, "Doughnuts for everyone!"

Moshe frowned. "No, just team and you and your Christian dog. You come tomorrow morning, coffee too."

I could not get the smile off my face.

Suddenly, the earthquake stopped.

I turned down the offer. "Cody and I can't do doughnuts. He's too young and I'm too old."

Moshe threw his unlit, half-chewed cigarette on the ground, crushed it and bear-hugged his boy who greeted me with a smile.

"Where's Cody," he puffed, "did he see my home run?"

I pointed to the now-empty bleachers. Cody was still out.

Suddenly, Mrs. Cohen was there–hugging her boy and rushing back to the bakery. Beaming, she whispered, "Nice to see you" and squeezed my wrist as she left.

I said, "Cody, come."

Immediately, he was up and out. He stretched, yawned, shook and stood beside me. I said, "Release" and he went straight to Frenchy.

I stuck out my hand. "Great game, kid!"

He was glowing and his team did not want to leave.

He was catching his breath. "Thanks, I was just lucky enough to get that one."

Moshe winked again. "My baby son is very lucky and also very good!"

Cody was gently mouthing Frenchy's wrist.

I apologized. "He wants to play. Must have forgotten he's working."

"No," Moshe shook his head, "you are the one who said, 'Release.'"

I turned to Frenchy. "Son, I gotta question. When you crush a ball like that, does it sting like crazy?"

"No sir," he smiled. "It's real sweet and smooth. Don't feel a thing."

I smiled, sat on the bench, petted Cody and took a deep breath. "That's what I thought."

The crowd was leaking out, glory already fading.

Suddenly, it was just the Cohens and Cody and me.

I said, "Maybe you guys don't want to talk about this, but I heard those voices today, same as you."

Moshe's shoulders slumped. His voice was tired. "Best to leave it alone or it gets worse."

Frenchy looked like a loser. He did not speak.

I looked at the ground. "Okay, we'll leave it alone. We won't talk." I looked up. "But, I'm going to say a few things and if what I say is true, put your right thumb up, otherwise leave it down. This is just between us." I paused. "One more thing. Don't lie. I'll know it. Don't hesitate. Probably means you're lying. And, even if your thumbs lie, the rest of your body will tell the truth. Remember gentlemen, you can't bullshit a bullshitter."

Moshe shrugged and Frenchy laughed.

I laughed too. "Now, don't look at each other. Moshe, look at the parking lot and Frenchy, you look at centerfield."

Moshe said, "Suppose we don't want to do this?"

I shrugged. "That's okay. Nobody said you had to want to do this. I don't care what you want. You are free to want whatever you want. Who am I, God? But, while you're busy not wanting to do this, let's do it! Okay, quick now:

1. I've received threatening letters or notes. (Frenchy, up.)

2. I've received threatening phone calls. (Frenchy. up.)

3. My property has been damaged. (Two thumbs up.)

4. My pets have been hurt or killed. (Two thumbs up.)

5. I have plans to defend myself and I have a weapon. (Two thumbs up.)

6. This has been going on for more than two months. (Two thumbs up.)

"In the last two months:

1. Trouble sleeping/sleeping too much (Frenchy)

2. Trouble concentrating (Two thumbs)

3. Bad dreams (Two thumbs)

4. Headaches (Frenchy)

5. Short temper (Moshe)

I heaved a big sigh. "We're done."

Moshe spoke, "What does this all prove?"

8

"On one hand," I said, "not much. It's pretty rough. On the other hand, there are a few things you better take to the bank:

1. Little problems, if ignored, do not go away. They get bigger.

2. You have both been under a lot of stress and each of us has a breaking point. It's not if, it's just when.

3. These people are cowards, but they aren't going away. They are dangerous—and it might get much worse before it gets better.

4. Take care of yourselves.

• Do not go places alone.

• Use cell phones. Let people know where you are.

• Be on the lookout for anything out of the ordinary.

• Alert your neighbors, friends and family.

• Get as many people as you can to take a self defense class with you.

• Maybe get licensed for pepper spray."

The father crossed his arms and planted himself, blocking the sun. "Perhaps you make too much of this."

Frenchy walked over, sat next to Cody and began petting him. I stood and walked a bit to loosen up. Cody left Frenchy and came to my side. I grabbed the end of the leash and wrapped it around my palm.

I looked Moshe in the eye. "I might be—but monkeys might fly out of my butt, too."

Moshe shook his head and rubbed the back of his neck, Frenchy cracked up and Cody cocked his head in my direction.

I pushed my advantage. "Can we afford to be wrong about this?" Before he could answer, I pushed again. "You gotta report this or I will. Lieutenant Kenny Sorrell, Police Department. Good kid. In my class a thousand years ago. Tell him I sent you."

Moshe caved. "I will."

I said, "Call when you get home. Maybe a patrol car can show on your street tonight." I pushed one more time. "Look, I'm worried. Promise me you'll talk to a shrink about this—all of you, everybody."

Frenchy asked, "Why can't we talk to you?"

"Lots of reasons. Main one: I don't do it anymore." I looked at Moshe. "I'll call Esther tomorrow and give her three names to call."

He nodded. "Tonight I talk to her. Tomorrow, I will talk to the crew."

I returned to the bench and motioned for everybody to huddle up. Cody stuck his nose in also.

"I want to remind you guys that God saves us through more things than He ever saves us from. Remember:

'I walk through the Valley of the Shadow of Death and Thy rod and thy staff, they comfort me.' (Psalm 23)

'Some trust in chariots, and some in horses; but, we will remember the name of the Lord our God.' (Psalm 20)'"

It was quiet.

I reached inside my shirt and pulled out the silver Star of David attached to the chain around my neck. "Moshe, remember when you gave me this a few years back? I was struggling and I read about Joseph's brothers selling him into slavery. He says, 'They meant this for evil, but God meant this for my good.'"

Moshe's eyes twinkled. "You are right. God thwarted evil and saved him. But, do not forget. Joseph was a self-centered little jerk."

We all laughed.

"My point exactly!" I said. "See, there's hope for you!"

Laughter subsided.

I prayed, "God, we know you love the Cohen family. Please keep 'em safe. Amen."

The Cohens began walking toward the parking lot. Moshe yelled, "Tomorrow morning, you come! Take up your old, low down ways and corrupt the dog as well."

I yelled, "Trying to corrupt me? I thought you were a good guy!"

Moshe laughed. "Who told you that?"

****

The entire park now in shade, I looked at the field. In my mind's eye, I saw a field from my childhood. Beautiful, too, but in a different way.

Cody nudged my knee.

I stood, grabbed the leash and headed toward the car. As soon as we arrived, I opened the door and gave the command. Cody jumped into my seat, crossed the center console and settled in the passenger seat. I turned my back on him, sat in my seat and glanced back.

I swiveled, grabbed my right leg, pulled it in, shifted my weight, pulled my left leg in and began wrestling everything into place. I followed Cody's line of sight: He was locked on a squirrel some thirty yards away.

I used a firm voice, "No. Leave it."

Cody cocked his head toward me.

I spoke softer, "No chance, pal. No rematch today."

My legs and feet were straight and my canes were next to Cody. I leaned forward, brought my seat-back to a 90 degree angle, pulled the seat itself forward, locked my seat belt and closed the door. Another fifteen minute victory.

I get to heaven... I swear. First thing I'm gonna do is hurry.

I laughed.

Talkin' to myself about heaven. Psych tests will say I'm crazy.

I pulled out of the lot, fully intending to hit the drive-thru on my way home. I swore the retriever to secrecy and then shared, "You know, as weird as it seems, I really did play baseball as a kid. I did lots of stuff. You shoulda been there. You woulda loved Rocket and Renfro. They are the reason I got you."

He looked interested.

I sighed. "What do you know? You're just a dog."

He looked at me as if to say, "Hey, I know a lot."

I popped in a CD. Paul McCartney sang sweet and clear.

I'm fixing a hole where the rain gets in
And stops my mind from wandering
Where it will go,
I'm filling the cracks that ran through the door
And kept my mind from wandering
Where it will go

I picked up my drive thru contraband. All that stuff I am not supposed to eat because of all of my old guy ailments. I drove about half a mile and parked next to the golf course, shaded by one of its biggest trees. I bribed the retriever with a French fry.

The music, the food, the dog and me: We all made each other better. I replayed the song until the cheeseburger, French fries, chocolate cake and evil Coca-Cola were gone.

Somewhere in those replays, my mind floated to another hot July some fifty years ago...

Chapter 2
Baseball, Kool-Aid and Housecoats

MID-JULY MORNING, LATE 1950's, California's Central Valley sweltering. Shimmering heat waves rolling up from the sticky asphalt, I stood on the chalk-circle mound at one end of the street where the bottle neck begins to open on the cul-de-sac. I leaned in toward the chalk-drawn home plate, rested my weight on my left side, left hand holding both of my canes tightly. The ball in my right hand, my tee shirt already ropes of sweat. I tried to wipe my forehead and eyes. No good. I looked behind me: Everybody focused and noisy, outfielders backed up to concrete curbs fronting neighborhood yards.

The rule was simple: Any ball hit out of the cul-de-sac was a home run. Outfielders were allowed to run to the curb, reach over it or step up on top of it and jump for the ball. If the fielder made the catch while in the air, the batter was out. If the fielder landed first and then made the catch, the batter circled the bases for a home run. Neighborhood legend hung in the air, stories of sprawling, tumbling catches, of sacrifice-your-body, head-first-dives, of crushed hedges and scrambled rose bushes.

Both the ball and my pitching hand were wet. I took turns wiping each on my right thigh. No good. The ball was a piece of work: hard plastic, solid through and through. Long ago, after a few broken windows and most particularly a broken windshield, we were forced to give up the traditional hard ball and wooden bat in favor of plastic all around. But, in those days, a bat and ball of solid plastic could do almost as much damage.

We had been playing since 8 o'clock in the morning. By 10:30, bottom of the ninth, two out, bases loaded, score knotted at 4, best hitter in the neighborhood coming to the plate. Andy Anderson was a thin kid, medium build, better than average looking. He had strong hands and wrists and lightning reflexes and was the most well-liked kid in the neighborhood.

I was a pitcher because it was the only position I could play. Born three months premature, I was diagnosed with Cerebral Palsy. Having endured many major surgeries, hundreds of hours of physical therapy, stretching and weightlifting, I was a strong kid. I was out there because I was expected to contribute. That said, a few accommodations were made for me: In the field, if a ball hit me while in the air, the batter was out. At the plate, I batted with one hand and a teammate ran for me.

Andy stepped to the plate, took a few practice swings, and smiled. "Hey, it's game over time for you! Besides, I want some of that cherry Kool-Aid over there." He jerked his head toward a tree in foul territory shading a 5 gallon barrel supplied by the twins, Danny and Davie.

I grinned. "Shut up!"

My catcher squatted, waggled the first two fingers on his right hand and slapped the inside of his thigh. I came straight overhand and snapped off a curve. Andy swung so hard he staggered and fell to one knee: Strike one.

I looked in again. "Nice swing, loser! Want some Kool-Aid now?"

The catcher squatted again, waggled one finger this time and patted the air, palm down. I came side arm and fired a fastball, low and outside. Again, Andy swung from his heels—and this time he connected.

Instantly, a scorching line drive crushed my right ankle. I couldn't get enough air to scream. I crumpled to the ground, sticky asphalt burning my left arm. I looked at my right shoe. A thin, razor-sharp steel pin had exploded through muscle, bone, sock and shoe, sticking up about an inch.

Everyone gathered, eyes wide, mouths open. I got some air and started yelling about the street. Suddenly, hands from everywhere lifted and we moved awkwardly and settled under a nearby tree. Somebody ran to get my dad. He looked at my shoe, took out his handkerchief and told me to look away. I felt a sharp jolt and it was over. He held up a steel pin about four inches long. He wiped his face with his handkerchief, laid the pin on the grass and opened a first aid kit. He carefully removed my shoe. Surprisingly, the bloody sock came off easily. No big pain, more like a cramp. No more blood, just a tiny dark hole. My dad cleaned the area with alcohol, covered the spot with a band aid, carefully tested my ankle and replaced the shoe. "Let's see if you can stand." He lifted me. I took a step or two and smiled. He smiled back.

Suddenly, fire yelled from my left arm. After a minute or so, hot water cleared the neighbor's garden hose and my dad began rinsing blood, dirt and asphalt. The arm felt better as long as the water covered it. But as soon as the water stopped, the scrape burned and looked angry.

My dad covered the area with gauze and adhesive tape. I told him I was okay. He patted me on the back, picked up the pin, told me to be careful and headed home.

Andy yelled, "Cherry Kool-Aid!"

Everyone roared. Nothing ever tasted better. I gulped down a glass, wiped my lips with a forearm and looked at Andy. "You were out on that line drive."

He laughed. "Rematch, right now. Same teams."

I walked out to the pitcher's circle.

Jesse Parker was a small guy with crooked teeth, dirty blonde hair, a surly attitude, a foul mouth, a splotchy complexion and a reputation for lying.

He spat in my direction. "What in hell is wrong with yer foot? Shit, man! Shit coming outta yer shoe?! That is messed up."

I looked where he spat and glared. Part of me wanted to kick his butt.

When I was little, my feet turned out bad. Doctors put six steel pins in each ankle to make everything straight. When the casts came off, they pulled out two from each foot. The others were supposed to stay forever. The one today was one of the forever ones.

Jesse spat again. "Hey, I never told you guys about the operations I had on my kidneys, did I?"

Groaning and grumbling everywhere, eyes rolling. The twins, Danny and Davie, spoke like a chorus. "You," they smirked, "are a lying piece of crap!"

"No," Jesse protested, "I mean it! It's true. I swear to God. I ain't shittin' you guys. You can ask my sister."

Fat Jim, a really nice kid who was simply fat, picked up his glove. "Let's just play, okay?"

Fielders started moving.

Jesse screamed, "What do you know about anything, fat ass? Shut up, before I kick your ass!"

Jim shrugged. Andy stepped in. "We don't want to know anything about your dumb-assed kidneys, Jesse. Shut up."

Jesse picked up his glove and started home. Over his shoulder, he snarled, "Jerk off losers! Don't need you anyway. Live with my cousins in LA for a whole month, go to Dodger games for free every night. So, screw you guys, alla you!"

We watched him go.

Andy shook his head. "Dumb-assed liar."

In spite of his troubles, we had reasons for putting up with Jesse. Loser or not, he was still one of the guys and he wasn't going anywhere. Plus, he

15

would often seem sorry for his ways. So, when all was said and done, who cared? He'd be better tomorrow or not.

But, the most powerful reason for putting up with Jesse was his 16 year old sister, Jade. She was two years older and she was fearless. She would do things other girls would never do. Not because anybody dared her, but because she wanted to. A few pounds lighter and she would have been drop-dead beautiful. Her face was pretty, but hard—even when she smiled. Like her brother, she wanted attention and she didn't mind picking a fight. She'd walk by in a razor-thin bikini and slow down. If you didn't look, she'd smirk, "Gay boy," and laugh. If you did look, she'd stare daggers. "Take a picture stupid, lasts longer."

Jade adventures were the stuff of many late night confessions and lies. My own "Jade Episode" was neither confession nor lie. It was more like an eyes-wide-open dream.

On an otherwise meaningless Saturday morning, my mother sent me across the street to borrow a cube of butter. I rang the doorbell and waited. Jade answered and asked what I wanted. She was wearing a quilted housecoat, unbuttoned, nothing underneath. I was speechless. My universe stopped.

She widened her stance, placed her right hand on her hip and fully opened the housecoat. I did not move. I did not blink.

Irritated, she again asked me what I wanted. I stammered something about a cube of butter. She told me to wait right there. She returned in a minute or so with a cube of butter—and absolutely no sign of a housecoat.

She smiled, slowly turning a complete circle. "What's the matter? Don't you like what you see?"

I whispered a crunchy, "Yes."

She gave me the butter and closed the door. I could hear her laughing. I somehow made it back home. I was buzzing. I didn't care that she was mean or hard or scary. She was the most beautiful thing I had ever seen. I simply wanted to remember everything. And though the images faded, their effects lasted forever. For this reason alone, I put up with Jesse Parker.

Cherry Kool-Aid finished, we lost our rematch 5-4 in ten innings and I walked home. I took off my shoe, looked at the small hole in my foot, put the shoe back on and thought about Jesse and Jade and the housecoat.

Chapter 3
I Show Up Early

CODY NOSED THE bag of French fries and jolted me back to the present and the golf course. I quickly saved him from all that bad nutrition, but his sweet face and gentle stare broke me down. I could feel my resolve leaking. I could almost hear him.

"I'm your best friend, your buddy. And I'm out in the cold on the French fries? I thought you were better than that."

I caved. "I can't leave you out, pal."

Wait a minute. Forget about emotions. Think, McFly. Think!

Trainers say that dogs get as much reinforcement from one pat on the head as twenty, as much pleasure from one small treat as twenty big ones.

How do they know that? Some psych dweebs out in a field somewhere giving dogs single and multiple pets and treats—counting how many trials it takes for the response to extinguish? Maybe the dogs are counting how many times the dweebs give treats, until the dweeb response extinguishes. Good idea for a Far Side cartoon... Too bad he retired.

I reached to the bottom of the bag, searching for the runt, the fry that would give my dog the most pleasure and do the least damage. I found it and held it out. Cody took it gently and settled. I ate a few and I settled too. It was quiet and comfortable.

For a moment, I thought about the Cohens...

I hope this thing doesn't blow up. I can't be the only one who heard those idiots...

In a bit, I returned to my memories. It was an easy return. I've heard the stories so many times—from everybody who was there. These memories are as real as anything I know...

****

It was just a flicker past the end of World War II and she was an early-bloomer, a 14 year old who looked 25. My grandparents signed off on the marriage. A diminutive 5' 4" with curves in the right places, my mother was a young woman who knew what she wanted. And on this nasty, cold, cloudy, wet October day, she wanted to get this over. Her water had broken some ten minutes ago and her younger sister, my aunt Coleen, sat next to her in the back seat and tried to shield her from the muddy, sliding, bumpy insults of the 20 mile roller-coaster to the nearest hospital.

My mother sat on soaking towels, held on tight and tried to smile. "You gotta hurry up! Please!"

It was all she could do to get those words out. She thought she was screaming, but neither her sister, nor my 21 year old father (sweating in the driver's seat) heard her. The old car simply lumbered forward, wipers useless against the rain, tires useless against the unkempt pavement.

My mother shrieked. So, my father put the accelerator to the floor and tried to assure everyone. But, unable to turn his head, his words also went unheard. His heart refused to settle and every now and then he remembered to breathe. He had married because that's what people in 1945, in California's Central Valley did.

My father was a skinny, handsome, angular, dark-eyed, dark-haired boy with fine features and a tenth grade education. He worked 10-12 hour days at 40 cents per hour in the packing sheds, six days a week—and he was going to be a millionaire. He joked with friends, "I just gotta work enough hours!"

Everyone laughed. But, secretly, in his own 21 year old mind, he meant it.

My mother screamed again and she pushed. She tried to will everything to a halt, but there was no stopping. In a flood of blood and water, the baby was out, cradled and covered in a towel. My aunt held the bundle. There was no crying baby, only the whining of an old, overworked transmission. Ten minutes later (two hours in my mother's mind) the old car lurched into the hospital parking lot.

Jumping out before it stopped, my father left his door open, sprinted through the Emergency Entrance, grabbed someone in a white coat and said, "Better get out here quick! We gotta dead baby out here!"

The doctor came running, opened the passenger door, smiled at my mother and gently took the bundle from my aunt. She turned back a corner of the towel, immediately flipped the baby face-down and began clearing his breathing passages.

"This baby's alive!" she said, cutting the umbilical cord and continuing to clear mucus. "We've got to be quick about this."

She turned to my father. "You come with me, now."

To my mother, she smiled. "Congratulations, you have a fine boy! You wait right here, we'll send some folks out to get you. Are you okay?" She didn't wait for an answer. "We'll get you checked out, right away."

She turned away, nodded in my father's direction and headed quickly to the Emergency doors. She held the baby close, shielding him from the rain.

My father hurried too, barely keeping pace.

My mother did not see me again for a week and only then, through a window. Masked, smiling nurses held a cigar box to the glass. I entered the world at three pounds and two ounces and immediately lost weight to two pounds eight ounces. My mother walked two miles every day—one up and one back—to the nearest pay phone. Every day she heard those same words, "He's still here! He's doing fine!" My given name was Ronald but everybody called me Randy. I do not know why.

My mother held me for the first time, exactly eight weeks after that bloody day in the parking lot and I came home four weeks later, sporting a full four pounds and five ounces!

The intensive care nurses cried when I left.

****

The day after I was born, my father visited his favorite neighborhood bar, "High Pockets." A tall, neon cowboy, High Pockets himself, stood on the roof above the doorway and waved his hat. He was nothing if not welcoming.

Ten o'clock at night, after a 14 hour day in the sheds, my father waved one arm-full of cellophane-wrapped cigars, each proudly sporting a red and gold foil ring proclaiming, "It's A Boy!" In the other arm, he held a mass of blue metal buttons which also declared the cigar message. He was so stuffed with cigars and buttons that he needed help opening the door. Once inside, he saw a few friends and began plowing his way through the smoke and noise, motioning with his head and body, smiling and saying to one and all, "Take a button, have a cigar!"

Trailing quietly behind him on the sawdust covered floor, a thin line of caked-on mud falling from his hair, shirt, pants and work boots. He was smiling through the smoke, like sunshine through rain. Folks were hugging him, slapping him on the back. He was losing some cigars and some buttons—and some more dirt. He emptied what was left in his arms on the bar and someone gave him a tall glass of cold beer.

Everyone raised a glass and someone yelled, "Hey, whadya have?"

My father trumpeted, "A boy!"

Someone clunked money in the juke box, punched A-14 and yelled, "This here is for your boy!"

Suddenly, Hank Williams' plaintive, "Your Cheatin' Heart" blared and everyone laughed. Before my dad could speak, the voice came again. "Sorry! Meant to punch A-15." Quiet settled for a moment and out came Hank's "Jambalaya."

A few beers later, someone asked, "So, just how big's this new boy?"

My father stood and saluted. "Three pounds, two ounces!"

They laughed my father out of that bar.

Chapter 4
Saw Horses and Stretching Boards

AFTER NEARLY TWO months, her figure now recovered, my mother rescued her baby from the professionals. Itching with fear and excitement and fiercely defensive, she simply did not know what to do. Home was a dreary little place: 800 square feet, one bedroom, cardboard-thin construction with a crumbling, motley, composition roof.

No yard, only a postage stamp of scruffy dirt. No trees or intended plants. A two-sided, broken down chain link fence in the front, the third side a shoddy grape stake. The place was a life-sized roach motel: The cheap linoleum floor, freezing cold at night, cracked like crinoline under the lightest step. And whatever the cold left in-tact at night, the blazing sun blistered in the day time.

In the beginning, everything seemed fine: Happy baby, good appetite, aware, responsive. But by seven months, something wasn't right. When placed on a rug or floor, the baby didn't crawl, but rather dragged himself from place to place using his forearms. His legs were stiff and returned to a constant scissor position when not physically corrected. The legs looked fine and although the baby showed no distress, his parents worried.

The company doctor for DeCarlo Farms set broken bones, passed out pills, applied ointments and bandages, and occasionally amputated a crushed or otherwise severely mangled limb. But he was over-matched in matters concerning me.

By contrast, my grandmothers were wise women who offered encouragement and minimized as much else as possible. Both came to California from Oklahoma's dust bowl. The Great Depression had stolen youth, drained beauty, taken loved ones and preyed on their minds. Each carried the fire of heaven in her eyes. Yet, in small, secret looks, they, too, were afraid for me.

My father's mother, Ruby, died of cancer before I was one year old, so I knew as little of her as she did of me. On the other hand, my mother's mother, Marie, lived until the end of my eighth grade year when she, too, died of cancer.

She had been dying for some months, when I decided to go see her. I was apprehensive. My mother said the decision was mine and though I needed her help, somehow I couldn't ask.

I entered a dark, cramped little house and went down a tight, dark hallway to a small, nearly-empty room. The bright September outside made me almost blind in that room. I stood in the corner, my eyes slowly focusing.

My mother spoke, "Mamma, Randy's here to see you."

My grandmother had been lying on her side. She turned, momentarily, to me and then turned away. She may have been crying.

I never spoke. What I saw attacked me.

Where is my grandmother?

I saw something shriveled and diminished in every way: A very tiny person, like a baby.

Where is my grandmother?

I saw paper-thin skin, and a translucent, blue, useless shower cap. The bed covers were flat.

Where is my grandmother?

Her eyes were watery and sunken, almost violent. My mother moved toward the door. I followed, paused at the doorway and looked back. My grandmother's face was buried in a pillow. I never spoke. Years later, I was told that my grandmother had requested no visitors. She could not bear to be seen. To this day, I regret my visit.

Where are my grandmothers today? At this very moment, they are alive and well in a place where perfect is as effortless as breathing. Memories healed and restored, they are not limited by space and time. If happiness is the pursuit of virtue, then my grandmothers are finally happy.

From that frantic, fear-laden drive to the hospital, to my bloody entrance that day in the parking lot, my grandmothers prayed and waited and decided that the best way to help me was to help my young, lost parents.

So, as I neared seven months of age, both my grandmothers accompanied my mother and me to the hospital. Covering the same dusty, erratic twenty miles, in the same flimsy car, the only thing different was the quality and texture of the fear. This time the nagging question was not about my survival, but rather, what kind of life I might expect, given whatever my problems might be.

Enter any pediatric ward and check the doctor's notations on the clipboard at any newborn's bed and you will often see one or both of these very cryptic messages: "FLK/GOK." After all of the poking and prodding, after all the consulting and questioning, the considered opinion of the current medical brain trust regarding this child comes down to FLK—Funny Looking Kid or GOK—God Only Knows. While FLK didn't fit, all my mother could think was "God Only Knows."

Fifty-plus years ago, my young parents didn't know that low birth weight, premature birth and a very young mother make for a bad outcome, what some doctors call "a bad baby." The diagnosis for me was quick, if not clean: Cerebral Palsy. Then, as now, CP was and is a "garbage pail" term used to identify a range of disorders unified by two criteria: 1) brain damage occurring at or near birth, and 2) damage limited to motor skills alone: all higher order mental functioning, by definition, unharmed. So, depending upon the degree of damage, CP presents very differently across a spectrum. Mild to moderate cases include balance, coordination and/or posture issues which call for using canes, crutches or other walking or sitting aids. Movements are often asymmetrical and awkward. Severe CP includes all of the mild signs and adds the following: spasticity, facial contortions, uncontrolled head movements, difficulty biting, chewing or swallowing, excessive sweating and the over production of saliva. Severe CP demands wheelchairs, physical restraints, protective head gear and computer-assisted speech technology.

In the months that followed our return to the hospital, my mother and grandmothers learned more about how life was going to change for me as well as them:

- The baby will not recover, nor will he ever be cured.

- He will never be "normal" as that term is typically used.

- Immediate as well as long term medical intervention is required.

- His overall level of function and quality of life can improve.

- His symptoms can be managed.

My family also learned the pain of mistaking a predicament for problem. By definition, a problem has a solution just as a question has an answer. But, more importantly, a predicament, also by definition, has no satisfactory solution. We can find out who served as the fourteenth President of the United States and we can know with certainty the number that results from adding 5 plus 4. But, what about the death of a friend or the deep insatiable need for the baby with Cerebral Palsy to be whole and healthy? These last two situations are predicaments whose reality must eventually be accepted, lived and managed. There are no satisfactory answers for predicaments.

Looking endlessly for non-existent answers only destroys those who do so.

****

When we returned home from the hospital the second time, nothing happened. Managing my Cerebral Palsy would not begin for another six or seven years.

In the meantime, my grandmother Ruby died and even though I was not allowed to attend school, I learned to read. A combination of billboards, milk cartons, cereal boxes, newspaper headlines and the constant drum beat of television commercials did the trick.

When we finally moved those messy twenty miles to the city so I could attend school, the State of California required that I—as a fully literate seven year old—spend one full year in kindergarten, playing with clay and pick-up sticks and learning my letters and numbers.

The year of kindergarten also marked the beginning of my quest to manage Cerebral Palsy: It felt like going to war. My weapons included:

- Steel Braces: Full-body (feet to armpits) with leather straps and buckles securing unruly knee, ankle or hip joints. These braces (along with ugly orthopedic Buster Brown shoes) were to be worn 24 hours a day, seven days a week, taken off for a one hour bath on Saturday. These braces were heavy and cumbersome and they hurt.

- Long, Solid, Rubber Tubes: They ran along the outer edge of the brace with metal clamps attached at the hip and ankle. The idea was simple: Twist the ankle end of the tube left or right and re-attach the clamp. Thus forcing the ankle in or out, as desired. More twists on the tube, more force on the ankle. My ankles turned hopelessly outward and it sometimes took two therapists to get enough twists. The tubes were effective but they were mercenary and relentless—and painful.

- The "Stretching Board: A medieval contraption of padded, upholstered boards laid out to approximate the bottom half of a human form, hips, legs and ankles. At the joint intersections, the boards were equipped with metal hooks and eyelets, leather straps and a small metal device resembling a skate key.

Let's use the ankle joint as an example. I sat on the floor, each of my legs strapped to a long board, knees locked. A smaller board supported my foot and held it at a 90 degree angle. Straps near my toes were connected to hooks on the board near my ankle. Every turn of the skate key tightened the straps, pulled my toes toward my chest and stretched the living daylights out of my Achilles tendon. Turning various skate keys stretched my Achilles tendons, hamstrings and other nameless muscle groups for one hour every single day. This was a nasty hour.

- Two kid-sized saw horses were my first crutches: an A-frame at either end of a three foot long wooden cylinder. But, after laboring a few weeks—alternating steps of steel and wood— my rather elegant "horses" soon became nothing more than "saw turtles." Yet, slow or not, I was happy to be vertical.

As I look back, these braces and the crutches generated far greater value for me than anything practical or pity-inducing. For me, these primitive technologies created a paradigm shift in my world view. They were "game-changers." They moved forward my ability to be a human being. In short, from this time on, I saw life as a person rather than a crawling animal. My horizons, literally and figuratively, changed for good, forever.

Chapter 5
Eight Years Old in the First Grade

IN THE FIRST grade, I spent a large part of my day at something aptly called, "The Standing Table." It was a chest-high four-legged gentle beast with a two inch lip and a half moon cut out on one side. I simply stepped into the cut out, locked my knee braces, hooked a safety strap across the opening and stood there, working.

The unpainted table top was warm and clear and clean. The school room was equally clean, shiny and welcoming: Splashes of color on poster covered walls, sunshine flooding through double-sized, spotless windows, and freshly waxed tile floors. There were three additional standing tables in the room and twenty traditional desks. For each desk, a wooden top sat on a metal frame and opened to expose a large storage compartment for books, papers, pencils, rulers, crayons and other supplies.

A dark green strip of expensive-looking tag board ran across the front of the room, background for beautiful white scripted letters. At the other end, the cursive was stunning. I looked closer. Tiny arrows followed the correct shape of each letter. I secretly decided that cursive was an illusion, a beautiful fraud.

My daily routine required an hour of "guard duty" at the Standing Table followed by an hour sitting at my desk. My standing table buddy was a kid named Albert. Tall, stout and African American, Albert, like me, wore full-length leg braces. He had a round, pleasant face with smooth skin and a perpetual smile. His eyes were bright and his teeth looked as if they had been professionally whitened. He always wore the same clothes: blue jeans rolled up at the cuffs and a lumberjack shirt.

Albert never spoke. He would cock his head to one side, smile and drool. He would shake his head yes or no and he would laugh. Otherwise, he was silent. It drove me crazy! Drool never seemed to bother Albert. Adult aides would come by periodically and set him straight, to no avail. Now, while Albert, like me, had Cerebral Palsy, I must say that I never understood his "other problem."

It was silent and for the most part harmless, yet "deadly." At some point during our table duty (without warning and apparently without provocation) Albert would simply begin urinating. Kids would yell and scream and adult folks would come running at him from all directions as if they were converging on a bomb.

"No! Albert, stop it! STOP IT!"

For his part, Albert never broke character. He just smiled, drooled, and like the Energizer Bunny, kept on going and going and going. The running and yelling were meaningless. The Pee Train had left the station. Boys looked and laughed—and laughed some more. Girls looked away, whispered and raised their desk tops.

Mrs. Blankenship, however, did not laugh. "Class, this is NOT funny." she'd glare. "Do NOT encourage him."

I always thought the same three things:

1) This is too funny, 2) Why can't he ever do this when I am at my seat? And 3) There's no desk top on this stupid table!

Mrs. Blankenship taught grades 1, 2 and 3 for handicapped children: all three grades in the same room. She was a careful, controlled, no nonsense woman. She expected these children to do their school work and to learn. She was not in the room to fill time or kill time or make any friends. She was not a warm person and I never missed her when I graduated to the fourth grade. She was a well-dressed, immaculately groomed perfectionist. The Albert episodes simply unhinged her: jaw set, teeth clinched, face hard, eyes narrowing. She came undone every time that boy did his thing. I felt a little sorry for her.

The Pee Train ran on an intermittent schedule, but its destination remained the one and only, Pee Lake located somewhere just south of Albert's ugly orthopedic shoes. For my part, I merely watched the mayhem in front of me. In deference to Albert, I also did not speak. But my concerns were heart-felt. I did not want that Albert-Made Lake moving in my direction.

Happily, each episode ended as it had begun: Albert back at his table, changed and smiling, the air having exchanged urine for Lysol. I tried to understand. But, I simply did not get Albert.

Today, I still wonder. Was there a physical problem? If so, why wasn't he on a catheter? Since he often signaled and used the restroom successfully, was this just his way of saying, "Piss off?" Or "Piss on everybody?" Did he do this at home? If so, did they punish him? How? Did they make him stay in the wet clothes until they dried? Or, did they, too, just make everything fine?

I used to think Albert was stupid. I do not know what became of him. But I do know what became of me. And, in some ways, I had nothing on old Albert. Over the years, I, too, made a mess: flooded my life with fears and lies and stood by silently at a table of indifference where I unwittingly murdered my own innocence.

I did these things partly out of ignorance and partly because that's the way I'm wired. Today, I know better. I know that to be real, innocence must be tested. It's the only way Pinocchio gets to be a real boy. As for my natural wiring, I win some and I lose some. As for my innocence, some days I think he can make a comeback. Other days, not so much. To this day, Lysol still conjures up vivid images and memories of old Albert. Wherever you are buddy, I wish you well.

While grades one through four trudged on rather unremarkably, one thing stands out. During this time, my mother was relentless in her dedication to my getting better. More than once I heard her deflect criticism and soldier onward. Someone might say, "How can you make that baby wear those heavy braces all the time? Can't you see he's miserable?" Sometimes my mom would not answer. When she did answer, she'd say something like, "I know it's hard, but he's just got to do it. That's all there is to it." For this, my very young mother was a hero.

It's hard to watch a baby hurt when you can stop it any time. It's even harder to know that in order to get better, your baby must hurt.

****

Suddenly, I could hear McCartney again: Still fixing that hole. The retriever cocked his head in my direction.

I had no satisfying answer.

Hurting is a hard part of the human equation. It can be redemptive or destructive, sacrificial or selfish, but it cannot be avoided. All humans are handicapped: Some damages show and some are hidden.

I released the retriever to go after squirrels. The golfers were gone. After a minute or so, I remembered my "therapy wars."

Regarding "getting better," time was my ally. In today's vernacular, I pounded the program. It began to pay off: Braces went from under my armpits, to my waist, my thighs, my calves and then gone. I went from saw horses to conventional wooden under-arm crutches, to aluminum Canadian crutches clamped at the forearm, to traditional wooden canes.

The point of these progressions was simple: independence. Fewer braces meant more strength, skill and movement. Canes forced more weight bearing on legs and demanded more balance.

To complement the therapy program, I also underwent a number of major surgeries. But, by the end of the seventh grade, I was free of braces and operations. That said, the daily tortures of stretching and weightlifting continued.

Chapter 6
Operation Catch Up

To ENTER THE eighth grade on time, I had to complete two grades in one year, twice. The architect of this achievement was my teacher for grades five through eight, Mrs. Anna M. Langley. Barely five feet tall, graying and sporting a chunky, matronly figure, she was the childless widow of a World War II fighter pilot, a Phi Beta Kappa key holder and a summa cum laude graduate from Tufts University.

Drab conservative clothing and antique heavy black shoes notwithstanding, she was a brilliant, colorful, creative person. Her voice had a nasal quality and she breathed like those little dogs with smashed, up-turned noses. She wore plain glasses and soft grey fuzz on her face. She had probably never been pretty. But, she was funny, energetic and very comfortable in her skin. She was happy with herself and settled in her life. She had nothing to prove and everything to give. She was approachable and friendly but children did not cling to her. And, although I never thought of her as my mother, she was indeed just that—my "other mother." To orchestrate four grades in one room, she used rules and expectations. Rules guide your outside self and expectations shape your inside self. A Rule: To speak, raise your hand. An Expectation: Be kind.

Concerning my school work, she never pushed and I never felt pressured. She would hand me a new book and say, "See what you think about this."

As soon as I finished the spelling, math or history for one grade, she'd hold up my books and announce, "Boys and girls, this young man has just completed all of the work in this book and is moving on!" A round of applause (often begrudging) would follow.

Once the work for every subject was complete, she would move my desk to the seating area for the next grade. And while I do not remember direct praise, I do remember that she would smile often, laugh all the time, tell stories incessantly, and sparkle when I finished something. I liked her sparkle and I liked catching up. It was easy.

For the record, I struggled in Art. In the third grade, Mrs. Blankenship held up my drawing for ridicule. She laughed and said, "Class, this boy thinks this looks like an airplane!" For the remainder of the year, I did not do any art project involving realistic drawing. For this, I received C's in Art.

I also remember a shoot-out at the OK Art Corral with Mrs. Langley. In the sixth or seventh grade, I was required to draw a toucan for the cover on a report about South America. I stared at the blank page. I remembered the airplane. I wanted to cry, but I couldn't. After sitting at the art table all morning and missing both recesses, Mrs. Langley sat beside me and "talked" me through the drawing. When I was finished, she held up my drawing, sparkled, and said, "Class, this boy thinks he **can't** draw!" (applause).

Years later, I would learn much more about my struggle with drawing. As a 30 year old ready to enter graduate school, I expressed my doubts about Statistics and Research Design to my friend, Dr. Gary Williams. I had just completed his upper division course in Personality Theory and he was gently chiding me for planning to enter seminary in the coming fall. I reminded him that it was an interdisciplinary program designed to integrate psychology and theology. All he said was, "Listen, you are the smartest guy in the room. If you ever decide you want to be a real psychologist, look me up. I'll give you a job."

It was only then that I expressed my doubts. He said, "You probably have math phobia. Lots of psychology students do." When I said I wasn't sure about that, he said, "Well, if you really want to know, call my secretary and have her set up a time for me to test you."

He then said, "Don't be afraid."

I asked, "What scares you?"

He answered, "When someone tells me I'm about to learn the truth about myself."

I went home that night, scared. I was no longer simply worried that I might not be able to do the math but I was terrified that I had left my job, sold my house and was now risking the future of my wife and new baby son.

My fright soon turned to fury directed solely at myself.

"How could you be such an idiot, such an utter fool?"

The next morning, I made an appointment for testing. When I arrived, Dr. Williams escorted me to a Testing Room. It was richly appointed: lush carpet, textured wall paper, dark and finely polished mahogany furniture.

He sat on one side of a large table with a briefcase, answer forms and lots of other paraphernalia which I did not recognize. He told me that the tests would last six hours and that I would complete one half of the battery today and the other half tomorrow. We began.

I was asked to recite a series of numbers given to me verbally at one second intervals. We started with three numbers. Eventually, I recited nine numbers correctly. I was then given a set of numbers verbally, again at one second intervals, and asked to recite them backwards. I was able to do six numbers correctly. Next, a set of cards containing simple line drawings was placed in front of me. I was told that the cards told a story, but that the narrative was incorrect as set forth. I was told to arrange the cards correctly and recite the story. The timer began. I completed a series of five stories involving increasing complexity, difficulty and subtlety. Each effort was timed and Dr. Williams scribbled something on the forms.

There were two more tests on that day. The first involved manipulating nine multicolored red and white plastic cubes. Some sides of each cube were solid red, some sides were solid white and some sides were diagonally red and white. The cubes, each about four times larger than gaming dice, were placed randomly in front of me.

A booklet showing various red and white designs was placed in front of me. A design was revealed, the timer was again started, and I was told, "Make yours look like this." Even though the first design was simple, I could not reproduce it. I tried the second and the fifth and the last design in the sequence. I could not do any of them. This was bad. No place to hide.

The last test of the day called for me to be blindfolded. Once the blindfold was secured, I was directed to place various three dimensional wooden shapes into the appropriate holes of a wooden board in front of me. The timer began. I could not do even one. I tried desperately. After about five minutes, I started to hyperventilate. I was crying but without sound, tears streaming.

Dr. Williams stood, walked around the table and said gently, "I know it's not okay, but it's not as bad as you think." He paused. "It'll be better tomorrow. I promise." He paused again. "I'll give you a minute to collect yourself and I'll be back."

He left and I removed the blindfold. I looked at the board. I looked at all those pieces I couldn't make fit. I wiped my face with my forearm, got control of my breathing and tried to get out of the office without making eye contact. I slept fitfully that night, dreaming that I was trapped in a crowded swimming pool two feet from the surface.

I returned the next day, Saturday morning at 9:00 AM, only Dr. Williams present. This day was filled with verbal tests: General Cultural Information, Vocabulary, Abstract Verbal Reasoning, Comprehension, and a few others. I did very well. At the end of the day, Dr. Williams did a few calculations and told me that I had nothing to worry about.

I asked, "What's the prognosis for a person like me?"

He laughed. I didn't get it.

He said, "The prognosis for you is wonderful. The greatest predictor of your future is your past. Your past is stellar. Regarding these tests, your verbal IQ is two standard deviations above the mean and your performance IQ is about two standard deviations below the mean. When the two sides of your brain try to talk with one another, it's like Einstein talking to Cro-Magnon."

I asked, "So, what do I do?"

He said, "Use the Einstein part to compensate for Cro-Magnon."

"What?"

"Brain function," he continued, "while localized, is best understood globally. The brain will compensate for losses by creating alternate use sites, if possible. So, you can use your verbal skills to navigate some of your spatial reasoning issues. But, just write a philosophical rather than an experimental dissertation."

"But, how can I do the Block Design?"

"Use your verbal and abstract reasoning. Look at the design. You know that the most complex designs use nine blocks, three down, and three across. So, reproduce the drawing in thirds. Start with the edges first. Solid colors are easy, but when it comes to the diagonals, trace the direction of the diagonal with your finger and repeat it aloud. Say, 'This red block goes from the upper left to the lower right,' and do it."

As I slowly completed the most difficult design, I smiled. Dr. Williams smiled, too.

Suddenly, I remembered the toucan.

Chapter 7
A Pretty Girl, a Conversation and a Dream

I FIRST SAW her bright and early on one of those eighth-grade spring mornings when you can smell the green of new things. Looking out a classroom window, I saw a yellow cab open. She seemed to spill on to the side walk—full, shapely legs, small waist and all those other curves. She stood tentatively, squinting into the morning sun. I was certain that she could not see me. She had short, light-brown, wavy hair with small flip curls. She was wearing a sleeveless, pale yellow sun-dress and tan flats. She carried a matching yellow clutch purse and wore a tiny yellow butterfly barrette above her right ear. She was fair with light blue eyes, an oval face, perfect teeth and full lips.

The driver came around to open the door, but he was too late. He refused a tip. She turned to say something to him.

I could see her perfect silhouette.

That's no girl, that's a woman. And, even if she is a girl, she's still a woman.

As she headed for the classroom, my breathing became shallow and I noticed that she favored her right leg. She stepped carefully through the open door and headed straight for Mrs. Langley's desk. I could only hear pieces of the conversation, but Mrs. Langley was effusive in her enthusiasm as she gave Christy her books, showed her to an assigned seat and explained the day's schedule.

Since it was only 7:30 AM, Mrs. Langley instructed Charlotte (a black girl upon whom I had an intense, but unrequited crush) to show Christy around the playground. At 8:00 AM, the bell rang, everyone was seated and Mrs. Langley introduced our new classmate.

"Class, I want to introduce Christy to you. She and her family have moved here from Oregon. She is in the eighth grade and wants to be a journalist. She enjoys riding horses and reading romance novels and says that she has a big crush on her favorite movie star, Troy Donahue. You may also notice that she has a prosthetic device for her right leg. She has cancer and is currently in remission."

Mrs. Langley then interrupted her introduction.

"Just a moment here, Christy. All of you fifth graders raise your hands. Now, do you all know what the words 'cancer', 'prosthetic' and 'remission' mean?"

They explained cancer but passed on the last two words. The sixth and seventh graders also passed, but the eighth graders were quick on their dictionaries and came through. She closed the interview this way:

"Class, Christy believes that she can beat her cancer and she is praying for that. She also told me this morning that she wants to have five children with at least one set of identical twins. Well, Christy, since there are already two sets of twins in your family, I can tell you that there's a good chance you might just get your wish. Of course, you've got to finish school first and then find a good husband!"

That said, with a wave of her hand, Mrs. Langley concluded. "Christy, we are very happy to have you with us for these last few months of the year and we look forward to getting to know you better."

Mrs. L. then spoke to us. "Class, let's welcome our newest friend and classmate, Miss Christy Engle!"

We applauded, whooped and whistled! Christy smiled, but her eyes refused to settle. I couldn't tell if she was shy or embarrassed or worried. At that moment, all I knew for sure, from the bottom of my eighth grade heart, was that I wanted to be Troy Donahue.

Christy spent her first week huddled with girls. That was on purpose, like taking it easy your first day aboard ship. Some days later, whatever it was that needed to wear off had worn off and whatever it was that needed to settle in or settle down, or whatever, had done so.

Lunch had just ended. I sat on the dark green wooden bench at the far end of the newly-oiled dirt playground.

A thin, sticky film covered my shoes and pants' cuffs.

Trouble about these pants when I get home.

I started thinking about the Dodgers new nineteen-year-old bonus baby, Sandy Koufax.

Man, he's fast and he's left-handed. But, he's so wild! If he ever gets his control down, look out, brother.

Out of nowhere, Christy appeared. Cheerfully, she plopped down next to me, smiled and fluffed her skirt.

"Hi. Want to talk?"

"Okay," I said.

After, "Okay," I was stuck. I waited for her to start.

Her voice was a bit unsteady. For my part, I simply had no clue as to why she might want to talk to me. As far as I could tell, she thought most boys were stupid. She talked about her family. Handsome 21-year-old brother Tommy was a cadet at the Air Force Academy in Colorado and was also her biggest cheerleader.

She grinned. "If he wasn't in my family, he's the kind of guy I'd want to marry."

"Does he worry about you?"

She nodded. "But he doesn't want me to think he does."

She went on to say that Tommy was one of the best people she had ever known, kind and sweet and "a real heartbreaker." It scared her to know that he felt guilty about her cancer. She didn't like to think that she might cause such a mess inside another person.

She told me about her little sister. Amy was eight, good with dolls and animals, including insects and bugs of all types. When Christy had been very ill, just prior to the amputation of her leg, Amy had refused to eat and had to be hospitalized. When Christy rallied, Amy recovered.

Christy smoothed her dress. "If I believed in reincarnation (which I do not) I'd say that Amy and I were twins in another life."

I thought she was going to tell me about her parents. But, she never did. She talked about her cancer, how she hated getting sick and losing everything: weight, hair, friends and family. She hated the way "the leg" looked.

I said that I didn't want to argue, but that I thought the leg looked okay, "as far as fake legs go." I added that I needed a closer look at the good leg before I could give my final opinion. She howled with laughter and hit me in the chest, hard. She told me to shut up and called me a stupid boy.

I had to agree. She might hit me again.

She then got quiet and asked me if I thought it was wrong for a person to want to die. I said I'd never thought about whether it was wrong or not, but that it made sense to me that someone might think that.

She coughed. "Catholics say you go to hell for that stuff."

I smiled. "I don't know. I'm not a Catholic. I'm not anything."

"Yes, you are," she laughed. "You are a stupid boy."

Suddenly the bell rang and we returned to class. I did indeed get in trouble that night for oily cuffs. I told my mom to write Mrs. Langley a note so that I could stay inside. She said she would, but never did.

Two weeks after our lunch talk, Christy left school and never returned. Mrs. Langley said she'd suffered a relapse and doctors were considering more surgery.

One month later, after lunch one afternoon, Mrs. Langley announced, "Class, I have some very sad news. Yesterday, at 4:30 in the afternoon, Miss Christy Engle passed away from complications connected with a surgery."

Mrs. Langley passed around a sympathy card for Christy's family and we all signed.

That night, I had a difficult time getting to sleep but I dreamed. I was with Christy in some strange place. It didn't seem like heaven and it didn't feel like hell. Everything seemed cloudy and murky, a slight breeze coming from somewhere. Christy seemed to be sleeping comfortably. I stood at the foot of her bed. She wore a sheer dress and I could see her "prosthetic device." I moved forward, knelt and softly kissed the calf of her artificial leg.

Immediately, the room was engulfed in a blinding light and a rushing sound filled my ears. We seemed to be moving. Christy awakened and looked down at her leg. She smiled and threw back her head, curls flying.

I looked for her artificial leg and I saw instead a perfect girl.

The dream disappeared and I awakened. I never told the dream to anyone.

Chapter 8
Sandra Dee

IN 1959, I was 14 years old and in love with baseball, the Dodgers and Sandra Dee. She was beautiful, perfect and utterly unattainable. Blonde hair, blue eyes and a sweet figure, she was the original "Gidget."

One Saturday, while waiting for the guys at the theater, I carefully studied the larger-than-life poster in Coming Attractions. Balanced on a surfboard, in a scanty, (yet somehow innocent) yellow bikini, pigtails flying—even her feet were perfect. Other guys in the neighborhood liked Annette (from the Mickey Mouse Club) and I did too. But, I never dreamed about Annette. Time was passing and the guys were nowhere.

I began thinking.

This is a set up. Waiting here all morning... Very funny, I'm just sure! Well, for the record, I was never here.

Suddenly, someone tapped me on the shoulder and I jumped as if I'd been shot. I almost lost my balance.

"I'm sorry," gasped the theater manager, "I didn't mean to scare you."

I just looked at him.

He asked, "What are you and your friends going to see today?"

"Bucket of Blood," I blurted.

"Well, come see me when you are ready to leave. I've got something for you."

"Okay," I smiled.

Maybe it's free stuff. Candy, coke, popcorn...

At that moment, the guys showed up with tickets, courtesy of Tim Bradford's Uncle Hank. Tim's dad, "Big Tim", owned a motorcycle shop and on this Saturday morning, the shop had septic tank problems. Of course, "Little Tim" was supposed to dig out the septic tank for no money—which he did.

Apparently, during the last hour of work, good old Uncle Hank showed up to watch and heckle and drink beer. But, once the job was done and the beer gone, Uncle Hank stuffed twenty theater tickets in Tim's pocket and said, "Take some friends to the movies!"

Once inside, I spent my only quarter on a small package of "Flicks." I shared my milk chocolate drops with Shane for a few drinks from his coke. *Bucket of Blood* was a complete bust! There simply was no bucket of blood. It was a silly story about a shy, loser guy who accidentally kills his neighbor's cat, covers it in clay and becomes a hit artist at a local coffee house.

As we entered the snack bar area, the Manager waved me in his direction and from his office produced a life-sized silhouette of Sandra Dee. Beaming, he explained that he had no open display space and asked me if I would like to take her home.

There she was more beautiful and mysterious than ever. But, as a 14 year old, Sandra Dee was the least of what I didn't understand. For starters, I didn't know:

- Technicolor was too real to be true.

- Disney's Little Golden Book's colors were too real to be true.

- The Mickey Mouse Club was too black and white to be true.

- Most secrets come out.

- Most people eventually get exactly what they deserve.

- I was God's idea and not the other way around.

- It might be true, even if it never happened.

The hardest thing I didn't know as a kid was that both Sandra Dee and Annette were also too real to be true.

Yet, to this day, I close my eyes and I can still see Sandra Dee in "Glorious Technicolor" as the most beautiful girl in the world—including her perfect feet.

Chapter 9
A Summer Ritual

TWICE A DAY, every single summer day, at precisely the same time, the same battered white station wagon with black wall tires entered the cul-de-sac and our own Kabuki Theater would begin. Once in the morning, just after 8:00 AM and once in the afternoon, just after 3:00 PM, the newspaper man would wrestle his old locomotive into the mouth of the cul-de-sac, scrape his way around the circle, tail pipes dragging, spitting rancid, black exhaust. The black shades decorating his sweaty forehead matched his exhaust. Without slowing, he could hurl a paper with stunning accuracy through any one of his four open windows. He wore nondescript, over-sized, short-sleeved shirts with no undershirt and his Popeye arms and Bluto beard were things of beauty.

The morning script read like this: As the station wagon entered near the third base chalk square and turned right toward home, a couple of infielders gathered near the pitcher's circle, gloves shielding mouths and faces. All other fielders scurried to porches or front doors readying themselves to catch or duck.

The newspaper guy said the same thing every morning. "You guys playin' this early?"

To which we always replied in chorus, "Yep."

One time we said, "Hell yes." That was a mistake.

The last throw each morning proved to be the most challenging. As the news wagon chugged dutifully toward the third base exit, Henry, Mrs. Sanderson's beautiful two year old English sheep dog, planted himself firmly behind three rose bushes near the front porch, prepared to launch all sixty pounds of his furry self toward the incoming. Henry's competition, two invincible fourteen year olds, readying themselves behind the big Redwood on the other side of the porch.

The news man's goal was to hit Mrs. Sanderson's front door on the fly, eluding both boys and dog.

Having inevitably missed the paper, Henry would immediately reload and attack the nearest fielder's glove. Tug of War eventually became Keep-Away-from-Henry which finally became Sit-On- Your- Glove-And-Wait-'Til-Henry-Goes-Away.

The matinee performance mirrored the morning with a few exceptions. Every afternoon, the news man would ask, "Man, ain't you guys hot? How can ya stand it? It must be at least 110 degrees out there!"

To which, we always replied, "It's 115! It's fine."

But, on this particular afternoon, there was much to come which would not be fine in the least.

The sky was high. Fly balls were going to be trouble, sunglasses or not and it was at least 110 degrees. The sun zeroed in on the back of my neck. I leaned in, squinted through the sweat and flipped a slow curve toward the plate.

Ugly little Jesse with his dirty blond hair and his dirty mouth (who couldn't hit the air with a couple of practice swings) swung so hard his shirt came unbuttoned. Accidentally, he ripped a line drive which glanced off Mrs. Sanderson's wagon wheel mail box in deep left field. Foul by less than a foot, it had home run distance.

He didn't even have time to drop the bat before everybody screamed, "Foul."

Immediately, he slammed the bat off the street. "Shit! Damn it! Son of a bitch! Shit!"

He paced behind home plate, muttering, screaming and spitting words in every direction, shaking his head.

The catcher sprinted to me. "Hey, asshole. You throw that thing again and I will kick your crippled ass clear to Clarkston. Who the hell is Jesse anyway, your long lost brother?"

"Maybe he's your girlfriend," yelled the shortstop.

"Yeah," I yelled back, "and, maybe he's your mother's girlfriend."

The catcher also yelled, "Shane, maybe Jesse is *your* mom's girlfriend. That would make Jesse your step-daddy, right?"

Everybody laughed. Shane turned his back and stared toward centerfield.

Jesse glared. "Hey, I ain't nobody's F-ing girlfriend and I sure as hell ain't nobody's Goddamn step-daddy. You're all a bunch of faggots anyway."

Suddenly it was raining epithets:

"You're the faggot."

"Dickhead, faggot"

"Faggot's girlfriend"

"Takes a faggot to know a faggot."

"Hey, get off the faggot thing. Some of Jesse's best friends are faggots, right Jesse?"

"Screw you."

"Screw yourself."

"Shut the fuck up."

Suddenly, a cloud or two appeared and it got quiet. The air was so hot that it was easier to breathe through my mouth. Jesse looked serious and pointed toward centerfield.

At first, I didn't get it.

Jerk. Thinks he's Babe Ruth. Jesus.

"Hey jerk off!" I bellowed. "News Bulletin: You ain't Babe Ruth, okay? So knock it off!"

Jesse kept pointing toward centerfield. I looked over my shoulder. Everyone was doing the zombie walk toward Danny in centerfield. I stuffed the ball in my pocket and started toward the outfield. I was the last to arrive at the cluster and I couldn't see a thing. Lots of milling and mumbling and looking at shoes. I pushed my way to the middle of the group just as Mr. Kellen was directing everyone to circle-up. Near the street side of his lot, a perfectly shaped thirty foot tall Modesto Ash gave welcome canopy to the deepest part of centerfield.

On most days, Mr. Kellen, a divorced, retired railroad detective, spent the afternoon huddled on his front porch, clutching his ever-present brown paper bag.

We called him, "Old Man Crotch." His clothes were always dirty— as mismatched and disheveled as his life. He made no pretense of personal grooming: Matted filthy hair, rotten teeth, splotchy skin and watery, mean blue eyes. He wore a ragged, wide-brimmed canvas hat that was at least as ugly as the rest of him and he had a slouching stagger that made it difficult, if not impossible, to tell in which direction he might stumble.

But today, as he leaned unsteadily against the trunk of the Modesto Ash, his slurred speech, glaring eyes and contemptuous smirk made him strangely focused and clear.

He began by berating us for swearing. "What makes you kids think you c'n talk like that? 'Goddamn this, F-that, SOB this, bastard that'... I mean, hell! Jesus, Joseph and Mary! What the fuck are you thinking?! Don't you know people can hear you?! Shit, people can HEAR YOU."

We stared holes in the tops of our shoes. In the 110 degree heat, we froze. We did not look up. We did not breathe. He seemed oblivious to us. He gathered momentum.

"I mean," he coughed and spat blood and phlegm on the street. "Dumb little mother fuckers. Do yer mothers know you talk like that?" He screamed, "Well, do they?! Goddamn it all to hell!" No one answered. But, he didn't wait. "Do they fucking know you talk like that?! Well, they're gonna fucking know! I c'n tell you that. What've you got to say for yerselves, now? Little shitheads."

He coughed and spat some more. Still, no one answered. I peeked. He looked at me. I saw snot and tears on his face. He took a swig from his paper bag and I saw disgust and hatred in his eyes. He pushed off the tree and moved toward me. I tried to look down. He thumped me in the chest with his grimy forefinger.

I was afraid he was going to knock me down.

"And you," he shrieked, "you of all people should be the most ashamed. Crippled little bastard! Are you so Goddamn dumb that you just don't get it?!"

I wanted to run, but I couldn't. I wanted to cover my ears, but I couldn't.

His eyes were crazy.

He thumped me again. "YOU should be the most ashamed because these normal boys here are giving you a break by, by even letting you play with them!"

He spat the word "normal" as if it were just so much phlegm.

"As a matter of fact," he leaned near my left ear and whispered through clinched teeth. "Yer an accident of the universe. Yer a big fucking mistake. If I was yer mother, I'd hang you on a nail in the closet and charge admission!"

His whispers slapped me.

I don't exactly know what happened next. He kept saying more things. I saw his lips move and I saw his yellow teeth. I couldn't hear a thing. His breath was rancid and I was dizzy. I watched a big, anonymous, black bug crawl past my shoes. I couldn't tell if it was moving or dead. I blinked and still couldn't tell.

After some minutes, how long I don't know, it was quiet. I looked up and everyone was gone. After a minute or so, I wandered home and sat on the curb under the big tree in my front yard. I wasn't thinking anything. I wasn't feeling anything.

My mom was on her way to the mailbox. "What's going on?" she asked, "Why aren't you playing baseball?"

"Everyone quit," I mumbled.

"Oh, that's nice," she said, heading back, reading her mail.

I never spoke to anyone about the events of that afternoon and Mr. Kellen never spoke to my mother.

The neighborhood's final word on Old Man Crotch was delivered one afternoon by none other than Mr. Jesse James Dean Parker.

He said, "That old man's breath could knock a buzzard off a shit wagon."

Everyone howled with laughter.

Andy rolled his eyes. "Jesse, don't say, 'shit wagon,' say, 'crap wagon.'"

I laughed.

For once, Jesse makes sense..

Chapter 10
Old Man Crotch: Past and Present

IN TRUTH, JESSE'S sign-off was far from the last word on Mr. Kellen. Rumor had it that some thirty years ago Mrs. Kellen, a real looker, had an affair and ran away. Her name was Loretta. But, her spelling was all over the place. Sometimes she'd write "Lorretta," but other times she'd write "Loreta." She changed it on a whim, like a schoolgirl practicing her future married name. She said she did it so no one could forge her signature.

The rest of the story goes that she left two young daughters, along with a note saying neither of them was his.

Mr. Kellen then drank heavily and his daughters were placed in foster care. How he made it to retirement as a railroad detective is anybody's guess. Guys said he never washed his clothes because he carried his wife's old underwear stuffed in his pockets. Andy claimed the underwear was like a charm that helped the old man believe that she might someday return. Shane said he heard the underwear was a charm alright, but that Old Crotch used it to deliver a curse on the ex-wife. I figured it was a little of both. There were other speculations about the underwear, but they are better left buried.

It was also widely accepted that the old guy once shot and killed a man: one bullet right between the eyes. Folks also said he also emptied all six slugs into the guy, just because.

Often, he danced and sang loudly, late into the night. One summer night we were playing a type of Hide and Go Seek on steroids, called "Ditch-'Em." There are no geographical boundaries. One team hides, the other seeks. As soon as a hider is discovered and tagged, he must then become a seeker and help catch those remaining. If a hider can successfully elude capture, that is, "ditch" everyone until they stop looking, he is the winner. On this night, I chose to hide behind a vine-covered trellis, surrounded by hedges bordering Old Man Crotch's front porch.

It was just after midnight on a cloudless July night on a cul-de-sac lit only by the moon. We heard the bell tower from St. Luke's. I had just carefully positioned myself behind the trellis and settled in with my back resting against the stucco wall when a 1936 Dodge truck clattered around the corner. It was an old beater: no windshield, no paint, loose steering wheel, half-flat tires and more dents than the moon has craters.

Suddenly, a hail of water balloons buried the porch and soaked me in the process. Old Man Crotch appeared at his door, bellowing and flashing his silver 32 caliber pistol. As he stepped from his doorway, the old man's face and mine were separated by no more than three inches of trellis and ivy.

If he turns his head, I am dead as hell!

Suddenly, for reasons known only to God, I felt an irresistible urge to laugh. The moment of inevitability approached. I knew that I would fail. My laughter would explode. It would hit the side of his head. He would then turn and shoot me. Justifiable homicide: trespassing, harassment, disturbing the peace and property damage.

I could see his half-shadowed, jagged profile in the moonlight. He turned and looked right at me. I didn't move a muscle. I didn't breathe. He waited, grumbled, stepped back inside and closed his door.

My heart was pounding.

What?! How could he not see me? I should be dead right now!

I could hear my friends' whispered screams.

"Get out!"

"Hurry, Goddamn it!"

"God, come on!"

I was all set to do my version of running away when the door reopened and the old man shuffled down two steps and began a systematic search of his front yard, flashlight in one hand, gun in the other. He searched for what seemed like forever, but never in the flower bed or the trellis. He returned to the porch, raised his right arm and fired twice, sending two bullets directly overhead. Then, he went inside. After about two minutes, the house went dark.

I couldn't move. That's all. I could hear more whispers, but I couldn't move. I whispered, "Help."

I heard thumping on the wet grass, but I couldn't see. I leaned forward and hands yanked me from behind the trellis and dragged me, rugby style, from the Old Crotch's front yard to the Sanderson's next door. Our pile of people hit the ground sprawling and laughing.

Suddenly, I realized that one of my canes was lying on Old Crotch's porch.

Andy grinned. "I'll get it."

He was gone in a flash and returned in seconds.

It was late now, long past midnight.

Shane said, "I gotta get home now."

Andy's eyes grabbed us. "Hey, let's all go home and get flashlights and sleeping bags and spend the night in the fort. Get whatever money you can scrounge. We'll hit Don's Market on the way. Meet in 30 minutes. If you're not there, we'll figure Old Crotch got you."

Chapter 11
The Log Fort

PARTLY OUR CREATION, the log fort was mostly a gift from Mother Nature. Our street was anchored by the cul-de-sac at one end and an empty field at the other. Long ago, a rare mid-summer deluge ripped down a 40 foot tall tree in the northwest corner of the field and slammed it across a recently created sink hole. Roughly four feet deep, five feet wide and eight feet long, the hole needed only a few finishing touches. We dug underneath the tree (what we called a log) to get crawling clearance from one side to the other. We swept the floor clean and hollowed out chairs on the interior walls. We completed a patchwork roof with discarded lumber, plywood and sheet rock. We camouflaged everything with tumble weeds. The entrance was a dirt slide from ground level, hidden from outside eyes.

I took Andy and Shane with me to ask my parents for permission to sleep out, a strategy that can easily backfire. But, on this Friday night it worked because my parents were busy with friends. We got my sleeping bag and pillow, a flashlight and my mom's transistor radio (I had to sneak it out.). My dad actually volunteered one dollar in quarters from his change stash. We arrived at the fort a little after 1:00 AM, slid in, scratched around and got comfortable. We tried out the flashlights and my transistor radio. Dion & the Belmonts were unhappy about being "A Teenager in Love."

Four other guys showed up a bit later and it was suddenly crowded. Andy suggested that we pool our money and that he and Davie go to Don's Market, an all-night neighborhood grocery store with jacked-up prices. At first, we tried to agree on what to get. That soon fell into chaos.

Finally, Andy demanded, "Hey, just trust us, okay? We'll get good stuff."

I pointed. "No black licorice, no horehound candy, no jawbreakers and no Kool-Aid Straws."

"Okay," Andy fidgeted. "We gotta go now or it'll be dawn when we get back."

Danny said, "You should be back in 30 minutes."

They left and we listened to Fabian, Frankie Avalon, Bobby Rydell, Ricky Nelson, Shelley Fabares and Elvis. It was interesting to me that after his early success as a wild man, Elvis reinvented himself by imitating all of his "cleaned up" imitators.

I marveled.

Wow! That's genius!

Over in a corner, Jesse was quiet. He was studying a *Playboy* centerfold which had appeared from inside his sleeping bag. We started to converge.

"Just hold it," he yelled, "keep yer pants on! I'll pass it around. Two minutes, each. I'll time it up."

We settled back.

Shane poked. "Where'd you get that?"

"Old man's closet. Got a million of 'em, never miss it."

Fat Jim snorted. "I ain't gonna miss it neither. Start timing."

Andy and Davie returned, took a quick look at Miss July and began passing out the goodies: Cokes, candy bars, Cracker Jacks, red licorice, Oreos, potato chips and hot dogs for all. Jesse put the magazine safely away and tackled his hot dog.

Trouble at the Fort

Andy took a long drink and asked, "Hey, you guys know who those guys were in the truck in front of Old Man Crotch's?" Before anyone could answer, he said, "The McKinley boys and their friends."

Everybody got quiet.

The McKinley bunch lived five blocks west of The Fort and they were in their early 20's. Ben and Ike stole beer from the delivery truck outside Don's Market and every afternoon they took money from junior high kids. High school drop outs living at home, they ran a cock fighting ring in their backyard on weekends.

They drove their father's '36 Dodge without a license. Each had failed the test three times and been disqualified twice for cheating. As youngsters, they cut school, threw rotten fruit over fences and tried, unsuccessfully, to set a cat on fire. The cat escaped, Ben burned his left arm and Ike lost part of an eyebrow.

Ray, the neighborhood cop, said it best. "The McKinley's? Forget 'em. Too stupid to cheat an' too lazy to work. Not even sure they can read. But, I do know one thing. They can at least sign their names."

****

"So, it's them, so what?" shrugged Fat Jim.

"Well," said Andy, "we ran into 'em at the market and they gave us some crap."

"What'd ya do?" Danny chimed in.

"Ignored 'em. But, they know we're doing a sleep out from all the stuff we were buyin' an' they know where this fort is."

"Think they'll come here?"

Andy's eyes sparkled. "If they're bored, sure. Look, it's just after 2:00 AM. If they're comin' (an' I think they are) we got two and a half to three hours to get ready. Their idea of fun is to wait 'til we're asleep, like 5:00 AM. Only, we ain't gonna be asleep."

After some discussion, we decided balloons would be best. We figured the McKinleys would stay with balloons because that's what they used on Old Crotch, plus they already had a monster launcher set up in the truck bed. Davie mentioned that he thought he saw Bobby Blazer in the back of the McKinley truck.

"Well," Andy sighed. "That little albino twerp is gonna get what's comin' to him. I hate that skinny, back-stabbing little bastard. I can't wait."

The plan began simple and became complex. Instead of waiting for the McKinleys, we would provoke them. Davie returned to the market to buy 1000 balloons. Danny and Shane went to re-dig and reinforce the dirt defenses of two near-by 2' x 3' x 2' holes. We used these in our own war activities regularly. But, tonight, they would serve a special purpose. The McKinleys had no idea these spots even existed.

Fat Jim and Andy went to Jim's to get his father's portable generator, air-compressor and three gallons of old, unused paint. Jim said his dad would never miss it. They brought the generator in a wagon and made separate trips for the compressor and the paint. Jesse and I went to his house for 250 feet of extension cords from his father's truck: five fifty-foot cords. Andy and Fat Jim set up the generator, compressor and paint in one of the nearby dugouts. Jesse and Shane connected the extension cords, stretched them to the edge of the field, threaded the line through the chain-link fence marking Polly Sanders' backyard and plugged into an outlet on the backside of her garage. Davie passed out the balloons.

Jesse looked at Jim. "How do we know this shit's gonna work?"

"We don't asshole. But, you better worry about your own shit. First thing I'm worried about is how loud this is gonna be. I don't even wanna think about the trouble if we wake up the Sanders."

Andy lifted his cap and wiped his forehead. "I think we're okay. I mean, we're a long ways out here and I think the dirt might muffle the sound. There ain't too much moonlight an' that one light on the telephone pole is so far away it don't even touch the field. Anyways, all we can do is try it." His eyes found Shane. "You an' Jesse go back to the fence. If you see lights or hear people in the Sanders' house, pull the plug, okay?" He looked at all of us. "Now, listen, ever'body, they pull that plug, you all hit the dirt like you're dead. An' don't move or breathe 'til I say. Ever'body got that?" He waited. "Anybody not got that?"

Shane asked, "Jesse an' me supposed to drop right there by the fence or haul butt back here?"

Andy coughed. "Haul your asses back here an' drag the cord with you. But, stay low. Don't move so fast that you fall down an' don't trip on the cord."

Once Jesse and Shane were in position, Fat Jim turned on the generator, fired up the compressor and waited: 15 seconds... 30 seconds... He pulled out a balloon, carefully stretched it over the compressor nozzle and squeezed off a short burst. He then gingerly removed it, tied it and held it up. There it was for all to see, perfectly filled with Columbia Blue paint. In that small flashlight-filled hole, eyes were as big as the moon and clown-smiles were everywhere.

Andy carefully handed the first balloon to Jesse. "Gonna give you three more. Ya carry four?"

Jesse nodded. "Uh huh."

Andy cleared his throat. "Don't go yet. We gotta get set. Remember, when ya throw, take your time, nice and easy, good throws. Try and hit the truck. Don't hit the house. Be quick, but don't hurry. Know what I mean?"

Jesse spat. "Yeah, I got it."

"After ya throw, make sure they see which way you go. Make sure they follow you but cut through the Jamison's back yard and haul ass back here."

****

Jesse waited while Fat Jim filled balloons. In line three times, four balloons per guy, twelve balloons total: 96 in 30 minutes. Andy checked his watch.

It was now 3:00 AM.

The next half hour Fat Jim got faster: one balloon every five seconds with five guys tying them off and two guys delivering them to pre-arranged sites. 12 balloons per minute, another 360 filled.

Fat Jim's fingers were cramping. "I gotta quit for a while."

Andy stepped up. "I'll take over. We only got about 30 left in this first bag. 'Bout ten of 'em broke. But, that's almost 500. That's good for now."

When the 500 were finished, Fat Jim stayed with me in the side bunker and opened the second bag.

He complained about his fingers and handed me the bag. "I need some of these for me. You fill, I'll tie 'em off."

In no time, we finished 30. It took more than a few trips to deliver his 30 to the main fort. He returned one last time and opened the second and third gallons of paint. The moon was bright and glowing, and even though it was July, I was getting goose bumps.

He took a shallow breath. "Don't breathe in these fumes, if you can help it."

I nodded. "What else?"

"On full blast, this thing'll shoot maybe 50 feet, more or less. When they're in front of the fort, you're only about twenty-five feet away an' they won't be expectin' nothin' from over here."

"Why?"

"Can't be seen from here an' they don't even know about this spot."

"What do I do? How does it work?"

He said, "Easy, all ya do is pull this trigger." He scratched his head. "Here comes the important part."

I leaned in and he did too. "Wait 'til they get to that line of cans and bottles in front of the fort. Make sure ya don't hit our guys. Do a few bursts at a time. The paint goes fast. As soon as yer outta paint, yell and we'll get your little ass outta here."

My hands were sweaty and dirty and I needed to talk. "God, Jimmy, I hope I don't screw this up."

He grinned and shook his head. "Naw, you'll do good." He crawled out and pointed at me. "Remember, hold on to that nozzle mother real tight. It's gotta kick."

He left and suddenly I was alone. The fort was deserted except for Jim hiding behind the roof. Some guys were up near the street; others were scattered around the field, 20 feet apart, each with a pile of 60 balloons. Paint is heavier than water, so a small amount goes a long way. A paint balloon is more stable than water and the thrower is almost always more accurate. But, a lot can go wrong. I checked my watch.

It was now 3:30 AM.

Andy signaled everybody in for one last talk. Everybody huddled up near me. Moonlight bright, he spoke just above a whisper.

His voice was electric. "We're gonna cream these bastards! We're gonna take *their* lunch money! Be as careful as ya can. If we get 'em in a cross fire, that's good, but make sure ya got some protection. Tumble weeds are easiest, but use whatever. The other thing is, don't move around too much. You'll be a target and ya might mess up your ammunition. You know what I always say—"

Everybody whispered, "Be quick, but don't hurry."

Suddenly, I saw a new problem. "What if we get hit with paint? Gotta get that stuff off."

Andy snapped his fingers. "Simple. Ever'body take off your shirt. Davie put 'em in that old chest. You know, on the back side where ya crawl under."

Just like that, shirts were off and Davie was gone. He was little and it was an easy in and out for him.

Jim spoke up, "No matter what happens, meet back at my garage later. We got rags and paint remover stuff."

Andy added a few more things. "When they're outta balloons, I figure they'll split. When that happens, everybody head for Jim's. Don't go in a big crowd and don't all take the same way. Don't talk or make any noise – and don't yell when you're throwin'."

He looked at me. "Danny and Tim and me, we'll be back to get you in the wagon. We'll leave the paint stuff and the extension cords here."

I nodded. "Don't forget me."

Andy continued. "An' when we get to Jim's"…

Somebody interrupted. "You mean, Fat Jim's."

"No!" barked Andy, "I mean Jim's. After tonight, it's 'Big Jim' or just 'Jim.' Everybody got that?" He stared around the circle, eyes sparkling in the moonlight. "Anybody ain't got that?" Silence filled the space and his stare lingered. "From now on, anybody says 'Fat Jim,' they got a problem with me."

Jesse laughed. "Maybe he's *your* girlfriend now."

Andy stared dead at Jesse and waited.

Finally, he whispered, "Go now" and Jesse slipped out. Andy pulled at the bill of his cap. "Davie, as soon as you're out of ammo get back here and help Randy."

Davie saluted.

Andy turned to me. "Go easy on the paint gun unless you can hit the truck. Save some paint if guys want to reload."

"Reload?" I laughed. "My God! Everybody's got 60 balloons."

"Okay, forget that," he paused. "Everybody go." Suddenly, he took a deep breath. "One last thing, throw everything you got. Don't save nothin' an' don't chase the truck."

Instantly, everyone vanished.

I asked, "Whadaya think the McKinleys'll do about this? I mean… later."

"I dunno," he sighed. "Right now, I'm worried about what they're gonna do tonight."

I looked at the moon. "Me too."

Suddenly, I was alone again. We were all waiting on Jesse now. It was quiet and soft. Clinching my teeth and shivering, I imagined screaming while I blasted the McKinleys.

****

"Excuse me, sir. Is there anything wrong? Are you okay? Can I help you?"

I had no idea how long she had been standing there. The first thing I understood was not a word but the intensity in her voice. It was her intensity that pulled me into the sunshine and the present. It took me a few seconds to connect with my questioner. Cody was backing away from her and nudging me.

I could see a frown under her pale blue sun visor. I shook myself and tried to sound credible. I knew I was interrupting her jogging. Her suit matched her visor. I didn't want to sound drunk or senile.

I answered quickly and energetically. "No ma'am, there's nothing wrong. I'm fine. I don't need any help. Thank you for asking."

She stepped back, still on the sidewalk but closer to the golf course. She was elderly, slender and agile. She spoke louder than needed. Her hair was grey, short and stylish, her facial features fine. I kept thinking Kathryn Hepburn.

"Well", she squinted, "it seemed like there might be something wrong. You were just sitting there, staring at the dashboard and you didn't answer. I thought you may have had a stroke."

I smiled. "No, nothing like that."

"Well, I noticed you had a service dog, vest and all, so I wondered."

I kept my smile. "No, I was just doing a bit of day-dreaming about the good old days of my youth, the escapades of my fourteen year old alter ego. I guess I was really concentrating."

She relaxed. "I am glad you are okay. Your memories must be very good, to hold you that way."

I kept smiling. "Thank you and thanks for checking on me."

With that, she was on her way. I looked at the house on the corner, checking the window for a possible snitch. Someone might be making that call on me at this very moment.

Cody cocked his head.

I said, "Hey, looking cute ain't gonna save you! Where's the warning, eh? You know, the Lassie, Rin Tin Tin stuff?"

He licked my arm.

I grinned. "So, here we are at a golf course and she thinks I might be having a stroke. Get it?"

He came across the console and tried to kiss my face.

I pushed. "Hey, no more kissing."

He curled up in his seat and cocked his head again. I gave him a tiny piece of a French fry. He gently accepted. I started the car and turned on the air-conditioner. He jumped to the floor and yawned.

I couldn't wait to get back to the McKinley brothers paint night—like a favorite movie where you know all the parts. Over the years, every guy there had recited his personal adventure many times, much to my delight. So, I clicked a switch in my memory and there I was—right in he middle of Jesse's part.

****

Suddenly, it was a thick and cloudy dark. No moon.

Jesse approached the ram-shackled McKinley mess that passed for a house, the old truck parked on what should have been a lawn. Light in the empty kitchen, the rest of the house dark.

Outside, Ben, Ike and Bobby Blazer were playing cards in the truck bed with two others that Jesse did not recognize. They were playing by lantern light on a makeshift table of wooden packing crates.

As Jesse crept closer, he saw clearly.

Shit. They're playing strip poker and drinkin' beer!

Jesse was the right person for this job. He was small, wiry and fast. He had nerve. He would mouth off to anyone, anytime, anywhere for any reason. If adults complained, Jesse's dad, Floyd, would whip him mercilessly with a razor strap. But, it never mattered.

Jesse got within ten feet of the old truck and carefully placed his balloons on the ground in a horizontal line about five inches apart. He wiped his throwing hand on his jeans, took a deep breath and let it out slowly. He thought of himself as a sniper. Smoothly and quickly, at one second intervals, he released four nearly-perfect strikes. The first throw exploded just below what would have been the old truck's back window, if it had any glass, which it didn't. The second and third throws blew away the lantern and exploded the table. But, his last throw was the best. He couldn't be sure, but he thought it smashed dead into Ben's sternum. Paint and balloon confetti splattering everywhere.

Jesse stepped out of the shadows, made sure Ben and Ike saw him, and flipped them off. He then turned and scampered away into the darkness.

The McKinley gang spat and cursed and wiped blue paint from faces and hands. They rushed into the darkness, intent on tearing Jesse limb from limb. But, he had vanished. Ben and Ike returned to the truck, filled water balloons at a furious pace and soon had over 100 resting carefully in card board boxes in the truck bed.

In the bushes close by, Jesse heard them counting and cursing.

"Let's go, Goddamn it," screamed Ben as he struggled to turn the old motor over. Suddenly, everything caught, coughed and shuddered to life.

"They're at their shitty little fort," he raged, as he wrenched the old truck through a Y turn and headed toward The Fort. "I know right where they are," he muttered, teeth clinched. "And I'm going over there right now and shove this truck right up their asses!"

Jesse waited. He had to make sure they followed. He heard the old truck cough itself to life, stepped out, yelled and gave a repeat performance of his special one finger salute. Only this time, he took off for real. As he cut through the Jamison's yard, he heard the old truck grind and clatter behind him. He crossed the open field on a dead run and slid safely into the fort.

"They're coming," he gasped.

In a minute or so, the McKinleys scraped around the corner and took dead aim on the fort. At the same moment, our advance guys, Andy, Tim and Davie stepped from behind an abandoned refrigerator at the field's edge and tattooed the old truck with ten out of twelve shots. The cab was dripping in blue paint. A couple of shots traveled through the open windshield, drenching Ben.

The truck slowed, turned into the field, and continued, the four in the truck bed now hurling wildly into the dark. From stashes on route to the fort, our guys reloaded and followed along, firing as they moved. The mid line guys, Danny and Shane, were half way between the street and the fort. They pelted the old truck from both sides, slopping it in more blue paint.

Ben screamed, "I can't see! Goddamn it! I can't see shit!"

Bobby yelled from the back. "Keep going. Don't stop. 100 feet straight ahead. Go. Go!"

Suddenly, Bobby himself began slipping and sliding from one side of the truck bed to the other. His slippery blue hands couldn't grip and he landed in the middle of a box of balloons.

Now, our last line of defense joined in. From behind the fort roof, Big Jim began firing at one second intervals, methodically and smoothly. It was raining blue paint. Bobby, Ike and company continued slipping, unable to use the launcher.

At 15 feet from the fort, Ben again stopped the truck. He opened the driver's side door and I smacked him with a three second blast. I knew I hit him. He screamed and spun away, soaked from head to foot, dripping in glorious, thick Columbia Blue. I heard the door slam shut, open again, and then again slam shut. It continued to rain Columbia Blue from all sides, a torrential downpour. Ben restarted the truck and began a slow circle of retreat.

The moon returned and spotlighted the scene. I again blasted all parts of the truck as it rotated in front of me. I emptied every drop of paint from all buckets.

Ben's foot kept slipping off the brake and accelerator pedals. He only had ragged control. The more things slipped, the more he cursed and the more he cursed, the more it rained Columbia Blue.

Guys were now out in the open, hammering the truck as it struggled toward the street.

****

We cleared the fort as quickly as possible. Andy and Shane loaded me into the wagon along with two empty paint buckets, one 50 foot extension cord and two canes.

Andy hustled. "Come back later for everything else."

With Andy pulling and Shane pushing, we were flying across the field like ghosts. Suddenly, the front right wheel took a violent jolt and the wagon rolled wildly to the right, spilling its contents like abused bowling pins. I did the tuck and roll as best I could, but my right shoulder slammed into the ground, followed closely by my right ear. The paint buckets flew away from me and the wagon flew over me. But, I hit and rolled and my right arm and hand were trapped underneath me and they were pretty scraped up, as was my right ankle. I settled and began taking inventory.

Andy whispered fiercely, "Goddamn gopher holes, shit! Are you okay?"

I whispered back, "Hell no, I'm not okay. I'm dead, whadaya think? Goddamn gophers, I hate 'em!"

In the dark, voices were like darts.

Andy fired. "You okay or not?"

He was resetting the wagon and Shane was helping me sit up. "I'm okay. Where are my canes and the extension cord?"

Shane whispered, "I can't see anything."

Andy spat. "Shit, we shoulda brought a flashlight."

Shane jumped. "I'll be right back."

"No," Andy flashed. "Wait! Our eyes are getting better. See, over there?"

He pointed to two disoriented paint buckets about ten feet away and moved toward them.

Shane shot another whisper dart. "Look out! Snakes!"

Andy froze. "What?"

Shane refocused and mumbled, "Sorry, shadows."

By the time Shane retrieved the extension cord, Andy had the paint buckets.

I moaned, "Never gonna find my canes."

Suddenly, Jesse stepped out of nowhere, flashlight pinned to his chin, a wedge of light distorting his nostrils, cheekbones and yellow-toothed grin. "Oh, yes we will, Dumb Shits," he bellowed.

We nearly jumped out of our skin.

"I'm gonna kill you," promised Andy.

Shane laughed.

I spat. "Shut up, Jesse and find my canes! Andy, Shane, let's get outta here."

Jesse pulled down his flashlight. "Don't worry. I got 'em."

He shined a beam behind me and took off. We reached the street safely and arrived at Jim's backyard shortly and I was reunited with my canes. Davie was throwing tee shirts while guys positioned sleeping bags on the lawn under some giant fruitless mulberry trees.

Andy looked at Jim. "Let's go back an' get the generator and compressor."

As they turned to leave, Danny said, "Get anything else we left, okay?"

Davie laughed. "Yeah, like all our food."

"And," I added, "my radio."

Davie volunteered. "I'll go with."

I was studying my scrapes. "Hey, Jim, before you go, I need some wet paper towels and a few Band-Aids."

He returned in a few minutes and helped me clean up. Other guys were using the hose to clear paint splatters.

Jim was untouched. "Hell, they never even saw me," he laughed. "Like shooting a pig in a poke."

I said, "You mean 'fish in a barrel'."

"Yeah, yeah, I guess." He said, "Whatever you say. Fish, eh?"

My scrapes were light but they stung and the Band Aids helped. Jim threw the paper towels away and signaled to Andy and Davie that he was ready to go. We settled into our sleeping bags and began reliving everything. We were excited, exhausted and scared. Our victory had been complete, but its full weight was only just beginning to settle.

I rubbed my eyes.

The McKinleys are gonna kill us. We got 'em too good. This is bad, real bad.

We scooted deeper into our sleeping bags, sucked in the cool, damp summer air and shivered. The moon was back, sitting in the trees.

I rubbed the back of my neck.

Never shoulda done this.

Apologizing was out of the question.

Oh, yeah! Let's say we're sorry and then they'll say, 'Okay, assholes.' Then, they'll kill us.

The crickets were going off like smoke alarms, the grass was wet and the trees were dripping. It might as well have been raining. I kept wiping my face and head with my shirt and scooting deeper into my sleeping bag.

We were clustered in a rough circle when Andy, Davie and Jim returned. They dropped candy bars, cookies, potato chips, a six pack of soda and a radio in the middle of the circle before laying out their bags. I grabbed my radio, a candy bar and a can of soda. Everybody grabbed something.

Andy tore into an Almond Joy. "Well, we gave 'em a real ass-whippin' boys, that's all I can say." The candy bar was gone in three bites. "An', they won't know we're here tonight and that's good. We can't let any of those guys grab us. An', we all know one other thing for sure. They are pissed."

After much discussion, we decided to spend the next few days at our individual houses, mention nothing about the night's adventures and play dumb, if asked.

Finally, sleep-loaded smiles arrived. Sometime after daylight, the backyard sprinklers signed in, peppering us with over-splash from long arcing shots periodically passing overhead. We ignored the artificial rain and dug deeper into our sleeping bags. Sometime later, the sun pounding, (along with our heads) we crawled out into the steamy light of day.

We imagined horrific McKinley revenge but nothing ever happened. In fact, we never saw Ben and Ike again. Two days after our victory, they were arrested for stealing beer from the delivery truck at Don's Market. There they were in living black and white on Don's newly-installed security cameras. They helped their cause by typical McKinley behavior: resisting arrest and fighting in the holding tank. They would be gone for a long time.

And, while Ben and Ike never returned, we often saw old man McKinley driving his ancient, Columbia blue, 1936 Dodge truck. I don't know if he ever knew how his truck got blue.

Chapter 12
Halloween Night

SUMMER ENDED BEGRUDGINGLY that year, as it almost always did. It was 95 degrees on October 31st and we argued about whether we were too old to trick or treat. We decided it didn't matter. If you were little like Davie or Jesse, no problem. If you were taller like Shane or Andy, just wear a full costume and keep quiet.

Jesse wanted to fill a paper bag with dog crap, set it on The Crotch's front porch, light it on fire, ring his door bell and hide to watch the fun. Everybody agreed that it was a good idea, but nobody wanted to do it. Jim said Jesse didn't need a costume. Disgusted, Jesse went off to collect candy.

****

We met at the fort late, plenty of candy in tow. Dark and cool inside, it was still 90 degrees outside. Spots were staked out, goodies passed out and coins flipped to see who would get veto power over the next song on the radio. Somebody vetoed The Everly Brothers "All I Have to Do Is Dream" and the radio was off for the rest of the night. Our parents had OK'd tonight's sleep out a week earlier, so the fort was fully stocked. Some candy trading, but not much. Everybody liked and hated the same stuff. Most chocolate stuff was best, unless it was old. Abba Zabbas, Cracker Jacks, Look Candy Bars, Mother's Sugar Wafers, Orange, Cherry and Lemon Slices, all good. All hard candy, anything powdered, anything pure wax and that God-awful orange, white and yellow candy corn—buried on the spot or thrown into the weeds.

Danny grinned. "Candy corn looks like teeth."

Jim frowned. "Who wants to eat teeth?"

At straight up midnight, Andy looked around the flash-lighted circle and spoke quietly and deliberately. "When was the last time you were really scared, I mean, little-girl, pee-your-pants, run-home scared?"

Jim blurted, "Tonight, when I saw Jesse!"

The room laughed, including Jesse.

"Naw, I ain't kiddin' now," Andy whispered, "when were you guys really scared?"

Some were scared walking home alone, late at night. Everybody agreed that pitch dark changes everything. Some feared getting caught for stealing, smoking, cussing, lying, cheating, pulling fire alarms, toilet papering stuff or listening in on phone calls.

But when Jesse talked, his eyes got big. "I was in the closet in my momma and daddy's room with a flashlight. Busy lookin' at the old man's magazines and, uh…"

We looked at each other.

"I wasn't in there just but a few minutes when my momma an' sister come lookin' for somethin'. I thought, 'What am I gonna do now?' I shut off the flashlight. They come real close. I hear 'em real clear. Takin' 'bout sandals. I'm hunkered down in the corner behind the long coats, sittin' on sleepin' bags. I get underneath quick, knees up. But I can't breathe, can't think what to do with the magazines. All of a sudden, my sister busts the closet door wide open, pushes a long coat across the rack. Then, she reaches down an' her hand bangs right up against me. I'm thinkin', 'Shit, I'm done for'. Then, she grabs some sandals, slams the door and they take off." Jesse paused. "I didn't come outta there for 'bout an hour."

At this point, usually guys would start punching holes in Jesse's lie-infested story.

Tonight, after a few quiet seconds of respect, Andy broke the tension. "Jesse, that is as scary as hell." He paused a moment while everybody agreed and then continued softly, "For me, it was last night when I went passed the old Jefferson place. I swear, I never been so scared in all my life."

****

Out of the blue, a horn clobbered me into the present. Cody was standing and alert. An immaculate, pearl-white 1957 Thunderbird convertible screeched to a stop behind us and my unmistakable friend, Lee Allyson, exited the driver's seat. He ran to my side and whacked me on the back.

"Buddy," he smiled, "fantastic to see you! How you guys doin'?"

A retired male nurse ten years my senior, Lee and I became friends during my internship at a psychiatric ward in a V.A. hospital in Washington State thirty years ago. He was a big, jovial man, in good physical condition and surprisingly agile and light on his feet. His clothes were rich/casual.

His major claim to fame came courtesy of his $40 million dollar lottery prize. Forced into early retirement by co-workers who criticized him for keeping a job someone else needed, he returned to his California roots and began living happily ever after. That was twenty years ago.

He pointed to Cody and kept talking. "Cody woulda liked Paris. Sure wish you guys woulda come."

At the mention of his name, Cody wagged his tail and sat. Lee laughed.

I asked, "When did you get back?"

He said, "Three days."

I grinned. You really want to impress me? Next time, don't beat me to death with the horn. Just roll up with Suzanne Sommers next to you."

He raised his eyebrows. "Huh?"

"What?" I faked mild shock. "You don't remember the mysterious, beautiful blonde in the pearl-white '57 T-Bird in *American Graffiti?*'

Lee scrunched his face. "Man, how could I forget?" He paused, "But, she's out of my league, pal. I might be old enough to be her daddy."

I cracked up. "40 million bucks! Nobody's outta your league!" I paused, "Unless… Please tell me you didn't blow it all."

He grinned. "No, I still got it and a little more to keep it company." He sighed. "Speaking of money, you gotta pretty car an' a beautiful dog. Why you sleepin' under a tree?"

"Not sleeping. Reminiscing."

"You mean like about when I introduced your new little scared Intern ass to 'Mr. Cool' and 'Jesus'?"

That blast from the past sent us both laughing.

Having encountered schizophrenia only in textbooks, I was scared to my socks to meet such folks in the flesh.

"Mr. Cool" looked like a slimmed-down version of Michael Douglas in the 1990's movie, *Falling Down*. His daily uniform: white shirt, narrow black clip-on tie, dark pants, black shoes and thick black glasses. His daily regimen: frenetically pacing restrooms, chain-smoking and flushing toilets. If restrained, he would project guttural flushing noises and blow imaginary smoke in peoples' faces. If challenged, he became agitated, smoked faster and repeatedly spat out "Shoot your damn head off!"

By contrast, "Jesus" was an apparently big man who got smaller before my very eyes. Sporting wild dark hair, a full beard, piercing green eyes and a thick wool sweater in June, he shook my hand we and sat at a table facing one another. He was quiet.

I smiled. "Well, Jesus, this is certainly a big day for me. You know, I think you might be the most well-known person on earth. People have been seeking you, worshiping you for two thousand years."

He smiled and spoke softly, "I am glad to meet you. I'd like to introduce you to my disciples."

He then stood and began methodically removing sweaters, folding and stacking them neatly. With each sweater came a name. "Matthew, Mark, Luke, John…"

I reminded him of his reputation as a great teacher and I asked him what he wanted me to learn from our meeting.

He again spoke softly and his piercing eyes never left mine. "Being good to people is free, but it will cost you everything."

****

Lee said, "Those guys weren't bad or dangerous. The more I knew them, I thought they were hurt and tragic."

I took a deep breath. "Yeah, they were psychotic alright: hallucinations, delusions, bizarre thinking, obsessive-compulsive. But, I agree. They were sad, unfinished people. Like somehow, people made a baby with no real person inside. Or a person so tiny that reality just swallowed them alive."

"So," Lee smiled, "they didn't end up scaring you at all, eh?"

"No," I said, "they didn't. But, the sociopaths sure did. They'll hurt you for fun or because they're bored. They really are crazy."

Lee reached over and scratched Cody's ear. "You did a real good job with that pretty twenty year old. The one so far gone she didn't know who her own arm belonged to—thought she was in hell."

I nodded. "I remember. Classic YAVIS: Young, Attractive, Verbal, Intelligent—can't remember the S right now. But, she also fit the pattern for getting well: acute onset, blah, blah, blah… The S might be for sophisticated."

Lee grinned. "Kid's married and owns a flower shop in Santa Barbara. Her mother is one happy lady. She asked about you. Said her daughter was dead and is now very alive."

"A flower shop? That's great. They were a good family. If anything, they tried too hard."

Lee rubbed the back of his neck. "Hey, I didn't mean to mess up your meditation time but I had to stop and say hello."

I reached out and we shook hands again. "It was great. I was just in the middle of remembering Halloween night when I was fourteen and our adventures at a spooky old house."

He patted Cody on the head. "Sounds like a fun memory. Let's have lunch sometime."

As he turned to leave, I hugged Cody and eased back into my Halloween memories. The history of the old house came back in living color.

****

The Jefferson house had been abandoned and boarded up for years. Built on a spacious double lot, it had once been the neighborhood showplace. Jefferson was a master carpenter who managed enough energy and resources to work on his own place after hours. In just three years, his masterpiece was complete: gentle lawns and meticulous hedges circling a gleaming white Victorian, trimmed in forest green. The replica was as stunning as it was out of place.

A softly-swirling, Confederate-gray wrap-around wooden porch (six feet wide) hugged every inch of the place. Three large, circular, ground-floor rooms stabilized the many other odd-shaped enclosures making up the second floor. The third floor attic sported two signature medieval-styled turrets, complete with flags.

The windows were a creation unto themselves. Some bold many-sided rectangles—five feet tall and three feet wide—others simply quiet squares, fun portholes or mysterious triangles. Jefferson also layered outside surfaces with traditional Victorian gingerbread.

In daylight, the place was eye-popping. At night, it was magical.

A four foot-tall white picket fence cast shadows thrown by a majestic, single-globe lamppost at the base of the front porch steps. Smaller globes hung every five feet and a shiny brass doorknob made the otherwise imposing front door a bit more approachable. Padded swings framed the doorway and padded chairs sprinkled the remaining spaces. The porch itself was defined by a simple white wooden railing.

An interior circular staircase anchored the structure and gave it an air of invincibility. And yet, the structure was anything but invincible.

The All American Babysitter

As a high school senior, Scotty Jefferson was a three sport, four year varsity letterman with a full scholarship to the University of Southern

California. A 6'3" 215 lb. blonde-haired, blue-eyed assassin, Scotty could take his pick of football, basketball or baseball. He was charming, soft-spoken and easy going.

For us, he was also the best baby-sitter of all time. We were all five or six years old and he was fifteen. For two years, he played with us endlessly: King of the Hill, Championship Wrestling, Roller Derby (without skates) or Frankenstein.

The game never mattered. We always ended up being thrown around like rag dolls. We bounced off Scotty like pinballs. In tickle fights, we laughed so hard we wet our pants. He let us stay up late and read to us or told us stories.

But, more than athlete or baby sitter, Scotty was his parents' only child.

This is where the story got lost for us, or mostly lost. We had no details, only rumors. What we did know is that on his birthday seven years ago, the fun stopped.

Scotty put a loaded gun into his mouth and pulled the trigger, leaving a fine mist of blood, bone and grey matter on his second story bedroom walls. We knew he left a large pool of blood. We knew he was dead. But, we simply could not get our heads around it. Everybody said that he was secretly seeing a thirty year old woman and when she refused to leave her husband and children for him, as promised, he "ate his gun."

It made sense, but it didn't.

Within a year, the Jeffersons divorced. One year later, Mr. Jefferson boarded up the place and left. It was as if a neutron bomb had dropped, killing everyone inside, leaving the building without a mark. But, with the boy dead and the family gone, five years of neglect killed the house as well.

The spirit of death hovered over the Jefferson's corner—nagging, unfinished business hanging in the air. Passers-by hurried, heads down, taking cheap tiny glances. I never walked on the Jefferson's side of the street by myself and neither did anybody else.

No matter the season, day or night, the closer to the old house, the darker and colder.

Chapter 13
Inside the Fort

Everybody leaned in.

Andy drew the moment out. "Last night, near midnight. I'm walkin' home. I'm not thinkin'. And I look up, an' there I am, face to face with the old Jefferson house. I swear! I stopped breathin.'"

Davie whispered, "What happened?"

Andy shrugged. "I dunno. I was kinda starin' at the house an' then I couldn't see it. It disappeared. An' then it came back."

"What?"

"You heard me," he snapped. "But that ain't the worst of it. I think I seen somebody up in that second story window. Somebody had a light on."

Through an avalanche of curses and questions, Andy made it clear that he couldn't make anything clear. He kept going back and forth. He saw something, he didn't see something. He heard a voice, he didn't hear a voice.

Jesse spat. "Shit. Let's jes go over there an' see. An', let's go right now, unless you ladies are scared."

Jim laughed. "You bet yer sweet ass, I'm scared. I ain't goin'. Send me a post card, pal."

There was grumbled agreement and it got very quiet. From the back corner, on the other side of the log, Tim Bradford, a kid who never said a word, suddenly declared, "I'm goin'."

Jesse smirked. "Ain't no motors to run away on, Timmy."

Tim fired back. "I don't need no damn motorcycle."

It got quiet again. The argument shifted from going or not going, to going now or in the morning. Jim spoke for the morning people.

Then Jesse spoke, "Listen, jerk offs. You go ahead an' tell me there's a better damn time to do this than on Hollow-F-ing-ween."

Silence.

He looked around the cave-like space. "Shit."

I spoke to no one in particular. "Hey, I need the wagon. I mean, if we need to get outta there fast."

Andy was matter of fact. "If we're goin', we gotta do it right." He looked at Jim. "Go get the wagon."

The dark felt like an extra layer of clothing. The moon was a weak, flickering flashlight. "Anything goes wrong, you guys get me out, okay?"

Andy punched my shoulder, hard. "Don't worry, Missy, we will protect your sorry little butt."

Shane smiled. "Don't worry."

In my head, I could hear my mother.

Well, what did you think was going to happen? Haven't you been told a thousand times to think ahead?

We thumped into the street and my mother left my head. The dark was thick and wet and the wagon wheels screeched enough to wake the dead. We knew the streets well, but night swallows things. Everything becomes a shape shifter. The lamppost saved us. Without it, the harder we looked, the less we saw.

Suddenly, we reached the corner, looked across and there it was. After a minute or so we crossed over.

****

A shipwreck floating in darkness, the Jefferson house was a twisted shadow of its former self. Jagged glass, charred wood and bullet holes everywhere. Rats, cockroaches and the filth of countless squatters... Overgrown weeds, dead trees, garbage and gopher holes... It stunk of decay and death. We hesitated at the once beautiful now battered picket fence. We stared at Scotty Jefferson's second story window.

We waited, we listened, we shivered. We saw nothing. The old place simply swallowed the shaky moonlight. But, we heard plenty: ugly, skittering sounds. Andy whispered that we needed gloves, boots, flashlights and hard hats. He told everybody to hustle back with whatever they could find.

In an instant, everybody melted away and I was alone, wet and cold.

I got out of the wagon.

If a monster is going to get me, at least now I'll get a whack at him... Hey, why him? Aren't there any girl monsters? Does the 50 Foot Woman count? She was supposed to be bad, but man, she looked good.

In a couple of minutes, I had a plan.

Halloween. Best way to handle fear? Scare somebody else.

I crossed the street and hid behind Mrs. Alvarado's 4' tall hedge. It was maybe a foot and a half wide. Her front yard got some coverage from the street light but her hedge was a coffin. I fished three empty glass jars from her garbage.

Suddenly, the street light failed. The dark swallowed me. After a while, it got better. Guys trickled in: the twins, Danny and Davie, plus Tim and Jesse. Stumbling around, they banged into the wagon, argued about looking for me and decided to wait for the others.

But, a few seconds later, they broke into pairs and set off in opposite directions, whisper-yelling my name. A mangy old calico cat jumped out of nowhere and complained his way across the street.

All four guys jumped like they'd been shot. Just for fun, I yelped like a yodeler with a hernia and made myself laugh. The four froze, looked around and started again. This time holding hands, they split up and moved in opposite directions. Soon, the pairs were about thirty feet apart.

My hiding spot was dead center between them. I stood, grabbed an open jar by the lip, swung my arm back like a bowler and launched my own "bottle rocket." Full follow through, release at the top of the arc. Straight up, hidden by the night. No sound until it exploded in the street. The next two were just as perfect, smooth and easy, seconds apart. BOOM… BOOM… Glass crashing everywhere.

Like a bird-dog flushing quail, guys fluttering, flailing, yelling and running into each other. This was my chance. I took a deep breath and launched a blood-curdling, gut-wrenching shriek, as if somebody was pulling my teeth with pliers.

Halfway through the scream, I slammed on the brakes, scrunched against the hedge and waited. The whispering was urgent.

"What the hell is going on?"

"Where's Randy?"

"Why would he take off?"

"He wouldn't take off."

"Maybe he got scared and went home."

"Uh-uh… We'd a seen him."

"We coulda missed 'im."

"Maybe somebody took him."

"Okay, Sherlock, who?"

"How do I know?"

"Hey, where the hell is everybody?"

From behind the hedge, I reached down for my deepest voice and bellowed, "BOOGA! BOOGA!" I stretched out the words (emphasis on the BOO) to make it more scary. I wanted to sit tight and silent, but I couldn't. I laughed so long and loud. I exploded the quiet. I shredded it.

Suddenly, they were looking again.

I heard Jesse. "Alright, Goddamn it! Whoever you are and wherever you are—we are gonna kick your ass."

He was close. He came around the hedge, moving slowly in my direction. But, he never looked down. Two feet from me, he stopped. I held my breath. He turned away.

I grabbed his leg and screamed, "ARRAGH!"

He tried to kick loose but tripped and fell.

Suddenly, something grabbed my neck and shook me hard. "ARRAGH YOURSELF!"

The sound hit like lightening. I used the turtle defense: arms in, shoulders up, head tucked.

And then, just like that, the screaming stopped.

Andy spoke sharply and whacked me on the back. "Gotcha!"

I nearly jumped out of my skin.

Jesse grinned and shook my hand. "Man that was good. Good Halloween. Scared the crap outta me."

It took me a minute to put myself together. After I congratulated Andy on scaring me to death, he took a bow. Everybody loved my disappearance, said it was a great Halloween. But, they couldn't figure out the lamppost.

I got a quick lift out of the hedge.

"Boys," I grinned, "the lamppost trick is for me to know and for you to figure out."

We crossed the street to the Jefferson's yard.

****

With everybody going home for tools, we could still only get enough stuff for three guys. We substituted football helmets for hard hats and Jim brought three face masks and flashlights from his father's painting business. Andy, Shane and Jesse suited up first. The rest of us waited at the wagon.

Shane said, "We can take turns. Go in, look around. Then, you guys."

Davie asked, "What, e-zactly, are we lookin' for?"

Andy shrugged. "Dunno."

"Well," Jesse urged, "Let's go."

Jim asked, "Whatcha gonna do if ya meet a ghost?"

"We're gonna kick the crap out of it with this!" Andy waved his helmet in Jim's face.

Everybody laughed, punching and shoving. The wind kicked up and a dog howled in the distance. Suddenly, the lamppost came on.

A beady-eyed bird stared at us from a nearby overhead power line.

I wish I had a .22 right now. Shoot that bird right through his stupid eye.

"Hey," I offered, "We should get our 22's."

But, it was too late. Andy, Shane and Jesse were cautiously picking their way toward the collapsed front porch steps, their flashlights puny against the darkness. A battered mess, the once-majestic front door hung askew on twisted hinges, its once-impressive brass knob, now a gaping hole.

We waited and waited. Suddenly, we were tired of waiting. It felt like forever. Davie was getting ready to throw rocks.

Tim had another idea. "Hey, let's throw glass. Ya know, chunks. Hit glass with glass."

"Sure," Danny smirked. "That's just great. Throw glass at windows when they're in there right now, by a window."

Tim shrugged.

Danny rolled his eyes. "Wanna kill somebody or somethin'? Jeez."

A while later, all three came out. Andy first, followed by Shane and Jesse. All three pulling off masks and taking in full breaths. Andy held up a small box, no more than six inches long by three inches wide and two inches deep. Everyone was crowding.

He pulled the box away. "Let's go back. We can look at it better once we get away from here."

There was a short argument about others getting a turn inside the house but one look at the used face masks ended that. Jim said he could get more masks and that we should come back in the daylight.

Andy was shaking his head. "It's a mess in there."

Tim was having none of that. "What is so bad? You just did it."

Andy coughed. "Tell you guys everything once we get back."

At the fort, everybody settled in. Andy's play-by-play account was fantastic. Here are Andy's experiences in my words.

****

75

The air was rank, thick and damp. The dirt on the floor was almost mud. Decay and destruction everywhere: bottles, cans, food containers, paper bags, makeshift beds, torn mattresses, pieces of plywood, broken needles, piles of ashes, cigarette butts, rotting tissue paper and lumpy dead things in corners. Broken-glass-shadows seemed first like one thing, then another. The spiral staircase stood some distance from the door.

Andy whispered into his mask, "I hope this thing'll hold. Let's go, before I change my mind."

The other two nodded. The stairs groaned and creaked and gave a little, but held. Breathing shallow and loud, they reached the second floor.

Shane panted. "I can hear my heart in my ears."

"Yeah," Jesse scoffed. "An' I can hear your ass pucker, so we're even."

Suddenly, Andy pointed and shoved. "There's Scotty's room."

Jesse's right toe pushed the door. Inside the room, time had stopped. A tableau soaked in dust and perfectly preserved: pennants, pictures and posters on walls, a large four poster bed near a window, a tall chest of drawers in one corner, everything exactly as it had been, minus the damages done by wind, sun and rain. Everything seemed smaller. Clothes still hung in a closet. A watch, wallet, books and papers were still stacked on a desktop, and a stuffed glass trophy case still stood guard.

After a few seconds, Andy whispered, "There ain't no tracks in here, no footprints, nothin'. It's like nobody was ever in here at all, except Scotty. It's weird. I swear, I seen somebody up here yesterday."

"Well," Shane sneezed. "The cops were here but that was a long time ago."

Then, they all saw it at the same time. To the left were piles of what had once been flowers, wreaths and bouquets.

Andy said, "Let's look under the bed." He shined his light on more dirt and cobwebs. "I'm done."

Jesse ran his flashlight beam along the wall of dead flowers, up to the northeast corner of the bed. For an instant, the beam flickered. He ran it backward and again it flickered. He stepped to the corner and concentrated his beam.

Andy's head snapped around. "Find somethin'?"

Quickly, he was beside Jesse. With two beams, they saw it. Snugged against the corner rested a small box with a brass clasp.

Jesse reached through dirt and cobwebs.

Andy grabbed an arm. "Watch out for black widows."

Shane joined in. "Yeah, and snakes and rats and squirrels. They got rabies."

Jesse flinched. "Awright! You get it! Besides, I thought ya said don't touch nothin'".

Andy grumbled, "I did, stupid. But, I meant don't touch other stuff."

In one fluid move, he stepped around Jesse, squatted and retrieved the box.

"We can't look at this here. We gotta get. Be quick, but don't hurry."

They retraced their steps and met us outside.

****

Andy looked around the room, everybody finally on the same page, snugged up in our dirt hideaway, flashlights glowing. He reached inside his jacket, produced the small box, wiped it as clean as possible with his gloved hand and set it on his sleeping bag.

The box was cedar. He removed his gloves and reached for the clasp. He opened it and stared inside.

Andy's head dropped. "It's empty."

All the air left the room.

Jesse slumped. "Shit."

Suddenly, Andy's voice lifted. "Hey, wait a minute!" Carefully, he lifted a scrap of paper. It was folded and torn. "Shine some more light over here." Again with great care, he unfolded, squinted and read aloud. "**His name was Scotty.** "Andy shrugged. "His name was Scotty?'"

Nobody said anything for a while.

Jim said, "We all knew that. So what?"

"I don't know." Andy refolded the paper. "But, must be important. Somebody saved it and hid it."

I said, "The guy is dead. We all liked him, but he's dead. And, we all know just how he got dead, don't we? It's just his name on a piece of paper."

Andy was clear. "We gotta go back there tomorrow."

A few card games peppered with a bit more idle talk and we called it a night. The main accomplishment? Easy: Guys had survived the Jefferson house. We woke up the next morning and the night before seemed like a dream--with one exception: Right there, in the middle of the floor sat the little cedar box and the tiny piece of torn paper.

But, box or no box, we did not go back to the Jefferson place that morning (or any other morning) for a long time.

Chapter 14
The Thanksgiving Parade

EVERY YEAR ON the Saturday before Thanksgiving, Don's Market sponsored a neighborhood parade, complete with prizes. Although the theme was Thanksgiving, Don welcomed any costume celebrating Americana.

It was special for us in another way. Show up at Don's parking lot early on parade Saturday and make some money. Minimum wage 25 cents per hour. The jobs included setting up tables with multicolored umbrellas, marking the parade route with colored tape, preparing and serving hot dogs and soft drinks and organizing the parade or taking pictures.

Don "hired" us unofficially for these jobs. He called us 'volunteers'. He called our wages 'a gift.' I kept a sign-in list for participants, assigned numbers, and lined them up, little people first. I also took my turn in the photo booth and served as Don's "second set of eyes."

Don also took a page from Disneyland's playbook and dressed his 'volunteers' in the most popular costumes of the day, right off the TV screen. Andy, Shane, Jim and I became Davy Crockett and Jim's sisters, Jane and Jenny, became Annie Oakley.

The Davy Crockett outfit featured a muslin shirt, fringed buckskin jacket, matching leggings and coonskin cap, topped off by a Daisy Air Rifle, Long Version. In those clothes, I *was* Davy Crockett.

The perfect Annie Oakley outfit sported a blonde wig, pigtails with dark blue ribbons, a long-sleeved white shirt, (red arrow embroidered on the pocket) a dark-blue kerchief, a dark-blue suede vest and skirt (with white fringe) black boots, a tan cowgirl hat, leather gloves, pearl-handled pistols and brass bullets. In those clothes, Jim's little sister, Jenny was beautiful. Suddenly, it hit me. Not only was Jim not fat anymore, but Jenny wasn't so little.

One other character was very popular: Rex, The Wonder Horse. A feisty pinto pony, he came straight from a catalogue. As soon as Don saw the pictures, he was sold. Davie played the head and Jesse the tail. Everybody said that seemed about right.

Don's prices were fair.

Thanksgiving Parade Bill of Fare

❖ Picture with Davy and Annie	10 cents
❖ Picture with Rex, The Wonder Horse	10 cents
❖ Hot Dog	25 cents
❖ Soft Drinks	25 cents
❖ Pastries	25 cents
❖ Ice Cream	15 cents
❖ Assorted Candy	25 cents
❖ Airplane/Yo-Yo/Lone Ranger Mask	25 cents
❖ Paper Dolls/Puzzle/Kite	25 cents

Our Special Contestant, Louie, the K.

Louis Kerensky, AKA "Louie, the K." was older (17) and smaller (thirty-six inches head to toe.) Medically, Louie was a dwarf. In every other way, he was "The K." Stuffed into a tiny wheelchair, he was an impressive figure: A cross between a miniature Buddha and an escaped gargoyle, his bowling-ball head was simply jammed onto his shoulders while his deep-set dark blue eyes surrounded his pug nose.

His dirty-blonde crew-cut ran away from his high forehead and his pock-marked skin looked like discarded moonscape. Stuck in a perpetual crooked grin, his thin mouth was flanked by tiny, low-set cauliflower ears. And his short arms and Popeye forearms were punctuated by fat, little, cartoon hands. His rounded back hunched him permanently forward.

And, he was deaf. Not completely, but enough to frustrate. He had hearing aids—more decoration than business. His voice had an artificial quality like the voice box for hole-in-the-throat-smokers. All of this meant that Louie always spoke too loud.

One last note: Louie cussed. He cussed incessantly about everybody and everything. He did not curse. He cussed and he was a liability in public.

He had moved from San Francisco to the neighborhood three weeks earlier. Each morning he rode the bus with me to the other side of town where handicapped kids attended special classes. Originally, it was my idea to enter Louie in the parade. But, it was Andy's genius to dress him as Uncle Sam. Mrs. Sanderson created his nearly infant sized costume from red white and blue silk-like material and Don provided his tiny white shirt and top hat. Louie provided his ever-present, menacing/impish looks and his resident grumpiness.

Tim Bradford, the only guy working off site that morning, took on perhaps the toughest job of all: getting Louie to Don's parking lot, in costume and ready by 11:00 AM. At 10:30, I got worried and asked Don if Andy and I could go check.

He scanned the lot. "Okay, but get back here quick, Louie or no Louie."

No one answered Tim's front door. We went around back. No one there. We turned to leave and Andy heard something. Ten yards away, a second gate opened onto a secondary yard. Under a massive tree in the far corner, Tim was standing on a wooden dining-room table, gently swinging a laundry bag, its drawstring tied securely around the thick branch above his head. He was talking to someone. Louie's tiny, empty wheelchair sat nearby.

Andy yelled, "Timmy, where's Louie?"

"Up here. He won't behave. I told him he ain't comin' down 'til he promises to behave."

We were now standing near the table.

Andy rested his hands on his hips. "We gotta get him over to Don's right now. I dunno that much about dwarves, but he ain't that strong. We don't wanna hurt him."

Tim slumped. "Okay."

Andy jumped on the table. "He's awful quiet."

"Well," Tim grumped, "he was cussin' like a sailor."

Andy and Tim untied the drawstring and gently lowered the laundry bag. Andy widened the opening and pulled down the canvas. On the table sat one steamed dwarf, arms folded in a huff, a scowl planted on his forehead.

Andy yelled, "YA OKAY?"

Louie huffed and looked away, arms still folded.

Andy screamed again, "YA OKAY?"

Louie grunted, "SON OF A BITCH" and glared at Tim.

"WHADAYA MAD AT TIMMY FOR?"

Louie studied Andy's lips. "BASTARD MADE ME WEAR THIS."

He fussed and tugged at his Uncle Sam jacket.

He was sitting on the tails. "LOOK LIKE A GODDAMN CLOWN."

Andy smiled. "NO, YA DON'T."

They carefully lifted Louie into his chair and adjusted his shirt, pants and jacket. Clothes dazzling, his frown looked scratched in for all time.

Andy grinned. "YOU DON'T LOOK LIKE A CLOWN. YOU LOOK LIKE UNCLE SAM."

I yelled, "YA LOOK GREAT. YOU'RE GONNA WIN THE PRIZE."

"WHAT?" Louie raised his eye brows.

"YOU'RE GONNA WIN THE PRIZE."

"WHAT RISE?" Louie smiled—ragged yellow teeth.

"PRIZE... PRIZE," I yelled.

Andy and Tim laughed.

"SPIES? TRIES?" Louie shrugged.

I gave up for the moment.

Andy squatted, looked Louie in the eye and gently placed Uncle Sam's top hat on his head. It rested just above his eye brows, the brim touching his ears.

"YA LOOK GREAT."

Louie glared. "WAIT? WAIT FOR WHAT?"

Andy looked him in the eye again. "NOW, LOUIE, LISTEN. THIS IS IMPORTANT."

Andy looked at Louie eye to eye, his hands on the dwarf's shoulders— and blasted. "WHEN WE'RE IN THE PARADE, YOU'RE NOT GONNA CUSS, RIGHT?"

"HUH?"

"IN THE PARADE. YOU'RE NOT GONNA CUSS, RIGHT?"

"WHAT?"

"CUSS IN THE PARADE! YOU'RE NOT GONNA CUSS—RIGHT?"

"WHAT'S HE DOIN?"

Louie pointed to Tim threading the wheelchair spokes with red white and blue crepe paper.

Andy sighed, leaned in nose to nose with Louie, took a deep breath and bellowed, "CUSS! CUSS! CUSS! YOU'RE NOT GONNA CUSS IN THE PARADE! ARE YA?"

Louie paused and milked the moment. "YOU'RE DAMN RIGHT I WON'T!"

I laughed so hard I almost fell. Tim walked away.

Andy threw up his hands. "Shit. Let's go. We gotta get back."

We left the yard and hurried two blocks over to Don's.

As we walked, Andy muttered, "We're screwed. He's gonna cuss, sure as shit."

To no one in particular, Louie grunted, "WE'RE NOT POSED TO CUSS."

I cracked up. It was Andy's turn to glare.

Tim said, "Hey, I thought he couldn't hear."

****

As we entered the parking lot, Don waved. "Hurry. We're ready to start the parade and the judging. Put Louie in front. Tim, you push."

Louie won a one dollar gift certificate for Best Newcomer and was the all-around crowd favorite. He wanted to do the parade route again, all by himself. We each made two dollars that day and spent all of it at Don's Market. I was glad Louie won something.

Afterward, we ate at the park. It was my job to help Louie. It was hard for him to hold stuff. His hands were too little and he couldn't get his fingers to work right. Sometimes, stuff hurt his teeth. Chewing was work. His tongue was too big.

Feeding Louie was okay, but there were rules. The number one rule was One-for-You, One-for-Me. I told Louie taking turns was okay but not from the same candy bar. Louie was dropping crumbs from a Snickers Bar and trying to bite my fingers.

Jesse smirked. "Shit. You should try dressing the little turd."

"I AIN'T NO DAMN BIRD," snapped Louie.

Jesse was on a roll. "Try putting pants on a pile of worms. Try putting Jell-O in a sack."

"I AIN'T JACK", protested Louie. He looked at me. "MY TURN."

I stuffed an extra big chunk of Snickers into his mouth. His eyes got big and he looked crazed. I flared at him, stuck out my tongue and made a sour face. In truth, it wasn't so bad feeding Louie, but taking him to the bathroom—that was a three man job. I was sometimes one of the three and it was often nasty and noisy.

Louie wrestled down his bite and looked at me like I was his butler. "TELL JESSE I HATE HIS DAMN GUTS."

Jesse laughed. "I ain't talkin' to turd-boy over there. Ridin' around in his little turd-wagon. Tell him that next year he can be 'Stinker Bell, the Turd Fairy' an' he won't even have to dress up."

Louie looked from Jesse to me.

I shrugged. "He's crazy."

The dwarf answered, "I'LL BE A TURD, BUT I AIN'T GONNA BE NO DAMN FAIRY."

Jesse yelped, "Hey, I thought he couldn't hear."

Chapter 15
An Emergency Meeting
and a Treasure Chest

THREE DAYS INTO Christmas Vacation, cold and wet with fog, I answered the telephone.

Before I could blink, my mother said, "You aren't going anywhere in this wet and cold today."

As I brought the phone to my ear, I nodded and said, "It ain't cold."

On the other end, I heard, "They're gonna tear down the Jefferson house. Meet at the fort at 2:30 this afternoon. I'm callin' everybody."

Andy sounded out of breath. Before I could say okay, he hung up. I stayed on for a few seconds, looking serious.

"Who was that?"

"Andy. Wants to know 'bout a sleep out tonight.

"I told you, it's too cold"

"We're not gonna walk around and everything like that."

She looked up from her movie magazine. I saw Natalie Wood, Tuesday Weld, Warren Beatty and Sandra Dee on the cover. I stared at Sandra Dee, no legs, just her top half.

I explained, "We're goin' over there right now and get everything set up. Once we get inside, it's warmer than the outside."

"That can't be right." She put the magazine in her lap. "How could it be warmer?"

"I dunno," I shrugged. "It's science is all I know."

"Who's going to be over there, besides you and Andy?"

"Everybody."

She was reading her magazine again, talking from behind it. "Who's everybody?"

"Everybody."

"What about dinner?"

"Baloney sandwiches."

"Did you clean your room?"

"Yeah. I mean, yes. All done."

"Did you do your homework?"

"Mom, it's Christmas vacation."

"Well, let's just wait for your father."

"Mom, it'll be too late."

She looked up from her magazine and waited… "Listen, you be home by 11:00 in the morning, without fail."

"I promise," I grinned. "Nice magazine, mom."

Before she could change her mind, I called Andy and told him to get over to my house right away and help get my stuff.

****

We arrived at the fort in the late afternoon, everything cold, wet and gray. Shane, Jim and Jesse met us at the entrance. Jim had a fist-full of new masks.

Andy asked, "Anybody else coming?"

"You should know," poked Jesse. "You called 'em."

Andy ruffled a bit.

Jesse shrugged. "Hey, you asked. Don't get your panties in a bunch at me."

Andy looked away.

Shane said, "Danny and Davie are coming."

Andy lifted and reset his hat. "That only leaves Tim and Louie. Tim is grounded, so he's out. But, I talked to Louie's mom and she says he can come but we gotta keep 'im safe and warm and do all the stuff and take care of him. So, Shane and I will go get Louie."

Jim coughed. "We shouldn't bring Louie. For one thing, how we gonna get 'im down here?" He pointed to the fort. "For another thing, we can't take him to the Jefferson place. He can't go in there. And, you know he'll make noise outside."

"That's right."

"Right, that's true."

"Yeah."

"Uh huh."

Andy ignored the general agreement. "Suppose it was you instead of Louie? Would you want Shane an' me to come get you?"

Jim looked at the ground. "Yeah."

Andy looked at every guy. "And so would the rest of you."

Danny and Davie arrived and Andy told them to find a piece of cardboard about Louie's size. He told Jim to clear out a special spot close to everybody.

He said, "We'll use the cardboard like a slide and we'll slide him down just like we do, only slower with guys holding on. Once we get him inside, we can put the cardboard underneath his sleeping bag. Be warmer."

Everybody nodded.

He smiled. "Any you other girls want cardboard room service?"

Everybody grinned.

"Now, about the Jefferson house," Andy continued. "You're right. He can't go in there. Somebody's gotta stay with him. We'll work that out."

In a few minutes, the place was packed.

Andy spoke with energy, "What I heard is they're gonna bulldoze the Jefferson place in two weeks."

Jim was surprised. "Ain't no sign or fence or nothin'."

Andy answered. "My dad says two weeks and he should know. He does all that treasure huntin' stuff with this magnet thing that picks up coins. He looks in the paper every night where they're gonna tear down stuff."

Danny added. "Maybe we can use it."

Andy was quick. "Nope. Not a chance. Still too new. He'd kill me an' then every one of you one at a time."

"No he wouldn't," Danny protested.

Jesse laughed. "Yes, he damn well would. He would."

Andy cut things off. "Listen. We gotta go over there and have another look, but no use goin' in the dark. Go there in the morning. See better."

Jim was lying on his back, looking up at sheet rock and tumble weeds. "Other people see us better too."

"Not," said Andy, "if we do it right."

The final plan wasn't very popular. Andy, Shane and Jesse would return to the Jefferson house for a closer look and send for the rest of us if they found anything. The strength of this plan was that it would draw no outside attention. Its weakness, of course, was that the rest of us would simply wait. Since nobody had a better idea, the plan stood.

We demanded a detailed account upon their return. Shane volunteered to take his notebook but I couldn't see the point.

Can't see in there, can't breathe. How can you write?

Jesse looked at Andy and Shane. "Screw this! It's 4:00 o'clock. Let's just go."

In seconds they were gone. We played cards, listened to the radio and waited. In less than an hour, they returned. As promised, we got a detailed report and Shane's notes actually helped.

Here is my version of their report on the second visit to the old house.

****

The Jefferson place looked more miserable than scary. Even in the late afternoon, the ghost of a dead friend lingered. Passing the house was strange. Still, nobody discussed Scotty's suicide. It was more than bad. It was creepy. No need to understand death when you can feel it and taste it. Entering the yard and climbing up the porch steps was both exciting and unnerving. Either way, you might throw up.

On this trip, every move was quicker, every step more deliberate: Through weeds and debris, over gopher holes, around dead trees and up the dilapidated front steps. Nauseating smells hit as they neared the front door.

Masks, gloves, flashlights and helmets in place, Andy muffled, "Try an' walk in our tracks from before."

Jesse argued, "Why?"

"Because I seen it on TV."

"Why?"

"Because I was watching it, stupid."

"Naw, I mean, why'd they do it?"

"I dunno. They done it so we should too."

Andy entered the house, flashlight on. He stepped lightly on prints he thought were his. The others followed, taking care to move slowly and give each other space.

A sickening rot wrapped itself around them. They were faster than the night visit and soon re-entered Scotty's second story room. Everything looked as it had before—only more sad than scary.

Andy directed, "We gotta look through stuff. Jefferson ain't ever comin' back an' they're gonna tear this place down anyway."

Jesse and Shane checked the bed: Nothing in the blankets, pillows or mattresses except gagging dust and dirt. They were closing eyes, waving arms and ducking away. Andy began in the closet, going through pockets.

Shane, trying to write, sneezed. "Don't forget about spiders and rats and lizards—and rabies."

Jesse spat. "Hell with 'em. I'm ready boy!" He proudly produced a can of industrial strength Raid. "Got it from my dad's station."

Andy and Shane chorused. "He'll never miss it."

Jesse raised his eyebrows. "How'd you know?"

Shane examined a pair of sneakers and smiled under his mask. "We're psychic."

Andy finished with Scotty's clothing and realized he couldn't close the closet door until he pushed the hamper flush against the wall. To avoid a face full of musty gunk, he twisted awkwardly to his right.

That's when he saw it.

He sputtered, "Get over here."

"What?"

"Huh?"

In the corner sat a shoebox-sized toy treasure chest. Shane said, "Maybe we should leave this stuff alone. Isn't this stealing?"

Andy laughed. "Kiddin' me? Can't steal from a dead guy. Besides, whole place is goin' down. Get the thing and let's go. I can't breathe."

Shane grabbed the box. Dirt and cobwebs filled the air as they entered the hall. Andy again lead the way down the staircase and out to the front porch.

They tried to scrape years of neglect from the small chest. There was no sign of a key and the brass lock was old and rusted shut. After a few minutes, they knew they needed tools. No one spoke as they hustled toward the fort.

Suddenly, Shane motioned that he was turning right. "I'll get a hammer."

Andy added. "Get a board, too."

Shane waved. "See ya there."

****

Jesse and Andy arrived at the fort, prize in hand. They slid through the entrance and interrupted a card game.

Suddenly, it was Christmas.

"Open it."

"Yeah, open it."

"Hurry up."

"Let's see what's in it."

Andy held the box above his head and yelled, "We gotta get the lock off. Everybody down!"

Jesse laughed. "Shit, you guys are like a bunch of little kids."

Danny's eyes narrowed. "Let's go outside and find out who's little."

"Anytime, little man," Jesse smiled. "Anytime."

I said, "You guys shut up."

Andy stared at them. "Knock it off. We got business."

Jesse shrugged and Danny looked away.

Andy set the chest in the middle of the floor. He explained that they tried to open it and heard a jingling sound. He picked it up and shook it. Everybody nodded. Suddenly, Shane slid down the entrance. Breathing hard, he dug in separate pockets and produced a hammer and a brick.

Andy looked at him.

Shane shrugged. "Couldn't find a board, so I brought a brick."

Andy took the brick and measured it against the bottom of the chest. Not a good fit. He hesitated with the hammer.

Davie pushed. "Dudn' matter if ya smash it to hell."

Andy agreed and was readying himself.

Suddenly, Jim yelled, "Hold it. We can't."

Andy held up. "Why, who says?"

Jim looked around. "'Cause we gotta go get Louie."

Andy dropped the hammer. "Shit. We forgot. Go get 'im right now."

Jim was already moving. "I'll go."

Shane, Jesse and Tim also volunteered.

Somebody from the back yelled, "Hell, let's all go."

It was also decided that Louie should hold the treasure chest on the way back.

****

Beaming bright as any sun, Louie's mom answered the front door. She wheeled Louie out and handed his stuff all around: sleeping bag, flashlight, food, plus a urinal and a bed-pan wrapped in a blanket. She started to hand Tim a roll of toilet paper but Jesse stepped quickly behind Louie, put his finger to his lips, intercepted her handoff and whispered, "We got enough of this stuff at the fort already."

Louie was stuffed into a yellow down parka with a hood trimmed in white fur. He looked like a deranged Kewpie Doll. Hands folded on his lap, fingers laced, elbows planted on his wheelchair's arm rests, blue eyes blazing, he was ready.

Andy stepped behind the chair and Louie's mother quickly removed his hood and placed one quick kiss on the top of his head and another on his cheek. He started to protest, but the crime was done and the hood already in place. He huffed a little.

Mrs. Kerensky reminded us not to lose Louie's hearing aids and fussed over us about how wonderful this was for Louie. We nodded and smiled and got out of there.

It was dark and wet-cold. Breath like horses, our noses and cheeks were pink under the street lights. We got to the end of the block and Andy stopped.

He made eye contact with Louie. "YOU CARRY THIS TREASURE CHEST."

"OKAY."

I was watching and thinking, shifting my weight.

Maybe Louie will be good tonight.

Jesse said, "I know what you're thinkin' an' you're wrong. He ain't gonna be good."

Shane piled on. "He's right. You are wrong. He ain't gonna be good—and that *IS* what you were thinkin'."

I mumbled, "That's not what I was thinkin'."

They laughed. "Liar."

At the fort entrance, Danny and Davie laid out a stretcher-sized section of cardboard and Andy and Shane carefully set Louie in the center. Andy sat behind with his legs around the little gnome. Jesse sat in front. Tim grabbed the cardboard from the back and lifted. Jim lifted gently from the front and Danny and Davie grabbed the sides. Evenly and carefully, everyone pulled. I did my best to shine a flashlight path. In a few minutes, Louie was safely deposited. He gripped the small treasure chest throughout.

Everybody settled in for the evening. Flashlights hung overhead made the space look warmer than it was. Jim crawled by and thumped Louie. The dwarf growled and grinned. They shook hands.

Davie complained. "Whadaya doin'? Gettin' married? Move it."

First order of business: Open the chest.

Andy set the chest on the brick, put a piece of cardboard over the top and gave the front edge a sharp whack. He removed the cardboard. The hinge had pulled away from the chest a bit, but the lock itself held. There was a small crack running the length of the top. He replaced the cardboard and whacked again. The little chest splintered and fell to pieces. The contents appeared unharmed. For a moment, no one moved. Then, the whole room launched.

Andy raised both hands. "Let me handle this stuff. I'll hold it up so you can see, but a lot of people shouldn' touch it."

He cleared the mess to one side, picked up a gold locket and opened it. "There's a picture of a pretty woman an' some writing… but I can't read it."

Jim dug a magnifying glass from his pocket. "Got it from my grandpa."

Andy used the glass and read aloud. "All My Love, Linda."

Danny blurted, "That must be the woman he killed himself over."

It was quiet. Andy set the necklace aside and picked up a gold, male ID bracelet. Engraving on the top: SJ + LL.

Andy looked up. "SJ is easy but who is Linda L?"

Nobody spoke. Louie was eyeing every item and reading lips.

Next, Andy held up a small silver skeleton key. "Any ideas about this?"

Tim grinned. "It's a key to somethin'."

Everybody laughed.

Jesse smirked. "No shit, Sherlock."

Everybody laughed again.

Andy collected the necklace, the bracelet and the key and tucked them in his jacket pocket.

He picked up the broken box. "Well, that's it. Let's eat."

Shane asked, "What did that other note say? The one we found in that little box."

"His name was Scotty,"

All of a sudden, I understood. "These are clues. It's a mystery. Somehow it fits together."

Jesse attacked some red licorice. "Okay, Sticks, what does it all mean?"

I fired back. "Don't call me 'Sticks.'"

Jesse exploded. "Dumb Shit."

I laughed, grabbed a handful of cookies. "If you had another brain, it would be lonely." (Laughter)

Jesse leaned in my direction. "You're so smart. What does it all mean?"

I popped an Oreo in my mouth. "Did your mamma have any kids that lived?" (More Laughter)

Jesse laughed too. "See, you don't know nothin'."

I ate one more cookie. "When you were born, they took one look an' slapped your mamma." (More Laughter)

Jesse attacked. "I'm still right, no matter what you say. You ain't got nothin' figgered out an' don't nobody else neither."

I laughed. "Jesse, I was wrong before. Truth is, when you were born, they kept the afterbirth an' threw you away." (Explosions of laughter)

"Awright!" He held up his hands. "Jesus, just shut up!"

He crawled back to his bag, looked over his shoulder and yelled, "Sticks!"

I saluted. "Pretty good. I got no come back."

Jesse smirked. "Thank you."

I waited a beat. "I got no come back because I never engage in a battle of wits with an unarmed man." (Laughter)

Suddenly, Andy screamed, "The treasure chest had a false bottom!" He flashed a quick look. "Don't start! I aint talkin' about nobody's butt."

I asked, "Anything in it?"

"Yep, another note."

He held it up and read aloud: "The problem is below and the answer is above."

Jim threw up his hands. "What does that mean?"

Davie frowned. "What problem? Below what?"

Danny followed. "What answer? Above what?"

I snapped my fingers and looked at Danny. "The problem is easy. Gotta be the girl. That's why he's dead, right? Because of her?"

Andy agreed, partly. "Okay, she might be the problem, but how is she below? Below what?"

I had an idea. "Maybe it means she's dead. You know, six feet below? He killed her and buried her somewhere."

Shane reached for the potato chips. "Nobody knows who she was. You guys ever hear anybody say her name? All I ever heard is that she was a lot older and married."

"My God," Tim's eyebrows shot up, "Scotty wouln' kill somebody. Nobody kills somebody they love"

"Oh, yes they do," Jesse piped up. "These bastards kill each other all the time. My mom likes this movie where some lady kills her old man for the insurance money. The insurance guy is in on it. They are pretty good but they get caught."

I surprised myself. I agreed with Jesse. "We already know Scotty would kill somebody."

Andy shook his head. "That's different, doin' it to yourself."

Jesse scowled. "How? How's it any different? Killin' is killin'."

Andy opened a Coke, took a long drink. "I don't know. Just is…"

I said, "Maybe 'below' means below the treasure chest, you know, where you found it. Where did you find it?"

"In his bedroom closet," Andy flashed. "Maybe it's something under that spot, another false bottom thing, only in the closet."

Jim announced, "Well, I'm goin' this time. My masks, ya know."

Tim added, "Me too. My turn."

Andy looked around. "Okay, we go tomorrow. And, all you guys who waited last time, you're up. Everybody else outside."

I reminded. "You better check above the treasure chest too."

Jesse shook his head. "Can't stay in there. The smell would gag a maggot. Gotta take two trips."

"Right," said Andy, "You're both right, gotta check above an' get out quick."

Louie growled, "I'M HUNGRY."

Andy looked at me. "Yer up."

Louie looked at me. "I GOTA SNICKERS."

I shook my head. YOU CAN'T START WITH THAT."

Jesse defended the dwarf. "Yes he can, if he wants."

They both stared bullets at me.

I dropped it. "Yeah, you're right."

Louie honked, "HUNGRY."

I got Louie's stuff and my stuff and positioned myself in front of him. His eyes locked on my every move.

I lectured. "ONE BITE FOR YOU. ONE BITE FOR ME."

He glared. I got my baloney sandwich and his Snickers.

I nodded to Jesse. "He gets the Snickers. I get my bite of baloney first."

Louie grumbled, "ME FIRST."

Jesse busted up.

I looked at Louie and shook my head.

I thought he couldn't hear.

The dwarf smiled and everybody ate. Shane, Danny and Andy did restroom duty with Louie. We got set to play cards. Jesse pulled his deck with pictures of naked French women. I knew we better play with different cards. Louie might tell.

Jesse agreed and we played with Louie's oversized cards. We played war and Louie got mad if he didn't win every hand. The radio played rock and roll Christmas songs. Suddenly, it was warm.

We played for a long time and after everyone dropped off, I talked with Andy.

"You really think he killed her," I whispered.

"It's gettin' too hot in here." He crawled to the entrance and lifted the blanket for a blast of cold air. "God, that's better. Uh, I dunno if he killed her or what, but somethin' sure as hell happened."

I settled, hands behind my head, moonlight leaking through the roof. "Well, I think 'The problem is below' might not be about the treasure chest. The below might be about the bed where you found the cedar box."

Andy said, "We looked there twice and there's nothin'."

I suggested, "Maybe it's a false floor."

"How could it be? It's a second story bedroom."

I asked, "Think Scotty coulda built a storage place?"

"To store what? If a girl's dead body is the problem, then a body is what ya need to store an' there ain't no body up there. Cops woulda found it. They were all over that place."

"Well, not too much. My mom says it was quick. Suicide, slam dunk. Said they found a handwritten note right in the middle of his bed. A gun. Everything."

"My mom says the same. I never heard nothin' about the girl."

"How'd they know she promised to marry him an' didn't?"

"In the note, I guess."

"Think the girl in the note is the Linda in the picture?"

"Sure, why not?

"I wish there was a way to get that picture blown up and ask around if anybody—I mean any grown-up— recognizes her."

"I dunno how to get it blown up."

I decided to switch things up. "Forget about 'the problem is below.' What about The answer is above?"

"If the girl was the problem an' ya killed 'er, then wouldn' that be the answer? An' then, wouldn' the note say that the answer is also below?"

I said, "Stay on above. Above what? The bed, the house?"

Andy scratched his ear. "Like in the attic?"

"Yeah, I guess."

He thought for a moment. "Weird little rooms. Least that's what I heard… Hey, didn' everybody say she was a lot older than Scotty? Does the girl in the locket look older? He was 18 or 19 or 20 when he died."

He got the locket and opened it. I shined the flashlight. We stared at it from all angles: too small, too fuzzy. But, after a minute we realized, even if she was older, she didn't have to give him an older picture. Plus, what if she was just a young looking 30? We put away the locket and shut off the flashlight. It got quiet.

My head was spinning.

Would I kill myself if Sandra Dee promised to marry me and dumped me? Maybe. Would I kill her for dumping me? Never.

I closed my eyes and there she was. Perfect feet and all.

Chapter 16
An Accident and a Perfect Breakfast

EARLY MORNING, EVERYTHING dripping wet. We scrambled outside two at a time. I helped Louie with the urinal and Jesse volunteered to empty it.

He picked up the urinal and looked at Louie. "HEY, I LOST A BET."

I looked around. Shrugs and headshakes. Louie pointed. He needed help with his zipper, button and belt.

From the back, Jim sat up. "Sorry man. My turn to help Louie, I just forgot."

"Wanna help with his pants?"

Jim started crawling over people. "Yeah."

As he got to Louie, I got out of the way. Danny grabbed my hands from behind and pulled me back about two feet.

Jesse stuck his head inside, and held out the urinal. "Any you ladies need this, before I put it away?"

Louie growled, "I AIN'T NO LADY."

I scratched my head. "I thought he couldn' hear."

Jesse thumped the back of my head. "Ain't so smart, are ya?"

I scrunched my face. "No, I guess I ain't."

Jesse shook Louie's hand and said to me, "Thought he couldn' hear nothin'."

Suddenly pillows were flying. Pillows, I could handle. The urinal was another matter.

****

Louie got out the same way he got in, minus the flashlight. I started pulling myself up the slope, toward the entrance, using my forearms.

Behind me, Jim offered help. "Hey, I'll bend over, get low, grab yer ankles and lift ya up, like a wheelbarrow."

Before I could answer, he bent forward, reached for my ankles—and fell. From the corner of my eye, I saw him going down. I rolled onto my left side. My top or right leg escaped but his full weight landed flush on

97

my left ankle. I heard something like knuckles cracking and fire shot through my foot.

I screamed at the top of my lungs, pulled at my left pant leg and slugged my thigh. I slugged the ground. "Goddamn it! Shit! Goddamn it! Oh, help me. Oh, God, please help me. Shit! Really hurts. This is really bad."

Jim moved quickly, but the damage was done. I faced the entrance and tucked my head inside my left forearm. I could smell wet dirt. I clinched my teeth, set my jaw and tried to breathe through my nose.

I lifted my head and screamed, "Shit! I broke my fucking ankle! Jesus. I hate this!"

I wanted to run from the pain. I started to hyperventilate and panic. *Why can't I ever run away from this shit?*

I screamed, "God! Help! I don't want to be hurt anymore!" I looked up at faces. "Pull me out." I could hear Jim saying it was an accident. I could hear others saying, "It's his ankle again."

Andy asked, "Want us to get your dad?"

"NO."

"Whadaya want us to do?"

"Nothing. Leave me the fuck alone."

"Huh?"

"Just pull me out, now."

I could feel hands everywhere.

I yelled, "Don't touch my foot or ankle."

We labored up the slope awkwardly, a bumpy arrival at ground level. It was cold and wet and gray—a bad day. Frightened faces everywhere. The ground was messy and scarred. The sun was trying to break through but it was not going to make it.

I gritted my teeth. "Get my sleeping bag." I winced. "Lift me up and slide it under."

Once on the sleeping bag, I laid on my back, forearm over my eyes. The pain went from stabbing and tearing to throbbing and aching. I concentrated on breathing.

Not so bad...

Until that moment I had avoided looking at the ankle.

It's gonna be all twisted the wrong way, blood and pins.

I thought about my dad and shook my head. I uncovered my face and asked Andy and Shane to help me sit up. I forced myself to look. The shoe was half off but still tied.

Goddamn ugly Buster Brown orthopedic shoes.

The sock was twisted. No blood, no pins. Suddenly, I was shivering, teeth chattering, jaw aching. I still couldn't get enough air.

I groaned, "Untie my shoe, straighten out that sock and get the shoe back on."

Andy hesitated. "You sure?"

"Yeah. Do it. Do it now."

I gave instructions. "One of you get on one side of my ankle and one on the other." I waited. "Andy, untie the shoe. Slowly, loosen the laces. We're not gonna take the shoe off. Just straighten the sock and get the shoe all the way back on."

I told Shane, "Hold the foot straight. Grip just above the ankle and don't let it roll or twist. Start real easy... That's good." I exhaled. "Now squeeze a little harder. That's perfect. Hold it."

"Andy, hold the heel of the shoe with your left hand. Now, softly move the shoe 'til it's lined up straight. Pull the tongue out. Sock straight. Now, put two fingers, from your other hand, into the pull-loop at the back, near the top of the shoe. You might be touching Shane, but that's OK."

Andy hesitated. "We might hurtcha."

"No, it's okay. It ain't broke. If it was, I wouldn' be talkin'. But, it's gonna swell up quick and it'll be real good to get it in the shoe."

"You sure?"

"Yes, yes, I'm sure. Hell, it's my ankle! Come on, girls."

I looked at Jim. "Yer probly gonna be carryin' me aroun' for a week." I looked back to Andy and Shane. "You guys ready?"

They nodded. Everybody took a deep breath.

"Okay, when I say three, Andy you start a slow, steady push with your left hand and use the same steady pull with your right hand. Just kind of ease the shoe back on. But, no matter what, don't stop, unless I yell.

"Shane, you just keep doin' what yer doin'. It helps. But, when the shoe slides on and that high top comes up, get your hand out quick, okay?"

He nodded. "Uh huh."

Suddenly, I noticed I was sweating. On the count of three, the shoe slipped perfectly into place. I told Andy to slowly, carefully tighten the laces and tie the shoe as tight as he could.

Everything felt okay. Sore, but okay. We decided to get the wagon, haul me around a while and let the ankle and foot settle.

But, before we got the wagon, we ate breakfast: candy bars, chips, cookies, cola and cereal. Danny brought a bowl and a sack of corn flakes. He had no milk, so he substituted cola.

"It's great," he grinned, "I swear."

When he finished, three guys lined up to use his bowl and spoon. There was more than enough cereal.

Louie had that hungry look.

I said, "DON'T," and then I thought.

I ain't goin' for this yelling again.

I looked at Louie. "Don't look at me. I'm hurt."

Jim jumped. "I got Louie. I'll get his stuff." He looked to Uncle Sam, the parade winner. "Hey, Louie, wanna start off with Snickers?"

"GODDAMN RIGHT!"

I thought.

Perfect breakfast.

Chapter 17
The Cardboard Box and Other Clues

WE ENTERED THE Jefferson yard from the back side: more jungled up, less traffic. Jim passed out masks for himself, Tim, Andy and Shane. No gloves, helmets, shovels or rakes but plenty of flashlights. As long as I stayed still, the ankle was a dull, steady ache but not a big deal.

Andy gave orders. "Split up. Me an' Jim upstairs to the attic. Shane, you guys recheck the bed and the closet in Scotty's room. Remember above and below."

Shane hesitated. "We should get gloves. It's bad in there."

Andy balked. "I'm goin' now. It'll be okay. Flashlight's like a weapon."

Jim was moving. "Wait ten minutes. Be right back."

Gone before anyone could say a word, he was back soon, huffing and puffing. Sitting next to me in the wagon, he waved two fists full of gloves.

He play-slapped Louie, threw the gloves on the ground and dug four crumpled painter's caps from his pocket. "I remembered gloves in the box in back of the fort, but I forgot I left these caps in there, too."

Andy repeated instructions. "Me and Jim upstairs, Shane and Tim recheck Scotty's bedroom an' remember above and below. Okay, let's go."

We made the same agreement as before for an inch by inch account. The adventure took about an hour and here's my version of how it unfolded.

****

The search party left, scurrying to the front of the house. The darkness and the rotten dank hit like a heavyweight fighter. They stepped lightly up the crumbling staircase and parted company at Scotty's bedroom, Andy and Jim continuing to the attic.

In the bedroom, Shane and Tim decided to work together. No talking, just shallow mouth-breathing. Shane pointed to the northeast corner. An icing of thick dust and cobwebs covered the bed while noisy, unknown creatures ran open-eyed in the space underneath.

Shane signaled to grab a post on the headboard and slide the bed away from the wall. It did not budge. There was no place to wipe their gloves. They shifted to the posts at the end of the bed and pulled together. The bed moved three feet. They flooded the area with light. Nothing. They stomped on the floor, heaving and coughing and spinning away from dust explosions. They shielded their eyes.

Dizzy, Tim put his head between his legs. He was thinking about animals that hang upside down (bats and sloths) when he saw something move.

He grunted, "Snake!"

Shane sputtered. "Move the bed back a little."

Tim straightened up. "Whadaya mean back? Where?"

Shane pointed toward himself. On three, Tim pushed and Shane pulled. Again the bed moved.

Suddenly, a small snake flashed and was gone in an instant. But, in its wake, Tim saw a message carved carefully into the hardwood floor. He used the heel of his hand to clear away dust and through his mask, he mumbled, **"It Is A Sin."**

Shane looked at the carving. "Let's push the bed back and get outta here."

"Why?" Tim frowned. "I mean, why push the bed back?"

Shane huffed. "Because, I said."

Within seconds they were on their way. They did not wait for Andy and Jim. Instead, they hurried down, ripped off their masks, and began gulping air as soon as they hit the outside. After a minute or so, they ran to the back of the house. They were covered in dirt.

Shane was breathing hard. "You guys can wait here if you want, but we're goin' back to the fort."

We looked at each other and headed to the fort.

Danny asked, "Find anything?"

Shane puffed. "Tell ya when we get there."

****

Here's my version of the other play-by-play account we were promised.

The attic was exactly as described, a marvel and a maze. The short stairway was dark and twisted. Andy and Jim had to corkscrew themselves upward.

Jim grunted a whisper, "This place gives me the creeps." He squinted. "No fast way out."

Andy coughed. "At least it don't stink so bad up here. Just smells old, like bad dirt."

Flashlights twittered like weak fireflies. The darkness was choking. Andy pushed on the overhead trap door. It did not move. He pushed again.

Jim looked up. "Somethin' wrong?"

"Door stuck."

Before Jim could respond, Andy smashed the butt of his flashlight against the edge of the door. It rained dirt. Both boys ducked and turned away. Hands on the wall, flashlight in mouth, Jim squeezed around Andy and steadied himself. He took the flashlight from his mouth, wiped the handle and offered a quick, focused, upward blast. Again dirt rained down, but this time the trap door gave. It sounded like painter's tape ripping. Jim heaved himself up, lifting the door with his neck and shoulders. The hinges screeched and the lid fell backward. Jim climbed two more steps and stood waist high in the hatch. He moved his flashlight slowly, left to right, up and down.

Andy grunted. "Move, go!"

Jim tried to avoid touching the floor with his hands. But the ceiling was low and he crouched. Andy followed. Once inside, it was difficult to make sense of things. The space seemed strange: a circular cubbyhole, filthy windows and window seats. It was impossible to see out and it was nearly impossible to move.

The Jefferson's life was littered everywhere. There were stacks of labeled cardboard boxes: Taxes, Toys, Baby Clothes, Pictures, Checkbooks, Games, Children's Books, and Letters. On one side of the room stood an antique, up-right, 1930's Philco radio; on the other side, a five foot tall, wooden cigar-store Indian. In good daylight he might have been majestic, but in this gloomy haze, he was threatening. There were broken things everywhere: Tools, furniture, mirrors, phonograph records and unmatched sets of dishes.

Andy looked in all directions. "I dunno 'bout the other two rooms up here, but this place would be cool fixed up, ya know. Cool to stay here."

"Maybe, if it was clean and sunny," said Jim, "but right now, it ain't cool. Barely move in here."

"Yeah," Andy whispered, "but if all this junk was gone… Kinda feels like a cabin on a sailing ship, you know, if all these windows were clean."

Jim nodded. "Maybe."

They looked closer—moving, touching and kicking things. Spiders were everywhere, alive and well. Flies were also everywhere, dead. Next to one of three cracked mirrors, Andy lifted a rotten blanket. It came apart in his hands. Underneath, he saw a jackpot: A cardboard box labeled, "Losing Scotty."

Andy exhaled and whispered, "Holy Crap!"

Jim pushed. "Open it!"

Andy put up his hand. "Not here. Later. Come back with the wagon."

Jim nodded.

Andy looked closer at the box and then glanced to his right at the broken mirrors. That's when he saw something else: A business card wedged underneath the frame of the second mirror. He lifted the card but neither he nor Jim could make any sense of it.

"Can't read it here. Let's go."

"Yeah, we'll be back later."

Jim held up an index finger. "Gimme a minute, I'll check these two other doors. Be right back."

Andy agreed and Jim duck-walked his way to each door, stuck his head and flashlight inside and returned.

He shook his head and coughed. "Nothin' except enough dirt to choke a horse."

Andy's eyebrows shot up. "Enough to cover a body?"

"Not hardly."

Jim was struggling to breathe. It took a minute or so before he was ready to move on. They shoved the "Scotty" box near the Indian so that it would be easy to find and returned as they had come, without incident. They were surprised that Shane and Tim were gone. But, they were more surprised that everyone else was also gone.

Jim sighed. "Guess they all went back."

Andy nodded. "Yeah, let's go."

Chapter 18
Richard Diamond, Private Detective

HALF WAY BACK, Andy and Jim caught up. The soggy gray cold began to squeeze. My ankle was now throbbing steadily and swelling by the minute. The wagon magnified every bump. I knew I had to get an ace bandage around the ankle soon. I also knew I needed to get up and test it.

I winced. "The ankle is stiffening up and I gotta wrap it."

A quick look at the ankle and everybody agreed.

Jim spoke. "I gotta ace bandage. Go to the park an' I'll meet you there."

I smiled. "Thanks."

Andy urged, "Be quick, boy! We gotta talk."

Jim took off.

I was glad.

Get the bandage tight enough so I can get around. Mom won't even notice.

****

The park was a bad idea: fog-soaked tables and benches. So, we headed instead to Shane's garage, happy for a pool table and dry couches. We picked up Jim along the way.

He walked beside the wagon, huffing. "Got it! It's real wide and long. My dad uses it."

He tossed it in my lap.

I said, "Thanks. You got the connector things. Those little metal clips?"

"Rolled up in there somewhere."

"Yeah, good."

Jim said, "I know how to do it. I mean, wrap your ankle."

****

Shane's garage was filled with light and warmth: thick dark-blue carpet, used brown leather couches and an over-sized pool table. Thin, honey-colored pine paneling everywhere. An antique, cathedral style upright radio sat in one corner, a classic Coke vending machine in another and finally, a full-sized juke box in a third—none of them working. Immediately, the couches filled and three guys grabbed pool cues. Jim asked Shane for a pillow to prop up my leg while we wrestled with the ace bandage. We wrapped the ankle tightly, shoe and all.

Standing was simple enough. I knew the drill: Leg straight, knee locked, drag the foot.

Every muscle works overtime, including eyelids.

Take your time. Be careful. Don't lift the foot.

I was happy. Nothing seemed broken and the pins seemed okay. This was particularly good because sometimes (even without an injury) the pins would shift and cause trouble.

Jim speculated. "We should wrap your knee, too."

I agreed and Shane offered a second ace bandage. It was a delicate operation: Jeans down, butt on the couch, bandage on, jeans up, butt back on couch. I was sweating. But wrapping the knee made everything better. I felt safer. I thanked Shane and Jim.

Shane handed me a hand towel. "No big deal."

Jim smiled. "I owe you."

Davie came over and asked, "This the worst thing ever hurt ya or was that time the pin come out worse?"

"Neither."

"So what was it?"

"You don't wanna know."

"Do too."

"Maybe some other time."

Andy sat on the edge of the pool table, legs dangling, and reported. "We found a card." He held it up and moved it slowly from left to right. "It's messed up. Crunched on one corner and torn a little in one place. Real dirty when we found it. Wiped it off some. Ya can read front and back."

Questions came like popcorn.

"Where'd ya find it?"

"What's it say?"

"See any ghosts?"

"Or dead bodies?"

Andy answered in order. "In the frame of a mirror, stuff on both sides—tell ya in a minute—an' no an' no." He continued. "The card is from a private eye, Richard Diamond Investigations, Los Angeles, California. There used to be a telephone number an' a license number, but both of 'em are pretty gone."

I waved. "Richard Diamond is a private eye on TV. How can that be?"
Andy shrugged. "Beats me."

Shane added. "He was on radio, too. When I was little I heard it at my grandpa's house. I just played on the floor, while he listened. He'd say, 'That Diamond is a real tough guy.' An' then he'd make me say, 'That Diamond is a real tough guy.' Then, he'd laugh."

"So," said Davie, "if there ain't any real Richard Diamond, only radio or TV, what's with the card?"

Jim wondered. "Maybe there's a real Richard Diamond who let 'em use his name for radio and TV."

"Well, if there is," Jesse laughed, "I wanna meet his secatary. TV one's called 'Sam.' Never see her, just her legs. I bet the real one ain't as good as the TV one."

I looked at Jesse. "Secretary", not 'secatary.'"

He flipped me off.

I ignored. "Maybe there's a real detective, who's just using the name, Richard Diamond."

Jesse jumped. "I can get my cousins in LA to look 'im up in the phone book."

Danny spoke deliberately, with emphasis. "Your cousins, Mr. Parker, cannot read."

Everybody laughed. Jesse flipped Danny off.

Andy ignored.

He was still interested in the card. "Maybe this ain't a real card at all, just a made up one that you can buy, like the one for Have Gun Will Travel. You can buy those an' they sure ain't real."

Tim grabbed a deck of cards. "Who cares? What else does it say?"

Andy turned the card and squinted. "As near as I can tell, it says, Ans. is y Sorry kid."

The room again jumped with questions. But, unlike before, some simple answers came—even if they still didn't help very much.

"Ans. is 'Answer.'"

"Y is 'yes.'"

"The answer is yes," said Andy.

"So, what's the question?"

"Who's sorry?"

"For what?"

"Who is the 'kid?'

"'Kid' is Scotty."

"Wait," Andy yelled, "Let's just lay this out… Somebody asked somebody, maybe a real detective, a question. And the answer is yes. The 'somebody' who asked the question is the kid. You guys think the kid is Scotty."

The room nodded. Louie watched and nodded, too.

Andy studied the card again. "There's more but it's all smudged. Looks like a smudge and an 8 and more smudges an' a 4."

Nobody said a word.

Andy turned to Shane. "Wha'd you guys find?"

Shane came to the front. "We found somethin' under the bed alright but we couldn' bring it with us. It was scraped, uh, carved, into the floor. Nice 'n neat, once you wipe the dirt off. You could read it real clear: It's A Sin."

"No," Tim corrected. "It said, **It Is A Sin**."

"Yeah," agreed Shane, "That's right."

Again, machine-gunned questions bounced off the walls.

"Who carved it?"

"Why scrape it into the floor?"

"What sin?"

"Who sinned?"

Andy waved his arms for everyone to be quiet. He looked around the room and heaved a big sigh. "There's somethin' else. We found somethin' else in the attic."

"What?"

"Where is it?"

Andy put his hands up again and motioned like he was settling the air. "Hold on, gimme a chance." He looked around the room one more time, heightening the tension. "We found a cardboard box marked, 'Losing Scotty.'"

Now, he answered quickly, cutting off questions. "We don't know what was in it, what is in it, 'cause we didn't open it. We figured we'd need a wagon to get it. It's gonna be hard to get it out of the attic and down that shaky staircase. It's pretty heavy."

Jim added. "We need a rope. Tie it up an' lower it down real slow."

Andy nodded. "Might work."

Everybody wanted to go back to the Jefferson house right then.

Jim objected. "Gotta get Louie home"

I sighed. "Me too. I gotta get home too."

"OK," Andy carefully placed the card in his pocket. "But, let's meet at the Jefferson place tomorrow, late morning"

Everybody wanted to meet earlier, but Andy had chores. So, everybody agreed on later. And that from now on we would only go to the Jefferson place as a group.

Shane volunteered to help me get home while Jim would take Louie.

Chapter 19
The Polar Bear Doctor

WE GOT TO my house and decided to use the back door.

Shane helped me out of the wagon. "You OK?"

"Yeah, just sore."

"You walk?"

"Think so. Gotta be careful."

The ankle was hot, weak and painful but I kept everything straight and locked and I dragged the foot. It made no sense that the ankle hurt more when I took weight off, but it did. I made it to the porch step. Those four inches of concrete might as well have been four feet.

I whispered, "Let's go in quiet. Less my mom sees this ankle, the better."

Shane grabbed my shoulder. "Let me lift you up."

I gritted my teeth. "Okay, good, but you gotta lift straight up and come down easy. Don't bang the front of my shoe on the edge of the step."

"Okay."

Shane was much taller and he was strong. So it was easy for him to wrap his arms around my chest, under my arms and lift from behind. But, from there, it got tough. The toe of my shoe scraped the front edge of the porch and I came down sharply on the step.

I grimaced and sucked air through my teeth.

Shane whispered, "Jesus. Sorry. You Okay?"

I grunted, "I'm OK."

I looked down and saw the threshold.

Maybe I can drag my foot over it.

Shane opened the kitchen door and pointed to the threshold. "Can you make this?"

I nodded. "Think so."

I gritted my teeth, tensed every muscle, shifted my weight against the door jamb and inched my left foot over the threshold. I carefully dragged the right foot over as well. Shane picked up my stuff from the wagon, stepped inside behind me and closed the door.

From the living room, my mother called, "Randy, is that you? Who's with you?"

We stepped from the kitchen into the living room.

"It's me and Shane."

Arms full, Shane stepped around me and smiled. "Hi, it's just me."

My mother smiled and asked, "How are you, Shane?"

"Fine."

I said, "He's just helping me bring my stuff in."

We started toward my bedroom and my mother scowled. "What's wrong with your leg? Are you OK?"

"Just twisted it a little. It'll be good."

"Well, be careful."

Inside in my bedroom, Shane put all my stuff away and tapped my shoulder. "Jefferson place tomorrow. Careful, okay?"

"Yeah. Thanks. See you tomorrow."

After he left, I rested on my bed and tried to make sense of all the mysterious clues:

What was the sin? Was it suicide or murder or something else? Who hired a detective, and why? Was there a real Richard Diamond and what was he investigating? Who was the kid? Did 'Ans. really stand for 'Answer'? What about the 'problem below' and the 'answer above?' What did the small silver skeleton key fit? Who was Linda L. and what happened to her? Why did Scotty's dad board up the house and disappear?

Suddenly, I felt very tired. Everything ached and I was shivering. I pulled the bedspread over my torso, up to my neck and stared at my ankle.

Not even close to hurting me the most—not even close.

I closed my eyes, put a pillow over my face and slept.

The dream was all too real.

****

I was nine years old, sitting in a wheelchair in the hallway of the county's regional hospital. My mother sat on a wooden chair to my right. The hallway was dark to the right, but on my left, the July sun marched right through massive glass doors.

The walls were institutional green, matching the flimsy, open-backed hospital gown now bunched on my lap. The black tile floor was mirror shiny.

The stark white of the baseboards and door jambs had once matched the casts covering my legs and feet. But, six weeks later, my below-the-knee casts were a sorry shadow of themselves: cracked, crumbling, battered and bruised.

My doctor, all 6'7", 300 lbs. and size 16 shoes of him, was surprised at the casts' condition.

"What happened here?" He thumped my right calf. "These aren't walking casts."

My mother told the doctor that I had been visiting my cousins on a dairy farm and they had taken me to the top of a haystack and accidentally dumped me out of my wheelchair.

"That's a new one. I guess you're OK, huh? That's the most important thing, right? Eh?"

I nodded and smiled.

He messed my hair (Can't mess a crew cut.) He had a soft voice, his eyes sparkled when he talked and he moved like a polar bear. When he said things to me, he sounded like he was thinking aloud, like he was thinking about something else: The way adults sound when they lose their place reading to little kids.

He sat next to me in the empty chair opposite my mother. "Today these casts will be removed and we'll be checking the progress of things. As we discussed, to straighten your son's ankles there are six pins positioned at cross-angles in each foot. Today we will be removing two pins from each foot because their job is done. We will then re-cast the feet so that the remaining pins may stabilize permanently, assuming he stays away from the top of haystacks." He smiled and winked. "Is that right? Did I get that right? You think you can stay away from haystacks for six more weeks?"

I smiled. "Yes."

He looked serious. "I need to tell you about what to expect today, okay? When these pins come out, it's going to hurt a lot."

He paused. I looked away.

He sighed and continued. "I have a few things I have to do and I'll be back. While I am gone, you are going to go into the room behind us," he pointed "and we will get your casts off and see how things are. We'll give you some shots for pain and take out the pins you don't need. We'll put on a new cast and send you on your way."

He paused again. "Is there anything you don't understand, anything you want to ask me?"

I asked, "Why is it gonna hurt? Won't the shots do it?"

"The shots will help some but they will not stop all the pain."

I was quiet.

He looked down for a moment, made eye contact, put his hands on my shoulders. "Listen, during this procedure, uh, I mean, if it gets too much and you want to stop, you just tell me and I'll stop, okay?"

"Okay." I looked away.

He took my mother and me into a nearby room and introduced us to a man with a hand-held electric saw. Two nurses lifted me to a padded, leather-covered table and the cast specialist placed plastic drop cloth underneath. He explained that the saw would cut the cast without cutting me because I was protected by a roll of cotton padding on the inside.

The saw reminded me of barber's clippers with a small stainless steel disc at the tip. It made a high-pitched, narrow, screeching sound. When the blade touched the cast, screeching became grinding, plaster-sprinkles and dust everywhere. We breathed through thin paper masks. There was a lot of vibration and shaking as the wheel made its way down the center of my leg, first on the inside and then the outside, going over my ankle and ending just where my toes stuck out.

My toes were dark and dirty and I felt ashamed.

I should have cleaned my toes.

I hoped my mother wasn't thinking the same thing.

The saw tickled my leg when the blade touched the cotton. When both legs were completed, he used shiny, silver pliers to wedge open the thin line made by the blade. He was gritting his teeth and clinching his jaw as the cast groaned and cracked.

He grunted, "Kinda like cracking lobsters, ya know."

I smiled. I didn't know what a lobster was or why he would want to crack one. I was surprised that the cast pulled apart evenly. But, when he lifted the top half of the cast (leaving my legs to rest in the bottom) and pulled away cotton, I was even more surprised.

The room was immediately filled with a sickening, rotten smell: The smell of dead flesh. I looked at my feet and ankles. Mask or no mask, it was hard to breathe. I saw thick, green, scaly mucus covering everything. It was oozing in places. I thought I was going to throw up so I looked away.

My doctor walked in, took one look, asked a nurse to take my mom out of the room and began giving orders.

He spoke to my mom. "I'm going to have you wait in the hall while we clean and disinfect everything and remove these pins. You can watch through the small window in the door if you wish but I would recommend that you not."

I was shivering, teeth chattering.

Nurses suddenly appeared with stainless steel pans of warm water, bottles of liquid soap, soft cloths, cotton balls, towels and a red liquid disinfectant. They spoke quietly to one another, worked quickly and smiled at me through masks. I could see smiles in their eyes.

The doctor said, "Let's get him a few warm blankets, eh?"

A nurse nodded and left.

He stepped near me. "Until she gets here, I'll just hold on to you for a bit."

He wrapped his polar bear arms around me from behind and I leaned against him. "This okay with you? You don't have a girlfriend who might get angry or jealous do you? One of these nurses might be your girlfriend, eh? Then, I'd really be in some trouble, right?"

Even though he was behind me, I could tell he was smiling, because all of the nurses were smiling. I could see the shadow of his big, wavy black hair and his big head and face. Everything about him was big.

I was smiling too.

I shook my head. "No, I don't."

The nurse returned with the blankets and she and the doctor wrapped me tight and snugged the edges. I felt better. The doctor was studying my legs and feet. Stuff in the pan looked awful but my legs and feet were looking okay. Underneath the mess was nice pink skin.

My toes looked like they belonged to somebody else.

The doctor turned to one of the nurses. "I'm going to scrub up. Have the tray brought over, set up the lights and get me six male nurses. Also, procaine hydrochloride, six altogether, three for each foot. You'll be here to assist me. Make sure somebody stays with him."

I was worried about my heels. A pin was sticking out from the corner of each—about one fourth of an inch. It was hard to tell that it was a pin because it was covered with clotted blood, scabbed-over dead skin and other junk. I was told there were two other pins sticking out, but I could not see them. As soon as everything was clean and dry, one nurse stayed with me.

She tucked my blankets and asked, "So, you don't like girls huh?"

"Nope."

"So, what do you like?"

"I'd like a Sheriff's Badge. I really wish I had one."

She smiled again. "Well, maybe someday, you'll get one."

"Yeah," I said, "but I don't think so."

A nurse came in with two trays on a cart: one with syringes (each with a very long needle) and a second with shiny, chrome-covered tools. I had

---

never seen such long needles. A minute or so later, another nurse delivered a large, overhead light on a rolling platform.

My doctor returned in full uniform, looking very much like a masked polar bear.

He said, "Let's get started, here, shall we?"

He sat on a chair with wheels and rolled toward me. He moved the lighting platform near the foot of the table and twisted the goose neck on the overhead light, positioning it directly over my legs, a bit above his head and to his left.

He spoke to the nurse quietly. "Let's lay him down and get a pillow, please. Also, let's get his arms out in the open, so they're just at his sides there. By the way, where are the others?"

She said, "They are on the way."

He looked at me. "I guess I look pretty funny to you, eh? Yeah?"

I shook my head.

"No? So, you think I look good?"

He was picking up a syringe, thumping it with his finger, pushing the plunger and forcing out a few drops of liquid.

"Okay, you're going to feel this a bit, a little pinch is all, maybe more, not much."

I looked away and closed my eyes. I looked up and saw a skinny, long window near the ceiling. I tried to breathe and not think about anything. I could feel sharp cramping and tugging. I clutched the blanket.

The door opened and six men entered. They were dressed in hospital green: caps, masks and gloves. My doctor waved them over. They were tall, all of them. Not as tall as my doctor, but tall. They surrounded the table. One of them began with a syringe. My doctor picked up another.

He said, "These big guys here are nurses. You believe that? It's somethin' eh?"

I said nothing.

He said, "They are going to help you be safe on this table."

He picked up one last syringe. He stuck the needle in a bit, twisted it to the right, pushed the plunger a bit, twisted the needle to the left and pushed the rest. The other male nurse was fast. He, too, was finished.

My doctor stood, pushed his chair back, stepped to his instrument tray and picked up a pair of pliers and a vise grip. The nurses gripped my shoulders, arms and thighs.

Suddenly, my body jolted itself into one long, rigid convulsion. I bit my lip and screamed. I twisted my head from side to side, grinding it into the pillow. Every muscle in my body resisted and trembled. I was drowning.

A female nurse tried to wipe my face.

I screamed, "Stop!" but it continued forever. It never stopped.

When I came to my senses, the big male nurses were gone. I seemed to be hemorrhaging oxygen. I was suffocating in the blankets. Mucus and sweat everywhere. Blood everywhere, all over me, all over the doctor, splattered on the nurse's cap, splattered on the table.

Pulling off his bloody gloves, my doctor said, "Let's get some help in here, fast."

The nurse nodded and left. He stepped to the table, wiped my face and lip with a wet cloth and placed a dry towel beneath my head.

He said, "Your lip OK?"

I jerked my head away.

The nurse returned with two others and they flew into action.

My doctor spoke to the nurses. "Let me know when the cast is on and he's ready to go. Is his mother outside? Don't let him leave until I see him."

Soon everything was clean and new. New casts, clean clothes. The nurses lifted me from the table and settled me into the wheelchair. I hurt everywhere. My muscles were still twitching.

My doctor entered the room. I looked down, clinched my teeth and gripped the chair's armrests. He squatted near the chair, just to my left.

I looked directly at him. "I hate you. You lied to me. You said you'd stop but you didn't. I hate you."

I turned away.

He whispered in my left ear. "I'm sorry. I stopped but you never knew it. After a minute, I had to go on and finish."

I looked at him. (Tears in his eyes.) "You stopped?"

He nodded, wiping his face, resetting his handkerchief.

He leaned forward, pulled me toward him, placed his arms around me and whispered again. "What you did today was brave. You are a very brave boy. I love you."

He kissed my cheek, settled me back and stood. He took a big sigh and so did I.

We shook hands.

On the way home, my mother said, "I watched some of that through the window today. I couldn't watch all of it. I am very proud of you."

Ron McCraw

I said, "Can I have a Sherriff's Badge?"

****

I woke up in a near-blinding sweat. I threw back the blanket.
"It's 1:00 in the afternoon. What the hell am I doing?
I looked at my ankle.
Hurt me the most? Hell, I'm okay. Next time, better dream about Sandy Koufax or Sandra Dee.
And, I wondered…
What really happened with Scotty Jefferson?

118

Chapter 20
The "Losing Scotty" Box

WE DID NOT return to the Jefferson house the next day. The five days before Christmas were a mess. It was not until the morning of the day after that we again gathered in Shane's garage. The long layoff helped my ankle. I was nearly 100%.

Comparisons of holiday loot choked the air. It was not simply a question of who got the best stuff, but also who got the most.

Tim Bradford's haul usually topped the list. His father owned a motorcycle and muffler repair shop and his parents seemed to have no spending limit on toys. While others showed off a cable-controlled, propeller-driven Mustang Electra Airplane, a magnetic dart board, an electric football game with plastic players who vibrated across the field, a football helmet, a baseball glove, an electric train, a plastic bowling and shuffleboard set or a Monopoly game, Tim rode in on his own kid-sized, gasoline-powered motorcycle.

It was a gleaming mass of candy-apple red fenders, matching jet black hand-grips, seat and foot pedals and cream-colored "white-wall" tires. Its wire wheels were chromed as were the engine compartment, handle-bars and tail pipe. It roared, deep and full. Its idle was like something alive.

I smiled.

As beautiful as Sandra Dee... almost.

Everybody circled the bike as Tim came to a stop and switched off the ignition. He took off his candy-apple red helmet and waved a black glove. Nobody spoke.

Tim grinned. "This ain't the best thing I got. I gotta exact model of Howdy Doody. Just like the real one, strings and all."

Immediate, exploding laughter.

Tim got off the bike, wacked the kick stand and set everybody straight. "I can't give nobody no rides. Don't ask. I can't let nobody ride it. Don't ask. My old man will beat my butt, take the bike away and sell it."

Jesse grumbled. "He'll never know. We go out to the foothills."

Tim shook his head. Everybody groaned.

Jesse shrugged. "What? What'd I say?"

Louie winked. "JUST MY SIZE."

Andy interrupted. "Timmy, we gotta go over an' get that box from the Jefferson place. Take your motor on home an' meet us. Nothin's safe over there."

****

The plan involved lowering the box marked "Losing Scotty" from the attic to the Jefferson second story by rope and from there, out the window to the ground. Four guys would lower the box and three guys would grab it at the bottom. But, before anything else, Andy would hammer out the remaining glass in Scotty's window. Only guys with leather or cloth gloves could even get near the rope or box.

Louie and I would wait by the wagon and watch the show.

Entering the Jefferson place was new each time, but it always looked and smelled bad. Suited up with painter's caps and masks as well as gloves, both teams headed for their spots: the attic and Scotty's bedroom.

It was an overcast day with sloppy fog and a bit of wind.

Andy said, "I'll go with you guys to the bedroom and knock out the window and then I'll head on up to the attic."

Jim hung the rope over his shoulder. "I'll take this up. You guys in the bedroom might as well give us a five minute head start, no use waiting inside."

Five minutes later, Andy waved. "Let's go."

Later that afternoon, the guys gave Louie and me a play-by-play account of the adventure inside the house. Here's my version. It reads like a movie.

****

Jim was faster the second time. It took a few minutes to adjust to the darkness, ugly smells and creepy sounds. But, once he reached the attic stairway, he lifted the hatch, pulled himself up and used his flashlight to direct Jesse and Tim.

He pulled the coiled rope from his shoulder and set it on a dust-covered stack of magazines. The space was overstuffed and standing was impossible. Movement was difficult.

Jesse wiped muddy fog from a window. "Hey, look! It's Ray."

Jim whispered, "Yeah… Crap! Is he stopping or what?"

"Yep," said Tim, "He sure is."

All three ducked and peeked over the window ledge.

****

Andy's group moved quickly through the blackness and stench, up the weak, winding staircase and into Scotty's bedroom. Moving toward the window, they too saw Ray's patrol car. Andy ducked and motioned everybody down..

"God," whispered Andy, "We are in one big pile of crap, right now."

****

Outside, I waved to Ray.

Louie pointed. "IT'S THE DAMN COPS."

Ray's patrol car slowed to a stop.

He yelled, "You guys okay?"

I answered, "Yeah."

"What are you doing out here?"

"Uh, we're gonna meet a bunch of guys and go to the park."

"Well, this is not a good place to be. You should be someplace else."

"Okay."

Louie was nodding.

Ray continued. "It's dangerous. You could get hurt."

"Yeah. We're goin' to the park."

"Do your mothers know you're here?"

"They just know we're goin' to the park."

Louie nodded again.

Static belched from Ray's car radio and he said something to the dispatcher.

He turned to me and Louie. "You guys better stay away from this old wreck. That means all you guys. You tell 'em I said nobody goes in there for any reason. I better not see any of you guys around here."

****

The attic guys fidgeted with masks. The air was thick and so was the conversation.

"What the hell?"

"What's he doing?"

"Why doesn't he leave?"

Jesse ripped off his hat and began violently scratching his head.

"What's wrong?" hissed Jim.

"Goddamn head itches. I can feel prickly things on my neck and ears."

Tim grinned. "What kind of things?"

Jesse blushed. "Shut up!"

Jim threatened, "You both better shut up, right now."

****

In Scotty's second story bedroom, the air was heavy and wet, the talk was quiet and the peeking intense.

"He didn't see us, did he?"

"Naw, I don't think so."

"I think he did. I think he's getting out of his car."

"No, he's not. He's just taking off his hat."

"Yeah, but he's talkin' on his radio."

"So what?"

"Whadaya mean, 'so what'? Look, idiot. He's callin' other cops."

"Nope," said Andy, "He ain't callin' no other cops."

Shane thought for a minute. "He might be callin' our moms."

"Yeah," said Andy, "He might but I doubt it. Too much hassle. Too much bullshit."

"Yeah," said Danny, "besides, it's just a warning. They always give a warning."

****

On the ground, the mist was getting thicker.

I looked right at Ray and didn't blink. "You don't gotta worry about us. I'll be sure an' tell everybody."

"Son," he said, "I gotta worry 'bout everybody in this neighborhood. It's my job."

I nodded and smiled.

"You cold?" he asked.

I shook my head. "Nope. I'm fine."

Cold didn't matter. In my white tee shirt and new royal-blue Baltimore Colts jersey, white shoulder accents and Johnny Unitas' number 19, I would have been fine in a snow storm.

He asked, "You gonna make it to the park? Need any help?"

Louie yelled, "ONLY IF YOU USE THE SIREN."

Ray laughed.

I laughed too. "No, we got it."

He waved. "Next time ya can tell me what you got for Christmas. I mean, besides the jersey."

As the cruiser slowly pulled away, I looked at Louie. He smiled and made his vampire face, like he was going to bite me. "THAT COP IS DUMB."

I looked at Louie and shook my head.

I thought you couldn't hear.

****

After five minutes, Louie and I saw shadows in the attic. After ten minutes, we saw glass splinter and fly from Scotty's window. It sounded like the crack of a whip. Suddenly, about five feet in front of us, it was raining glass.

I stepped behind Louie, yelled "Duck," spun his chair away from the house and shoved him about ten feet. The ground was sloped and lumpy and the chair struggled and bounced. I thought he might fall out.

I looked at Louie's chair banging along and suddenly, Marx Brothers mayhem was running through my head: I saw Old Crotch chasing Louie's chair helter-skelter.

I laughed, staggered and sprawled on the ground. I flopped on the ground like a fish. My stomach on fire, I gritted my teeth and tried to hold my breath.

Louie screamed, "WHAT'S THE MATTER?"

I laughed harder. My sides were killing me.

Gonna pee my pants! Help!

Andy yelled, "You hurt?"

Suddenly, it hit me.

I am laughing at nothing!

That was it. Another blast of killing laughter smacked me. I was gone.

Jesus, please help me.!

Louie shook his head and gave me his dwarf vampire look.

****

By the time Andy got the glass out and cleared from the window sill, Jim's group had the box secured. His scout merit badge in knot-tying showed.

Andy started up the attic's corkscrew stairs but Jim stopped him. "Hey, no room. Stay there. We're gonna lower it down real easy right now."

Jim, Jesse and Tim lined up on the rope behind the box like a tug-of-war team. Jim slid the box to the edge of the hatch, told Jesse and Tim to hold and yelled at Andy, "Here it comes."

He gripped the rope, looked at the other two and carefully nudged the 20 pound treasure into space. The taught rope against the hatch gave the boys good leverage. Jim controlled the slow and steady release of the rope. In about twenty seconds the box was safely in Andy and Shane's hands. The boys in the attic let the rest of the rope drop and climbed down to the second floor.

Andy and Shane moved the box near the window.

Andy warned. "Watch out for glass."

Shane looked up, sneezed and waved for Danny and Davie to follow him outside.

"We'll be ready."

The tug-of-war rope-line reset with Andy and Jim at the front. They nudged the box over the window ledge, held it for a moment, rope taught, then carefully rested it against the outside wall. Guiding the box down was surprisingly easy, a minute or so from start to finish. They could see and feel the box safely into Shane and the twins' hands. The boys on the ground set the box in the wagon and collected the rope.

Andy cupped his hands and yelled, "Let's get outta here before Ray comes by again."

The grey sky rained gloves, masks and hats.

Soon after, the second story bunch arrived.

Jim yelled, "I got Louie."

Jesse shook his head. "No. I got Louie."

They each grabbed a handle of the wheelchair, pulled and glared. Louie looked from one to the other.

Andy said, "Jimmy, call it." He flipped, caught and slapped a covered quarter on the top of his left hand.

Jim called, "Heads."

Andy said, "Tails, Jesse pushes."

Jim stepped away, hands in the air. "Okay, but I getta take 'im home from Shane's."

Louie smiled. "YEAH."

Jesse thumped Louie's right ear from behind. Louie turned with surprising speed, snarled his vampire look and grunted. Everybody laughed.

Jesse grouched. "Quiet, ya little fairy turd or I'll thump your other ear."

Louie looked at Andy and me, rifled a pudgy little thumb in Jesse's direction and winked. "HIS TIME OF THE MONTH."

We laughed hard and Andy saved me from falling.

Suddenly, everybody yelled, "I didn't think he could hear!"

It took a moment or two for the laughter to die.

"Hey," Andy looked at me. "That reminds me, what happened to you? Saw you rolling around, couldn't hear a thing."

Others nodded.

I smiled, "A personal problem. Tell ya later. We gotta get goin'."

Andy said, "Right!"

We left the Jefferson's yard and crossed the street only moments before Ray's cruiser rolled by.

He smiled, waved and tipped his hat. "Have a good day boys. And stay away from the Jefferson place."

We smiled and waved back. Everybody yelled.

"Oh, we will."

"Yes."

"Yep."

"Sure."

"You got it."

"No problem."

Chapter 21
Inside the Box

WE ARRIVED AT Shane's garage near noon. By the timeless overcast, it could have been 8:00 AM or 4:00 PM or anything in between. The argument began as soon as we settled in and ended almost as quickly.

Andy announced, "You guys wanna eat, go ahead. I'm gonna open this box right now."

That was it. Nobody moved.

Suddenly, Tim declared, "I got ten bucks from my grandma for Christmas. After we look at the box, we all go to the GAD for lunch on me."

He waved the ten dollar bill above his head and everybody whooped it up. The GAD or Great American Diner, a converted railroad car, was the best.

"OK," Andy cleared his throat. "Let's do this."

He began by using a Wisk broom to attack years of dust. He wiped the surface, sides and bottom with a cloth. So much for spider webs and egg casings. He lifted the box from the wagon and set it on a towel on the pool table.

Shane warned. "Black widow spiders."

Andy took a breath. "Yeah" and began working the lid.

It was stuck as if it had been glued shut. He gently worked first one side and then the other. After a minute or so it broke free. He lifted and set it aside. Everybody moved forward.

Louie tried to crane his neck, but he couldn't. Nothing to crane.

"GODDAMN IT, I CAN'T SEE."

Andy sounded like a dog trainer. "Everybody sit. I'm gonna take stuff out one at a time and Shane's gonna write a list of everything we find."

Shane stepped up. "Ready."

Andy said, "I'm gonna hold things up and I'll say what it is and set it on the table. Don't ask no questions right now. We can talk about everything at the GAD. Shane'll bring the list. Here goes."

For the next twenty-five minutes, everybody saw what was in the box:

A small stack of blue, crocheted baby clothes and booties

A rubber-banded, yellowed stack of elementary school report cards, a few high school ones included (all A's)

Valentines, lots of them

Mother's and Father's Day cards

An Olympic style junior high gold medal for track, attached to a red, white and blue over-the-neck ribbon

A silver referee's whistle

A high school football All-American lapel pin

A high school diploma

Bronzed baby shoes

Three picture albums: birthdays, holidays, vacations

A baby book

A scrapbook of newspaper articles about Scotty in football, baseball and basketball

A letter of acceptance to the University of Southern California.

A framed picture of Scotty standing next to the Tommy Trojan statue at USC, holding up a cardinal and gold jersey, number 23

A small, plastic, yellow and red toy Jack in the Box

A framed, smiling, family high school graduation picture with mom and dad

A file folder of a child's drawings and handwritten notes

A selective service registration form, 1A classification

Three Achievement Award Certificates for Perfect Attendance

A tiny combination lock

Cracker Jack Prizes: A collection of five 1" tall three-dimensional plastic red, blue, yellow, green and purple cowboy-on-horse statues, each on a plastic standing pedestal.

Four high school year books

An infant's Super Man Tee Shirt

Baseball cards: Duke Snider, Willy Mays and Mickey Mantle

A file folder of class school pictures

An autographed picture of Larry, Moe and Curley, signed "To Our Pal Scotty"

Two, 2 lb. silver disc weights

A small, metal, yellow toy bulldozer

An envelope of letters, apparently from Scotty, bundled with a thin red ribbon

A box of Cub Scout and Boy Scout merit badges and patches
A blue and gold Cub Scout kerchief with a silver eagle clasp
A red Boy Scout kerchief with a gold eagle clasp
Eagle Scout Award and ceremony pictures
Medical records from 1941 describing a still-born baby girl named "Evelyn."
A toddler's plastic drinking cup
A proof set of US coins for the year 1939
A child's worn out outfielder's glove
Two sixth grade mimeographed newspapers with Scotty's column on sports
A County Lifeguard Certification
Silver metal pin-on kid's pilot's wings from United Airlines.

That was it. The bottom of the box was filled with dirt, rat droppings and other odd scraps. Andy took the box outside and banged it on the ground. When he returned, guys were arguing.

He tried to cut the argument off. "We might be able to use the envelope of letters but, that's all. So cut the crap an' leave the rest of it alone."

Jesse would not back down.

His little eyes were on fire. "I want the pilot's wings and the Cracker Jack Cowboys. Hell, none of this stuff matters, these people are all dead."

Andy threw up another roadblock. "We should leave this stuff alone, put everything back, even the letters, after we read 'em."

Jesse would not fold. "I say we flip for the stuff we want and throw the rest of this crap away."

Davie yelled, "I want the baseball cards."

Andy stood his ground. "I say we ain't messin' with this stuff. It ain't ours. Besides, I found the box and I say it all goes back after we read the letters."

Jesse stuck out his chin. "It's America. Let's vote."

Andy's eyes flashed and he moved toward Jesse. "I don't care if it is America, we ain't votin' on this."

Jesse backed up a step. "You ain't the only one found the box. Jim did too. Whadya say Jim?"

Jim shrugged. "I'm with Andy. Put the stuff back after we read the letters."

Jesse raised his hand. "Anybody who thinks we should vote put up your hand."

He looked around. No hands.

His eyes were full of black fire. "OK, forget it."

He sat in a corner, arms folded across his chest.

Room temperature and energy levels dropped. Shane started putting things back in the box. He handed Andy the envelope of letters and the red ribbon. Andy re-tied the ribbon, stuffed the bundle inside his jacket and turned to help Shane. Suddenly, things didn't fit. It took a few extra minutes of re-arranging to get it right.

As we were about to leave, Shane's mom stepped through a side door. "Hello boys," she smiled, "I thought I heard voices out here. How are you all?"

Some nodded, others waved, a few just smiled and one or two mumbled.

Shane spoke, "We're just leavin' Mom."

"Have you thought about your lunch, then?"

"We're goin' over to the GAD."

"Have you got your money, then?"

"Uh huh."

Shane's family was different. His mom was from England. She called people "love" and finished lots of her sentences with "then." She called trucks, "lorries" and she called the bathroom, "the W.C." If she spoke quickly, she was impossible to understand. Shane's father, an American, a fighter pilot in the RAF in World War II, had returned to America with his bride. Shane also had an older sister, Leslie, who was smart and sweet but plain. Always a bit nervous, she wore too much make up and tried too hard.

After a pause, Shane's mom made a suggestion. "Maybe your sister would like a go at this GAD place."

He snapped, "No, Ma." But, he caught himself when he saw his mother's face. "I mean, uh, she probly wouldn't like it, I mean, with us."

There was another brief pause.

Abruptly, Louie sounded off. "SHE CAN GO WITH ME."

Shane's mother blanched and quickly recovered. "That's quite nice of you, then, dear, isn't it? Perhaps another time, then."

Shane fidgeted. "We gotta go now, Ma, okay?"

"Alright, dear. Have a good time, then."

She looked at the rest of us. "Nice to see all of you."

****

Once outside, everybody fell apart.

Andy squared up with Louie. "WANNA GET US KILLED?"

Louie shot Andy the vampire look. Andy threw up his hands and nodded to Jim who smiled, grabbed the wheelchair and set off to the Great American Diner.

It was still overcast and drizzling, the sun struggling through only now and then.

Andy looked at Louie and then at me. "What's he askin' about Leslie for? I thought he couldn't hear."

I laughed. "Yeah, me too."

We reached the corner of Blake and Poplar, crossed the parking lot, continued down the tree-lined sidewalk and entered the GAD single file, Louie first.

Chapter 22
The Great American Diner

A CONVERTED PASSENGER rail car, the GAD (The Great American Diner) was a work of art: a mass of chrome-plating, stainless steel, glass and color. The daytime logo, classic royal blue art deco set below bay windows, drew visitors' cameras like a magnet. At night, its backlit, blue neon twin rested softly above the roof.

Once inside, our eyes never stopped moving. Our images were reflected in everything: shiny black and white checkerboard floor, candy- apple-red tables with coin-operated juke boxes, Coke-a-Cola swirl vinyl seats with etched glass backdrops, tinkling chandeliers—and the stunning inlaid copper ceiling.

Multi-colored celebrity posters drenched every inch of wall space: John Wayne, Marilyn Monroe, Elvis Presley, Chuck Berry, Little Richard, Fats Domino, Ricky Nelson, James Dean, Elizabeth Taylor, Mickey Mantle, Roy Rogers, Buffalo Bob, Howdy Doody, Shirley Temple and many more. Painted metal signs made you want hamburgers, Coke-a-Cola, French fries and milk shakes.

We entered from the west end. Booths lined the window side, mirrored by a long row of vinyl-covered stainless steel stools guarding a long candy-apple-red counter top. Red and white ceramic tiles sparkled below the counter. The east end of the counter was anchored by an enormous three-tiered stainless-steel-framed glass house, home to doughnuts, fried pies, cakes and cookies.

At the west end sat the cash register, a mahogany antique of clanking keys, pop up numbers and a ringer-banging change drawer. A red and black rotary pay phone was mounted on the wall near the restroom. Above the phone sat a black cat neon clock.

Behind the counter, owner Reggie manned the galley. The business end was all stainless-steel: double sink, grill, stove, toaster, mixer, oven, deep-grease-fryer, two double-door refrigerators and a walk in freezer. Utensils hung from metal hoops.

We were greeted and seated four on a side with Louie's chair parked at the open end. The waitress, Daisy, was friendly and beautiful: Light honey blonde hair, full red lips, a matching glossy manicure, perfect teeth and a movie star figure. When she moved, her red and white polka dot skirt swirled and her white blouse pulled at her waist. She kept tucking it in.

She held nine menus, "You fellas got money, right?"

She glanced in Reggie's direction. He waved at us.

She flipped pages in her receipt book. "You gotta be serious here. No playin' around boys, right?"

Tim waved his $10 bill.

"Great," she smiled, "would you like water and are you ready to order or do you need menus?"

Andy answered. "We decided on the way over. No thanks on the waters and we don't need menus."

She looked relieved. "Now, who wants what?"

Andy answered again. "We all want the same thing. Cheeseburger, French fries and Coke."

"Well, that's easy," she smiled and left.

Davie grinned. "Let's trade out the salt and pepper."

"Get thrown out," warned Jim.

I shook my head. "Nothin' to put it in while yer switchin'."

Andy removed the shakers. "We ain't doin' that. We ain't gettin' thrown out. We'll be lucky they don't remember Jesse."

Jesse laughed and Jim grinned. "Oh, they remember him."

Danny was staring at glasses of water like he wanted one.

He started digging in his pockets. "Hey, do we got enough money?"

Tim cleared his throat. "Sure do."

Andy was quick with the math. "Add these up. Cheeseburger 45 cents, Coke 20 cents, Fries 25 cents. That's a total of 90 cents."

"Right," Tim added, "and since there's nine of us that's 9 times 90 cents which is $8.10 total."

Jim added the last bit. "Tax about 15 cents."

Tim shook his head and wagged a finger. "18 cents, exactly, I know."

Andy clapped. "So, we got it an' some left over."

Shane cleared his throat. "Gotta tip. Ten percent."

Tim was on it and spoke out loud and clear. "82 cents. Total $9.10."

Out of nowhere, Louie bellowed, "GIVE 'ER A DOLLAR. SHE'S GOOD LOOKIN'."

All heads snapped to the dwarf instantly.

I announced, "My count, on three."

The chant rang out, "I thought he couldn't hear!"

The table exploded. Louie laughed too—and hard. It was the first and last time I ever heard him laugh. And, his laugh was funny, like Chip & Dale being put on the rack.

The food arrived. She carried three plates on each arm, returned with the last three plates and then brought nine drinks on a platter. She set the platter next to Louie (who stared at her legs) and hand delivered each drink.

I asked, "Why don'tcha have a picture of Sandra Dee on the wall?"

She said, "I really couldn't say. Maybe you should ask Reggie."

Shane spoke for everybody. "They should have your picture on the wall."

"Yeah."

"Right."

"Now yer talkin'."

"You bet."

She blushed. "Thank you all. That's very sweet. Enjoy your meal."

I was lost.

Look at that hair! I wish I could touch it. Forget it. Don't even know how to talk to a girl. I really liked Angela, couldn't say a word. How am I gonna marry a girl when I can't even talk to one? Can't reach the ketchup on the top shelf. Gotta be able to do that. That's the kind of stuff that dads do. Fix things, know things, get money and get ketchup off the top shelf. Open lids that are on tight... Probably do that but that's not enough.

"Hey," Andy was poking my shoulder.

He whispered, "Stop lookin' at her ass and eat your food."

"I wasn't lookin' at her ass," I whispered, "I was just thinkin'."

"Yeah?" he continued, "Then stop thinkin' about her ass and eat."

"I wasn't thinkin' about her ass."

"Okay," he whispered again, "I give. What were you thinkin' about?"

I spoke softly and deliberately, "I'll look at what I want and I'll think about what I want. You gotta problem with that? We can settle it outside right now or later. I don't care."

I surprised myself.

Why the hell am I so mad?

Andy sat back. "What's the matter with you? Take it easy."

Louie barked. "TAKE IT EASY."

135

Andy and I smiled. Jim came around the table, told Davie to move to the other side, set his plate down and hip-checked me about a foot to his left. He pushed my plate along, too.

"Sorry, but, I got Louie."

He picked up his knife and cut a bite from Louie's burger. "This about right?"

"TOO BIG."

He cut the bite in half. Louie nodded. He placed the bite in Louie's mouth.

He turned to his own plate. "My turn."

Louie scrunched his face. "WHY BURN?"

Jim stopped in mid-bite. "You heard me."

I looked out the window and focused on the parking space nearest the door. Pete Decker swung his turquoise and white '55 Chevy Bel Air convertible into the lot next to Reggie's restored burgundy and cream 1930 Model A rag top. The Ford was exciting and fun, a life-sized toy. But the Chevy was larger than life: All sleek and smooth, all color and chrome and curves.

Pete Decker was a nineteen year old, muscle-bound paraplegic, Marlboro soft pack filters rolled up in his tee-shirt sleeve, always the same tan fisherman's hat. He swung his car door open, swiveled in his seat, reached behind with one hand, lifted his folded wheelchair out and slammed it down.

I knew Pete Decker the same way most minority folks know each other. And, even though I did not like him, we came from the same world of braces, weights, therapists and doctors.

In a tight spot, he might help me, maybe.

Jesus, what an arrogant asshole. God, how do you do that? How can you be arrogant and paralyzed? I'll tell you how. You are Pete Decker. That's how.

His face was big and square, pale and puffy. He shook the chair out and tossed a square pillow inside. Then, in one effortless motion, one hand on the car seat one on the wheelchair armrest, he lifted and transferred himself. During the transfer, his spindly legs dangled like Howdy Doody's and scraped the ground. Once in the chair, he reached down, slammed first one foot rest and then the other into position. Next, he grabbed a fistful of jeans just above the knee-cap and jerked each foot into place.

He flicked the car door shut with his thumb and spun his chair toward the entrance. He ignored the ramp and took the stairs instead. Gripping both wheels in the front, near the ground, he jerked both wheels backward violently, stopped his hands abruptly about even with his hips and shoved forward in a short, hard move. This whiplashed the front wheels into space and balanced the chair on its back wheels at a 45 degree angle. Once balanced, Decker moved up the steps, all five, without a hitch. When he reached the porch platform, he let the front wheels drop, opened the door, pushed inside and greeted Daisy.

"Hey, Good Lookin'."

"Hey Pete," she sighed.

"Wanna dance?"

In the background, the Coasters sang, "Charlie Brown, he's a clown." She ignored the invitation. "What'll it be?"

"It's not on the menu, baby."

She rolled her eyes, sighed again, and glanced in Reggie's direction.

"Okay, Okay," he apologized, "I didn't mean anything. Just jokin' around. You know."

"Yeah," she sighed. "I do know."

"I'll seat myself."

He waved off the menu and headed toward our booth. "I'll have a cheeseburger, fries and a coke and a chocolate milk shake and a fried berry pie."

She scribbled and left. He parked at an angle, next to Louie and spoke to me, "Hey kid. How's it hangin'? Gettin' any lately?" He turned to Andy. "Whatcha got there, Shmoe?"

He pointed to the letters.

"Letters," Andy answered.

"I can see that, Shmoe. Who are they to?"

"They're from Scotty Jefferson."

"No shit? I mean, no kidding?"

"Yeah."

"The kid who blew himself away? That kid?"

"Right."

Pete thought for a moment. "Hand 'em over, Kokomo."

"Nope. Uh-uh."

"I just wanna look at 'em for a minute. He was my friend, too, ya know. Just two years older than me."

I tried to look intense. "Shove off Pete, your food's ready."

Pete straightened up and stared at me. I did not look away.

Andy stared too. "Your food's ready."

Pete glanced over his shoulder and saw Daisy waiting.

He backed up a bit, looked at Daisy and muttered, "Follow me." He hesitated and squinted, "I thought you wanted a ride in my car."

I whispered, "Not in this lifetime."

I was shaking.

"By the way," he smirked. "I know a secret about our friend, Scotty but you wouldn't be interested, would you?"

He laughed and left.

Andy whispered, "I hate that guy."

Jesse grimaced. "I'd like to kick his crippled ass."

Tim cautioned. "Uh, I don't think so."

I grinned. "He'd throw you around like a rag doll."

"No, he wouldn't," Jesse protested.

Andy leaned back. "Randy's right. He'd throw you around like Raggedy Ann and all of us together couldn't help you. You best leave him A-L-O-N-E."

Jesse rolled his eyes.

Andy popped in a French fry. "Let's look at these letters. I'll pass 'em out. Everybody read yours to yourself an' then we'll see what they say."

Louie did not take a letter.

I whispered to Andy, "Wonder what secret Decker knows."

He leaned close. "Nothin'... He's bullshit."

I had three letters to read. Most guys got only two. The first was from eight year old Scotty at summer camp. His cabin was called "Sherwood," his camp nickname was "Hawkeye" and he missed his mother. The printing was big and messy. The second was just a postcard. Twelve year old Scotty was at a two week football camp, passing league two-hand touch. He liked everything and was the number one quarterback so far and was eating a lot. No mention of homesick. The third letter meant something. It was addressed to someone called, "D.G." and it was dated May 15th 1954, a bit more than a month before Scotty died.

Dear D.G.

Please don't do this. I'll do anything to make things right. You know I never meant to hurt you. Can't we just talk this out? We used to talk all the time. Why not now? What are you afraid of? Why can't you face me? Why do you hate me now? Why are you doing this? It doesn't have to be this way. Please. Talk to other people. They will tell you.

I can't eat and I can't sleep. This is killing me. We may have done some wrong things. But, this is just not right. Everybody knows something is wrong. My parents are asking questions. I can't concentrate in school. I'm afraid I'm not going to graduate. How can I go to graduation parties? How will I ever be happy again?

Maybe I should just disappear like you. Why did you do that? No note, no phone call. You said you would always love me. Was that a lie? Was it all a lie? Did you ever really love me? Just tell me that. Tell me to my face that you never loved me.

Listen to me. You're smart. Think. You know two wrongs or a million wrongs won't add up to anything right. You know that. I don't mean that it was wrong to love you. It was (and is) the best part of my life. And, I'm not talking about the sex. I'm ashamed about that, but I'm not ashamed that I fell in love and that I love you with all of my soul at this very minute. Losing you is like being dead without being buried. Please come back. You don't have to be back with me. Just come back and see if there's a better way. I know you understand me.

I will always love you,
Scott

I was half way through the letter for a second time when Decker stopped by on his way out.

"Hey kid. You still pissed at me? Listen, I didn't mean nothin'. You know I didn't mean nothin'. Right?"

He faked a head slap. I ducked. Suddenly, I was tired. Everybody was waiting for something to happen. I could see Reggie staring, Decker couldn't.

I sighed. "It's okay, Decker. Let's just drop it, huh?"

"Okay, if that's what you want."

"Yeah, that's what I want."

"You still want that ride?"

"Yeah, I guess so. It is a real cool car."

"You bet yer ass it is."

He wore his full, peacock smile. "You remember last year when I drove up and you about shit yer pants right there in the driveway?" He looked around the table. "Never seen me in nothin' but a wheelchair and thought it was a miracle, thought I got healed by Oral Roberts or Kathryn Kuhlman. Some shit like that." He touched my shoulder. "Hell, I showed ya the real Goddamn miracle, hand controls. Nothin' to it."

He laughed. Nobody else did.

He hesitated, gave a thumbs up and thumped the table. "Well," he sighed, "just to prove there ain't no hard feelings, I'll tell you my Scotty secret."

He leaned forward and whispered, "Old Scott had another girl friend. Not the blondie, Linda, but a Mexican girl."

He winked and left.

I watched from the window. This time he took the ramp and balanced on his back wheels all the way to his car. Everything was now the reverse of before. He just did it faster. The transfer was complete and the chair loaded (one-handed) in no time.

That son of a bitch is really strong.

Jesse watched Decker and whistled. "He is fuckin' strong."

I laughed. "Just how strong is that, Einstein?"

Jesse grunted, "Who's Einstein?

I looked away.

Jim also watched from the window. "He never has anybody in that car with him."

Tim added. "Never has anybody with him anywhere."

Jesse sniped. "Tells girls he got hurt in the war."

Andy surveyed the table. "Five more minutes and everybody tells about their letters."

Jim spoke through a mouthful. "Somebody's gonna hurt him alright. But, it ain't gonna be in no war."

I sighed. "Decker's a pain in the butt, alright. But, he's okay. He's just pissed at God 'cause he got polio. Besides that, mess with Decker, you better bring some help. He ain't stupid like the McKinleys."

Jesse stuffed a mouthful of fries. "Maybe God's pissed at Decker. Ever think of that? Maybe that's why God give him polio."

I shook my head. "No, that ain't right. God don't curse people like that."

"Well," Davie said, "Satan does."

Jesse attacked me. "How do you know God don't curse people?"

Tim talked with his mouth full. "Satan don't curse people, just deceives 'em."

Davie screwed up his face. "How in hell you know what Satan does?"

I punched back at Jesse. "Because God loves people, even you, asshole. That's why he doesn't curse 'em."

Tim answered Davie. "I learned about Satan in church."

Jesse grinned at me. "If God loves people, why does he give Decker polio? An' look at you an' Louie."

Louie blurted, "THEY WON'T LET ME GO TO CHURCH."

Jim pointed at Jesse. "Parker, if we're lookin' at people, let's look at you. Why would God give anybody a face like yours?"

Everybody laughed, except Jesse.

I answered Jesse. "You are right. I dunno about Decker or me or Louie or you."

Jesse saluted. "Thank you, Brainiac." He turned and stared at Jim. "And you. Any more cracks about my face and you'll be damn sorry."

Jim shrugged, laughed and returned the stare. "Anytime, pal... crack, crack, crack."

I grabbed Jesse's arm and my eyes grabbed Jim. I whispered through clenched teeth. To those near, I'm sure it seemed like we were sharing important secrets, maybe we were.

"Hey, idiots, listen. Cut this grab-ass crap. We got free food in a nice place. Eat. If you wanna fight, get the hell outta here and fight. Don't sit around here waving your panties at each other." I paused and talked directly to Jesse. "And, you pal, better watch yourself. Just between you and me, about the only thing you can do better than Jim is run. Take a good look. He ain't the same guy. He ain't little anymore and he ain't fat. He'll kick your ass. And, when he does, I'll laugh."

Jesse scowled and sulked.

I turned to Jim, softer. "Hey, wise up. Don't waste your time. Besides, you get me banned and you and me are gonna have our own problem and you know I don't care what you can do. I will hurt you."

Jim grinned. "I'll do this later not here." He took a breath, leaned in, and winked. "Besides, after you hit me once, I will kill you."

I smiled. "I don't care."

Andy touched Louie's arm. "Why won't they let you go to church?"

"I DUNNO. MA SAID THEY DON'T WANT ME."

Andy groaned, "That is screwed."

Everybody agreed.

Danny took a long drink. "Louie, If I ever start a church, you can come."

Louie smiled, blue eyes sparkling, bad teeth showing yellow. "YEAH."

Davie snapped. "On 3...

Everybody screamed, "I thought he couldn't hear!"

It took more than a few minutes for the booth to settle down.

I took a drink. "There's another reason Decker is mad. He wanted to be a priest when he was a kid our age. They told him no because he wasn't 'a full man.'"

Jesse chomped a fry. "What the hell does that mean?"

I shrugged. "Beats me. Guess they figure you ain't a full man if you're crippled."

Tim motioned for Andy to pass the salt. "Maybe it just means you can't do all the priest stuff if you're crippled."

Jesse laughed. "Maybe he's gotta dick that works overtime. Priests ain't posed to have dicks that really work."

Andy glared. "Jesse, shut up! You hear me?"

Jesse nodded.

Andy looked in my direction. "When did Decker tell you that?"

"Coupla years ago. He was my counselor at a summer camp for crippled kids."

"An' he told you all that 'not a full man' stuff?"

"Yep."

"Was he a good counselor?"

"Nope, mostly, he was mean. But, never around other counselors."

Jesse asked, "Any good lookin' girls there?"

I shrugged. "Didn't care about girls then."

Andy thumped the table. "Enough. Take five more minutes. Finish your letters and be ready to tell."

Everybody got quiet and read.

After three minutes, Louie growled, "I WANNA MILK SHAKE."

Everybody looked up.

Andy pointed. "Not now. Quiet gnome."

Two minutes later, Andy started. "I got nothin.' Postcards from camp."

We continued around the table.

"Thank you notes to grandma."

"Letter to Uncle, thanking him for a gun." (We were all wondering the same thing.)

"Letter to Columbia Record of the Month Club."

"Order form for white sweatshirt with purple Bullwinkle Logo: Whatsamatta U."

"Birthday invitations."

"Letter to USC Athletic Department."

I was the last person. What I held in my hands was 1000 times more powerful than anything we had yet discovered. I took my time. I read the letter aloud, twice. Nobody said a word.

I set the letter on the table. "The letter makes sense but who's D.G.?"

Andy scratched his head. "His girl was Linda, Linda L. not D.G."

This was a bomb.

I pushed my plate away. "Decker was right. I guess Scotty did have another girlfriend, somebody named, D.G."

Andy was about to say something when Daisy set our bill on the table. Tim passed his money forward.

The beautiful honey blonde leaned in. "Fellas, I couldn't help but overhear the letter. I knew Scotty too. I'll be back with change and information."

Daisy headed toward the register. We looked at each other, eyes wide.

I couldn't wait for her to return.

What information could she possibly have?

If Andy was particularly interested in Daisy, he didn't show it.

He held the letter up and studied the envelope. "Looks like this never got sent."

I pulled my plate back. "Think he wanted to send it, but died before he could?"

Andy shook his head. "He didn't know where to send it. Doesn't he ask where she is?"

I knew that letter inside out. "Not really. Just says, 'Why did you disappear? Why did you do that?'"

"Okay," he agreed, "But, he don't know where she is. So, he couldn't send it."

Shane said, "Maybe that's why he had a detective. You know, lookin' for her."

Daisy returned with the change.

Louie honked. "KEEP THE CHANGE. YER REAL GOOD LOOKIN'."

Andy laughed. "Don't mind him, he's crazy."

From the far end of the booth, we heard Tim. "He ain't one bit crazy. He's right. Keep the change. Merry Christmas from my grandma."

Daisy blushed again, scooped up the change and edged a chair up next to Louie. He rolled his eyes and stared at her legs.

Her voice got low, her eyes got hot and she talked fast. "I don't know who the D.G. is in that letter. But, I do know that he loved Linda. Her last name was Rilley or O'Reilly, somethin' like that. They were only in here twice maybe and two things were real clear: 1) They loved each other and 2) They were scared of somethin', maybe her old man. I don't really know."

Davie interrupted. "Scared of her father?"

"Her husband," Andy corrected.

"Yeah," Daisy nodded, "husband." She looked toward the grill. "Be right back. Be ready to order a dessert."

As she moved away, Andy stuck out his hand. "Okay, you heard the woman, ante up, boys."

Jesse whined, "Why? She already got all the money."

"Hey," I disagreed, "It ain't about the money. If we're gonna be in here all this time, we better be buyin' stuff."

"Sure," Andy tilted his head. "See ole Reg over there? He can't have us in here, if we ain't spendin' no money. 'Sides that, you guys wanna get Daisy in trouble or what? So, let's see some money boys."

Louie announced, "I WANNA KISS 'ER."

Everybody laughed and money started rolling in.

I smiled and touched a shoulder. "Louie, every guy at this table wants to kiss her but that ain't gonna happen. It doesn't happen that way."

He raised his eyebrows. "EVEN YOU?"

I leaned toward his ear. "What?"

He gave me the wild eyes and croaked, "I THOUGHT YOU COULD HEAR!"

I never heard such laughter before or since. I thought it would never stop. It hit like lightening and rolled like thunder. I almost fell off my seat. An old lady with blue hair gave Louie the wolf stare. He gave it back double.

Andy elbowed me. "He means you. Even you want to kiss her, right?"

I looked at Louie and leaned in close again. "Right now, buddy, I want to kiss Daisy more than I've ever wanted anything in my life."

His blue eyes flashed, deep and bright. In the chandelier light, he looked magical. He smiled and stuck out his small, stubby-fingered, pudgy hand. We shook and I smiled. I was careful not to squeeze too hard. It was one of the happiest moments of my life.

Louie pointed to his pants pocket. Andy reached inside and pulled out a carefully-folded one dollar bill. With Louie's contribution, we easily had enough for nine fried pies, five berry, four cherry and waters all around.

Daisy returned, and took the order. "Be right back."

144

She winked at Louie and left. He smiled and puffed up with a fierce satisfaction.

Andy grabbed a fry. "I think the D. might be for Daisy."

Danny took a fry from my plate. "Yeah, but her last name is Clover."

Chapter 23
The Kiss

DAISY RETURNED AND checked for Reggie. He was nowhere to be seen. She again sat next to Louie and quickly read the letter. Then we ate and she talked. It was a magical space.

"I always liked Scotty. He was a real nice kid with a real nice future. But, I wasn't surprised when I heard he took his life. When that Linda girl (woman) wasn't around anymore, he died. I mean, died before he died. Know what I mean?"

We all nodded, eyes riveted.

"No light in his eyes. Seemed to hurt when he moved, like an old man. He'd come in, order black coffee, get the paper, lay it on the table and just stare out the window. Sometimes for an hour or more.

"Never drank the coffee, never ate anything. Never read the paper. Just left it on the table or threw it away on his way out. Reg made me change out the coffee every 15 minutes anyway."

Andy asked, "Always by himself?"

"For the most part. But, the last time I saw him in here, he was with another guy, an older guy, a stranger. For some reason, I thought the stranger was a body guard or newspaper man. I don't know why I thought that. They sat in a booth and talked secret-like and looked at some pictures."

Shane asked, "Could the stranger have been a detective?"

"Maybe," Daisy paused, "I dunno. But, I do know that Scotty didn't have any other girls. Now, in his junior year, he did go to the prom with a girl named Delores Graham but, they were just friends. Over the years, she hung around the diner a lot, especially after Scotty died. I got to know her. She loved Scotty, but there was never any romance. (Not that she didn't want it.) Of course, as far as I could tell, every girl in that school wanted a romance with him."

I jumped in. "Ever get a look at the pictures they looked at, Scotty and the stranger?"

"No, any time I got close, they got even more quiet."

"Dolores still around?"

"Sure is. Works at the Anytime Cleaners on 5th Street, family business."

Andy asked, "Think she'd talk to us?"

"Maybe one or two of you, not the whole bunch. I don't know if she knows anything. But, I will tell you this, she's a shy person."

Andy touched the bill of his cap. "Thanks for your help."

Daisy nodded. "You know, it might help if you knew a little more about Delores. You can tell her I gave you her name. I'll see if I can jot down a bit about her before you leave."

I smiled. "Thanks."

Daisy said, "Can I ask where you got those letters?"

"Sure," I answered, "in a box in the attic at the Jefferson place."

"That's all you found, letters?"

"A few other things," Andy said, "but, nothin' big."

Daisy took one last look at the letter. "Well, it's a mystery, that's for sure." She stood and paused, "Listen, I have to go. But before you leave, we do have a special contest you can all enter. Each of you pick a number between one and one hundred. Quiet now. Wait 'till I ask. Think hard, it's a very good prize."

Everyone picked and she came to me last. I picked 23, Scotty's USC number.

Daisy smiled. "The winner is # 23."

Before I could react, Daisy leaned close.

She whispered, "Tilt your head back a little. We're gonna do this like in the movies. Don't pull away until I do. I heard your wish. Sometimes, it does just happen."

Suddenly, her lips were touching mine, soft fire everywhere. I could feel the heat. I held my breath. It was the longest, shortest five seconds of my life. She smelled and tasted like cherries.

She stepped back and smiled. "That," she said, with authority, "was a movie star kiss."

I didn't move a muscle. I couldn't see or hear very clearly. Everyone sounded far away and I felt weak. I couldn't think.

She touched my cheek and whispered, "Thank you. Bye."

I was numb all over and a bit lost. I felt good, but not very much like myself. It seemed like I couldn't get the inside me connected to the outside me. I just wanted to sit and be quiet for a while. It took a while for guys to finish up. Every once in a while I'd catch one of them staring at me and

I'd just smile. As far as I could tell, everybody else was pretty quiet too, nothing from the dwarf or Jesse.

Andy tapped me on the shoulder. "Come on boy. Let's go. Gotta getchu outta here. Son, you do not look good at all."

Daisy came by once more, gave Andy an envelope and said to keep her informed. Everybody thanked her again. I could barely whisper. I don't remember leaving. I do remember everybody yelling and pounding on me as we made our way back to Shane's.

I looked at the little wheelchair.

Louie, buddy, I owe you forever. Without you, this never happens, never in a million years. What did she say? Sometimes it does happen...

Late afternoon, in the garage: pool, checkers, chess or cards. Jim playing "War" with Louie's over-sized deck. Louie winning four of every five hands.

"Louie, you cheatin'?" Jim cocked his head. "'Cause if you are, you're goin' right back in that laundry bag."

The dwarf's blue eyes sparkled. "WHERE YA GONNA HANG IT?"

"Don't know yet but nobody'll find ya."

Louie flipped over the Ace of Diamonds, taking Jim's King of Clubs. "HA HA."

Jim squinted. "Louie, I mean it. Laundry bag."

Louie grinned and turned over the Ace of Hearts. "LAUNDRY BAG THAT," he grunted.

Jim rolled his eyes, sighed and turned over the Ace of Spades.

Eyes locked, they yelled "WAR," flipped over three cards, face up, as fast as they could and then stopped dead.

Jesse frowned. "Posed to take turns putting down three cards, one at a time, face down, so ya don't know what yer losin' 'til ya turn over that fourth card."

Jim growled, "Shut up."

Shane wandered over to the pool table. "Wish we had a Carrom board."

Tim banked the three ball in the side pocket. "Had one. Sister stepped on it."

Jim slowly turned over his fourth card, held it high in the air and slammed it on the pile: Queen of Spades.

"HA yerself, ya little cheater. Take that!"

Louie tapped the top of the deck with his pudgy, little cartoon index finger and slowly turned over his fourth card... The Queen of Hearts.

Everybody screamed, "DOUBLE WAR."

Tim dropped his pool cue. "All right," he laughed, "double war. This is good."

Jim grabbed his head with both hands.

Louie barked. "DON'T BEND MY CARDS."

Jim collected himself. "Okay, this time, we put 'em down, face down, one at a time, like Jesse says. That way, it builds up, see."

In no time, the card pile grew by six more face-down soldiers.

Louie pointed. "YOU GO FIRST."

Jim cleared his throat. "Only right, little man, only right. Beauty before age."

Louie flipped him off.

Jim made a face, mocking, wide eyes. "Easy, little man."

Andy touched Louie's shoulder. "Just a game buddy."

Louie scowled and grumbled.

Jim smiled. "It's okay, Louie don't mean nothin'."

Louie suddenly announced, "I WANNA BET."

Jim leaned in and locked eyes with Louie. "Huh? We are bettin'. We're bettin' our cards."

Louie cranked his little bowling ball head. "NO. I WANNA BET."

"What?" Jim shook his head. "Money? I ain't got none."

Louie rolled his eyes. "NO MONEY."

"What then?"

Louie's eyes twinkled. "THE LAUNDRY BAG."

"Huh?"

Shane came over. "I get it. Louie wants the loser to go in the laundry bag. Right, Louie?"

"YEP."

Jim scratched his head. "I can't fit in no laundry bag."

Shane snapped his fingers. "I got it. We can use a sleeping bag."

Jim frowned. "How?"

"I mean duffle bag. My dad's got one from the war. It's big, it's canvas and it's got big handle things that we can put a rope through and hang it from the patio roof."

Jim looked around the room.

Andy agreed. "Sure. We can do it."

Jim reached for his card. "OK. Here goes."

"Wait." Andy grabbed Jim's arm. "Loser stays in the bag 20 minutes."

Jim nodded, gave a big sigh and turned over his card: Ten of Diamonds.

Louie studied the enemy card. Guys pulled in tight over his shoulder. Carefully, he turned over... The King of Hearts.

Instant shouts of victory, everybody back-slapping Louie.

Jim shook his head, groaned and threw his remaining cards in the air. "Louie how in the hell are you doin' that? Huh? Nobody wins like that."

The dwarf, all bowling-ball-head-and-moonscape-skin of him, realized the moment.

He smiled, surveyed the room, tilted his strange head, gave an evil wink and said, "I PRACTICE."

As soon as the room put itself back together, Jim said, "We'll do the duffle bag thing tomorrow, okay?"

Louie frowned. "NAW. FORGET IT."

Jim put his big paw out and hid Louie's whole hand. "Little man," he smiled, "you are a big man."

Andy and I sat in an over-stuffed, dark brown leather couch in a corner in front of what we called, "The Ex-Juke Box."

He put his arm around my shoulder. "Son, we gotta talk an' I mean, serous, S-E-R-O-U-S, serous."

"Right," I said, "but you mean, serious, S-E-R-I-O-U-S, correct?"

"Nope. My uncle Billy says if you really serious, down deep, then you SEROUS."

I grinned. "Is he the one?"

"Yeah. The one with the pretty nurse in the hospital."

We looked at each other and began to laugh.

Danny laughed too. "What's so funny?"

I looked up at Danny and crumbled.

Tim grinned. "What's so funny?"

Danny pointed at me. "He's worthless."

Head down, I laughed harder each time I peeked at Andy.

Shane put his hand to his forehead. "Don't encourage them, trust me."

Jim looked at Andy. "Go ahead, tell it."

Everybody suddenly chanted: "Tell it... Tell it... Tell it."

Andy waved his arms for quiet. I was doubled over in semi-silent, happy misery.

All eyes settled on Andy.

He began slowly. "To know this story, ya gotta know my uncle Billy. Every few weeks, my aunt Pearl and Uncle Billy come over to visit my parents and have dessert and play that stupid-assed marble game, Aggravation. You guys know that one, right?"

Everybody nodded.

"Well, after the game, they'd always sit around and drink beer and talk and they usually run us kids off. But, about half the time, I'd hide behind that huge planter in the hallway. You guys know, not only is it five feet high, but it goes across the whole hallway, just enough room for one person to slip by.

"I'd scrunch up in the corner behind that thing for hours an' hear everything. Sometimes I'd peek out from behind it, down low along the floor. I could see faces. People even went right by me on their way to the bathroom.

"And, that, boys, is how I heard this story—behind that planter. And, I can tell ya right now, long as I been big enough to understand talkin', I been bustin' a gut over my uncle Billy. Funniest person on this planet, I swear."

Jesse blurted, "How you know he's the funniest? You met ever'body on the earth?"

Danny snapped. "Shut up."

Andy took a deep breath, hands on hips. "Jesse, my uncle ain't the funniest. You are… Funniest Goddamn lookin'!"

Jesse looked down.

Louie bellowed, "TELL THE STORY."

Andy looked around and chuckled. "We know what we're all thinkin', right?"

Everybody smiled and Andy continued. "My uncle Billy, he's a kind of a little guy 'cause he ain't tall, but he's a big guy 'cause he's got a big ole gut, a big head and a big red face and a big ole nose that's kinda smashed in and up, like one of them old-time cartoon Porky Pigs. You know, the ones with the big eyes an' no clothes. His hair is buzzed so short you might think he's bald but he ain't. An' the other thing is that his gut ain't soft, like a grandma. It's hard as a Goddamn rock. I know. Tried to punch 'im once. He laughed an' knocked me silly. My aunt Pearl tried to act like she was mad about him throwin' us aroun'. But, I think she really thought it was okay.

"I mean, she let 'er own son, my cousin Benny, put his eye out. Not that she did it on purpose, nothin' like that. Don't get me wrong but she let it happen. Even though it was an accident, I don't know how old Benny was, maybe ten, but he was old enough to know better. He took a yoyo string and wrapped it around the business end of a butcher knife and began sawin' up toward his face. As soon as the blade came through, whack! Right there in the eye! Cut his cheek, eyebrow and forehead too.

"My uncle tells about Benny. He says, 'It's the Goddamndest thing you ever saw. Bled like hell. You'd a thought they killed somebody. Towel fulla blood. I just made the boy lay down in the back of the truck with another towel an' I hauled his ass off to the doctor. I told 'im, I says, 'I guess you'll learn now, wontcha?'

Andy was smiling and laughing and it seemed like he became Uncle Billy. Everybody else was smiling and laughing, too.

Andy said, "My uncle would say stuff like that. Like he did about Benny. An' my aunt would always say, 'Now William O. you don't want these folks to think you were only mean to the boy.'

"'Well now,' he'd say, all out of breath, 'what I said and done, is what I said and done, ain't it?'

"An' she'd always roll her eyes, give him this, 'You piece of shit,' look and then she'd smile an' say, 'Go on with your story. Don't let me interrupt you. I was only trying to help.'"

Davie asked, "Was Benny okay?"

"'Pends whatcha mean. If ya mean, did he die? No. If ya mean was he messed up forever, yeah, that too. I mean, he gotta glass eye. Looked like it belonged in somebody else's face, always goin' someplace he wasn't. He hadda wear this black eye patch. Kids called him, 'Black Eye' and 'Patch Eye, the Pirate.' He had to fight every day for about a year. Guys sayin' stuff an' tryin' to pull that patch off.

"My uncle wasn't mean, just tough. He ain't afraid an' don't think his boys should be neither. He got a purple heart in the war, shot in the leg by a sniper when he was clearing a landing strip. He walked on the shot leg.

"So, here's the story I love. Coupla years ago, my uncle's in the hospital with a pendicitis. I can imitate my uncle Billy real good. I can sound just like 'im. He tells it like this:

Suddenly, Andy really became Uncle Billy. He puffed out his stomach, stuck a toothpick in his mouth and hooked his thumbs under imaginary suspenders. Even his face seemed to change. It seemed to get red and puffy. He spoke, huffing and puffing, as if every sentence was work.

'I'm in the hospital, boys, an' I'm hurtin' real bad see. So, I just figger I gotta do it. So, I kinda lean forward, grunt real hard, ya know, eyes poppin.' out an' all—an' I rip off a real good one. Long, loud, like a foghorn. Felt real good.'

Briefly, Andy spoke as himself:

"Here, my uncle's eyes are startin' to water and he's grinnin' real big, his face gettin' redder, an' he keeps right on."

Again, Andy became Uncle Billy:

'Then, I think. That poor guy's on the other side of the curtin. An' I feel bad, see, but I'm hurtin' agin. So, what am I gonna do? I gotta go agin, right? So, I rip off two more beauties. Long, loud, ugly. I feel some better, but I use the pillow to cover my face. An' there they come. Two more real good ones an' the same thing agin.'

Andy became himself again, eyes dancing:

"My uncle's slappin' 'is knee now, head down, laughin'."

Andy became Uncle Billy:

'I'm breathin' real hard, see, when the guy on the other side calls the nurse with his blinker light. She comes down and looks on my side of the curtin. She's real cute, bouncy-like an' real sweet, all shiny-like. I point to the other side an' she smiles an' goes over to him.

I'm thinkin'...

Jesus in heaven! How in hell can she take this?'

'She says, 'What seems to be the problem?'

'He says, 'I'm in excruciating pain and discomfort. Bloating, cramping.'

'She looks at his chart for a minute an' thinks a bit an' says, real sweet like a bird, 'Well, fart, honey.'

The garage exploded. Everyone pounding one another, as well as the floor.

Andy waited for calm and resumed as Uncle Billy:

'Boyz, when she says that, I start laughin' see? An' ever' time I laugh, I rip one off, like a little machine-gun burst, see?'

The garage was now a mass of howling and tears.

Andy laughed and snapped back into Uncle Billy:

'Well boyz, I don' need to tell ya how bad that was. But it got worse, see? That little nurse, she says, 'Well now, she says, 'what in the world was that?'

More howling and screaming... guys melting into the floor.

Andy picked up again.

'Well, boyz, when she says, 'what in the world was that?' I'm a deadgoner. I just let 'er go! One big, long amazin' blast. An' the curtin moves, I swear!

'I'm thinkin' again.

Jesus in heaven.

154

'Right then, she pulls open that curtin an' starts slidin' it to the end of the bed. She looks at me an' smiles. Then, she says to him, 'See honey? You just do like Mr. O. an' you're gonna feel fine.'

'He looks at me an' I blast another. I cain't help m'self. She's all shiny agin. 'See there,' she says, 'that's the way.' She's all smiles. An' the poor guy in the other bed still looks bad. All bound up.'

'Well, she looks to me an' says, 'I'll just bring a little air freshner. It's called 'Country Flowers.' After a little pause, she says to me, 'Honey, do you think you might need a bed pan?'

'Well, boys, I laughed agin. An' I shouldn't have, if you know what I mean.'

'She just crinkles up 'er nose real cute an' says, 'I'll be right back with that air freshner.'

'I look across. The other guy's still no good at all.'

'She says, 'I'll just close this curtin.'

'Well, she come back later with that spray an' the bed pan but I played like I was asleep. She was real sweet, though. She puts that bed pan on the stand next to my bed an' whispers, 'Just in case.'

'Once she left, I listened for the other guy. But, I never heard one sound. Boyz, for all I know, he's still there. Hurtin' to beat the band.'

Andy bowed to a screaming, yelling, clapping, room-rattling, standing ovation. He stepped to the couch and pulled me up.

I finally got air. "Funniest thing I ever heard."

Andy grinned big. "I know. I love the guy. Kills me every time."

He paused, got serious and whispered, "Listen, we gotta talk about all this. The letter, D.G., the kiss."

"What about the kiss?"

"I dunno, you know, just about it, that's all."

"You mean you wanna know what it was like, right?"

"Yeah, an' more."

"Okay. When? Where?"

"Tomorrow afternoon, my house."

"Okay. What about Jim in the duffle bag? When we doin' that?"

"We ain't doin' that. Louie said forget it."

"That Louie, he's OK."

"Yeah, he is."

Andy paused and asked, "Wanna go to the GAD tomorrow, later. Just you an' me?"

"Can't, no money."

"It's okay. I got money. When I got money, you got money an' the other way around."

I sighed. "Yeah, but I ain't ever got any money."

"I don't care."

"I do."

Andy pleaded. "I know, but, just go this one time."

"Why?"

"Doncha wanna see Daisy?"

"Stupid question."

"So?"

"Okay, after we talk. We'll go."

"OK."

I went home to think about Daisy and D.G. and a little about Uncle Billy.

Chapter 24
Dobie Gillis and the Twilight Zone

I GOT HOME in time for a Swanson chicken pot pie with burned crusts. My parents were getting ready to go out to the K.C. Steakhouse.

I was all set to watch one of the big new TV shows of 1959, "The Many Loves of Dobie Gillis." Dobie is always chasing the same three things: money, popularity and the beautiful but selfish Thalia Menninger. Even though she is poison (and he knows it) Dobie still wants Thalia. I understand. To me, the real life actress Tuesday Weld looked a lot like Sandra Dee. Who wouldn't want her?

It doesn't matter to Dobie that smart and trustworthy Zelda Gilroy is crazy in love with him. It only matters that she is not Thalia Menninger. It doesn't matter to Dobie that it doesn't matter.

It doesn't matter to him that he knows it should matter—and that it should matter a lot. The only thing that does matter is that Thalia is Thalia and Zelda isn't.

I understood Dobie perfectly. Who wouldn't? It doesn't have to be right to make sense.

I wouldn't walk across the street to watch Zelda Gilroy bleed to death, even on a real boring Tuesday. Thalia Menninger or Sandra Dee? I'd eat a mile of asphalt just to say, "Hi."

My mom was putting on her lipstick.

Suddenly, I had an idea. "Can Andy an' Shane an' Jim stay over tonight?"

"You're with them all the time. Don't they have homes?"

I didn't answer.

She finished her lipstick. "Ask your father."

I went down the hall and asked my father through his bedroom door.

"What did your mother say?"

"She said to ask you."

A few seconds passed. "It's OK with me if it's OK with her."

I went to the phone as fast as I could and made the same call three times. "My parents are goin' out, can you stay overnight? We can watch Dobie Gillis an' The Twilight Zone"

I got three quick answers.

****

I found my mother changing her stuff from one purse to another. She looked up, smiled and left half of her stuff in the old purse.

"You look happy. Your father said yes?

"Uh huh."

She set the old purse aside and snapped the new one shut. "Now listen, this isn't summer and I don't care how hot you say you get in the middle of the night. You boys may not, under any circumstances, go outside. And, you may not, I repeat, not sleep on the floor in the hallway and turn on the cooler."

"Okay, we won't. I promise."

"You better. Last time those boys were over here, I think there were eight of you, you all slept in the hallway under the cooler and your father nearly killed himself stepping over people in the dark, trying to get to the bathroom. You can't move places in the middle of the night. Stay in your room."

"We will, I swear, I promise."

"Well, don't swear, just see that you do."

She was finishing her make-up. "You came in here. Did you want something?"

My mind went blank. I looked around and picked up nail clippers. "Uh… I kinda forgot. I needed these."

She was smoothing wrinkles from her dress. "What?"

I shrugged and put the clippers back. My mother frowned and shook her head. My father came down the hall, pulling on his suede jacket and grabbing his Stetson hat. The hat and jacket matched his new tan boots.

I was quick. "Hey Dad, the boots look real cool, like Roy Rogers."

He smiled. "Thank you, son."

He was adjusting his shirt collar and jacket. "Now listen boy, no horseplay in this house. No wrestling or any of that stuff. I'll light you up. You and your friends. You understand?"

"Yes sir, I understand."

"And absolutely no going out of this house for any reason or having any other people in here. Do I make myself clear? You are big enough now. You don't need a babysitter."

"Yes sir, very clear."

"And no sleeping in the hallway. I almost broke my neck last time."

My mother asked, "When are they coming over?"

"In about fifteen minutes."

"Well, we could be out for a while. So, if we're not back by midnight, you boys go to bed. Lock the door once the boys get here. You can call us at the K.C. Steakhouse if there is an emergency. The number is there by the phone. But, if you need help quick, you just call Mr. and Mrs. Shirley next door."

"I will."

My mom was out the door when she stopped in her tracks. "I almost forgot. I don't mind you watching "Dobie Gillis," but no "Twilight Zone."

"Aw, Mom, what's wrong with 'Twilight Zone?'"

"It's too scary."

My dad pointed with the brim of his hat. "Don't argue with your mother."

I mumbled, "Yes sir."

The guys arrived five minutes after my parents left. They brought sleeping bags, flashlights, comic books and stuff to eat and drink. I locked the door. They plopped everything on our new, first-time-ever, carpet.

I yelled, "Get any crap on this carpet, my dad'll kill all of us."

Everything stopped. Statues staring at me.

"It's what I call the 'Six Weeks Rule.'"

Andy dropped his sleeping bag. "Huh?"

"I figured outta long time ago that for the first six weeks my parents have anything new, it's gotta stay perfect. After that, who gives a crap..."

Shane set his sleeping bag on end and used it for a wobbly stool. "I know whatcha mean. New has to wear off."

Jim attacked the Oreos and pointed at Shane. "Your Ma keeps everything in clear plastic, even lampshades."

Shane shrugged. "I know... Makes no sense."

I looked everybody in the eye. "We mess anything up, I mean anything, my dad will 'light us up,' his own words, I swear."

Jim grimaced. "Light us up?'"

Andy flashed. "Beat our backsides with a razor strap."

Jim gulped. "Gotta be kiddin' me."

Andy grabbed an Almond Joy. "Nope. Serious as a heart attack. My dad uses it too. Hurts like a you know what."

I opened a Hostess Snowball. "He's right, you don't want no part of this."

Jim stuck both hands in the air. "I give. Gotta stay away from the strap."

Suddenly, Andy pushed his stomach over his belt, hooked his thumbs under imaginary suspenders. We could almost see Uncle Billy's pudgy, pink Porky Pig face with his Marine Corps crew cut.

Andy paused and wagged a finger. "Boys, this here is serous shit. S-E-R-O-U-S. Y'all better watch yer A double S. You mess with the razor strap, truth is, you ain't gonna have nothin' left to watch. Put yer head between yer legs an' kiss yer A double S goodbye. You know what they say. Breakfast in this life, dinner in the next."

We clapped and yelled. Andy took a bow, became himself and reached for a Coke.

Jim guzzled two thirds of a Cherry Nehi and blasted a mean burp. "What time does 'Dobie' start?"

I turned on the TV. "Right now."

He slugged the last third of his drink. "After this, we're watchin' 'The Twilight Zone'. Scares the crap outta me."

I stood in front of him. "My mom says we can't watch 'Twilight Zone.'"

"No," Jim bristled. "yer Mama says **you** ain't watchin' no 'Twilight Zone.'"

Andy stepped between. "Cool it. Let's just watch this, OK?"

Jim shrugged, stepped away and grabbed a grape Nehi. I sat next to Shane.

We watched.

"The Many Loves of Dobie Gillis"

As every episode begins, Dobie appears on camera in front of a replica of Rodin's Thinker and speaks directly to the audience.

****

"My name's Dobie Gillis. This park is where I come to think when things bug me, which is like every day. What bugs me is this. I like girls. What am I sayin'? I'm sayin' I really love girls: beautiful, gorgeous, soft, round, creamy girls. Now, I'm not a wolf, mind ya… Ya see, a wolf wants a lot of girls. But, me, I just want one.

One beautiful, gorgeous, soft, round, creamy girl for my very own. That's all I want, one lousy girl for my own! And I'll tell ya a sad, hard fact. I'm never gonna get a girl… Never… Why? Because to get a girl you need money. And standing between me and money is a powerful obstacle, a very powerful obstacle…

The camera pans to Dobie's glaring father.

"Caper at the Bijou"

In this episode, beautiful Thalia tells Dobie he can only have her if he promises an expensive evening at the prom. Dobie decides that his only chance is to cheat on the theater's cash drawing.

But, as his plan unfolds, his conscience kicks in. He has doubts, fears and regrets. He argues with Thalia, shreds his winning ticket and lets his perfect girl walk away.

He's upset. His only comfort is that he did the right thing. But, suddenly, his friend who "fixed" the drawing runs up and apologizes for being late. He says that he's sorry for messing things up, sorry that he didn't get the drawing rigged.

The camera pans from Rodin's Thinker. Dobie, head in hands, realizes what he has done.

"You mean I won? I won fair and square and I tore up the ticket for nothing?!"

****

Jim exhaled and shook his head. "Dobie's right. It ain't never, ever gonna work out for him."

Shane slapped a piece of cheese between two pieces of pepperoni. "Thalia's not worth it. All she cares about is money."

Jim mushed through a mouthful of chips. "What they all want, even if they don't say it."

Andy sighed. "Everybody wants money."

I asked Shane to make me one of his pepperoni and cheese sandwiches. He made me two.

I looked at Andy and shook my head. "Ain't the same. Girls want things; they want stuff, stuff that takes money an' only money. Things a guy wants don't take money unless she says so."

Shane was building a new sandwich: pepperoni, cheese and chips. We all copied immediately.

He spoke with a mouthful, "I don't understand why girls are so different than us an' why we can't just understand 'em. They don't understand us. They always say we're stupid. An' they talk about us. Why? I thought they didn't like us."

Andy waved his pepperoni at me. "You're right. It ain't the same. They gotta get somethin' from a boy, 'cause he's the one gettin' something an' they're givin' somethin'—their body."

Jim growled and chomped a stick of cherry licorice. "Ain't a boy's body worth nothin'? How come they don't think we're givin' them somethin' too?"

I laughed so hard Coke came through my nose. I coughed, used my shirt as a napkin and collected myself. "Uh, sorry pal, let's think. We got a guy's body an' we got Tuesday Weld or Sandra Dee. Do I gotta say more?"

Andy took a long drink, punctuated by a belch. "It's more than that. It ain't the same. It ain't even. My grandpa says, 'nine minutes for him, nine months for her.'"

Shane grabbed a red licorice. "That's right. It's not even 'cause we want it lots more than they do."

I grinned through my food. "Shane, difference is we get to feel good and she gets to have a baby."

Shane shrugged. "My uncle Patrick says, 'Love makes the world go 'round, but money greases the wheels.'"

Jim sneered. "Got that right. Hey, why do they tease, then? Come around all showin' off."

I stretched and pointed to the pepperoni. Jim was on it. I gave him a thumbs up and took a big bite. "Boys, we're in way too deep here." I took a drink. "All I know for sure, I just think Dobie's right. I love 'em. I love the way they look, all soft, sweet curves. What's he say, beautiful, soft, gorgeous?"

"Round."

"Creamy."

I smiled and gave my last word. "But, boys, I tell ya one thing right now. It don't matter to me what some girl wants. She looks like Thalia Menninger, I'm gettin her whatever she wants."

Andy fired an Ace of Hearts at an empty shoe. "Yeah, true. Sometimes though, I just want a girl so bad it hurts, pain in your body."

Everybody agreed.

Jim shrugged. "I'll say this. I ain't puttin' up with no girl who's just a big ole B."

I bounced a tennis ball off the wall and caught the rebound. "I still say I don't care. She looks like Thalia: blonde, curves, all that. I do not care, boys. I do not care."

Shane cleared his throat. "I gotta question. When Dobie says he loves girls 'cause they're so beautiful why does he say he wants 'just one lousy girl'? Why would he say, 'lousy?'"

Andy answered, "Sometimes it just pisses him off. It's all too hard."

Jim stood. "Boys, I gotta see a man about a horse."

Andy stood too. "Right behind ya. Gotta see my Chinese friend, "Ling Toy Let."

I yelled at Jim, "Can I have your Grape Nehi?"

He waved. "Go."

Shane picked up a Fantastic Four comic. "I still don't get it. Why can't things just work out? Dobie says things'll never work out. An' every week he's right."

I had those same thoughts.

Why don't things work out? Why is Louie messed up? Why am I messed up? Why is Decker paralyzed? Why'd Christy get cancer an' die? Why'd Albert always slobber an' pee?

I shook my head. "Makes no sense. Things happen."

"Some people just lucky?"

"Yeah or unlucky."

"This about that God an' Satan thing?"

I waited.

I need to be smart, have somethin' really good to say. Makes up for bein' crippled.

When nothing smart came to me, I told the truth. "Really, I dunno much about the God/Devil stuff, wish I did."

Shane was quiet. I fussed with my sleeping bag and pillow. Suddenly, I felt like crying. I fussed with the pillow some more. I was glad I had something else to look at and I was glad Shane couldn't see me. It was hard to get control. I made a show of clearing my throat and straightening my stuff.

My voice was too loud and didn't sound like me. "Know what really pisses me off?" I was breathing hard, trying to get air.

Shane looked up. "Uh uh."

"Jerks that drive through the street an' slow down to look at the crippled kid bat or pitch. God, I hate 'em. Think 'cause my legs don't work—"

Jim returned. "What you guys talkin' about? Thalia's boobs, I bet."

I said, "Nope."

Shane mumbled, "He gets mad when people look at him from their cars."

Andy came in. "Who gets mad?"

Jim nodded toward me.

Andy flopped on his bag. "Well, hell, who don't know that? Half the time you want somebody to hang a nice fat change-up, so you can smack the crap outta that son-of-a-bitch an' amaze them assholes in the car. 'Oh look honey that crippled boy just smacked the shit out of that ball.'"

I laughed, hard. So did everybody else.

Andy pointed at me. "That ain't all of it."

I sat up. "What?"

Andy shook his head and wagged a finger. "No, no, no. Friends too long. Everybody here knows."

"Knows what?"

Andy, hands on his hips. "Jim, tell 'im."

Jim stuffed an Oreo into his mouth. "You don't want people to think yer a retard."

Andy was on a roll. "That the exact words you heard?"

Jim stuffed another Oreo and shook his head. "Don't want people to think he's a fuckin' retard."

Shane stood and re-arranged his bedding. "Don't want 'em to think just 'cause your legs don't work your brain don't work."

I still couldn't get enough air. "What am I supposed to do, kiss their asses?"

Andy faked an offense, fluttered his eye-lashes, placed his hand on his heart and used his best falsetto voice. "Well now, Missy, I just don't know about that."

Jim stuffed one more Oreo and followed it with a slug of Coke. He struggled to get the crushed cookies from between his teeth. "We don't get mad at them car people. God made them stupid. They are dead wrong. They THINK yer a fuckin' retard. WE KNOW YOU ARE ONE."

Andy yelled, "Get 'im!"

Suddenly, I was pounded by pillows from all directions.

Things soon settled, the air cleared and I was breathing again.

I stared everybody dead in the face, my serial killer look. "One thing you guys are dead wrong about, an' I mean this. Next time you jerks wanna gang up on somebody, remember, NO STANDING UP IN A PILLOW FIGHT."

Andy looked at Shane and me. "Boys, forget pillows. I gotta say I'm disappointed. "You sure that when me an' Jim was in the head that you wasn't in here talkin' about Thalia?"

We shook our heads.

"Nope, not a word."

"Not a syllable, no."

"Well, then," Andy hung his head, "you boys just pushin' the air around."

Shane grinned. "Can't argue with that."

I smiled. "Me neither."

Andy brightened and adjusted his cap. "That's real smart, boys. Never argue with the Big Dog."

He moved toward the TV. "Now, let's talk about this Twilight Zone thing."

There was really very little talk. It was all about watching.

I explained to Jim. "Might scare me, too but I'm really thinkin' 'bout my dad's razor strap."

He smiled. "Never know unless you tell 'em."

Andy raised his hand. "One thing I say is, we get caught, we all take the strap."

I sighed. "Okay."

Jim sighed louder. "Whatsa problem, now?"

I threw up my hands. "No problem, unless you call my dad whippin' me an' my cousins silly for losin' his comb a problem."

Jim screwed his face up. "What the hell are you talkin' 'bout?"

Shane walked toward the bathroom. "He means his dad doesn't need a reason."

I touched the tip of my nose, like charades. "An' he don't care... After we got the whippin' for the comb, he found it in his pants' pocket."

Jim jumped. "Bet he was sorry."

"Bet not! Lose all yer money. 'Cause all he said was 'That was for somethin' that you gotta way with.'"

Andy was clear. "If we're gonna getta ass whippin' let's get it for somethin' we done. Let's watch this S.O.B."

"The Twilight Zone"

165

Every episode begins with a general introduction to the series, followed by an on screen or voice-over introduction by Rod Serling, the host and creator. Always a bit edgy, his voice creates tension by itself, not to mention the creepy things he might say. Each episode finishes with another edgy voice-over, the perfect ending to another cautionary tale.

Series Introduction

There is a fifth dimension beyond that which is known to man. It is a dimension as vast as space and as timeless as infinity. It is the middle ground between light and shadow, between science and superstition, and it lies between the pit of man's fears and the summit of his knowledge. This is the dimension of imagination. It is an area which we call "The Twilight Zone."

Escape Clause

You're about to meet a hypochondriac. Witness Mr. Walter Bedeker age forty-four. Afraid of the following: death, disease, other people, germs, drafts, and everything else. He has one interest in life and that's Walter Bedeker. One preoccupation, the life and well-being of Walter Bedeker. One abiding concern about society: That if Walter Bedeker should die, how will it survive without him?

The scene opens with Mr. Bedeker sniveling and complaining. From his bed, he yells and screams at his doctor and his wife, accusing them of wanting him dead. Suddenly, a rather large, well-dressed, pleasant-looking man, Mr. Cadwalleder, appears at Bedeker's bedside and says that he, too, believes that life is short and people deserve more.

Bedeker argues a bit about how Cadwalleder got into the room but is finally more interested in the subject of living longer. He asks the fat man what he has in mind and is told that it is possible for a man to live for any number of years, including forever, if certain conditions are met.

Eyes sparkling, Bedeker says that he's not a fool, he recognizes the Devil when he sees him and will not be cheated. The fat man smiles and says that he wants very little in exchange for immortality, something so small and unnoticed that it will never be missed: The hypochondriac's soul.

Bedeker is quick with conditions: life forever, no further aging, and invincibility. Curiously, the fat man quickly agrees and adds a condition of his own, an escape clause, one which allows Bedeker to request his own death at any time.

Once Cadwalleder disappears, the game is on. Bedeker places his hands on a live heater, drinks a mixture of rubbing alcohol and ammonia, throws himself under trains and off boats and survives plane crashes. So far, so good. But, he is getting bored. He is collecting multiple insurance checks, but that, too, is no longer exciting. He climbs out on his roof, preparing to jump. His wife tries to stop him and accidentally falls to her death. Bedeker is thrilled. He phones the police and confesses to murdering his wife. He is excited about experiencing the electric chair.

But, the unexpected happens. His excellent lawyer gets him life in prison without parole. A guard jokes that there is nothing to worry about, that Bedeker will be dead in 45 or 50 years anyway. Bedeker quickly realizes that he cannot spend eternity behind bars and summons the Devil to exercise the escape clause.

Cadwalleder appears; Bedeker nods, suffers a massive heart attack and slumps to the floor. The guard discovers the body and says, "Poor devil."

Closing Narration

"There's a saying, 'Every man is put on Earth condemned to die, time and method of execution unknown.' Perhaps this is as it should be. Case in point: Walter Bedeker, lately deceased, a little man with such a yen to live: Beaten by the Devil, by his own boredom and by the scheme of things in this, the Twilight Zone."

"Quick," I barked, "turn it off."

Jim jumped. "Got it."

As soon as the room was quiet, everybody breathed full and easy for the first time in twenty-five minutes.

Andy shook his head. "See the way he got smashed by those trains! I wanted him to go ahead an' jump off that roof after his wife fell."

Jim was taking apart an Oreo.

"Hey," I dared, "put a pepperoni in there."

Jim laughed. "Dare you to eat it."

He ate the icing and saved the cookies.

"Be great", I said, "if nothin' could ever hurt ya. Like Superman."

Everybody loved Superman, but he was not without problems.

167

I scratched my head. "Hey, explain this. Clark Kent goes in to the barber shop for a haircut. How do ya cut Superman's hair? Stuff's stronger than steel, right?"

Shane was on it. "Yeah, I mean, how would he shave?"

Andy finished some chips and picked up a cherry licorice. "He's invincible 'cause of the force field that protects him, that's why his costume never gets messed up. An' his hair can only be cut 'cause it gets outside the force field. An' he uses his heat vision reflected off somethin' for a shave."

I yelled, "Not gettin' the heat vision! Why doesn't the heat burn his face?"

Andy struggled, mouthful of licorice. "He's using his own power, his own heat vision, an' 'cause it's from him, it don't hurt him."

I shook my head. "Don't make sense. I mean, kinda does but not really."

Shane snapped his fingers. "I remember now! Superman's beard an' hair don't grow on any planet with a yellow sun, like earth. But, since Krypton has a red sun, his hair grows fine."

I gave that idea some thought. "That's better, but why even go to a barber shop?"

Andy sat up. "I got it. He can turn off the force field when he wants. So, he'd be okay getting the haircut. There was one time when he got hypnotized an' lost his powers because his force field was down."

I simply could not believe my ears. "You mean a dumb-ass hypnotist can wreck Superman? That ain't right. That's no good."

Andy held his hands up. "Hey, I know. Don't blame me."

Jim smiled. "I thought it was cool when that guy burned his hands on the heater, all smokin' and he wasn't even hurt. I think ya could hear his hands sizzlin' on the grill. You guys hear that?"

Nobody remembered hearing the sizzling sound.

Shane almost dropped an open can of Coke. "How'd that whiny guy get bored with his powers? I'd never get bored bein' invincible."

I jammed a couple of Oreos, gulped some Coke. "You would too. Everybody gets bored of everything, sooner or later."

He looked at me like I was crazy. "How could it ever be borin' to never be hurt?"

I ignored him. "Here's the deal: I'd rather be irresistible."

Jim frowned. "What's that?"

"Means nobody can resist you. Can't say no to ya."

Shane took off his outer shirt. "Why did that guy's wife stay with him? He was mean to her."

Andy punched his pillow. "Where's she gonna go? Got no job."

"See Jim," I smiled, "how cool is that? Ask people for money or stuff. Ask 'em to do stuff, they have to. It's called irresistible."

Shane picked up a handful of chips, careful about crumbs. "She's got a family. She could go there."

Andy yelled, "They don't want her. Would you go back? Yeah, you probably would."

Jim perked up. "Very cool. Ask for money, homework assignments, naked pictures, anything."

Andy snapped. "Hey, I didn't know ya wanted naked pictures of me!"

Jim rocketed a pillow passed Andy's head. "Watch it!"

Shane asked me, "Think you'd ever get bored bein' irresistible?"

"Yup. Sure would. No question. Done deal."

Andy rolled his eyes and retrieved Jim's pillow. "Who you kiddin"? This is us yer talkin' to."

"I know. But, I really do think I'd get bored of it."

"Why? Why would ya even think that?"

"Remember the Jamboree?"

Andy nodded. "Yeah, so?"

I said, "Remember ten thousand Boy Scouts an' Scout Masters all in one place for three days an' not a mother to be seen anywhere?"

"What's your point?"

"Remember my favorite thing back then?"

He shrugged. "Yoyos, gettin' new badges? Badges, I think."

I whispered, "No, don't be stupid. Think."

"Just tell me."

"Remember Snickers an' Coke?"

"What about 'em?"

Shane laughed, "Ya loved 'em. Couldn't get enough. Ate an' drank that stuff for days."

"Right," I yelled.

"Okay," Andy sighed, "so what?"

I pointed. "Shane, tell 'em."

He finished a mouthful of chips and took a drink. "After two days an' nights, ya got sick as a dog, went outside an' puked yer guts out."

"Uh huh," I laughed. "Puked so long an' hard. I remember thinking... Next thing comin' outta my mouth is gonna be my shoes!"

Andy shoved me in the chest. "I remember that. Where's the big deal?"

I fell back. "What you guys don't know is what happened next afternoon."

Everybody re-positioned themselves on the floor closer to me and reloaded on food.

Jim ripped open a new bag of potato chips. "Sorry, man, you're makin' me hungry."

I smiled and waved him off. "The next afternoon, I was in the tent by myself. You guys were off rope climbing an' I didn't feel good. In two days I ate twenty three Snickers and drank fifteen Cokes. I counted 'em."

Jim waved a handful of chips. "Yeah, everywhere ya looked there was these big metal tubs of ice with bottles of Coke stuffed in 'em. An' someplace near them tubs was always candy bars, mountains of 'em."

"So, like I said, there I was in the tent all by myself an' Bruno comes by."

Shane blurted, "Who's Bruno?"

"Tall kid from San Bernardino or Pasadena. Real thick glasses, always outta uniform. Remember? Big trench coat, twice his size, an' cowboy boots. Nice kid. Anyway, he comes in the tent, opens his coat wide with both arms an' says, 'Whadaya want? Whadaya need? We got it.'

"He musta had fifteen Cokes an' twenty Snickers hanging on the insides of that coat. I looked him dead in the face an' I screamed, 'I WANT MILK! I WANT MEAT!'"

Everybody laughed.

Jim asked, "Wha'd Bruno say?"

I grinned. "Nothin'. Bruno got the hell outta Dodge."

Jim crushed another mouthful of chips. "I know you ain't lyin', but you really said, 'I want meat?'"

"Uh huh."

Shane resisted. "Snickers or not, I'd still never get bored of bein' invincible."

We moved everything. The carpet and our backsides safe for at least one more night. My small, cheap-tiled bedroom was next to the even smaller bathroom. I took the lower bunk and everybody flipped for the top. Shane won and immediately planted himself. Andy and Jim staked out the floor.

Everyone settled in, lights out.

Andy whispered, "Jim, open the window."

Jim sighed, got up and reached for the curtain. "I was a little kid, there was a window over my head in the bedroom. I used to peek up at that curtin an' imagine a' ugly, murderin' monster just on the other side of the glass. Face all smashed against the glass with a a bloody, poked out eye."

Andy sat up. "Jesus, why'd ya think that?"

"Dunno. More I thought of it, scareder I got. Put my head under the covers, under the pillow."

"See it in a movie?"

Jim finished with the curtain, moved the glass. Cool air swirled into the room.

"I think I just made it up."

Shane tried to sit up, bumped his head and rubbed. "I don't think the devil is some fat guy. Where'd they get that?"

Andy shifted in his sleeping bag. "Devil is usually a scary guy with horns an' a pitchfork."

Shane shook his head. "That's just a kid thing for Halloween. Devil is supposed to fool people, tempt 'em into doin' wrong."

I gave my two cents. "Devil can be anything. Like that mean little kid in that other Twilight Zone, where he just made people go off in the cornfield if he didn't like 'em."

Jim rolled over and smacked a bag of chips with an elbow, a giant, ripping crunch.

He whispered, "Sorry, but I was gonna say about that kid, he turned off everything. Everybody was afraid 'cause he could go inside your mind an' make ya like a zombie, if you made 'im mad."

Shane turned, careful about his head. "What about the voice in your head that tells you to do bad things? Is that the Devil?"

I looked out the window. No moon. "Could be."

Andy unzipped his sleeping bag and folded it back. "No, that's your conscience."

I was trying to find a safe place for my canes and I clanked into somebody's bottle. Everybody jumped.

I laughed and settled down. "Conscience is how you know right from wrong."

Jim avoided the chips, grabbed his bottle and set it at the foot of his bag. "What about the voice in your head that tells you to do the right thing?"

Andy coughed again. "That's your guardian angel, the good voice."

Shane propped himself up on his right side. "Sometimes we do wrong even when we know it's wrong."

I fired quickly. "Any conscience that tells you to do wrong is a screwed up conscience."

Shane leaned in my direction. "Where's conscience come from?"

Andy was fumbling in the dark. "What I want to know is this. Can the Devil make you do things? Can he hurt people? The fat guy just fooled that whiny guy but that kid hurt people. He messed with his aunt's mind 'cause she did somethin' he didn't like, made 'er like a zombie."

Jim was crunching away. "That's what I said, he made her a zombie."

I unzipped my bag too. "When you grow up an' they teach ya right from wrong. That's your conscience."

Shane was now flat on his back, talking to the ceiling. "We should ask Father Phillip from St. Luke's."

Jim nodded. He's a really good basketball player."

I agreed with Shane. "He answers questions good. Never makes you feel stupid, like you're just a kid."

Jim said, "You know, I gotta say, if I saw a real guy with horns and a pitchfork, I'd not only be scared, I'd be butt-ugly scared."

Suddenly, Andy was on the move. "Boys, I'm on my way to China again, lovely people. And, when I come back, we're gonna talk 'bout what we shoulda been talkin' 'bout all along."

Jim looked around. "What?"

Andy whispered into the dark, "The kiss boys, the magical kiss."

I peered into the darkness. "Nope. Ain't talkin' 'bout that."

"Well then," Jim tried, "Let's talk 'bout the time you seen Jade Parker naked. That's a good story."

Shane groaned. "Everybody's seen Jade Parker naked."

I was quick. "Ain't talkin' 'bout Jade Parker, either."

Jim gasped. "Shane, you seen Jade?"

"Yes, I did."

Andy was back. "I tell you right now, I'd give my right arm—let 'em saw it right off—to see Daisy Clover naked. And, I wouldn't be lonesome for the arm neither."

Jim was fussing with his bag and pillow. "You saw everything? You saw the front, right?"

Shane coughed. "Uh huh, I did."

Andy held up his arms. "After all, that's why we got two arms, right?"

I thought about my best friend's willing sacrifice. "I was wrong before. There's lots of stuff I'd never get bored of. I'd never get tired of seein'

Daisy Clover naked an' I'd never get bored of throwin' a 100 mile an hour fastball."

Jim was beside himself. "How come I'm the only one never seen her?"

Andy whispered, "Maybe you should just ask her."

Even in the dark, I knew Andy was grinning.

In a soft voice, I cautioned. "Jimmy, better not do that. Bad idea."

Shane whispered, "Bad idea."

Andy poked and punched. "They just don't wantcha to see what they seen."

Jim mumbled, "Maybe I will ask her."

A minute of silence floated by.

Andy spoke softly, "Jimmy, second thought, better not do that."

"But, you said…"

"Yeah, but I was messin' with you."

"What should I do?"

"Nothin', I shouldn't've messed with you."

Shane changed the subject and spoke to me. "On that contest thing, I think Daisy just picked your number."

Hair stood up on the back of my neck. "Why would she do that?"

Shane needled. "I don't know but, I think she did."

Andy coughed and spat into the waste basket. "I dunno neither. But, I think she did, too."

Jim stared in my direction. I could feel it. "Me too, I always thought that."

I was lost. "You guys are crazy. No reason for her to do that."

Suddenly, we heard the front door open.

Andy whispered, "Parents…"

My mom came down the hallway and carefully cracked the door.

She whispered, "Good night, boys."

She closed the door softly.

Suddenly, there was no energy in the room. It was as quiet as dark.

The question stuck in my mind.

Why would Daisy do that? Maybe I should ask her? Nope… Bad idea…

The next thing I knew I was dreaming of another number-guessing contest at The Great American Diner.

Chapter 25
The Cleaners and the Secret Place

THE NEXT MORNING was another day of Christmas vacation—more cold, wet and grey. Last night's conversation belonged to another time and place. Brave and brash *(just go right up an' ask her)* became wrong *(bad idea)*. Darkness became daylight. The handsome boys became plain and the dream became a mirror.

Everybody slurped cold cereal. In a few short minutes, dishes were rinsed, bedroom stuff straightened and guys on their way.

Andy stepped to the porch and waited for Shane and Jim to reach the driveway. "Meet me at the GAD this afternoon? Say, one o'clock?"

I nodded. "Sure."

Lotta things we gotta figure out."

Okay."

"Nobody but me an' you."

"I'll be there. Bring a notebook."

****

Mist blanketed everything. Christmas vacation aside, the Great American Diner was nearly empty. I came down the tree-lined sidewalk, passed Reggie's restored 1930's roadster, up the wheelchair ramp and through the beveled glass doors. The crystal door-knob felt perfect in my hand, like a new baseball.

Even empty, the place was a circus of color and sound. Reggie was more than an owner or cook. He was an artist.

I claimed the booth across from the glass pastry house.

Daisy smiled. "Hey there, contest winner. How are you today? You look soaked."

My face felt hot. "I'm just all messed, uh, I mean, mist, uh... I'm all wet."

"Know what you want?"

"Glazed doughnut, hot chocolate."

"All we got left is a twist, that okay?"

"Sure."

"Waitin' for somebody?"

"Uh huh."

"I'll be right back. Nice to see you."

"Nice to see you."

Andy appeared from nowhere, shook the wet from his cap and set his yellow notebook on the table.

"Talking to your girlfriend?"

"An' you're Wolf Man Jack, right?"

Andy glanced at the big Wurlitzer 1015 Jukebox: All chrome and glitter, double arches of rotating light and changing neon colors, like a giant toy soldier from the Nutcracker Suite.

Suddenly, he challenged me. "Like that Bobby Darin record?"

"Mack the Knife?"

"Uh huh."

"Guess so, why?"

"He's married to your dream girl, you know."

"So?"

"Jealous? Broken-hearted?"

I leaned back. "You crazy?"

"Me?" He raised his eyebrows. "You're the one nuts 'bout Sandra Dee. Had a quarter every time you talked 'bout her, I'd own this place."

I laughed. "I am crazy about Sandra Dee. But, you? You're just plain crazy."

He asked, "You know the name of the longest song title ever?"

"What's a song gotta do with anything?"

"My Uncle Billy had me an' my cousins memorize the longest song title. Wanna hear it?"

I folded my arms. "Not really, but you wanna say it, don'tcha?"

"Here goes:

I'm a Cranky Old Yank

In a Clanky Old Tank

On the Streets of Yokohama

With my Honolulu Mama

Doin Those Beat-O, Beat-O

Flat-On-My-Seat O

Hirohito Blues"

I couldn't help myself. "Cool! I wanna learn that."

Andy did his version of a booth bow.

At that moment, Daisy placed the twist and hot chocolate in front of me.

Andy seemed hypnotized. She waited a moment and playfully waved an open palm in front of his face.

"Know what you want?"

He spoke in a flat line, "Cheeseburger, Fries & Coke."

"Coming right up."

She smiled and moved away.

Andy drummed his fingers on his yellow notebook, grabbed a handful of my shirt, pulled me close and whispered through clinched teeth. "I swear, that woman is flat out beautiful."

I twisted up my face, squinted and pushed my voice through my nose. "Hey Pal, lay off my girlfriend, see? Or I might have to get rough, see?"

Andy released my shirt. "James Cagney?"

I smoothed my shirt. "Edward G. Robinson."

"Tell you one thing," Andy smiled. "You ain't gettin' on Ed Sullivan anytime soon."

"Yeah? I think I'm pretty good."

Daisy set out Andy's order, winked and handed him the check. "Pay when you're ready, no hurry."

He smiled and paid her on the spot.

"Thank you, boys. Have a good afternoon."

I smiled, "You too."

Andy attacked the cheeseburger, jammed a fistful of fries and slurped some Coke. "Gotta go over everything."

I pulled the notebook to myself, took a bite of the twist, wiped the glaze from my fingers and printed the heading: What We Found.

I sipped some chocolate. "First, we write everything we found and then we write what we know."

Andy whispered, "You ask Daisy about another contest?"

"Huh? Course not, stupid."

The cheeseburger was disappearing. I grabbed some fries while I could.

"Hey, my fries!" Andy yelped. "And, I ain't stupid. This is excitin'." He whispered harder, "ASK HER."

"Okay," I whispered, "I will. After we do the list."

He finished the burger, put his hat on and rubbed his hands together. "Great. Let's get the list. Go boy! We gotta contest to find out about."

I rolled my eyes. "I'll start. You jump in when you want."

The list was interesting: long on questions, short on answers.

What We Found So Far

1. Boy's bracelet: Initials SJ + LL

2. Necklace & Locket: Fuzzy, small picture: "All my love, Linda."

3. Scratch on floor: "It is a sin"

4. Private Eye Card: "Ans. Is y. Sorry kid/ -- 8 -- 4

5. Note: "His name was Scotty."

6. Note: "The problem is below and the answer above"

7. Box of stuff: "Losing Scotty"

8. Letter to D.G.

9. Girl from cleaners: D.G (Delores Graham?)

"Wait," Andy flashed, "don't forget what Daisy said."

He grabbed the notebook.

I went blank. "What? About Scotty an' the stranger lookin' at pictures an' whisperin'?"

"Right." He scribbled: Stranger and Pictures.

We studied the list for five minutes.

Andy fidgeted with his napkin. "We gotta buy somethin' or get outta here."

"No we don't. Look around. Where's Reg?"

"Still..."

"No, there ain't no 'still.' We can't leave here 'til we figure somthin' out."

Andy waved to Daisy and said, "Gonna get another Coke, want one?"

"Yeah, thanks."

He pushed his plate to the side and looked me in the eye. "I been thinkin'."

"Good."

"Maybe not."

"Whadaya mean?"

Daisy arrived, full of smiles, turning pages in her order book.

I still wondered.

Was she making a fool of me and I was too stupid to know it? Did she simply feel sorry for me?

Andy's voice jerked me back. "You listenin' to that stupid Frankie Avalon?"

"Huh? You mean, uh, 'Venus'?"

"Yeah and stupid Frankie Avalon."

I frowned. "Let's just talk about stupid, okay? You even know what Avalon means?"

"Already told you what it means… Means a stupid singer with a stupid song."

"No, it doesn't. Truth is, you don't know."

"So, shut up and tell me."

I laughed. "Oh, that's smart! How can I tell you if I shut up?"

"That's what I mean, right there. Stop bein' a wise guy an' just tell me."

"Avalon is a magical island where Merlin comes from and where King Arthur goes when he dies. It's a place of healing and wisdom and it's almost impossible to find."

Andy adjusted his cap. "And since Venus is the goddess of love…"

"Now you're gettin' it."

Andy leaned forward. "You just get such a stupid look when you listen to it."

I leaned back. "Hey, that's my thinkin' look. Why is my thinking-face stupid? What am I supposed to look like?"

"Just don't go into the trance thing. It's creepy."

The words and music were swirling, harps filling the nearly-empty diner. The room felt lighter, softer and warmer. Daisy suddenly seemed to dance—as if she walked on air.

> Venus, make her fair
> A lovely girl with sunlight in her hair
> And take the brightest stars up in the skies
> And place them in her eyes for me
> Venus, goddess of love that you are
> Surely the things I ask
> Can't be too great a task

Daisy floated over with two new glasses of Coke.
She pointed to the table. "Clear these away for you?"

"Sure."

"Yeah."

Hands full, she asked, "Did you talk to Delores yet?"

We both said, "No."

Andy added, "Maybe we will today. We just gotta figure stuff out."

"Did you look at the notes I gave you? I think they'll help."

Andy grabbed the top of his cap and started to blush. "I completely forgot about your note. It's still here in my jacket."

"Well," she sparkled, "The letter is a mystery."

I nodded. "Sure is."

We stared as she turned away. Andy shook his head.

I wondered aloud, "Can you really tell me not to trance?"

Andy took a drink. "Trance might be just right when it comes to Daisy."

Suddenly, I understood.

I grabbed Andy's arm. "Hey," I whispered, "She cheated."

He looked confused.

I repeated. "The kiss. She cheated."

His eyes got big. "She felt sorry for ya?"

"No," I shook my head, "she told me."

"What?"

"Just before the kiss, she whispered, 'I heard your wish.'"

"What wish?"

"Remember, Louie wanted to kiss her? I told him every guy there wanted to kiss her."

"Yeah," Andy nodded. "He wanted to know if even you wanted to kiss her."

"Exactly! Remember what I said?"

"Uh-uh."

"I looked Louie dead in his screwy little face an' I told him, 'Right now, buddy, I want to kiss Daisy more than I've ever wanted anything in my life.' An' I said it loud—for Louie."

Andy's mouth was hanging open. "Holy crap! All you did was ask her."

"Yeah, but I didn't know that."

"I still think it was 'cause you're crippled."

The next song was perfect or close to it.

"Don't worry about me," I grinned, "they're playin' <u>your</u> song now."

He sputtered. "What song?

I laughed and toasted. "Here's to you, Paul Anka, 'Lonely Boy.' I sang along and salted the wound. "I'm just a lonely boy... lonely and blue."

Andy sighed. "Okay, okay, enough."

"Hey," I offered, "if you really think that's why Daisy kissed me, I dare you. Ask her, right now."

He looked away. "I'm not doin' that."

"No way I'm askin' her 'bout another contest either."

Andy drummed with his fingers and shifted in his seat. "Okay. We're even."

I grinned. "Not my fault you're jealous."

His eyes narrowed. "Better shut up!"

I pushed. "Ya really wanna be me? Crippled for life for just one kiss?"

He whispered, "Gonna cripple your little ass worse than it already is."

I raised both hands. "I give!"

Andy dug into his inside jacket and opened the pink envelope with Daisy's note. "Look at this."

We each read it and were about to discuss it when Andy whispered, "Hey! Here comes Decker."

Decker entered with his customary flourish, flinging the door wide and shoving his chair over the threshold. The door clanked shut.

He waved to Daisy, pointed to a booth at the far end and headed in our direction.

Andy yanked the bill of his cap and mumbled, "I hate this guy! I hate 'im! Like to paralyze his smart-ass brain to match his dumb-ass legs."

I nodded as Decker as rolled up.

"Well, well, well," he grinned big, "if it ain't Howdy an' Dilly Dally or is it Kukla an' Ollie? Wait, don't tell me. Frank an' Joe Hardy, right?"

I said, "Good to see you too, Decker. I was wondering, as an outsider, how do you feel about the human race?"

"Very funny kid."

Andy focused just above Decker's left shoulder. It was meant to annoy. Decker's purple LSU football jersey (yellow-gold number 1 painted on his chest) actually made his muscles look bigger. He thought he looked good in it and he was right.

Andy tilted his head. "Nice jersey Decker. Is that your age, your IQ or your shoe size?"

I laughed.

Decker smirked and turned to me. "How's the mystery? It is a mystery, right? Mysterious letters?"

"Just letters, no mystery."

"Not what Daisy says."

"Whadda you care?"

"Matter of fact, Kokomo, I don't. But, 'cause I'm a nice guy, sometimes I wanna help out. 'Sides, Daisy cares."

Decker adjusted himself in his chair and leaned forward, like he knew something nobody would ever guess. "I told you about Scotty's secret girlfriend, but I didn't tell ya about his secret place."

Andy jumped. "What secret place?"

"I don't know. That's why it's a secret, Shmoe."

I leaned back and looked at Decker. "What the hell are you talkin' about?"

"Easy, Howdy. No need for profanity. All he told me was that he had a secret place to take girls."

Andy exhaled. "Decker this is such crap. You know he never ..."

Decker laughed. "Hey, no reason to get all pissy. He was an all-star, Shmoe. Get girls anytime, anyplace."

I stared. "What else?"

"Nothin' really. No details. He'd just smile, wag 'is finger an' say, 'A gentleman never kisses an' tells.' I bugged hell outta him an' got nowhere. Said I couldn't go there, he'd have to carry me. Said he'd only do that when hell froze over."

Andy said, "I still think you're lyin'."

Decker looked over his shoulder and backed up. "Careful, Dilly Dally, you're on the edge." He doffed his hat, "You all have a nice day in Doody-Ville."

I said, "Decker, I believe you. You think of anything else—"

"Oh, I will, Howdy," he said, "I sure will." He turned to leave and winked at me. "Maybe you can cheer up Mr. Bluster."

Andy snapped, "Thanks, Clarabelle!"

Decker hesitated a moment and left.

I grabbed Andy's arm. "Wanna get killed?"

"I hate the guy."

"So, look at it this way: At least he didn't call you 'Princess Winter-Fall-Summer-Spring.'"

"Probably a fag himself."

"An' you're Wolfman Jack, okay?"

"I just hate the guy. Why'd you say ya believed 'im?"

"I don't want him mad at us."

Andy looked out the window.

I thumped his shoulder. "Hey, Bubba! You call Decker a fag an' he'll kill your ass right now. An' I mean right now, right here in front of God an' everybody."

Andy slumped. "Yeah."

I suggested. "You might outrun 'im."

Andy sighed. "Only if I'm far enough away when I say it."

The conversation turned again to Decker's believability. The real question was whether he had a reason to lie. After some feeble debate, we decided that Decker always had a reason to lie and that the better question was if he had any reason to tell the truth. We agreed that Daisy was a good enough reason. But, the idea of a secret place was as baffling as a secret girlfriend.

The list of clues gave us nothing.

I took a long drink. "Seems like we have all this stuff but we got nothin'."

Andy tapped the table. "Decker lies 'cause he can. He likes to stir it up."

"Yeah, but seemed like what he said was real."

Andy collected his notebook and cap, slipped out of the booth and waited for me. "Granma was slow but she was old. What's your excuse?"

Before I could defend myself, Decker came by again. "Can't stay long," he gestured toward the door, "but I did think of something."

Eyes bright, I said, "Great."

Decker was thoughtful. "One time Scotty was talkin' about his secret place and he said it was 'in plain sight.'"

Andy slipped back into the booth.

I knew what I heard, but I said, "Say that again, please."

Decker removed his hat and scratched his head. "I know, beats hell outta me, too. Thought he was screwin' with me. Never thought nothin' about it. But, seein' as how he offed himself, it's weird."

"Decker, did you say that he said his secret place was 'in plain sight'?
"I did."

There was a moment of indecision.

Suddenly, Decker saluted, "Gotta go," spun himself sharply and was out the door in seconds.

Andy opened the notebook and listed "in plain sight."

I thumped Andy's shoulder again. "Think that's a lie?"

"Nope, goes right along. Decker might make up the girlfriend and the place, they stir it up. But, not the in plain sight thing. For once, he wasn't actin' like a butthead. He was really talkin' to us."

Andy closed the notebook and waved to Reggie. "Gotta get outta here, outta money."

"Hey, thanks for all the stuff."

"Uh huh."

We waved goodbye to a suddenly busy Daisy, hit the door and headed for Anytime Cleaners. Late afternoon misting, the sun still prisoner, we took the short cut through the park to the Graham family business. The ground was sloppy, wet, hard and uneven.

I concentrated on the ground. "Catch me if I hit a gopher hole or any other surprise, okay?"

Andy nodded and moved a bit closer. I stopped to rest, re-adjust my wet hands and look around. The trees provided no overhead shelter. They looked more like giant wooden umbrellas minus fabric than anything a bird might nest in or a kid might climb. The flattened, matted ground was slick. Dark green weed clumps decorated the weak yellow grass like fallen ornaments.

"If I go down, I don't want to hit a tree with my face."

Andy laughed.

I stopped. "What's so funny?"

"You mean kiss a tree? You don't wanna kiss a tree, unless the tree cheats."

"Still jealous?"

"She still cheated."

"So, whadya wanna do, beat her up?"

"Maybe."

"What is the matter with you?"

"We ain't gettin' nowhere on all this."

"Sure we are. Look at all our clues, an' there's still Delores."

"How we gonna talk to her? She doesn't even know us. What is she? 23?"

"We just ask her if she's the D.G. in the letter. You got the letter, right?

"Yeah."

"We just ask her what she thinks of the letter an' we see what happens."

"Not me. Uh-uh. No."

"I'll do it."

The rest of the trip to Anytime Cleaners was semi-uneventful. One slip and one near miss with a hidden tree root resulted in two catches: The last one a swirling embrace. I hugged Andy close, struggling to regain my balance.

"Any closer pal," he was straining and laughing, "we exchange rings."

I was laughing too. "At the very least, we're goin' steady."

We laughed harder, I started to fall and we involuntarily hugged again. Andy stood firm, pushed back and steadied me. "Got it?"

"Yup." I was breathing hard.

Thirty more yards brought us to the edge of the park. We crossed the street and entered the southeast corner of the Anytime Cleaners parking lot. The persistent mist quickly moved to a drizzle and then to a light, steady rain. There was no nearby shelter.

An elderly woman passed by, stopped short and returned. She reached into the bucket-sized pockets of her bright magenta rain slicker, produced two plastic yellow and blue promotional umbrella hats from Norm's Tire Shop and pointed them at us. She did not make eye contact.

Her hands shook a bit as she spoke, "Take these," she ordered. "Catch death o' cold out here."

She was gone as quickly as she had appeared. The headband announced the after Christmas sale. Hooray for Norm. Even in the rain, an umbrella hat is foolishness, like someone shot and skinned a baby beach ball and stretched its polyurethane hide. Still, if the deal is foolishness for protection, take the deal. So there we stood, foolishness on parade, leaning against a corvette-red jeep, in the rain.

Anytime Cleaners was a droopy little place. Grime settled into every corner and crevice. The "N" and the "Y" on the neon sign were out: A**TIME. The big clock no longer kept watch over the Anytime logo. Its once-bright, always-moving hands now dark and dead at 11:00 o'clock.

Despite the rain, the door was propped open, fuzzy figures moving from counter to rows of clothes and back. Customers trusted thin plastic bags as they headed out against the rain. As we approached the open door, I thought about Daisy's descriptions of Delores. She told us a lot in a just a few words.

****

Suddenly, I felt something wet and cold on my right ear and the wet afternoon at Anytime Cleaners melted into my past.

I looked at my retriever's smiling, insistent face. It took a minute to relocate: golf course… Cohen's… summer heat…

Cody began chewing on my wrist and pulling. I understood immediately, opened the passenger door and let him out under the big shade tree.

I gave the command, "Get Busy" and he took care of matters. I took a quick look around. Was this a reportable offense? Hard to say. After a minute or two, Cody was back. I gave him a bite or two of my turkey burger, just the meat.

In tribute to my memories on this hot afternoon, I switched the Beatle CD for the Soundtrack to Forrest Gump. Poor Paul had worked enough on that hole. I began with (I Don't Know Why I Love You) But I Do, by Clarence "Frogman" Henry.

Does it get any better than a guy named "Frogman?"

My adult children humor me about these things. But, I love 50's and early 60's music for the simplest of reasons: It's fun and makes you want to dance.

Go "Frogman" wherever you are.

As I listened, I thought again about Delores Graham. I can tell you a lot about her today. On that rainy day I first met her, I knew little more than she was shy. If I were to briefly profile Delores today, it would sound like this.

Delores Graham: A dark-haired, green-eyed 24 year old, trapped in a single life, a family business, a plain face, a soft body and a sharp mind. Her life: over-examined and underactive. Emotionally and socially anemic. Like many shy people, she cycles through painful periods of quiet followed by dangerous outbursts followed by crippling floods of humiliation and renewed seclusion. Her friendship with Scotty, an accidental pairing of chemistry lab partners, is one of her best memories.

I looked at the retriever. He was expecting more turkey.

Cody would have been good for Delores: a safe place for her to express herself without fear of rejection, a nice building block for practicing social skills…

I gave Cody more turkey and decided that he could have the rest. As I broke off small bites, I encouraged my memories of that wet afternoon at The Anytime Cleaners to resurface.

****

We removed our umbrella hats and entered the open door at exactly ten minutes 'til 5:00. A buzzing bell rang somewhere in the back and Delores came to the counter. She was dressed in the store uniform: expensive black sneakers, crisp white pants and shirt and a light blue shirt-jacket with the ANYTIME logo embroidered just above her heart.

Her eyes were tired and her voice was polite, but forced. She looked like a girl who could be pretty but wasn't. Maybe she didn't try or was afraid to try.

"May I help you?"

I leaned against the counter. "Uh, are you Delores?"

I felt stupid.

Name's embroidered on her shirt.

"Yes, what is it?"

I spoke as quickly as I could. "My name is Randy an' this is my friend, Andy. We were friends of Scotty Jefferson. We found a letter from Scotty and we think you might be able to help us understand it."

I was out of breath. I focused on the top of her left shoulder.

She asked, "What makes you think I can help?"

"Daisy Clover said you might."

Suddenly, she relaxed. "I'm closing now but tomorrow's my day off. I can meet you at the Diner at 1:30."

Andy blushed. "We'll be there. Uh, thank you, ma'am."

****

We hurried across the parking lot. As soon as we reached the park, I shrieked, "'Ma'am'?! Have you lost your mind? And you blushed!"

Andy was pacing in a small circle, flapping his arms. "I dunno what happened. I dunno. I don't even know why I talked. Why did I talk? God! I really sounded stupid, huh?" He continued to spin slowly, looking at the sky for answers. "How could I be so stupid? So stupid. You couldn't help me, huh?"

I couldn't stop smiling, so I looked down. "Nope. You were gone."

He stopped spinning. "Whadaya think she thinks? Thinks I'm stupid? I'm a little kid?"

"No, because she's a girl an' 'cause she's older, she probably thinks you're sweet."

"You think?"

"No, stupid. I just said that to hear myself talk."

He seemed a bit relieved, but began pacing and flapping again. "Sweet, huh? You think? Boy, hot out here," he puffed.

I laughed. "Hot? Sure, out here in the fog and slop."

He ignored me. "Sweet. That's good, real good, huh?" He again stopped spinning. "Maybe you should just go there by yourself tomorrow. Take the letter, you know."

"Nope."

He stuffed his hands in his pockets, took them out and adjusted his hat. "Think she's pretty?"

I shrugged. "Not so much, not like Sandra Dee or Daisy. Nice big juggs. You think she is?"

"Kinda."

The rain stopped as we retraced our steps. Now and then a stubborn leaf, a small miracle holdout, would surrender. Everywhere I looked it was as bare as could be. The gusting wind slapped at everything. I was sliding along, barely lifting my feet, like an ice-skater.

"Stay close, "I reminded, "Don't wanna…"

"Yeah," he moved closer. "Kiss no tree." He put his hand on my arm. "Gotcha."

We reached the other side of the park, crossed the street to the sidewalk and the sky opened up. There was no place to hide and hurrying was useless, so we settled into a slow, steady pace. I could feel my shoes filling up. I had to turn my head to the side to see. It was getting dark.

I yelled, "Go on home. See you tomorrow."

Andy yelled back, "I am goin' home right now."

"Don't wait for me. Go."

"I am goin' right now. Ain't waitin' for you. Don't tell me what to do."

The post office was closed. We stepped underneath the overhang and away from the wind and rain. It was much warmer without the wind but my teeth were chattering. I discovered that I could control the chattering. If I "pushed" with my stomach muscles, the chattering would speed up, if I relaxed and held my jaw firm, it would stop.

Andy was shaking water from himself top to bottom, like a golden retriever hitting the river bank after a quick swim. He was also wiping his head frantically and using his fingers like a comb.

I stood by quietly dripping.

Wish I could shake. God, would it be such a big deal if I could just shake?

I laughed. Suddenly, I did shake myself, mentally.

Dumb ass. Suppose God decides to listen to you this very minute. You're one an' only shot at a miracle. An' you ask to be able to shake? You're not only crippled, you're a moron.

I laughed again, harder. Andy was tilting his head to the right and then to the left, pounding the water out of each ear.

"What the hell is so funny?"

"Just me," I grinned. "Just wishin' I could shake."

He continued pounding. "What?"

"Nothin', forget it."

He was about to blow his nose toward the wall.

"Don't," I yelled, "Might hit an innocent bystander."

He looked up. "Huh?"

I pointed to a nearby bush in a flower bed.

"Oh."

He placed his thumb and forefinger on his nose, sealed his right nostril and blew hard in the direction of the bush. He sealed the left side and repeated. He then cleared his throat, spat in the flowerbed and wiped both sides of his nose with his right sleeve.

The wind stopped, but the rain continued somewhat calmer. We stepped back on to the sidewalk and squished and squeaked our way toward my house. We got to the big tree in my front yard and it was very dark.

I was shivering and aching. "Need you to come in an' help me."

"How?"

Jaw tight, I could barely speak. "If you're there, she won't get mad, or only a little an' you can help me change real fast. She'll forget all about me bein' wet."

Andy was shivering too and moving around. "Okay, an' you can gimme a dry shirt and some of your cut offs."

"Why cut offs?"

"You're too short long-wise, but we're the same around an' the same in shirts."

"Okay. We can call your mom an' tell her you're gonna stay at my house 'til the rain quits."

"She might not go for it. Dinner time."

We went to the back door and entered the kitchen. My mom came down the hallway, started in on me about being late and wet, saw Andy and immediately lightened up. She told us to go straight to my room, change and put our wet stuff in the dryer. We both breathed a sigh of relief when she said that she would call Andy's mom and ask if he could stay for dinner. I mentioned overnight and she said she'd ask.

"Dinner," she said, "will be ready in thirty minutes."

We hurried down the hall, stepped into my bedroom and closed the door. Before we could say a word, my mom knocked on the door, set a stack of clean towels on the floor and left. We set a towel out on the bed to sit on and one on the floor to stand on.

Andy hustled. "I change quick, then I help you, then get this stuff in the dryer."

I stopped him. "Get the clothes out now."

"What? They're all wet an' we still got 'em on."

"No, I mean, get the dry stuff now."

He nodded and collected clothes for both of us. He undressed and piled his wet stuff in a corner. I took off my jacket, and shirt, undid my belt, dropped my pants and underwear and sat on the towel on my bed.

Andy asked, "Whadaya need help with?"

"Shoes, socks, pants, underwear. My legs don't bend an' my ankles don't turn."

"Why not?"

"Operations. An' everything's worse if I'm cold."

He was out of breath and almost dressed. He went to the corner, picked up his wet stuff and grabbed my shirt. "Be right back. Keep your shirt on," he laughed, "get it?"

"I get it, but, help me first, then go to the dryer."

He dropped everything and together we wrestled my wet clothing to a standstill. In fifteen minutes we were both dry and ready to go. I was still cold. My mom knocked on the door and offered to put our wet stuff in the dryer.

Suddenly, I was worried. "Where's the letter?"

"Huh?"

"The letter, the letter! Where is it?"

Andy grabbed his jacket, pulled his notebook from an inside pocket and rummaged through until the letter fell out. We exhaled. Everybody was safe and dry: Andy, me and the letter.

He made a show of placing it on my dresser. "Leave it here. Come by tomorrow an' we go see Delores at 1:30."

"Man, I got no money."

"Drink water, fool. Long as one of us is buyin' we're good."

"Okay, but we can't stay long."

"She'll know right away an' that's it."

"Hope so."

My dad was working late so we ate dinner with my mom: stew, vegetables and milk. As soon as we sat, my mom announced that Andy's mom was happy for him to stay the night. She was very tired and would appreciate not having to come out. Conversation was stuffed with awkward silences and those silly, obvious questions adults ask when they are trying too hard. But dinner finished without incident or dessert (It was a weeknight.) Mom cleared the dishes and said that she was going to watch a romantic movie—our cue to escape.

Halfway down the hall, she called us back and pointed to the sink. "Not so fast boys."

Andy grabbed a hand towel. "You wash, I'll dry an' put away."

We finished the dishes quickly with no casualties. My mom stuck with traditional dishes and glasses (the ones that break). I could not understand why she didn't want invincible Melmac, the Superman of dishes.

I volunteered. "I'll wipe the table, you sweep."

****

We headed down the hallway a second time.

Andy flopped on my bed. "You got the kiss, I get the bed."

The top bunk was out. It was stacked with storage boxes.

"Then you get the sleepin' bag, lay it out an' gimme a pillow."

Andy grunted, got up, jumped off the bed and belted me silly with a pillow. I hit the bed in a heap as he headed for the closet.

"Right back with your sleepin' bag, Missy. An', get offa my bed."

"Might have to hurt ya."

"If I'm scared, I'll bring a dog."

Andy returned, laid out the bag and pillow. "Whadya wanna do?"

For the next two hours we wore each other out:

- Checkers

- Chess

- H-O-R-S-E with rolled socks

- House of cards (building contest)

- Card toss

Suddenly, Andy's eyes sparkled. "Let's play Slap Hands."

Slap Hands is a test of nerve, speed and pain tolerance. The slappee places his hands palm down, hovering above the slapper's hands. The slapper brings his hands over to slap the top of the other's hands. If the slapper fakes and his opponent pulls away, the slapper gets a free hit. If the slapper misses, roles switch. The slapper can slap with either hand or both and may slap as often as he chooses—and every time the slapper hits, he gets another turn.

We sat in facing chairs.

It's the free slap that kills. Five minutes into things, my hands were turning red. I was getting hit left and right. Andy faked and I flinched and pulled away. I had to hold both hands out, palms down, and wait. Andy calmly raised both hands above his head and came down with deadly force.

My mind went numb.

My God, my hands just exploded. I have no hands.

We both looked at my hands and Andy spilled into laughter. My right hand flashed and I whacked him hard across the left side of his face and sent him sprawling.

He was complaining. I could see my palm and finger prints on his left cheek and ear. I reached for the sky and blurted, "I give up, I quit, you win! Sorry, I swear."

He whined, "Jesus, ya knocked out a tooth." He then hit me hard with a pillow and I went to the floor.

My mother called, "Boys what is going on in there? Settle down right now."

We buried our faces in pillows. After a minute or so, Andy put the chairs back at the desk and reclaimed the bed. I straightened my bag and positioned my pillow.

I asked, "You OK?"

Andy worked his jaw. "Cut my cheek inside." He looked at me. "You OK?"

"Yeah," I laughed.

He was tough and didn't rub.

We decided to read *Boy's Life*. For the next hour we read about football, hunting, whittling and stamp-collecting. We learned about Lafayette, Jacob and Esau and Davy Crockett.

Andy said, "Esau was stupid."

"Uh huh," I agreed, "but he was hungry."

"Still stupid."

"Yeah. Hey, you think George Mikan really wears Keds?"

"Bullshit… ya kiddin?' Just 'cause they put it in a stupid magazine?"

"Me neither."

I pushed the magazine aside. Andy sat up and snapped his fingers, eyes sparkling.

"Whatever it is," I said, "I don't wanna do it. My hands are…"

He waved his arms. "No, stupid." He leaned forward and whispered, "Next year, we should sell Christmas cards."

"What? To who?"

"Huh? Everybody."

"Like yer mom? 'Cause my mom won't buy 'em."

He jumped out of bed and began pacing.

Suddenly, he spun and pointed. "We could sell 'em in front of the GAD."

"Nope," I shook my head, Reggie—"

"We can ask 'im."

I shook my head. "These ads make it seem easy but ya get stuck with left over cards. You gotta buy all the cards before ya sell 'em."

Andy grabbed his head. "Huh? Gotta be…? Why would I want to make money sellin' the cards if I had the money to buy 'em? If I got the money to buy 'em, why do I need to make money sellin'?"

I shrugged. "Don't ask me."

"Don't make sense."

Andy climbed back on the bed, slugged his pillow and rested his chin on his hands. "What's somethin' else we can do?"

I started flipping cards at the waste basket. "You know, I wanted to make money last summer. So, I looked in the Bible. An' it's got a thing called 'Job.' Talk about stupid! Wasn't even nothin' 'bout a job in it."

"Then why'd it say job?"

"Another thing that makes no sense."

Andy brightened. "Hey, I got it. We can make a lotta money next Christmas, easy."

The plan was simple and would cost almost nothing. Collect and bag sprigs of holly for folks to use in holiday decorations. It was a very good idea. Mrs. Reynolds, an elderly widow who lived two short blocks from The Great American Diner, felt both blessed by her three beautiful, giant American Holly Trees and cursed by the overgrown backyard in which they were trapped.

Andy's idea was to clean and clear her backyard in exchange for all the holly we could sell. I could see no drawbacks.

He was off and running. "We use little brown lunch bags an' rubber bands and we got it made in the shade."

I smiled. "We're in the money."

We were getting sleepy. Andy looked down. "Tomorrow, you do the talkin'. Not me."

"You can talk," I argued, "Don't worry."

"No," he mumbled, "I ain't worried, but I ain't talkin'."

Suddenly, Frankie Avalon and "Venus" were in the room.

"Hey," I yelled, "Turn that thing off."

Andy moved. "Got that right. I hate that faggy song."

"Reminds me," I said, "I got somethin' for you to memorize."

He scowled. "What's that gotta do with faggy Frankie Avalon?"

"You asked me if I liked that Frankie Avalon song. Then you told me about 'Yokahama Mamma.'"

"So?"

"So, here's what I did in the fourth grade talent show."

I had two delivery choices: One involved a slow, painfully dramatic effort designed to dazzle with rhyme and the other a monotone machine-gun style designed to send the listener's head spinning.

I went for the machine-gun effect and recited the following:

Ladies and Gentlemen

Hobos and Tramps

Cross-eyed Mosquitoes and Bowlegged Ants!

I'm here to tell you something I know nothing about.

Admission is free But you pay at the door.

Pull up a chair and sit on the floor.

One bright day, in the middle of the night.

Two dead boys got up to fight.

Back to back, they faced each other

Drew their knives and shot each other.

The deaf and dumb policeman heard those shots

And came and killed those two dead boys.

And if you don't believe me,

Ask the blind man on the corner.

He saw it all.

Andy clapped. "Good!"

I did my version of a sitting bow. "Think so, really?"

He nodded. "Uh huh."

I paused. "Well, it ain't gonna get me another kiss."

He grabbed a pillow, fired at me point blank and missed.

I screamed, "No standing up, butthead cheater!"

He jumped from the bed, retrieved his pillow, reset, fired from his knees and nearly took my head off.

"You don't get to whine about a second kiss," he warned, "when some of us are still waiting for number one!"

He was right. I called "Truce" and gave him his pillow. We turned off the light and began to drift.

I spoke directly to the dark. "Whadya thinkin' 'bout?"

Andy fussed with his covers. "Same thing I think 'bout every night.

I said, "I wonder if Delores is the real D.G."

Andy sat bolt upright like his back was spring-loaded. "How could she be the real D.G.? We know he was in love with a blonde named Linda and we know that they really loved each other. Daisy saw 'em together more 'n once. I mean, she could tell 'bout that if anybody could, right?"

I nodded. "Right. So D.G. must mean something else. Must not be a person's name."

"Gotta be a name," Andy protested. "What else do ya start a letter with?"

"Suppose it's an insult. Like, 'Hey, Butthead or Howdy Bozo."

Andy was strong. "No, can't be. Nobody insults his girlfriend."

I tried again. "Unless he's mad. He had a lot of reasons to be mad. She made him look like a fool."

"So," Andy frowned. "D.G. might mean 'Damn Giraffe?'"

"No," I was shaking my head. "You're right. Makes no sense. Doesn't fit together with the rest of the letter. If it was an insult, the rest of the letter woulda been bad. But, it wasn't."

Andy said, "Let's look at this letter again."

He threw back his covers, stepped carefully into the darkness and moved toward the light switch. I pulled back so that I would not be stepped on. I could hear Andy's hand scraping on the wall in search of the switch. Suddenly, the light blasted us and we were squinting. He made his way to the desk and we read again.

May 15, 1954

Dear D.G.

Please don't do this. I'll do anything to make things right. You know
I never meant to hurt you. Can't we just talk this out? We used to talk all
the time. Why not now? What are you afraid of? Why can't you face me?
Why do you hate me now? Why are you doing this? It doesn't have to be
this way. Please. Talk to other people. They will tell you.

I can't eat and I can't sleep. This is killing me. We may have done some
wrong things. But, this is just not right. Everybody knows something is
wrong. My parents are asking questions. I can't concentrate in school. I'm
afraid I'm not going to graduate. How can I go to graduation parties? How
will I ever be happy again?

Maybe I should just disappear like you. Why did you do that? No note,
no phone call. You said you would always love me. Was that a lie? Was it
all a lie? Did you ever really love me? Just tell me that. Tell me to my face
that you never loved me.

Listen to me. You're smart. Think. You know two wrongs or a million
wrongs won't add up to anything right. You know that. I don't mean that
it was wrong to love you. It was (and is) the best part of my life. And, I'm
not talking about the sex. I'm ashamed about that, but I'm not ashamed
that I fell in love and that I love you with all of my soul at this very minute.
Losing you is like being dead without being buried. Please come back. You
don't have to be back with me. Just come back and see if there's a better
way. I know you understand me.

I will always love you,
Scott

I suggested writing our questions.

1. Who is D.G.?

2. What does he mean, 'never meant to hurt you?'

3. Why did she leave?

4. Why didn't she say anything to him?

5. Was there something she was afraid of?

6. What wrong things did he think they had done?

7. What did his parents know? What did they ask?

8. When he says come back, why say, 'You don't have to be with me?'

****

I asked, "Think he knew she was married? I mean, from the beginning? I do."

"Yeah," Andy agreed, "He was too smart not to know. He went around with her a long time, didn't he?"

"I don't know, but I think it would be real hard to tell your kids you're leavin' 'em. I think that's part of why she just took off."

Andy shrugged. "Maybe."

We worked our way through the questions and decided that Scotty was surprised that Linda was leaving, that she didn't talk to him because it wouldn't have made any difference, that he might have regretted getting involved with a married woman, and that his parents only knew he was depressed, not why.

I stared at the list. "Why does he say, 'Come back, but you don't have to be with me?' If that's true, why be upset she's gone?"

Andy laughed. "Easy. It's a lie. Just say somethin' to get her back. If I was him, I'd say anything."

I nodded. "Think there was somethin' goin' on with Dolores an' Scotty?"

Andy shook his head. "No, but we should ask her tomorrow."

"Yeah, I will."

Andy returned the letter, turned off the light and got into bed.

He asked, "Whadaya thinkin' 'bout?

I said, "Same thing I always think about."

I closed my eyes and there she was—with her perfect feet.

I smiled in the dark.

Wonder what Sandra Dee dreams about?

Chapter 26
Interviews, Passing League,
Arrows and Yearbooks

SATURDAY MORNINGS ARE easier than weekdays, even on vacation. Parents often sleep late and the day can stretch like a rubber band. From the sloppy, wet grey against the window, this day would be a continuation of the last seven. We dressed and Andy got his clothes. We cleaned my room, ate cold cereal, wrote my mom a note and went to Andy's to clean his room.

Andy sat at his desk, opened his notebook and found a clean page. "Let's write the questions for Delores."

He wanted a list of questions because he didn't trust himself in another face to face with the girl from the cleaners.

The list came easy:

1. Are you the D.G. in the letter?

2. If not, do you know who D.G. is?

3. Were you ever Scotty's girlfriend?

4. Did Scotty have other girlfriends?

5. Did you know Linda?

6. Did Scotty tell you anything when Linda disappeared?

7. Did Scotty ever mention a private detective, Richard Diamond?

8. Did Scotty ever mention suicide?

9. Did Scotty ever talk about a secret place?

10. Does "hide in plain sight" mean anything to you?

11. Does "the problem is below and the answer is above" mean
anything to you?

Andy set his pencil down and forced a breath. "What about all the
other stuff like the little silver key, the scratched note on the floor, the
bracelet, the locket an' the 'his name was Scotty' thing?"

I looked up and shook my head, "Never get that far. But, we should
show her the locket picture."

"Maybe the little key?"

I shrugged, "Guess so, sure. Why not?"

"Show Daisy that locket too?"

"Noooo," I frowned. "Gotta be careful 'bout Daisy. Reg knows
everybody comes in there to see Daisy. She can't get hung up with us."

Andy closed the notebook, reopened it and ripped out a page. "Let's
play Finger Football."

"Uh," I hesitated. "Let's play Passing League instead."

Andy threw the paper and tape in the desk drawer, grabbed the football
from the closet and headed toward the door.

He stopped. "Come on, Grandma. You wanna play or not? Don't
have all day. Good thing you got some guns, throw the hell outta the ball.
Otherwise, hafta put a dress on you, make you a cheerleader. Good thing
you can't step into a throw, you'd kill somebody."

I grinned.

Hooray for weight-lifting.

"Call the guys, meet at the park."

He shook his head, opened his dresser, pulled two sweatshirts and
threw one at me. "No need. Guys are already there. Trust me. Wait here.
Be right back."

He left and I put on the sweatshirt. I thought he had to use the rest
room. He returned in five minutes with a big grin and a victory fist.

He sat next to me and splattered $1.88 in change on the bed. "Who
says we can't eat at the diner today?"

I laughed. "I ain't complaining. You get that from the restroom?"

"Huh? You crazy? I turned the couch upside down, underneath the
cushions and inside the lining at the bottom. I was gonna do it when we
first got here, but I forgot."

He grabbed a hand towel as we hit the door.

****

It was mid-morning. The park was foggy, hard and slick. Passing League is two-hand touch football, every play a pass. The quarterback must release the ball in three seconds or suffer a sack. There are no first downs, only short, medium or long touchdowns. A team gets four downs and keeps the ball until it fails to score or its quarterback is intercepted or sacked. There are many ways to score:

Long Touchdown	4
Medium Touchdown	3
Short Touchdown	2
Quarterback Sack	3
Interception	3
Interference (penalty)	4
Tackling (penalty)	4
Tripping (penalty	4
Shoving (penalty)	4
Fighting (penalty)	4

We entered the park from the east side and immediately spotted Shane and Jim on the basketball court. By the time we reached shouting distance, everybody was there as if they dropped from the trees.

Andy waved the football. "Hey ladies, let's play Passing League."

Shane tucked the basketball under his arm and pointed. "Bobby Blazer is here with all those other guys. Let's play them."

Everybody screamed.

Andy threw the ball in the air and laughed. "If that comes down girls, let's go get 'em."

As we moved toward the west side of the park, the Blazer bunch appeared to be in some sort of scrum: pushing, shoving and cursing.

"What the hell?" sniffed Jim.

We stopped ten yards from the mess in front of us and stood in a rough line, watching. After a minute or so, the scrum broke and lined up, facing us. Although it was incorrect to call Bobby Blazer the leader of this or any other collection, he was easily the most recognizable. Nicknamed the Albino by his enemies, his skin was thin and watery, almost transparent. Skinny and spindly, he moved more like a marionette than a boy. He had an oval shaped head, topped by a longer-than-ordinary flat top of snow white hair propped straight up by a fourth of a pound of Pomade. Calling himself the 'Jester,' he sported bird-like features: beady eyes, a hawk nose, a thin mouth and baby teeth.

He took half a step forward, squinted, cocked his head and screeched. "Whatchu assholes want?"

Andy stepped up. "Wanna play Passing League?"

"Ha," he cackled, "You bet—with your mama."

He looked behind for approval.

Andy cleared his throat. "Bobby is that blue paint in your left ear?"

Blazer's head snapped around as if he'd been slapped, his eyes narrowed. "Let's just play, jerk off."

Andy stepped closer and pulled a quarter from his pocket, "Call it."

He flipped it, caught it and slapped it on his wrist.

Bobby squeaked, "Heads."

"Tails, we'll take the ball first."

We agreed to play to 20, marked the end zones and the lines for long, medium and short touchdowns and took positions at our goal line.

I stood five yards deep in the end zone. Andy dug inside his sweatshirt, pulled out the hand towel and stuffed one end inside my pants at the belt buckle.

"Wipe your hands on this."

I nodded, we huddled up and I studied the other side. Skill sets aside, they easily won the battle of the nicknames. Here is the Nickname Bunch line up:

- Richard and Robert Hughes/AKA Short Stack and Heavy Lunch

Chunky little stumps with fat faces, big stomachs and bushy eyebrows that grew together. They could have been twins but weren't. Always wore sweat-stained, faded, red baseball caps, forever drinking water and belching.

- Gary McRandle/AKA Daddy Long Legs/AKA Spider

Tall, fast but clumsy, body parts flying in all directions, he was a polite quiet kid who stuttered. He often defended himself against bedwetting rumors, all of which were true. His father and big brother were Marines.

- Carl Wakely/AKA The Assassin

Big, strong, athletic, fast, super hand-eye coordination, lost three front teeth to a hockey puck while visiting cousins on the East Coast one year ago, never repaired or replaced. High school coaches began talking to him in the sixth grade. He's a monster, plain and simple. He can hurt people anytime he wants.

• Kenny Morrison/AKA Smokey/AKA Michelin Man

Incredible arm strength, throws so hard he hurts receivers, began smoking cigarettes in the third grade and cigars in the sixth grade, no brothers or sisters, only alcoholic parents. Earned Michelin Man nickname when he stole a tire from Norm's Tire Shop and tried to sell it to buy a carton of cigarettes.

****

I looked around in the huddle. "The only guy I'm afraid of is Carl an' they know that. So, they think we'll stay away from him, use Andy as a decoy to take him away. That's what I'd do if I were us. Well, we are us, but we ain't gonna do that. Everybody listen up. You guys, all of you, on two, sell the left sideline fly and curl about ten yards down at the green bench. Andy, you're on the right, run the fly pattern full out. I'll hit you right at that Modesto Ash. To get it that far, there won't be much air under it but I'm gonna throw it as hard as I can right passed Carl's left ear. It should come to you about chest high. You might have to lay out. Remember if you go down an' no one touches you, get up an' go. Everybody stay in bounds."

Everybody went to the line. I stayed in the back of the end zone, leaning on my left cane with the football in my right hand. Why me at quarterback? Simple: Passing League quarterbacks cannot run and neither could I. Also, for Passing League we used a smaller, non-regulation football, easier to get your hand around. Everything was already wet. I wiped my hands and called signals.

On two, everybody exploded. I counted in my head: one thousand one, one thousand two and zinged the ball with full force. I never saw Andy. I was just throwing to a spot on the field. The ball left my hand cleanly, but in my follow through, I wacked the Albino right across the bridge of his nose and connected like a heavyweight. I heard a crunch and saw blood spurt from the middle of Bobby's face. It felt like I slugged a brick wall.

I flashed.

Jesus, I just broke my hand.

My arm was numb to the elbow, didn't even look like it belonged to me. Bobby was on his knees two feet in front of me, holding his face and screaming.

At the very instant I connected with Bobby, the Hughes brothers, Heavy Lunch and Short Stack, plowed into me left and right. Lunch smacked the canes out and sent me spinning while Stack ducked under my right arm and lifted me up and out of the end zone. Both brothers landed on me. Everything went blurry. My hips and the back of my head hurt when I hit the ground, all the air punched out of my stomach. Everybody was screaming. I could hear Andy whooping it up in the other end zone.

I started slugging, clawing, punching and elbowing anything I could reach. I could feel people pulling the Hughes brothers off me. I could feel weight shifting. I was worried about getting punched in the groin.

I tried to roll on my side.

Jesus, hope nobody steps on my ankles.

As Robert was being lifted to his feet, he stepped on my stomach with his left foot and stood there for half a second. I thought about biting his ankle, but he moved and Shane and Jim picked me up. I got both canes underneath me and looked around.

Everybody was screaming about some type of penalty. The argument centered on whether I had been sacked or not. If I released the ball late, the sack would count and there would be no penalty for contact. The touchdown would not count; the Nickname Bunch would score three points and get the ball. After much haggling, the long touchdown counted, plus two penalties on the Hughes brothers for tackling. Total: twelve points, plus the ball.

We huddled in the end zone. My hand was bleeding just above my knuckles. Andy stuffed the towel back in my pants and I wiped my hand. Bobby was tearing part of his tee shirt into little pieces and stuffing cloth into both nostrils. His eyes were starting to blacken and he whined that two of his teeth were loose. His nose was so clogged with blood that he was hard to understand. He spat blood on the ground and looked in my direction.

I flipped him off with my bloody hand and said, "Sorry! It was an accident."

The huddle laughed.

I looked at Andy. "Must have been a great catch. I never saw it. I was buried under blubber."

Everybody laughed again.

Andy said, "I did have to lay out, but it was easier than it looked. I just rolled, came up on my feet an' strolled in. Carl wasn't even in the same county but I think he thought he intercepted it. He kept sayin' he thought he had it."

I had my breath again and I leaned into the huddle. "Fly patterns right and left. Clear out for Robert."

Jesse asked, "Who gets the ball?"

I winked. "Robert."

I looked around again. "If stuff starts, don't stand around and don't let anybody hurt my ankles. Okay, on one. Let's go."

Everybody reached the line. Robert was standing in the middle of the field six or seven yards from me. Bobby was sitting things out.

I yelled, "Down, set," paused, looked around and screamed, "Hut!"

Everybody took off. Robert took one step toward me and I wound up and drilled him with all the power I could muster, full follow through, good release, tight spiral. As soon as the nose of the football hit him, center chest, he crumpled.

We huddled. I leaned in. It was a sweaty, happy group.

I whispered one word, "again."

The huddle broke and everybody reached the line. I stood in the back of the end zone and carefully called out, "Down, set."

Robert was in the same spot on the field only two yards closer.

I looked him in the eye and screamed, "Hut!"

This time, he took two quick steps to his right and Carl, the Assassin, dove across the middle hoping to intercept. Apparently Robert was supposed to draw the throw to his left. But, running to his right, he simply left Carl's lane of protection and I unloaded harder than before and drilled him again: same spot, same result, twice the pain. Carl lunged, slipped, grunted and took a rolling belly flop into the mid-field mud pit.

Carl glared at Robert. "Don't look at me. Your fault."

We huddled up. I leaned in, everybody breathing hard. I asked, "One more sprint?"

Everybody nodded.

I looked to Andy. "Hard count on one, go on two. Stand beside me. When they lunge on one, I flip the ball to you on two and you make people miss. Okay."

Andy made everyone miss: twisting, spinning, and changing directions. Spider McRandle got a hand on him, but not two. He shifted into overdrive for the second half of the field and left a trail of discouragement, the whole Bunch standing or sitting in mud: sixteen nothing.

As Andy jogged back, Kenny Morrison grabbed a handful of muck and splattered him.

Andy smiled, wiped off the mud and announced, "Penalty, four points. Twenty to zero, game over."

We walked east toward the basketball court. I stopped and looked back. They were stuck in the mud, like lost sheep.

I grinned at Andy. "Good day for the Mudville Nine, eh?"

He smiled, tossed the football in the air and caught it. "Sure is."

Jesse asked, "Who's the Mudville Nine?"

Andy stopped and put his hands on his hips. "Casey at The Bat, you know."

"Huh? I thought we were playin' football."

Andy rolled his eyes and turned away.

Shane shook his head. "Hopeless."

Jim echoed, "Hopeless."

Tim added. "No hope."

Jesse pleaded. "Hey, wha'd I say?"

We reached the basketball court and everyone headed home for water and a change of clothes. Andy and I agreed to meet at the Great American Diner at 1:00 PM. We would be early and he would bring the notebook and the locket. I got home, cleaned up, changed clothes and put a couple of Band-Aids on my right hand. My neck, back and ribs were sore, but it felt great to be in my new blue and white Baltimore Colts jersey. I felt good about nailing Robert.

Shoulda got him one more time.

The more I thought about it, I was surprised that Carl, The Assassin, had been so calm.

Maybe he really doesn't give a crap about those guys. Talk to him sometime when those jerks aren't around. It was good to smack Bobby's nose, too. What an asshole. Always has been, always will be.

I remembered spending an afternoon with Bobby once. Most guys (even jerks) have a good side, or at least a better side, but only when no one else is around. Not Blazer. Late afternoon, sitting next to me on a concrete retaining wall separating the Thompson and Mendez yards, Bobby took a long swig, finished the last of his Royal Crown Cola, blasted a loud, ugly burp, shrieked like Geronimo and without warning, fired his empty bottle through the Mendez' bedroom window. The collision sounded like a bomb.

He looked at me, eyes sparkling and laughed. "Better hurry crippled boy 'cause yer in big trouble. Me? I was never here, pal."

He then grabbed my bottle and threw it through the Mendez window as well. In a flash he was gone, over two fences and down an alley, as if he'd never been there. From the back, he reminded me of Brer Rabbit slapping his heels together and scampering away.

I thought about trying to run away.

What's the point? I don't do running.

I walked around to the Mendez front door and rang the bell. No answer. I walked to the Thompson front door, rang the bell and told the Tale of the Bedroom Window. Mrs. Thompson thanked me and said she'd tell Mrs. Mendez. She also had a few other choice comments about Bobby. I told her I agreed.

****

I looked in the bathroom mirror one last time before heading out to the diner. The jersey looked great but I wondered if I'd ever get muscles like Decker. I wanted to look good for Daisy even though I felt stupid about it. As I stepped into the hallway, the doorbell rang and my mom answered. I could hear Andy on the porch and I yelled that I'd be right there.

At the door, my mom asked where I was going and when I mentioned we might stop by the diner she wanted to know what I was going to use for money.

"At Andy's house this morning, he found a bunch of change in the couch cushions and we were thinking this would be a good time to spend it."

"That's very nice of Andy to invite you," she smiled, "Have a good time."

"I will. We'll be there for an hour, probably. Bye."

I stepped out the door, she closed it behind me and I smiled at Andy. "Thought we were gonna meet at the diner."

"Yeah, I just wanted to go in there together.

"Good."

We walked five blocks to the park and took the short cut. It was nearing 1:00 o'clock and the sun was making feeble efforts against the heavy overcast. The park was empty, one lone guy shooting baskets on the far side.

We covered the remaining three blocks to The Great American Diner in no time.

Once inside, I was grateful for the heavy-duty mat. Dry crutch tips would help avoid an Alice-in-Wonderland moment on the glossy black and white checkered floor.

The colors and sounds of the GAD were as warm and welcoming as Daisy's smile. She pointed us to our favorite booth across from the grill and mouthed, *Be right with you.*

We slid into opposite sides of the booth and Andy suddenly realized our mistake.

"I'll switch," he said, "both of us need to see her face."

If I entered The Great American Diner three times a day for thirty days or only once a year, the result would be the same: a sensory jamboree, a kaleidoscope of chrome, candy-apple red, copper and crystal. It was simply stunning. I could fill up on the sights, sounds and smells and never touch a menu.

Suddenly, Daisy was there, right next to me.

She smells like cherries.

Andy punched my shoulder.

"Honey," she smiled, "if you're not careful, you are gonna stare a hole right through me an' how good would that be?"

Andy chirped, "I'll have a cheeseburger, fries and a Coke an' so will he as soon as he learns to close his mouth an' open his ears, right buddy?"

I nodded and blushed. They both smiled.

She jotted the order and took a step back. "Uh, why are you two sittin' on the same side of the booth?"

It was Andy's turn to blush. "We're waitin' here, I mean, we're meeting Dolores here in a few minutes to let her read the Scotty letter."

"So, why're you both over on that side?"

"So we can both see her face when she answers."

"When she answers what?"

"Our questions about the letter, 'bout Scotty."

She stuck her pencil in her red and white polka dot skirt pocket. "Makes sense."

I added. "Also because if we sit on opposite sides, she has to pick one of us to sit next to an' that's not right."

Daisy smiled. "Boys, that is very thoughtful." She waited for half a count. "This order'll be right up and I'll bring her over when she comes in. Which one of you is buying her lunch?"

Andy stuttered, "We, wh—We both are. Why?"

Again, Daisy sparkled. "Very nice boys! I mean, gentlemen."

She headed to the grill and we looked at one another.

Andy whispered, "I got another 80 cents. We're good on this."

I whispered, "You are a stud."

He whispered back, "Tell me somethin' I don't know."

At that moment, Dolores entered. She fussed with her jacket and looked a bit lost. Daisy greeted her, brought her over, seated her across from us, served water and asked, "Do you know what you want?"

Dolores looked down. "Uh, whatever is fine."

Andy rescued. "Make that three of the same."

Daisy scribbled. "Will do."

I spoke to Dolores, "Thanks for coming. But, I thought this was your day off. You're wearing your work uniform?"

She took a sip of water, set her glass down and didn't know what to do with her hands.

She put them on her lap and mumbled, "One of our guys is sick."

Andy reached inside his jacket. "Here's the letter we found inside a box in the Jefferson—uh, Scotty's old house. We don't think it was ever sent, but Daisy thought you might know something."

Delores took the letter and awkwardly unfolded it. "I'll try."

Out of the corner of my eye, I saw Decker at the far end of the diner.

Just what we need—a muscle-bound big mouth bugging us. He's talking a lot, maybe he doesn't see us. If he sees Delores, we're dead. He'll be over here in a flash an' we'll never get rid of him.

I cleared my throat, caught Andy's attention and nodded in Decker's direction. As soon as Andy glanced Decker's way, his shoulders dropped and he pulled the bill of his cap down.

Delores was just finishing the letter when I spoke, "We'd like to ask you a few questions, if that's OK."

Andy reached inside his jacket and handed me the list.

"Uh, she hesitated. "I have to get back to work soon, sorry."

I smiled. "This will only take a minute or two. Here we go."

1. Are you the D.G. in the letter?
   No.

2. Do you have any idea who it might be?
   No.

3. Were you ever Scotty's girlfriend?
   No. He treated me like a kid sister.

4. Did Scotty have other girlfriends which you knew about?
    She shook her head.

5. Did you know Linda or anything about her?
    No. But, I heard that there was a woman and she was older, married and beautiful.

Daisy appeared with three plates balanced on her left arm and in her right hand a small round tray holding three drinks. She set the tray on the table, set a plate in front of each of us and then positioned a glass near each plate.

She picked up the tray and smiled. "Can I get anybody anything else?"

We were quiet. Daisy smiled, slipped the bill in Andy's direction and headed toward the grill. In the background, Bobby Darin sang, "Dream Lover."

I watched Daisy leave.

That jukebox! Perfect song for right now. Must be a ghost in that machine.

I was watching Daisy tuck in the back of her blouse when I suddenly became aware that Dolores was talking to me. My head snapped around and I could feel my face and ears getting hot.

"Do you like Daisy?" She smiled and picked up her cheeseburger.

I cleared my throat, but Andy spoke first. "Not really, just kinda. He's really gone on Sandra Dee, dreams 'bout her all the time."

Delores' eyes sparkled. "Oh."

I was finishing a bite and I didn't want to talk with my mouth full. Delores waited while I chewed as politely as I could.

I said, "Every guy comes in here thinks Daisy is the best, me too. Daisy is a lot like Sandra Dee."

"Yeah," Andy agreed. "An' every guy that comes in here is hopin' to see that blouse come outta that skirt. I swear, it comes out every five minutes."

Delores walked through the rest of our questions quickly. She knew nothing about Linda's disappearance, never heard of detective Richard Diamond, never discussed suicide, knew nothing about a secret place and the "problem below/answer above" phrase was meaningless to her.

The one thing she did remember was that "hide in plain sight" was some joke between Scotty and his father. She remembered Scotty saying 'hide in plain sight' and that he thought it was clever. But she couldn't remember any details about what it might have meant, although she thought it might have something to do with football.

She wasn't quite finished with her food, but she pushed her plate forward, wiped her mouth and began leaving.

She again avoided eye contact and spoke just above a whisper, "Thanks. I wasn't much help."

Andy reached inside his jacket. "Uh, you're welcome for the lunch but before you leave, could you tell us anything about these things? If you could just take a quick look."

He produced the gold picture-locket and the small silver key and showed them one at a time. Delores said she'd never seen either of them and didn't recognize the girl in the picture. She apologized again and hurried toward the door, head down. Andy stuffed the locket and key into his pocket, stepped around and took Delores' spot.

He marveled. "Her lips look cool, don't they?"

"You askin' or tellin'?"

He smiled. "Both."

As Andy settled, Decker rolled up. "Well, well," he said, "as I live an' breathe, if it ain't Ricky an' David. How are Ozzie an' Harriet, boys?"

Andy was already irked. "Is that what you call what yer doin', Decker? You call it 'livin', do ya? Coulda fooled me. Then again, I am slow for my age."

In a blink, Decker's right hand shot out like a spear, snagged Andy by the collar and pulled him nose to nose. Andy stopped breathing.

Decker snarled through clenched teeth and whispered, "Listen, Rocky, don't wanna ruin your TV career, do ya? Besides, without you, what'll Bullwinkle over there do?"

Decker's contorted smile gave me the creeps, but I knew he'd never hurt anybody while in the diner.

Andy was pale and silent, arms at his sides.

I leaned forward and whispered to Decker, "Pete, you're about to be banned from the diner for life. Smooth move, Ex-Lax."

Andy laughed and so did Decker.

Then, he hurled Andy back into the booth. "Well, Huey an' Dewey, been real nice seein' my little nephews today. Be sure an' say hi to your brother, Louie for me."

I threw words in his direction. "Hey, Decker, put an egg in your shoe an' beat it, make like a tree an' leave, make like a banana an' split, see ya wouldn't wanna be ya."

Andy's eyes were as big as silver dollars. Decker's smile melted and his eyes became bullets.

I waved toward the grill and yelled, "Hey, Reg, good to see you."

Reg smiled, tweaked his toothpick and gave me his spatula/parade wave. Decker's face became soft and bloated again. He smiled, turned and rolled leisurely to the door.

Andy and I looked at each other and exhaled.

I felt drained. "I need a drink."

Andy whispered, "You need your head examined."

I gulped water. "After you, Einstein."

Andy was about to speak when his words stuck. I looked to my right and Decker was back, crap-eating grin, cheesy sign in and all.

He leaned in close and whispered, "Now, don't take this wrong, Abbot and Costello but take it to the bank. If either of you ever smart-mouths me again, any time, any place, I will hit both of you so hard your children will be born deaf. You understand me?"

We nodded quickly. "Yes sir, we understand."

In a few seconds, he was gone. I looked at Reggie. He was not smiling. Daisy came by and asked if we needed anything else. Andy ordered two more Cokes and an order of fries to share. Daisy cleared the table and said she'd be right back with the drinks.

I pointed. "Pull your hat up, can't even see your face."

He smiled. "Does your face hurt?"

"No."

"It's killin' me."

I paused for a long time. "You wanna apologize to Groucho for stealing his stuff or should I do it for you?"

Andy pulled back and raised his eyebrows. "Me apologize? Hey, Mr. 'put an egg in your shoe and beat it.' You want me to apologize? Can't get stupider than that."

I looked away and then back. "Listen, I was stupid under a death threat. Tryin' to save your sorry butt. A death threat brought on by you. I thought Decker was gonna kill you an' you did too."

Another long pause. "You're right," Andy smiled. "I'll do it. 'Groucho, please accept my apology for stealing your sorry-assed stuff and using it so badly.'"

We agreed that baiting Decker was an all-around bad idea and that we'd better try to fix things with him next time. At that moment, we could only come up with "We're sorry."

Andy winced. "It's the right thing to say, but it sounds so retarded." He spoke in a halting, deep, slow voice. "Huh huh, uh… We're, uh… Uh, huh … sorry. So, please don't kill us Mr. big, strong, crippled guy, huh."

"I know you're right," I sighed, "but what else can we do?"

Daisy arrived with new drinks and fries. "So, how'd it go with Delores?"

I answered quickly. "We didn't get much of anything. She didn't really know anything."

Andy took the locket out of his pocket and handed it to Daisy. "Do you recognize the girl in this picture?"

Daisy glanced toward the grill. No Reggie at the moment, she slipped into the booth next to me. I peeked at her thigh. It was beautiful.

I tried desperately to think up an excuse, some way to touch it.

If you're gonna ask for a miracle, ask now.

But there was no time. She took the locket in her graceful hands with her perfect glossy nails, opened it, studied the tiny fuzzy image and handed it back to Andy.

She said, "That's her alright. No doubt about it, that's Linda."

She started to slide out of the booth, stopped, leaned toward me and whispered in my ear, "Can't touch my leg, sweetheart. I appreciate the thought. But, it is okay to look."

She then righted herself, exited the booth and smoothed her skirt.

She looked right at me and smiled. "That's a very pretty shirt."

And then she winked and left.

Andy was dumbfounded. "She winked," he whispered fiercely.

I could not speak.

He continued his fierce whisper, "What the hell did she say?"

I flat-lined. "She said, 'That's a pretty shirt.'"

Andy sucked air in through his teeth, adjusted his hat, rested his hands on the table top and leaned in. "I know that, you idiot. I was right here. What did she whisper? Tell me now or I kill you. I make it look like an accident but best friend or no best friend, I kill you, right here, right now."

"She called me, 'Sweetheart,'"

"That's it? 'Sweetheart?' What else? She was whisperin' a long time."

I took a deep breath and looked directly at my best friend. "I cannot tell you here. I cannot tell you now. But, I will tell you, unless you kill me here and now, which means I will never tell you. And, the more you bother me about it, the longer it'll be 'til I tell you."

For a minute, Andy did his version of Louie's crazed vampire but he said, "What goes around comes around, remember that."

I smiled. "I will."

We drank the Coke and demolished the French fries. As we were preparing to leave, the jukebox again played *Dream Lover*.

Andy was disgusted. "Stupid song, stupid jukebox."

Suddenly, I understood.

I almost screamed, "Not a stupid song at all. I got it! I got it! I know who D.G. is."

Andy's eyes bugged out, "Who is it?"

"Not here. We need proof and I think I know where to get it."

"What?"

"Hurry up! Got enough for a tip?"

Andy was digging in his pockets and piling change on the table.

From my pocket, I produced a quarter. "Here, add this."

"Don't need it."

I threw it on the pile. "As Louie would say, 'Give it to 'er. She's beautiful.'"

"She is beautiful alright." Andy stuffed the lining back in his pocket.

We headed for the door with a new urgency.

"Who do you think it is?"

"Quiet. You know I can't walk and talk at the same time."

Andy chuckled, "Let's make it real tough. Try chewing gum."

I laughed. "Shut up."

He opened the door and I stepped through. "Is the box of Scotty stuff still in Shane's garage?"

"Yeah, why?"

"No time now, gotta hurry. I need you to get me through the park, then go to the cleaners and see if you can get Delores to loan you her sophomore yearbook. Then, meet me at Shane's."

"She's at work. How's she gonna lend me her sophomore yearbook?"

"How do I know? Just get it, okay?"

Andy pulled his hat down. "Okay."

"Tell her anything. Tell 'er it's life an' death. Just get the yearbook."

We reached the edge of the park quickly. Andy stepped closer to me and put his hand on my arm. I started my slide-stepping technique and we were moving along at a brisk pace, at least for me. After ten minutes, we stopped to rest. I looked around for the first time. The park was deserted.

Suddenly, I heard and felt something whiz by my right ear. It sounded like a bee with a jet engine for a stinger. Instinctively, I covered my ear with my hand. In less than a blink, I also heard something thump the tree trunk less than a foot from my head.

Andy turned and looked behind us. "What the hell was that?"

I was shaking as I pointed to the tree inches from my face. "We gotta get the hell outta here!"

Andy looked around again and turned back to me. "Nobody anywhere."

He stepped forward and tried to pull what appeared to be an arrow from the tree. "No need to hide or duck. Second or third shots coulda killed us by now."

I rolled my eyes. "I feel so much better now."

Andy braced himself against the trunk and pulled. No luck. On the second try, he wiggled and pulled and forced it out. It was a wine-red aluminum arrow, no more than twelve inches long and ¾ inches in diameter, a steel point on its tip and bright yellow feathers on its tail. Despite the force of impact, its shaft was perfectly straight.

Andy carried the arrow in his right hand and we covered the rest of the park in record time. I was breathing hard and Andy was fidgeting.

I puffed, "I'll meet you at Shane's. I'll take the arrow. You just get the yearbook. See you there."

Andy was still fussing. "Sure about this?"

"Just give it to me and get going."

He began jogging in the direction of the cleaners and I slipped the arrow under my belt on the outside of my pants at a 45 degree angle on my right hip. It was snug and did not affect movement in any way.

****

Thirty minutes later I knocked on Shane's front door. His sister Leslie answered and invited me in. She seemed nervous or embarrassed. Suddenly, I realized that she wasn't bothered at all. In fact, she was quite relaxed, polite and sweet.

On the other hand, I was extremely nervous.

What in the world is going on? Why am I short of breath? Why am I sweating? Leslie isn't pretty. Why would I be nervous around Leslie? This is crazy. Maybe I'm in The Twilight Zone.

For the first time, I noticed that she had a very girl shape, all those curves.

Her voice was soft. "Shane's in the garage playing pool. You can come in this way, if you want."

I nodded and followed her down a dark hall.

She stopped and gave me a curious look. "Are you okay? You don't look so good."

"I'm OK. Stuff's just been happening today."

"Oh," she smiled.

She seemed so nice that at that moment I wanted to be in love with her.

The dark gave me courage. "Uh, well… Leslie, I know you are older than me but I just wondered if I could give you a compliment."

Her brow wrinkled and she smiled. "Sure, I mean, yes you may."

I took a deep breath. "Well, I never noticed it before, but you are a very beautiful girl. At least that's what I think."

I exhaled and my knees were quivering, like I'd been lifting weights too long. I could see light in her eyes.

She smiled, stepped forward, placed her hands on my shoulders, leaned forward, kissed my cheek and whispered, "That's the nicest thing anyone has ever said to me."

She stepped back and I whispered, "Somebody should have said it before now."

She stepped around me and opened the door. "Shane's in here."

I stepped through and she closed it softly.

Shane looked up from the pool table. "Hey."

"Hey, I gotta sit down."

"What's wrong, you okay?"

"Yes and no."

"What?"

I started to crumble on to the couch, caught myself, removed the arrow from my belt and eased my way down.

Shane pulled up a folding chair. "What's with the arrow and what's on your face and why are you sweating?

I grimaced. "1. Someone shot at Andy an' me today. 2. Your sister's lipstick and 3. I'm really not sure."

"Let me get this straight." Shane was very deliberate. "Why is my sister's lipstick on your face? And don't say 'cause she kissed you."

"I complimented her."

He smiled big, something he usually tried to avoid with a mouth full of braces.

He looked away from me and back. "That's it?"

"Uh huh."

I pointed to a ragged beach towel near the old juke box. "Could I use that?"

Shane quickly handed me the towel. "Stop complimenting Leslie."

My face was in the towel. "OK."

"Someone shot at you?!"

"Yes!"

I kept wiping my hands. "We interviewed Delores Graham at the GAD today."

Wha'd she say?"

I waved him off. "Quiet. I'll get there."

He put his hands up. "Sorry, go."

"When we left there I was pretty sure I knew who D.G. was and that's why I'm here."

Shane started to say something. I ducked my head and raised my right hand. He stopped, folded his arms and leaned back.

I took a breath. "We took the short cut through the park. "We stopped so I could rest and this thing (I held up the arrow.) came right by my ear and slammed into the tree about a foot from my face."

"Why were you close to the tree?"

"To lean against it to rest. It almost hit Andy, too. He pulled it outta the tree and we split up. I came here and he's gone to talk to Delores before he comes here. He's tryin' to borrow her sophomore yearbook." I took another deep breath. "We need to look in the Scotty box and get his senior yearbook. It's in there, right?"

Shane was already pulling the box from beneath the pool table. "Yeah, I think all his yearbooks are in here." He began digging. "Who would try to shoot you and what's in the yearbook?"

"I don't know who'd shoot us. But, it's not what's in the yearbook but who."

"Who?"

The real D.G."

He handed me the yearbook.

At that moment, the door opened and Andy bounced in, yearbook under his arm.

He was out of breath and talking fast. "Did he tell ya somebody's tryin' to kill us?!"

Shane nodded. "He also told me he knows who D.G. is and that he kissed my sister."

I began shaking my head. "No, no, no. I did not kiss your sister. For the record, she kissed me."

"What?" Andy almost yelled. He threw his hat on the floor, turned away, ran his fingers through his hair, released a long sigh and turned back to me. "I wish you'd stop kissin' people everywhere! Pissin' me off."

"I will. I swear, I will."

217

"Now," he said, "whadya wanna talk about first, the arrow or the yearbooks?"

Shane stared at Andy. "You know about the arrow?"

He retrieved his hat, sat and plopped Delores' yearbook. "My uncles are hunters an' I've read a lot of those hunting magazines and I've read a lot of those ads in the back. I know about 'em.' He picked up the arrow and began examining it. "This is an arrow that can take 150-180 pounds of pressure."

"What's pressure?"

"Not now, fools. Look it up, eh? Just listen. It's made for a crossbow not a long bow. It's aluminum and it's hollow."

"Hollow, why?"

"For poison. Aluminum is light, break away tips. Enter the prey easily, no surface damage. And, no matter what anybody says, these are arrows not bolts. People think crossbows shoot bolts and long bows shoot arrows. Wrong. Bolts have no feathers and are dumpy looking little things. Look how beautiful this thing is. Look at these perfect feathers."

He furiously dried his hands on the rug and told Shane to get a dry wash cloth. Shane was back in a flash. Andy dried the arrow and gripped the shaft firmly with his left hand. With his right hand safely shielded by the cloth, he began twisting and pulling on the steel tip.

In a moment or two it dislodged and separated. Andy opened the side door and pounded the open end of the tip on the door jamb. He was expecting to find powder. Instead, he found nothing.

"Guess I was wrong, dry hole."

Shane said, "Hey, look at the other end. Take off the feathers. They come away from the shaft don't they? I mean, the feather section comes off in one piece, right?"

Andy said, "Not that I know of."

He studied the feathers carefully and discovered that the shaft appeared to be altered: A thin line was visible just above the feathers. He took the shaft to the door jamb, held it in both hands and gave it a hard whack. No luck. He took it to the front porch, leaned it against the step at a 45 degree angle and stomped hard with his right foot. The shaft and the feather section separated cleanly. Apparently, because it had been pre-cut, the shaft itself was not damaged.

Andy returned holding both pieces. "No poison but I guess it's true that a cylinder is one of the strongest things. This thing is still perfectly round."

"So are arches," said Shane, "remember the Romans." He reached for the main shaft piece. "Let me look at that for a minute."

He stepped to the pool table and whacked the shaft against its edge: Three quick, hard thumps, each with greater downward thrust. On the third thump, he added a whiplash.

Suddenly, there it was on the carpet—a small clear gelatin capsule with something inside.

Our eyes sucked all of the air from the room and for a few moments no one moved or spoke. We blinked and checked. It was still there.

"Shane whispered, "Get it! You know about poison."

Andy dropped to his knees and looked closely. He picked up the capsule and took it to the pool table. Then, he glanced at Shane and they turned and pulled me up from the couch. We stood together at the table.

Andy said, "There is a message in here."

He was gently twisting and pulling two sections of the capsule which interlocked. "You can get these by the billion at the drug store. Empty, they're cheap. High school kids buy 'em to announce keggers. Tiny strip of paper, roll it, set it inside and pass 'em out. Teachers never catch 'em."

"God," I said, "You couldn't pay me to be a teacher. What a crappy job."

Shane was riveted on the capsule. "You got that right. If I ever think about bein' a teacher, slap me."

Andy grinned. "Here it is, boys."

He unrolled the narrow strip, smoothed it out and read the neat, fine printing:

"Let the dead bury the dead."

We stared at each other.

Shane snapped his fingers. "Be right back. I gotta get somethin'."

He was back in seconds, looking through a Bible. "Matthew 8:21-22: 'And another of his disciples said unto him, Lord, suffer me first to go and bury my father. But Jesus said unto him, Follow me; and let the dead bury their dead.'

I looked at Shane as if he were an alien. "How'd you know that?"

"We studied this about two months ago in Sunday school. But, I saw it before, way last year when I was getting the religion medal for Scouts."

Andy flinched. "There's a merit badge for religion? Never heard of that before."

"It's not a merit badge," Shane explained, "and it's not given by the Scouts exactly. It's a medal for God and Church or whatever, like the

Jewish Temple. You earn it through your church or whatever and the Scouts OK it and you get to wear it on your uniform."

"You got this medal?"

"Uh huh."

"So, what does 'Let the dead bury the dead' mean?"

"I can't remember."

Andy sat down. "Whada we do now?"

Shane shrugged.

I had an idea. "Call your Sunday school teacher. It's only 4:30 and it's Saturday. Ask him. It is him, right?"

"Yeah, Mr. Thompson. He's pretty cool."

Shane started to leave.

Andy yelled, "Write down the answer."

When Shane left, I asked Andy how he got Delores' yearbook. He said she didn't really want to lend it at first because she couldn't see how it could help. He told her we were sure it held a clue and we would find it quickly and let her know all about it. He promised to take good care of the book and return it Monday. After more thinking, she finally said she just couldn't lend it and Andy turned to leave.

Then, just as he reached the door, Delores said, "Wait a minute," pulled a phone from beneath the counter and called her little sister. Delores told her where the yearbook was and to give it to Andy when he came by. He went straight to the house, got the book and came to Shane's—piece of cake.

Shane entered in a flurry and said, "It's complicated so I wrote it down. Mr. Thompson says that the Jews used the word dead to mean more than not alive anymore. If something was dead to you, you didn't care about it anymore. If you didn't like football, you could say football was dead to you, meant nothing to you. So, it's like Jesus is telling this disciple to forget about everything else and follow him."

Andy grabbed the scrap of paper with the finely printed message. "I get it! This means buzz off, forget it, let this thing be dead to us. Scotty Jefferson is dead, leave it there."

"You're right," I agreed, "That's what it means alright."

For fifteen minutes we tried to come up with more answers. Who might be angry that we were asking questions about Scotty? Angry about what? What was our enemy afraid we might find? Should we tell somebody about all of this? Who? Could this be a joke done by the Albino or someone else? If so, we'd look pretty stupid running to our mommies for help. For now, we decided to keep everything to ourselves.

Andy sat on the edge of the pool table. "Shane, you think your mom would let us sleep over tonight?"

"Yeah, I think so."

They looked at me.

I sputtered, "I gotta go home and at least eat dinner. I might be able to get out 'cause it's still vacation but maybe not. I been gone all day."

Shane racked up, took the break and got a good scatter. "No different than any other day. We're gone all the time. It's normal."

I caved. "Okay, I'll try. But, we still got a little time. Lemme see Scotty's yearbook."

I grabbed the book and turned to the back pages, signatures everywhere. And there it was, just as I had suspected. I laughed and slapped the page. Emerald, D.G.; Gloria, D.G.; Judy, D.G.; girl after girl after girl, all D.G. Sally, Penny, Franny, Marsha, Anne, Carol, all D.G. There was not one girl's signature without the notation, D.G.

Andy and Shane were baffled.

I taunted them a bit and they threatened violence. "Okay, alright," I laughed. "To Scotty, D.G. is every girl. Either he calls them his Dream Girl or they call themselves his Dream Girl. Doesn't matter, a D.G. is a D.G."

Shane dropped his stick. "Why call every girl a Dream Girl?"

Andy answered, "Why not? He could have any girl and everybody said he was always nice to everybody, so why not?"

"So," I said, "the D.G. in the letter is Linda, his one and only real D.G."

Andy scratched his head. "How'd you figure out Dream Girl?"

I laughed again. "Bobby Darin one too many times today and it just clicked, Dream Lover/Dream Girl."

It was nearing dinner and I knew my mother would never go for a sleep over and I said so. I wasn't even going to ask. I hustled home as fast as I could. I was looking forward to dinner and TV. Saturday night meant one of my favorite shows, "Steve Canyon, USAF." It was going to be a good night.

Later I would listen to Wolfman Jack on my mom's transistor radio. I'd think about Sandy Koufax, Sandra Dee, Daisy, Scotty, Robert Hughes, Bobby Blazer and Leslie.

Maybe every girl really is a D.G. to somebody or should be.

Some nights are almost perfect. This might just be one.

Chapter 27
Wolfman, Sunday School and
the Mysterious Stranger

THE NIGHT WAS soft and calm, my mind a flying carpet of competing images: Robert crumbling twice and yet strangely, never complaining... Lost sheep in the mud... Pretty wet lips... Blood exploding in Bobby's face... The buzz and thump of an arrow... Dream Lover... Cheeseburgers... 'Good thing you got some guns'... Me in a cheerleader's dress... All those girl curves... Blouse coming out ... 'Hit you so hard, your children will be born deaf'... Beautiful thigh... *Jesus, I broke my hand...* A sweaty, happy huddle.

After a few minutes, I settled down.

Who would try to hurt us and why? Could Decker be that pissed off? Maybe, but forget an arrow. He'd do what he said, 'Hit you so hard.' Besides, how would Decker get away? Whoever shot that arrow got away quick. Blazer is stupid enough, crazy enough and maybe mad enough. But, the arrow took guts. Can't be Blazer. Afraid of his own shadow.

We're interested in Scotty, so what? Everybody around here is. Whoever shot that arrow is good. They wanna hit you, they hit you. I don't know anybody good with a bow or a crossbow. Maybe an old D.G. ? Who? Gotta go to sleep... Check out Delores' yearbook tomorrow...

Lying on my back, I looked up at my bedroom window curtains.

Maybe there is a twisted, slobbering monster with a burned face, rotten teeth and a bloody, poked out eye, his head all pushed up against my window... Holdin' his breath... Waitin' for me to move that curtain, that thin little cloth. Stupid Jim... Last time I ever invite him for a sleep over...

Pretty voices, soft music – violins, clarinets and guitars...

First a boy and a girl meet each other
and they sit down to talk for a while...

Suddenly, static crunched the small speaker on my pillow. Thump, a telephone picked up and that bright, gravelly, unmistakable voice filled the darkness.

Wolfman: "Hello! Hello? Who is this on the Wolfman telephone? Eh? How old are you?"

Boy: (voice cracks) "Whoa! This is Josh, uh, I'm thirteen. How old are you?"

Wolfman: "I'm only fourteen."

Boy: (pauses) "Ah... Boy, I love you, Wolfman."

Wolfman: (whispers) "Boys an' girls... The Five Satins' 'To the Aisle' on the Wolfman Jack Show...

Fade in... same beautiful music.

> In your heart, you want her for a lover
> While each step draws you closer to the aisle
> You may start with a simple conversation
> 'My darling please put me on trial.
> She says, 'Yes.' And your heart starts beating
> While each step draws you closer to the aisle.
> You ask her if she loves you, she answers, 'I do.'
> Your heart starts glowing inside...

Fade out...

Wolfman: (whispers) "Here's a Wolfman double play for you, baby. The Five Satins, 'In the Still of the Night' on the Wolfman Jack Show. Are you out there baby, in the still of the night, eh? Are you bein' still in the night? Huh, baby? Or are you runnin'' 'round on the Wolfman? Maybe you just runnin' 'round your room in your PJ's, eh? I see you." (Laughter)

In the dark, I laughed, too.

Cue deep vocal harmony...

Shoo dooten shoo be doo... Shoo dooten shoo be doo...

I love you too, Wolfman... What do you look like? Bet you look great. You are so cool. What if we were on the radio together? Play all that great music...

I saw myself in a room with lots of electronic equipment: control panels, knobs, levers, turntables, earphones, meters registering sound levels. Walls of shelves stuffed with record albums and boxes filled with 45 rpm singles. Fat black leather chairs for the Wolfman and me, side by side.

There were clocks on the wall to our right and left and a red light directly in front of us. Below the red light was a red neon sign, "On Air."

I listened so close to the pillow... It was all so real, more real than my real life. After a long time the music faded and my mind wandered...

Wish I could dance with Daisy. Maybe I'll grow up and be on the radio and a girl like Sandra Dee will fall in love with me. Teachers say you can do anything if you try hard enough. Not true. Close my eyes, imagine dancing. Can't. It's not fun. It's scary.

I was stupid to say what I said to Leslie. God, please let her forget what I said. Why would I feel bad for her? I'm the one looks stupid in my clothes. I look stiff and stupid, like a dumb Frankenstein without the bolts, only shorter. She's plain? Who am I kidding? Be just as good if that arrow did hit me in the head, right through the eye. One less stupid-looking fool.

I felt tiny and weak and lost and alone.

Can't get any tears. Can't even do that right. Old Man Crotch was right. No, he is right. I am a mistake and I should be hung on a nail in the closet. I look like a fool trying to bat or pitch or throw a football.

I turned off the radio and I cried a little, the hard kind of crying that hurts your head and chest and makes your spirit ache. Crying that makes tears in your mind.

One long bad dream or a series of disconnected ones, it didn't really matter: getting shot at, falling while dancing with Daisy, wrecking Decker's convertible, trapped in a Frankenstein suit, trapped in front of an ugly old drunk or on a blood-splattered table...

I awoke worn out.

I dressed, straightened my bed, ate a bowl of Rice Krispies and hurried out to the car for church. My mother wanted to know if I needed a Bible. I told her not to worry.

My parents drove for a couple of miles and dropped me off at a nearby church while they went out for coffee at a place called The Little Brown Shoe. The design got a lot of attention. The name sounded cute but it looked a lot more like The Little Brown Work Boot, something Grumpy, Sneezy or Doc might wear.

It sat in the corner of the parking lot and fronted the sidewalk, its rounded toe pointing west. If you approached from the east and glanced to your right, you could pretend the building was walking beside you. A beautiful wooden door anchored the boot's heel. To its left, a long skinny rectangular window (little more than a foot high) ran the length of the shoe.

My parents liked it because they knew the owner. As far as I know, they only went there on Sundays, after dropping me off at church.

I had a bad feeling about Sunday school. I hadn't been there in a while. The day was bright, clear and crisp, almost blinding. The sky was stunning. I squinted my way passed the sanctuary (light bouncing everywhere) to a small, dark hallway. I entered a square, drab, tiny, mint-green room barely big enough to hold its massive round table.

It took a few moments for my eyes to adjust. People were filling chairs. I recognized no one and found a seat quickly. Kids were staring at me.

I noticed the colorful booklet on the table, "Samson & the Philistines." I also noticed the teacher sitting on the other side of the room. She had a princess face with fine features: Short, dark hair, blue eyes, a graceful nose and soft, pink lips. Snow White except for the pink lips. She was all color and curves and her thin sheer dress hid nothing. I stared at her perfect breasts.

I could not look away.

They are perfect. I can see everything. They are coming out of her dress! They are coming out of her dress! What is she doing? This is Sunday school.

Class started and she prayed. It helped. I calmed down and concentrated on my booklet. We took turns reading around the table. When my turn came, she skipped me.

Without a word she skipped me and called on the next kid.

What? Why'd she skip me? Didn't she see me?

I fussed with my papers, felt my skin crawl and asked to be excused to the restroom. Once there, I occupied the same stall for the better part of an hour. Folks came and left without a second thought, each man or kid simply believing he happened to be in the restroom at the same time as me.

It was fool-proof but it was also a long time to count tiles and think.

They were all looking at me. They saw her skip me. Why did she do that? I know, same old story. Thinks I'm stupid. I'm not stupid, she's stupid. I don't even know her.

What did I ever do to her? Okay, I looked at her jugs. But, isn't that what she wanted? Who wears a dress like that to church anyway, a jug jailbreak dress? Who does that?

They don't want me? I don't want them. I'm never going back. Same people don't want Louie. Why? Makes some sense, I guess, maybe. But, God, I swear, I just don't get this. What do other people know that I don't? Just tell me…Tell me what to do…

God! What a lousy place to be on a Sunday morning. Get it? Where are you? Everybody says you're good and I guess you are sometimes. But, why don't you make things good all the time? If you can, then why don't you? If you can't, what's the point? I understand assholes like Bobby Blazer and Robert Hughes get what they deserve. But, do I deserve this? Okay, I know I looked at her jugs but, what am I supposed to do? I'm not the only one. I tried not to look. People say you're fair but how is this fair? I wish I could make her hurt.

In the corner, a small, trapped spider pushed frantically. In my mind, I saw again that big black bug mosey across my shoe while Old Man Crotch went crazy on me.

What about Jesus? How is that right? I mean he's good to everybody, except maybe assholes. And he gets killed? And he lets 'em do it? I swear, I try to get all that stuff but I am lost … And Scotty is dead because he loved a girl?

When I heard the release bell, I rushed back to class, picked up a few loose papers and met my parents in the parking lot.

"How was Sunday school?"

"Fine," I waved my papers and they smiled.

My strategy worked so smoothly that I did it the next Sunday as well only I cut out the middle man (or the middle princess.) I stuffed a Super Boy comic down my pants and when my parents dropped me off, I went straight to the restroom, stayed the hour, slipped by the classroom, grabbed a loose paper or two and zipped out to meet my parents. Wave the papers, everybody's happy. I attended The Church of the Restroom for the next six months without a blip.

****

Back home, I changed my clothes and attacked a baloney and cheese, no chips. Halfway through the sandwich, the phone rang and my mom picked up.

"He's here, but he's eating lunch. He'll call you when he's finished. What? Oh, I'd say five minutes or so."

I gulped a slug of Kool-Aid. "Who was that?"

From the living room, my mother answered, "Andy. Call him when you're finished eating."

I stood up from the table, put my glass and plate in the sink and headed for the phone. I picked up, heard other voices, hung up, waited five minutes, tried again, got an open line and dialed Andy's number.

He picked up on the second ring, "Hello."

"Hi, you called?"

"Yeah," he whispered, "Last night on my way home, I went by the Jefferson place."

I screamed, "You what? Are you crazy? Why?"

"I dunno. I just did."

"And?"

"And, all shit broke loose, that's what."

"What happened?!"

"I saw somebody up in Scotty's bedroom again with a light, looked like a lantern."

"You really saw somebody? I mean, last time…"

"I don't give a crap about last time. This ain't last time. This is last night. I saw an old guy. I think it was a guy, up in Scotty's room. He was wearin' a wide brimmed leather hat, I think. It was dark and hard to see. But, I think he had gray… wait… white hair."

I squeezed the telephone receiver. "So, wha'd ya do?"

"Are you kidding?! I did nothin'. I thought about throwin' a rock, but I was scared crapless so I just ran."

"I'd run too. Anything else?"

"No."

"Hey! Meet at Shane's in a half hour. You got Delores' yearbook, right?"

"Yeah, I got it. See you in a half hour at Shane's."

I hung up the phone and told my mother that Andy wanted to meet over at Shane's. She asked what the rest of the conversation was about and I said it was about some movie on TV. She went back to her romance paperback.

I walked to Shane's the long way around the park. As always, it was a tedious process, staring at the ground with every step, vigilant for a million killer obstacles: sand, gravel, holes, leaves, papers, uneven spots, water, mud and more.

There was a lot to think about.

Who could be up in that bedroom? And why? Should we tell all this stuff to Ray? Exactly what are we gonna say? We think we saw somebody in Scotty's room? We found stuff from him and his girlfriend?

So What? So far, nothin' we found has done one thing to change the basic story. The woman dumped Scotty and took off and he blew himself up.

How about the arrow? Looks like a stupid prank or maybe a real good one. But to a guy like Ray, that's all.

Everybody jokes. City Council makes Ray use rubber bullets. Somebody said he was a prize-winning shot. Right, uh huh. Somebody like Jesse. And what about "hide in plain sight" and the "above and below" notes? What about Richard Diamond? What about the stuff scratched on the floor?

What would Frank and Joe Hardy do? Joe'd be goin' crazy, runnin' all over, askin' questions and stirrin' stuff up. But, Frank would be thinkin' slow and careful. Joe is good, but when it gets down to it, put your money on Frank.

I looked up and knocked on Shane's door. Leslie answered, smiled and pointed me to the garage. I was afraid to look at her eyes but all those beautiful curves were right where they were supposed to be. My face started tingling, but I got to the end of the hallway. She never asked me if I was okay and I gave her no compliment. She opened the door, I stepped through and she closed it.

Shane looked up from the pool table, leaned on his stick and studied my face.

He grinned, braces and all. "Anybody kissin' you today?"

"No."

"Really? Then, why are you blushin'?"

"I'm not." (I was.)

Shane rolled his eyes. "Oh, okay, if you say so."

I huffed a bit. "I say so. So get off it."

In an overdone melodrama, Shane's hands shot up and he dropped to his knees. "Sorry, I didn' mean nothin' Mister! Don't hurt me, Mister! I ain't got no teeth!"

I laughed and threatened him with a finger pistol. Shane dropped his hands. "That reminds me. Anybody shootin' at you today?"

"No, but I did take the long way around the park."

"Good idea. Hey, where's Andy?"

I sat on the couch. "On his way over. We're gonna check out Delores' yearbook."

"Why?"

"We might find somethin' in there. We're gonna look where Scotty signed his pictures or if he wrote stuff on other pages. Andy's got some news, too."

"Like what?"

"I'll let him tell you."

At that moment, Andy stepped through the side door a bit out of breath, yearbook under his arm.

Shane looked at him carefully. "What's the matter?"

Andy sat. "Nothin'. I just ran through the park, that's all."

We relaxed.

He continued. "Everything seemed normal, I guess. I mean, I was runnin'."

I took a deep breath. "I was scared too. I took the long way around. But, last night wasn't normal, was it?"

Andy grimaced. "You bet your butt, it wasn't."

Shane leaned his stick against the table, thought better of it, got up and walked over to the wall rack. "What happened last night? Did you call? I missed it."

He racked his stick.

Andy adjusted his hat. "Too late. Besides, I knew I'd see you guys today."

"So, what happened?"

I jumped in. "He saw somebody in Scotty's room again."

Andy set the yearbook on the pool table and started pacing. "I was walking home last night and I ended up on the corner across the street, right under the lamppost. I wasn't hangin' around there or anything but one minute the place was totally dark and the next there was a light."

Shane walked back and sat on the pool table. "Same thing as last time?"

Andy frowned. "Last time it only lasted a second or so and was gone. Last night, the light was on a long time and I know I saw somebody. Looked like they had a lantern, like they were lookin' for somethin'."

"What else? Wha'd they look like?"

Andy looked at me. "Like I told you on the phone, I think I saw a guy: worn out face, floppy wide-brimmed leather hat, white hair. Skinny maybe. Tiny eyes, too, I think."

Shane stood and leaned against the pool table. "You sure you saw all this—skinny, tiny eyes. All that—at night from the street? I know there's a lamppost, but still…"

Andy turned quickly, spoke fast and pointed with his forefinger. "I am sure of everything except the skinny part. The face looked skinny, so I'm guessin' that the rest of him is skinny but all the other stuff, I know what

I saw. I got good eyes. I ain't sixty-five years old. Things stand out in the dark when there's only one light."

Shane shrugged. "Hey, okay. I'm just sayin'…"

I remembered Frank Hardy and I knew what to do. "Think about the hair. Was it long, short, bushy?"

He closed his eyes for a moment. "Bushy, I think. But there were shadows. Maybe his hair was stuffed inside his hat."

"Okay, now. Was there anything about his ears or his shirt or jacket?"

Andy closed his eyes again. "Nothin' about his shirt or jacket and his ears were in the dark."

"Could you see his hand as he held the lantern?"

"No, but there is one more thing."

"What?"

Andy paused and looked at us. "He saw me. He looked right at me, eye to eye."

Shane grabbed his head with both hands. "Holy crap!"

There was a lot of talk, "high talk" as my grandpa would say, about what to do. But we ended in the same dead place. There was simply nothing to be done with all of these watery details. No adult was going to take any of this seriously and that was that.

Andy said, "I could keep my .22 pistol with me."

I stared at Andy. Shane dropped his head. The silence was heavy and hard.

Andy shrugged. "Jesus, Joseph and Mary. I sound like Jesse."

We laughed and it got quiet again, softer this time.

I asked, "Who says, Jesus, Joseph and Mary?"

Andy said, "Uncle Billy."

Shane left the pool table. "Maybe the guy in the window shot the arrow."

I leaned against the table. "Yeah and maybe he didn't."

Andy handed me Dolores' yearbook. "Let's check this out but I don't know exactly what we're lookin' for."

"Before you got here, I told Shane we should look at where Scotty signed his pictures. I think there might be something. Remember, it wasn't long after he signed this yearbook and he was dead, two weeks maybe."

We sat on the couch and I opened Dolores' yearbook. Nothing in the first few pages in the front. We turned to the Senior Section and found the page with Scotty's picture. It was tough to tell that it was really him. His flashy signature swooped into his face. Thank goodness for typed names in the margins. Only part of the rest of his writing made sense. Above his picture he wrote, "Best Wishes," but below his name he wrote, "H.W.H."

We looked at each other, totally lost.

Shane pushed. "Look in the football section. His picture's all over it."

He was right, a three page spread for the League Champion Falcons and Scotty's picture everywhere: all-league MVP quarterback, all-league defensive back.

As we studied the pages with Scotty's notes, we saw H.W.H. a few times but we also saw the notation, "Hips" many times.

I said, "Delores must have made him sign this thing for fifteen minutes—football, baseball and basketball.

Andy was up and pacing. "I remember 'hips.' In the paper, my dad showed me. It was a nickname Scotty's dad gave him. Hips' for 'Swivel Hips' 'cause he was so good at gettin' away from people on the field, like 'Crazy Legs' Hirsch for the Rams."

Shane snapped his fingers. "Hey, I bet anything H.W.H means 'Hips Was Here.'"

We all smiled. That made perfect sense. We knew Shane was right and Andy's story about the nickname was as good as it gets.

Andy sighed, "Okay, good, but that still leaves us a big fat nothing."

I said, "We got two places left. Student Government and the blank pages at the back."

I looked in the Index and turned quickly to the student government pages. As Senior Class President, Scotty's picture was again, everywhere. But he had chosen to sign only once. He was pictured, gavel in hand at the head of a cafeteria table, chairing a meeting of the Senior Class Council. It was in the Faculty Dining Room and must have been taken mid-morning. Clean trays stacked at one end of the stainless steel counter, the buffet was empty. The shot was canned rather than candid, cheesy expressions all around.

Scotty's swirling signature dominated this larger picture just as it had the smaller ones. "D.G. Best Wishes" at the top and underneath the signature a note.

Kiddo,

To the best biology partner ever! Don't tell anybody I was afraid to dissect the frog, OK? (Our secret, a lover's pact.) Knock 'em dead next year. I'll be back to check on you. Go USC #23.

H.I.P.S./SJ – get it? (HA HA).

PS. My dad loves this picture. Me too.

We looked at each other. Nobody said a word.

I was at a loss. "Okay, let's play 'Retard, Retard, Who's a Retard?'"

Shane laughed. "I'm in."

Andy examined the picture closely and shook his head. "Retards 3, Smart Guys 0."

Shane studied the picture. "Let's try the back of the book."

I spun the book around and handed it to Andy. "You take over. Maybe break our bad luck"

He smiled, took the book and turned to the back pages. "Probly won't help, but I can try."

He sat on the couch between Shane and me. There were lots of long entries from girls but nothing more from Scotty.

We were lost.

Shane crossed the room, picked up his stick, racked 'em and made the break. I went to the dead Coke machine, pulled a deck of cards from the delivery tray and started flipping at the waste basket.

Andy was determined to read every entry in the last four pages. He buried his face deeper into the pages and began reading each entry aloud so he wouldn't overlook something.

He said, "Frank Hardy never quits. That's me."

Shane kept shooting and I kept tossing but our hearts weren't in it. He collected my misses for the third time, racked his stick and sat on the edge of the table. "It's about 1:00," he said, "at 1:30 I'm gonna be at Mrs. Reynolds' cleaning her back yard. She pays fifty cents an hour. You guys wanna come?"

Andy dog-eared the page and closed Delores' yearbook. "You sure she'll pay all of us?"

I shrugged. "If not, whatever she pays, we just split three ways."

Shane tucked his shirt, reached for his comb and ran it through his hair. "I'm pretty sure we're okay, there are only three of us and her yard is a mess. She's got gloves and all the tools."

Andy set Delores' yearbook in the Scotty Box underneath the pool table and we headed for the door.

Chapter 28
Mrs. Reynolds, Father Phillip
and Mrs. Kerensky

THE WALK TO Mrs. Reynolds' was quiet and comfortable all the way through the tree streets to 2211 Spruce, two blocks from the Great American Diner. This time of year, the evergreens are sensible. They keep their clothes on. Others drop every stitch.

****

Paul yelled, "Hey, buddy! What are you guys up to?"

Instantly pulled into the present, I squinted through the streaks of softening sunlight. A polio survivor and a farmer of forty years, my friend Paul lived with his miniature Doberman, Pinky. A second round of polio had confined him to a power chair in recent years.

I answered, "Just eating a bit and doing a little reminiscing."

He grinned. "Shall we let the boys run a while?"

I opened the door and out Cody blasted. Paul pushed his wide-brimmed straw hat back and marveled. The dogs flashed across the green grass, plowing through sprinklers and creating new spay patterns.

"Reminiscing, eh?" said Paul. "About what? Women, I hope."

He belly-laughed, blue eyes dancing. I smiled and closed the passenger door. He moved closer, draping Pinky's leash around his own neck.

I answered softly, "Well, yes, actually. I was thinking of a woman, an extraordinary woman, although not in the way you think."

He slid his sun glasses down the bridge of his thin nose. "As far as I'm concerned, there are only a few things worth thinking about concerning women, if you know what I mean."

He hit me with a wink.

I laughed through the glittering sunlight. "Now, why am I not surprised?"

He took mock offense, punctuated by more laughter. "Well, my God! I didn't even use any bad language."

I smiled. "No, you didn't. Good for you. But the evening is young."

Divorced three times, Paul was the father of two successful daughters but a polio relapse sent him scurrying to a potentially lethal combination of pain medications and alcohol. We had discussed his struggles often in the past. His rigidity was as much a function of his age as anything else.

I smiled again. "Buddy, are you in control on the meds and the booze?"

He took off his hat, rested it in his lap and brushed through what used-to-be hair. His sun glasses stayed on.

He grimaced. "I just hurt so Goddamn much all the time."

His emotion seemed to push the sunlight around.

I squinted. "What medications are you taking?"

He reached into his pocket and handed me a container of pills.

I checked the label. "These are for anxiety. What about the pain?"

"None of that stuff works. I've taken barrels of it. My doctor said I was anxious."

"About what?"

"I don't know. He didn't say."

"What do you say?"

"I don't know either."

"Sure you do. Anxiety means you are in pain but not the kind that a pill can cure. You are trying to live in the future. Nobody can live there. The pain is a warning system…"

He interrupted. "I am doing something! I'm trying."

I waded into the deep water. "Alvin says you're drinking a lot. Said you were so drunk last week that you were banging into things with your chair. Said you didn't even know whose house you were in."

His blue eyes were hard. "What the shit does Alvin know? Not a Goddamn thing, that's what! Hell with Alvin, an' the horse he rode in on, an' the guy that made the saddle!"

"Right," I grinned. "He's only known you for sixty years."

Blue eyes sullen. "Still doesn't know shit."

I paused, took a deep breath and charged another windmill. "What hurts?"

"My back. I can't sleep. That's why I drink."

My dog was rolling in the wet grass.

I spoke softly. "It's your mind that hurts and your mind doesn't need alcohol. It needs information, it needs facts. It needs less toxic ideas. Your heart lives on feelings but your mind lives on thoughts. Your mind is hungry for the truth not medication. I'm guessing that as soon as your mind feels better, your back will."

"Shrink talk. Bullshit! Talking makes no difference."

I changed directions. "Paul, if you can't get excited about a beautiful woman, where does that hurt? Does it hurt in your body or in your mind?"

Blue eyes scared. "Who said anything about that?"

"You did. Last week when you gave me that junk about being upset that you can't connect with any of the widows around here when all you want is conversation and friendship."

"Why didn't you say something?"

"Not the point. Listen. Life is full of necessary losses. Everything that life has given, it will systematically take away, down to the day you are dead."

He laughed hard. "You are one cold S.O.B."

I laughed too. "Thanks, I'll take that as a compliment."

"Well," he huffed. "That's not the way I meant it."

I shrugged.

Blue eyes friendly. "Well, what the hell am I supposed to do?"

"Be a man."

He winced. "That's what hurts. I can't."

"You think being a man is about the physical stuff?"

He laughed. "You bet your ass, I do. Don't you?"

"Sure, partly."

He fussed with Pinky's leash. "Where are you going with all this?"

I watched Cody chase Pinky through the water. "Before I answer that, I want to ask you a question."

He nodded, put on his hat and shoved his glasses up. I asked him if he was ready.

He grumbled. "Locked and loaded."

Blue eyes absent.

I pushed. "Actually, I have two questions: Is your back hurting now and was it hurting when you rolled up a few minutes ago?"

His glasses fell to his lap and his jaw dropped slightly. "No, doesn't hurt a bit right now but it hurt like a son of a bitch on my way over here."

I yelled for Cody and he came like a bullet.

I opened the door and hugged my wet dog. "Paul, you gotta read a little."

The old farmer grabbed his little Doberman and wrestled him into his leash. "What are you talking about?"

"Your mind needs some food, and then your back won't hurt so much. Your mind is starved for information, information about losses. That's what you're anxious about.

"How the hell do you know that?"

I shrugged. "What else is there to be anxious about? Loss of place, loss of face, loss of control… All anxiety is about loss or the fear of loss."

No answer.

"Listen," I continued, "I want you to read a poem and a book. The poem is called, 'Do Not Go Gentle Into That Good Night' by Dylan Thomas.

It starts like this:

> Do not go gentle into that good night,
> Old age should burn and rave at close of day;
> Rage, rage against the dying of the light.

"What about the book?"

"On second thought, no book. You're okay without a book."

He cackled. "What if I want a book?"

"Anything by Earnest Hemingway. He's always about 'grace under pressure, hold tight under pain'… sex, death, losses, fighting… good stuff—all the messy stuff."

Pinky began chewing furiously on his leash. The old man lost patience and harshly corrected his little dog.

He asked one more question. "I wasn't very good in school. I mean, school was a long time ago. This Hemingway write anything for kids? I might try that."

I scratched my head. "You could read a fable called 'The Faithful Bull' and we could talk. You can get this stuff at the library right here."

Paul grinned, doffed his hat and pushed the power button on his scooter. "I'll see what I can do." He paused. "We're off to the store. Thanks."

He was off in a flurry.

Suddenly, he skidded to a stop and spun to face me. "Hey, Alvin said you were at the game today an' some assholes were callin' Frenchy Cohen a kike?"

He was returning slowly. I squinted into the sun. He was a dark outline against a sea of bright.

I used my hand as a visor. "I couldn't tell who they were, but somebody in that crowd knew 'em. Hope they catch these S.O.B's before they hurt somebody. I told Moshe to get the cops in on it."

The old man's face turned a shade of purple I didn't think possible. He ripped off his sun glasses and knocked his hat off in the process. Cody pushed next to me and Pinky hid behind the power chair.

Blue eyes full of lightning. "Goddamn it... This is what we fought a fucking war over! To get rid of shit like this! Hell, my two brothers died."

I tilted my head, but I still couldn't see him clearly. He fumbled to get his hat. I couldn't tell if the muscle tremors were Parkinson's or fury. His eyes were tearing up.

"You are right," I said. "This stuff is evil. It's not a tragedy, it's not sad, it's not ignorance. It's evil and it's real. I am very sorry for the loss of your brothers."

It was quiet for a minute or so.

I broke the silence. "Listen, you are a hero of mine. I mean it."

He smiled, slapped his hat on and pulled Pinky out of hiding. "I remember... Dylan Thomas and Hemingway." His blue eyes were bright. "Before we take off, tell me quick about this woman you were remembering."

I smiled. "You mean, Mrs. Reynolds. Well, I was fourteen and she was elderly. In her younger days, she had wanted to be a stunt pilot, but ended up a circus performer."

His blue eyes flashed. "Was there a romance? There must have been a romance, right? I mean, God."

I chuckled. "She was elderly, remember? We did yard work for her every couple of weeks for a year and she helped us make a pile of money one Christmas vacation. During that year of working week after week, I learned everything about her."

"So, what were you remembering?"

"I was about to remember everything: walking to her house that first day, talking with her, and seeing her place. That's when you came by. We didn't know it at the time, but she had actually been crying just before we arrived. She was afraid to disappoint us. Like I said, I learned that later."

"I take it everything turned out?"

I nodded. "It was a fun time in my life."

"Well," the old farmer grinned. "Guess we better be moving along and leave you to your thoughts. Thanks for the ideas about the back pain."

I smiled. "You're welcome. I assume you've been to all the pain specialists, right?"

He moved his hat to avoid the sun. "Yeah, no help."

I squinted. "Did they ever suggest that you talk to someone about it?"

He answered, "Sure they did. I told 'em, 'No.'"

I smiled. "You take care of yourself. We'll talk soon."

Just like that, he and his little dog were gone. I looked at Cody and began to think again about Mrs. Reynolds. Slipping back into her history was as easy as breathing.

****

The neighborhood was older than she but not by much. It was a cluster of once-stately, two-story colonials which had not only seen better days but better decades.

The lawns, like the trees, were also "living or dead," those with rye grass and those without. Like many retired neighborhoods, there were also only two kinds of people: those who had outlived their money and those who had not.

Margaret Reynolds lived on the edge of these worlds. A widow of thirty-five years, she was a petite and fragile ninety with bright tiny dark eyes and grey hair the texture of cotton candy. Her voice was as shaky as her hands but her spirit as solid as the massive American Holly trees strangling her back yard.

Born in Wisconsin in 1880, as a twenty year old she ran away from home to join the Ringling Brothers Circus as a bareback stunt rider. She chose Ringling, she said, "Because it was known for honesty toward customers and kindness to animals; traits sadly lacking in the industry."

She once told us, "I was just a little slip of a thing but I looked good in the ballerina costume and I could stay on the horse."

After five years on the circuit, she caught more than the fancy of a young dentist in California. When he attended every single performance (afternoon and evening) for seven straight days, fates were sealed.

Her decision, she said, was "as easy as cake."

Married for thirty five years, she had one son, Kevin, named after his father. At age sixty, after walking home from his office, her husband suffered a massive heart attack and died instantly. Her son was killed in a car wreck on her eighty-eighth birthday on his way to see her.

He had never married and she counted no grandchildren as her "eternal heartbreak." Her greatest disappointment was "turning forty by the time lady pilots were barnstorming in bi-planes."

Her biggest surprise? "Easy," she'd twinkle, "I can't believe I'm still here. I should have been dead long ago. Everybody else I grew up with or knew as an adult is gone. Nobody should live this long. Why am I here?"

****

Some memories are watery. They slip and slide or they tease and hide, just out of reach. But my recollection of my first visit to Mrs. Reynolds was as clear as yesterday. I remembered being a few blocks from her place and suddenly, we were late. We had to hurry.

We crossed Elm, Oak and Ash. As we approached Spruce, we decided that Mrs. Reynolds didn't have much money or help and that we would work for her for one dollar, total.

We got to the front steps. Andy and Shane hoisted me to the porch and rang the bell. Mrs. Reynolds came to the door and we reminded her of our names and our mothers' names. She had spoken with one of our moms about today but could not remember who.

Still in her church clothes, she sparkled. She invited us to her kitchen table and offered us chocolate chip cookies and lemonade. She apologized for the lemonade more than once and we told her it was fine. We were not sure why she was worried, but she seemed relieved when Shane mentioned that we would all be working for two hours for only one dollar as full payment.

Andy finished a cookie, looked at Shane and me, cleared his throat and surprised us. "Mrs. Reynolds, what Shane was tryin' to tell you was we're workin' here today for cookies and lemonade, no money. That is, if it's okay with you."

Mrs. Reynolds was beaming. "Boys, I don't know what to say. You needn't feel sorry for me. I have the dollar."

Andy was quick to her defense. "Mrs. Reynolds, if it's okay, we've got a business idea for you."

She looked lost for a moment and passed the cookie plate again. "Well, of course. What did you have in mind?"

Andy looked at us and plowed straight ahead. "Well, we were thinkin' that we could make some money next Christmas vacation if we could sell holly from your trees. Bag it up in small bunches an' sell it for decorations."

"That's a fine idea, son but Christmas is over. It was last week."

"Yes ma'am, I know. We thought we'd come here today and work on your yard an' we'll come here once a month for all the year in exchange for bein' able to sell your holly at Christmas."

He took a deep breath and did not look at Shane and me. Mrs. Reynolds was radiant.

She passed the cookie plate a third time. "Well," her voice was almost dancing, "that is the most wonderful idea I have heard in I don't know how long. It is splendid. Shall we just shake on it or shall we write a contract?"

We shook all around and I wanted to say something nice to her, too. "Mrs. Reynolds," I was trying to chew and swallow quickly. I struggled and started again. "Mrs. Reynolds, you look so nice today. I was wondering if those are your church clothes."

"Thank you for that very beautiful compliment and yes, these are the clothes I wore to Mass this morning at St. Luke's." She took a deep breath and shivered. "This is as exciting as riding bareback!"

I was scared to try another cookie. "We just met the new priest, Father Phillip. He seems cool."

"Yes," she smiled, "he does seem very 'cool,' as you say. It seems to me also that he looks like that handsome young actor. What's his name? Oh me. He looks like Troy Donahue, only in a black robe."

We were quiet for a moment and Shane spoke, "We better get started. Did you want to show us what you want done?"

"Yes," she smiled," We can go right through this door and down the steps."

We left the kitchen and I got lifted down the back steps. We were stunned. It was hard to get located. What we saw resembled another world. Phrases like "tangled mass" or "over-grown jungle" simply proved to us that experience can outrun language.

What we saw resembled a Twilight Zone set. It was impossible to tell if the chaos started on the ground and went upward or the other way around.

We all saw the same thing in each other's eyes.

This is a monster. This is the belly of the beast. This is the place where ships sail off the edge of the earth. We need to change the contract this minute. If we don't change it now, we never will. Okay, who wants to crush the sweet old lady? Who wants to be that asshole?

Regular weeds were easy. They started on the ground and stopped at my shoulders. A solitary red brick here or there suggested the edge of an original flower bed. Mrs. Reynolds was a perky little bird, chirping her support. She provided gloves, hand tools, a kneeling mat for me and barrels. The ground was tough but more workable than it might have been in mid or late summer.

We worked as a team. One would disc up large chunks of dirt with a shovel and the other two would dislodge the weeds and throw them in the barrels. It took two hours to fill two barrels and to clear, clean and level a 10'x3' flower bed. Clearing meant removing surface weeds and cleaning meant removing roots three inches below the surface. Leveling meant making the surface uniform, smooth and attractive.

We returned all tools to Mrs. Reynolds' shed and made plans to return next Saturday. If we waited any longer, we would simply keep re-doing the same patch. As we prepared to leave, Mrs. Reynolds gave us cookies to take home and surprised us.

"Next time you come, I'll show you an original poster from the Ringling Brothers Circus."

We chorused, "Who's on the poster?"

She smiled. "Why, me of course!"

We could not believe our ears. Mrs. Reynolds just laughed, waved and stepped inside her front door. We headed back. We figured we could get more guys to help next time. It was going to take some time to guess Mrs. Reynolds' circus job but we figured it must be pretty good if it was on a poster. We ruled out the tattooed lady and the bearded lady right away but after that, it was anybody's guess: knife thrower, acrobat, clown, animal trainer? It never occurred to us that she would be standing (!) on a galloping horse. (Although, if we had listened carefully to her earlier, we'd have gotten it.)

Weeks later, when she shared about why she'd been so nervous about the lemonade, it only convinced me more that she was a great lady. After we'd worked for her a few months, she was very open about her beginning with us.

By 1:00 o'clock on that first cold Sunday afternoon, she was pulling a second batch of chocolate chip cookies from her ancient oven and setting the sheet on the counter to cool. The first batch (stacked symmetrically on the plate) waited next to a new pitcher of lemonade, napkins and glasses.

Suddenly, tears filled her tiny eyes.

Oh no… this is all wrong. It's winter. Children should be getting hot cocoa, not lemonade. This is all wrong. What have I done? Is there time to fix chocolate? Lord, do I have any chocolate? Help me find it.

She didn't hurry and she didn't scurry. But her heart and mind were fluttering in all directions.

Suddenly, she became worried about everything.

I hope I cooked these correctly. I hope they taste good. I just don't know how things taste anymore. I hope the temperature and time were correct. I looked at the clock and wrote it down. Where did I put that paper? I can hardly read my writing.

She was terrified of stereotypes. She kept her doors and windows open, mopped and waxed weekly, made sure that her clothes were clean and starched, that her make-up and hair were "presentable" and that her

243

things were dusted and polished. It worried her that she might use too much perfume or hairspray or not enough. "There's no fool like an old fool," she'd say and she didn't want patronizing politeness. She wanted meaningful relationships and authentic encounters.

She looked at that "pretty little slip of a girl" on the poster in her bedroom, jumping through the hoop and landing fast on that beautiful, gentle stallion's back and she sometimes prayed she might sleep and not wake.

After a few minutes of fussy indecision, she made up her mind, took out her handkerchief and dabbed her eyes.

Stop being silly now. Boys don't care what they drink, if the price is right. It'll be just fine. Don't act like a silly old woman. Invite them in before they work. Too messy afterward. How many boys did she say were coming? I do hope it's more than two but less than ten.

We finished our work on that first Sunday and left. Nearing the corner of Cherry and Tenth, we were feeling pretty good about ourselves and our money prospects. Helping Mrs. Reynolds was a good thing and our imaginations couldn't spend next year's Christmas money fast enough. The great thing was that we could spend the money over and over in a thousand different ways and never lose a cent.

We didn't really plan it, but we soon realized we had agreed to work a whole year for free. Truth is, if we'd gotten paid every week, we'd simply have spent it. So, all in all, it seemed okay. In fact, we might just be rich next Christmas.

Andy mentioned that we should stop by Louie's. He had been sick for a few days and his mother had called our moms.

Shane was still wondering about Mrs. Reynolds. "Do you guys think she coulda been somethin' like a monkey trainer? I think so because nobody'd ever guess that."

Suddenly, a friendly voice called just to our right. Father Phillip, exiting the rich polished oak doors of St. Luke's, seemed to wave with his whole self.

Securing the lock on the big doors, he stepped through the thick, pink adobe archway and spoke, "Hey, Shane! What's up, buddy?"

We stopped and waited while Shane shook hands. "Hey, Father. We just finished doing some yard work for Mrs. Reynolds."

"Sounds like a worthy task," the young priest smiled. "I don't believe I know your friends."

"Well, these guys here are my friends, Andy and Randy. Uh, guys, this is Father Phillip, he's new."

Everybody smiled and we shook hands all around.

As I shook his hand, Father Phillip said, "I think I've heard about you. Aren't you the kid who nearly decapitated Robert Hughes and broke Bobby Blazer's nose yesterday?"

I blushed. "It was an accident, Father."

"Uh, huh," he smiled. "I'm sure it was. I think I heard you say that."

Everybody laughed. I was confused.

He shook Andy's hand. "And, didn't you make a rather amazing diving, sprawling, finger-tip touchdown catch?"

Now it was Andy's turn to blush. "Yeah, how'd you know?"

Eyes bright, the young priest looked at all of us. "I was there."

"Really," said Shane. "'Where? We never saw you."

"Actually, I was walking through the park and I leaned against a tree just to your left about ten yards behind you." He was smiling again.

Shane changed the subject. "Hey, Father, remember that time we played basketball in the park? You and me and Jim? You said if there was ever anything we wanted to talk about, it would be okay?"

"You bet. Who wants to talk?"

Shane moved his hand in a circle, including Andy and me. "Us Father, us three."

"Is this conversation about God or something else?"

"Uh, sorta. It's more like God stuff."

"Sure, I think I get it. Are you guys Catholic?"

We shook our heads.

Andy said, "But our friend, Scotty was—an' that's kinda why we wanted to talk to a priest."

Father Phillip nodded. "You mean, Scotty Jefferson?"

Andy eyes widened. "You know about Scotty?"

The priest smiled. "Well, if you spend even a little time in this neighborhood, you will hear."

After a moment, Father Phillip took a small appointment book from his pocket and began fishing for a pen. "You guys have a few more days of vacation, right? How about day after tomorrow, that's Tuesday, say 2:00 o'clock? We can meet in my office. Uh, just come right here out front. I'll come and get you so you won't get lost."

We were quiet.

He hesitated. "You guys OK with this? Something spooky about St. Luke's?"

"Spooky" made us laugh and we agreed Tuesday in Father Phillip's office would be fine. We shook hands all 'round again and parted ways with the priest.

We crossed to Pine Street and looked back at St. Luke's. The church bulletin carried a perfect description: "… St. Luke's is a monument to Mission architecture and a neighborhood anchor for nearly sixty years, a place of mythic imagination."

It was a cross between the Alamo and Middle Earth: Massive adobe walls with broad unadorned stucco surfaces: low-pitched roof, wide eaves, thick arches, red clay roof tiles, stained glass windows depicting Jesus' parables and a signature bell and clock tower. The grounds were marked by curved, clean adobe-brick-edged flower beds and fiery green grass. The place was forested by an army of majestic pines. Soft-spoken evergreen giants who misted life and power.

In the sun-splashed late afternoon, St. Luke's felt magical, and when moonlight cloaked the nighttime with silver shadows, it felt enchanted and mysterious: Old and new at the same time.

****

We headed to Louie's. I winked at Shane and looked at Andy. "You know where the three hidden benches are at St. Luke's? The outside ones?"

"Course not," he sighed. "They're hidden."

"Wanna know?"

He pulled his cap down. "No, I don't. Let's go."

Shane smiled and kicked at a pebble.

I gently touched the bill of Andy's cap. "Hey, easy now. I'll tell ya."

He pursed his lips and huffed. "I don't want to know. I don't care."

I prodded. "Take a guess. No big deal if you're wrong."

He stared bullets, raised his voice, spoke slowly and opened his mouth in an exaggerated fashion. "What part of 'No' don't you get? I do not want to know. I never wanted to know."

"I can tell you," I promised with a sunny smile. "Really, I can. Wanna know?"

There was a long pause.

Andy waved his arms expansively, lifted his hat and ran his fingers through his hair. "Okay, okay, tell me! I wanna know, okay? I'm dying to know. Please, I'm begging you with all my heart. Tell me and then I can kill myself and die happy."

I dead-panned and quickly blurted, "I dunno! Beats the heck outta me! I never heard of the three hidden benches."

In a flicker, Shane was laughing as hard as he could and I was screaming, "Don't hit me! Don't hit me!"

Shane started to run. Andy paused, stepped to me and whispered, "I ain't gonna hitcha."

He then stepped back and gave me a hard two-handed shove in the chest and I went flying backward into a massive pile of leaves in the Bell's front yard.

At the end of the block, Shane covered up and laughed his way through a serious "hat whipping" about the head and shoulders.

After a minute or so, Andy quit and began the slow walk back. He arrived and sat next to me. A few seconds later Shane sat on my other side. Andy ran his fingers through his hair and readjusted his hat.

He was still breathing in gulps. "You okay?"

I nodded. "Yeah."

He grinned. "Jerk."

He looked at Shane. "You?"

Shane, still smiling, coughed. "Yeah, but I don't think your hat can take much more."

Andy grumped. "There's more where that came from."

I burst out laughing. "You sound like my dad. He whips ya 'till ya cry an' then whips ya 'till ya shut up."

Andy reacted. "Huh?"

I started picking the wet leaves off my back, neck and arms. "One time, my dad rips back the covers and I start screaming bloody murder. He says, 'What're you cryin' for? I ain't even hit you yet.' I say, 'I know, but it's gonna hurt.' He says, 'You're right.' "

We looked at the scattered leaves.

Andy asked, "Did you cry?"

I nodded. "You bet."

Shane added. "Did you shut up?"

I nodded again. "You bet."

Andy heaved a big sigh. "Nobody on TV ever gets a real ass-whippin'. Take 'Leave It to Beaver.' Nobody's dad's that nice. He always talks to 'em and understands 'em. And nobody's mom's that pretty."

247

Shane grunted and stood. "Huck Finn got his ass kicked, that's for sure."

Andy stood too, pulled me up and dusted me off.

He remembered the Book Lady. "Yeah, Huck got it all right. It's cool that the Book Mobile Lady had three copies."

"Good thing," I said, "We didn't do anything else last summer."

Shane stuck an index finger in the air. "Uh, except for Carol Atkinson."

Andy rolled his eyes and I shook my head.

"Shane," Andy corrected, "we did not 'do' Carol Atkinson. Trust me, I woulda remembered that."

"Right," I said, "that was the problem if I remember. Nobody did nothin' about Carol except drool and dream."

Andy laughed. "Uh huh, drool and dream."

Shane frowned. "You guys know I didn't mean it that way."

Andy said, "Okay, Mr. 'Wavy Hair.'"

Shane was combing his hair and blushing. "I meant that everybody was talkin' about her, thinkin' about her but nobody had the guts to talk to her."

Andy stopped laughing and paused. "You're right. Never shoulda thought what I thought. Carol is about the best girl I ever knew."

I said, "Me too. As I remember it, all we did was talk about Carol."

****

Carol Atkinson was a dark-haired, dark-eyed, olive-skinned sixteen-year old with a perfect face, perfect figure, perfect teeth and a perfect personality. Friendly and smart without being a pain, she was the kid everyone liked.

I never called her Carol. I always called her 'Pretty Perfect.' No mystery there. Her family moved to San Francisco and somebody said *Playboy* interviewed her and took some pictures. I never believed that, but I believe they should have. I'd swear on a stack of Bibles that girl did not look sixteen.

As far as boys went, Shane was right, no one spoke to her. I am not sure why others didn't. I never asked them. I just know why I didn't. She scared me and that's the truth. She was perfect and I was so far from that, it wasn't even funny. I always wondered if Carol knew she was close to perfect. As far as I could tell, it did not mess her up. She reminded me of Annette on the Mickey Mouse Club.

We agreed that she was prettier than Jade Parker. We also agreed that the idea of seeing her naked didn't seem right. Shane wondered if Carol was lonely. I reminded him that she had plenty of less-than-plain girlfriends.

I kept my other thoughts to myself.

Gotta try with girls, even pretty ones. Next time, go for it. Hurts either way, so just try.

We reached the corner and Andy said, "If we hurry, we can get to Louie's house in fifteen minutes, maybe twenty."

Shane asked, "Louie's really sick, huh? His mom called all our houses."

Andy shrugged.

I coughed and spat in Mrs. Whitten's hedge. Suddenly, there she was in her picture-postcard living room in front of her story-book Christmas tree. Glaring out her window, she looked like a statue with a hernia.

Too bad she's not as nice as her stuff.

It took a while to reach Louie's front door. Shane knocked and we waited. After a minute or so, he knocked again and stepped back. Again, we waited. After another minute or so, we turned to leave and the door opened and Louie's mom spoke. She had a bookish look: short black hair, green eyes, tiny nose, thin face, dark glasses, pretty teeth and a beautiful mouth.

She said, "Louie's not here, right now. But, if you could all come in."

She sounded stuffed up and her eyes looked red and puffy.

I was worried.

She has a cold or she's been crying or both. Why would she ask us in if Louie's not here? Jesus, is Louie dead? Please, God, don't let Louie be dead.

We stepped into Mrs. Kerensky's house and sat in her living room. There was no sign of a Mr. Kerensky. She took a breath and said she would tell us everything and answer any questions after she told us stuff. She then began.

"Louie's not here. He's in the Shriner's Hospital in San Francisco. He has lots of problems: liver, kidneys, and pancreas are all bad. He may or may not make it back here. But, even if he does make it back, he will not live very long. He is dying. There are lots of things going wrong." She started to cry and stopped herself. She struggled. "I'm sorry... uh, but... it's nobody's fault. This is just what happens... Sometimes when a dwarf... has lots of other health problems... like Louie has from the beginning..."

She was blowing her nose, wringing her hands, looking at the floor, talking as if she had said these lines a thousand times. She wiped her eyes with her forearm and stared without seeing. She couldn't or wouldn't lift her head.

She didn't know what to do with her hands. "I can't find the Kleenex box. I'm sorry. I'm so sorry... I should know where it is..."

She broke. She was now sobbing hard. Her face and hair were a mess.

Her voice was just above a whisper. "I know nobody else wanted Louie... but I did... He wasn't ugly to me. He wasn't awful to me..."

Her voice burst and she dropped her head into her hands, fists clenched, chest heaving. She tried to comfort herself by curling inward and rocking. She was shaking violently like a plane spiraling out of control.

It felt like she was talking to herself.

"He was my baby... my sweet, little baby... I don't know who taught him all those... I just don't want this... to... I should never have let him... I should...I tried everything. God... I went everywhere. You know, uh... I tried..."

She was gritting her teeth, grinding her fists into her tired eyes. Her face was wet and splotchy. She was twisting her torso, trying to escape her own body. Now, words seemed to rip from her throat.

Her breathing was erratic. "Somebody should have helped. What good does it do if ...Why even... He was just a little baby, a sweet..."

Suddenly, she was out of air and out of tears. We sat nailed to the sofa, staring at our shoes. No sound of breathing in that room. No heads turning, no legs fidgeting. It was hot and my head began to itch, like tiny flashing lights on a Christmas tree. I didn't dare move and I knew it. Somehow, if I moved, if any of us moved, it would be disrespectful to Mrs. Kerensky and it would shame her.

Suddenly, she remembered something and collected herself. She sucked in air. She found the tissue box. But, she looked like a fighter unable to answer the bell.

It took her a few moments. "I'm sorry boys, please forgive me. Sometimes these things swallow me up. But, I am okay now... I am. I want you to know that you are very important to Louis and I would appreciate it very much if you could each write him a letter. I will deliver them. Do you think you could do that?"

We said we certainly would. We were sorry Louie was sick. She used another fistful of tissue, stood, ushered us to the door and apologized again for her tears. We said we would have letters for Louie by Wednesday and that she could pick them up at Shane's house after 2:00 o'clock. We said we'd get other guys to write letters too.

She hugged us and it was messy and uncomfortable and then we left. It was dark. We started toward my house. Half a block from Louie's, we stopped in our tracks and everybody agreed. It was too dark, too cold and too scary. We were looking over our shoulders and jumping at shadows. I kept listening for that deadly bumble bee.

We hurried back, knocked on the Kerensky front door, and explained our situation. We each needed a ride. Mrs. K. understood and invited us in. We sat again and waited while she changed clothes. In a few minutes, we were in her car. From the back seat I could see her eyes in the rear view mirror. She looked better, maybe even a little happy. I only saw her eyes a couple of times. Soon, we were all home, safe and sound.

When I walked in the front door, my mother faked a heart attack and congratulated me for getting home, "pretty close to right on time." She was getting ready to be mad about my clothes, but as soon as I told her about working for Mrs. Reynolds for nothing and seeing Louie's mom cry, she was fine.

I cleaned up, ate dinner with my parents, watched "Maverick," took a shower and went to bed. Bret Maverick was my favorite. He just seemed the friendliest and the funniest. He wasn't like an old time cowboy like Roy Rogers or John Wayne. He was more like a today guy stuck in the Old West.

There was a lot to think about before I went to sleep. Tomorrow we had to make up a list of questions for Father Phillip and finish with Delores' yearbook. I was hoping not to dream about bad things. I wanted no part of Mrs. Reynolds' Twilight Zone yard or her doing some weird circus trick. Or worse yet, Mrs. K. crying and Louie being sick or dead.

But, I wouldn't mind dreaming about Blazer's exploding nose again or about hiding benches at St. Luke's.

But, mostly I wanted to dream about Sandy Koufax and Sandra Dee. Sandy wasn't very good yet but he was so fast. I knew he would be good someday. Sandra Dee? She was perfect, right now. Always had been, always would be.

Suddenly, something amazing popped into my head.

My two favorite people in the world have the same first name! If I ever do get married and have kids, I got two good names right there. Sandy for the boy and Sandra for the girl… pretty amazing. Wolfman would think it's amazing too. I bet he would.

Chapter 29
Secret Voices, Priestly Questions
and Secret Places

MONDAY MORNING SUNSHINE splashed through my bedroom at nine o'clock. It had been a restful, somewhat dreamless night, only shadowed flashes involving Delores' yearbook.

I lectured myself in the mirror.

If we don't find something in her yearbook, we're dead.

I brushed my teeth and read the note taped to the mirror.

Gone to pay electricity and telephone bills. Cereal is OK. Put the milk away. Don't drink from the carton. Clear the dishes and the table. Back about 11:00. Weed the front before you go anywhere. You have my permission to go to the park or Andy's or Shane's but nowhere else.

Love,

Mom

PS Boys may be in the house, but only to use the bathroom. Don't just watch TV. Make a sandwich for lunch if you are with other boys.

Leave a note.

I escorted my hand-me-down shirt and jeans to the kitchen, mixed the Sugar Crisp and Cheerios, ate like a man on a mission and headed to the garage for gloves and weeding tools.

Sooner I get the weeds… sooner I get outta here…

Suddenly, I heard scraping and whining. I opened the front door and greeted the prettiest guys on my block. Rocky and Renfro, two beautiful, three-year-old, dark-red golden retrievers, sat politely on the other side of the front porch screen. Colors swirling in the morning sun, fine shiny-smooth coats, glistening red and gold highlights, ragged ears, feathery tails and legs, they were magnificent: Stately heads, narrow faces, soft brown eyes and shiny black noses.

I spoke to them through the screen. "Hi guys, long time no see. Where ya been? Stay right there. I'm coming out."

They backed gently as I stepped on to the porch. Sleek, powerful and strong, each pushing ninety pounds, they strolled the neighborhood at will. I met them the first day they arrived: tiny, blonde panda imitations with dark red tips on their ears and chewing everything in sight. Occasionally, Rocky lived up to his full name and took off like a rocket after a bird or a squirrel. But, Renfro never broke character. For him, slow and steady won every race.

I asked, "You guys wanna help me pull weeds? Let's go get the stuff."

I went to the garage, put gloves and a short-handled tool called a "fishtail weeder" into a pail and began making my way to the front flower bed. Pail and cane in one hand, I looked down, a black nose near each of my knees. They flopped next to me as we reached the flower bed.

From out of nowhere, I heard a familiar voice. "Goin' to the dogs?"

Andy was smiling and the retrievers (tails wagging) were up and moving toward him. He squatted and petted them.

I smiled. "No, I'm goin' to the weeds. Gotta do these before I can go anywhere. Whada you doin'?"

Andy moved closer, looked around a moment and whispered, "I was gonna call you but something happened."

I looked up. "What? Another arrow?"

"No. I picked up the phone. You know how it is, an' I heard the end of a conversation. I don't think they knew but it gave me the creeps."

I dropped the fishtail. "Wha'd you hear?

"Two voices, men. I didn't recognize 'em. One says, 'They're just kids.' The other says, 'I don't care. I don't care one bit. I don't like it.' And then, the line went dead."

"Think that was about us?"

"Yeah, I do."

"No way to tell."

"Still, we gotta tell everybody."

I stuck the fishtail in and ripped through the roots of a big clump of weeds. "Bad idea. I mean, if it is about us, all the more reason we gotta lay low."

Andy rubbed the back of his neck. "Okay, but sometime we gotta do somethin'. We gotta tell somebody. More I think about it, they were talkin' about us staying away from the Jefferson place."

I shook my head. "If it's about Scotty, it's about more than the house. Remember, 'Let the dead bury the dead?'"

Andy grabbed the fishtail, drove it deep into the middle of a big chunk of weeds. "Maybe you're right. Leave everything alone."

I took the fishtail and pointed it at Andy. "Was one of the voices mad?"

"Yeah, but the other was more like pissed off."

I leaned forward, "If they were mad and pissed off, we must be getting close to something."

Andy sighed. "I'm gettin' close to my limit."

I dropped the weeder and wiped my forehead. "It ain't that bad."

Andy sat on the bricks. "Maybe we should just drop this stuff."

"Okay, Missy. You need to stay home with your mommy, I understand."

Andy shook his head. "Don't start on me. You know what I mean."

"I know what you mean. I do. But, I think this is real exciting, like the Hardy Boys, like Huckleberry Finn."

Andy hesitated. "Yeah, but this ain't no dumb book. This is real."

"I know," I almost yelled, "That's what's so great!"

"So, whadya think we should do?"

"I think we should just go right along. Keep our eyes an' ears open. Like today, we gotta get questions for Father Phillip and finish up on Delores' yearbook."

"I don't think we're gonna find much more in her book."

I shrugged. "Never know... Got any better ideas?"

Andy studied the flower bed. "Want my help on this?"

"Duh... Whada you think? I tell ya this much, I pointed to the sleeping boys in the red trunks. You gotta be more help than Mr. Moto and Haystack Calhoun."

Andy laughed. "Uh, where do I get the stuff?"

"In the garage on the shelf next to the back door: gloves and fishtail.

Andy said, "Be right back."

It was mid-morning when we got serious about the weeds. We finished them faster than Rocket could eat a tennis ball. Mr. Christiansen said he once saw Rocket finish one in an hour. We finished the weeds in forty five minutes, including clean up. We made two baloney and cheese monsters and added a couple of fists full of chips to each brown bag. I wrote my mom a note and taped it next to hers.

Andy said, "Drinks?"

I shrugged. "Water?"

"Uh-uh. Let's go to my house. We gotta case of Coke and some candy bars. We'll bring some for Shane."

We quickly made one more monster sandwich, added chips and set off for Shane's by way of Andy's. The day was bright, clear and cold. I felt like reintroducing myself to the sunshine. Renfro and Rocket decided to tag along. They would scout ahead for twenty or thirty feet, double back, check in and take off again. They were attention-magnets, friendly looks from everyone.

At corner of Emerald and Money, we were belted by the familiar toxic sounds and smells of Old Man McKinley's clumsy Columbia Blue '36 Dodge. We ducked and turned away as it clattered by, the air suddenly black. We held our breath and the retrievers disappeared. It took some minutes for the cloud of gunk to pass. We watched the old bucket of bolts limp away.

I waved at the air near my face. "Nice truck, eh?" I grinned. "You know, I really miss ole Ben and Ike."

Andy coughed. "Beautiful paint job, eh? Remember the night we painted it?"

I coughed and laughed. "Sure do."

Andy looked in every direction for our scouts and then glanced at the street signs. "Who names a street, 'Money'?"

I grinned. "Same guy who names another one, 'Easy.'"

Suddenly, the noise and the black air were as gone as the dogs, so we plugged on.

As we neared Fremont Park, Andy jammed to a stop. "Hey, wanna go to the GAD?"

"Huh?"

"The GAD. Wanna go?"

It took me a few seconds. "If you're afraid to go through the park, just admit it."

He backed up. "Did I say that? No. I said, 'Wanna go to the GAD?'"

"Hey," I smiled. "No shame here. I'll admit flat out. I'm scared crapless."

He set the paper bags down and shoved his hands in his pockets. "I'm not sayin' that I'm not scared, I am. But, I am also sayin' I wanna go to the Great American Diner."

I gently tapped his skull. "Anybody home?" I pointed to the bags. "We got lunch right here. Wanna go around the park okay or through it, okay but I ain't goin' to the Diner."

Andy said, "There's always Daisy."

"Hey Buddy," I paused. "You know I can't go. I got no money and besides, my mom's note says go to your house or Shane's."

Andy looked around. "There's enough people here today, let's go through."

We followed our original path. It was the shortest and most level. As the "arrow tree" loomed ahead, I heard a rushing and pounding behind us. Andy was looking in all directions. To avoid falling, I kept my eyes on the ground, listening for that bee with the jet engine. Suddenly, something smacked the back of my left leg and I went down.

Instantly, Andy was yelling, "No!" as two ninety- pound, breathing, electric blankets with tails, landed on me.

Our scouts were back. I heaved a sigh of relief and nudged them to my side. After a minute or two, Rocky and Renfro were quietly sitting next to me.

We petted the boys, reset our sites and hurried through the rest of the park.

We were happy to reach Andy's in one piece. His mom cheerfully added drinks, candy bars, raisins and napkins to our lunch bags. We took a few minutes to arrive at Shane's garage and Leslie again ushered us in. She said Shane would be in soon and that we should make ourselves at home. Rocky and Renfro parked in the dead jukebox corner. We laid out our lunch on the pool table.

Shane stepped through the door and went to the retrievers immediately. "Hey, what's up?"

Andy pointed. "We got lunch for you but we need a can opener."

Shane spun and headed back to the main house. "My dad calls it a 'church key.'"

I laughed. "Never heard that one before."

Andy fished around and pulled out his small notebook and pen. "We'll eat and get questions for Father Phillip."

I sat on the couch. "Yep, then we'll see about the yearbook and let Shane in on the phone call."

Shane returned and we ate sitting atop the pool table. We had to pull up our legs. The boys would just as soon chew pants or shoes. They settled under the table awaiting scraps. Andy filled Shane in on the details of the party-line talk. Shane agreed that we should lay low and he, too, was sure that the mysterious call was about us.

Food finished, we cleared our mess, fed the boys our left-overs and a few crusts and tackled the Father Phillip questions. We thrashed around and at one point, we had fifteen or twenty.

Shane looked at the list and started marking them out in bunches. "Boys," he looked at the retrievers. 'Sorry, not you guys.' This is way too much. We ain't got all day."

Andy was shooting eight ball and I was tossing cards. Quickly, my game became keep away from the retrievers.

Shane looked at us. "I cut out all the repeats and the Twilight Zone stuff and some other conscience stuff. So, we got three good questions."

1. If you commit suicide, do you go to hell?

2. Why does an all-powerful God let bad stuff happen?

3. Why do bad people get away with stuff?

Suddenly, we had no energy for Delores' yearbook. We ran through lots of games and sloughed them. Shane suggested telephone tricks. Those tired old things that everybody seems to have known since before the telephone itself:

"Hello, do you have Prince Albert in a can? Well, you better let 'im out."

Andy racked the balls and took the break shot. "Those are more fun to talk about than do. They don't work on a party line anyway."

I sneaked a wink at Shane and prodded. "Andy, you aren't the only one who heard somethin' on the phone."

Andy stopped shooting eight ball.

Shane played along and raised his eyebrows. "You heard something too?"

"You bet." I gave him the big eyes. "It happened when I was tryin' to call guys about letters to Louie."

Shane leaned in.

I looked down and spoke just loud enough to be heard. "I picked up the phone and Amanda Lacey says, 'Thank you for such a sweet kiss and some guy says, 'You're a sweet girl.' Then, click."

Shane grinned and scratched his head. "Amanda Lacey. Man, she's somethin'. Recognize the guy?"

I shook my head. "No, I couldn't figure the guy." I picked at my pants' leg. "But, Amanda did say he's 'very sweet'."

Shane shrugged. "Could be anybody."

"Really?" I raised my eyebrows. "Amanda won't kiss just anybody. Her dad hates guys."

We looked in Andy's direction. Our frazzled friend cleared his throat and shifted his weight. The garage was heating up. Andy held his stick like a javelin.

He fussed with his shirt and heaved a big sigh. "Okay. It was me alright. I kissed her last week. No details."

After a minute, I nudged him. "Pretty sweet, eh?"

Shane jumped up, gave Andy a pat on the back, grabbed the Scotty Box, pulled Delores' yearbook. "We gotta get after this."

We huddled around the book and began checking the last four pages, the autograph pages. Every page filled, seventy-five percent of the signatures were female and most of those included the sign off, "D.G."

Shane shook his head. "Every girl in school must have been in on the D.G. thing."

I shook my head, too. "How'd a shy girl like Delores get all these signatures?"

Andy said, "It's not like people really sign 'em for ya. I mean, they do but lots of times, people just stack 'em up on someone's desk and the person just signs as fast as possible. And, lots of times, you don't gotta talk at all, just shove your book in somebody's hand."

So much for the shy-girl signatures mystery.

We turned our attention back to the yearbook. Nearly one fourth of the last page contained an eye-catching but puzzling entry—a splashy, intricate and artistic fountain-pen line-drawing of what appeared to be a three-story gothic mansion. The drawing included spacious grounds and lush vegetation: tall stately trees and expansive flower gardens and hedges. In perfect script, the personal note was also delivered by fountain pen.

Hey Dolores –

Have a fantastic summer! Remember PE and those crazy dances? (Don't let 'em step on you.) I will miss you. We had good times in Art, didn't we? Don't worry. Like we said, there is a 'Scotty' out there for each of us. I'm looking for mine. Hope you find yours. Who knows? Mr. Perfect might walk into our life any day!

Good Luck,
Clarice, D.G. (H.I.P.S.)

Questions attacked us:

1. 1. Is this drawing a real place? If so, where is it and why is it important?

2. Who is Clarice?

3. Why would she use Scotty's nickname?

We studied the drawing from all angles. It was not familiar. We had no idea about Clarice, other than her notation as one of Scotty's many Dream Girls. As for her use of his nickname, we were dumbfounded. We decided that Andy should return Delores' book immediately and quiz her about everything. While waiting for Andy, Shane and I would get started on our Louie letters and see about calling others to remind them.

Both retrievers in tow, Andy tucked the yearbook under his arm. "It'll take me fifteen minutes to get to the cleaners. I'll get her on a break. If she's off, I'll drop by her house. If she's not home, I'll come back with the yearbook. I should be back in thirty or forty minutes."

Shane retrieved notebook paper and pens and we decided to use the pool table as a desk. We were stumped about how to begin: *Looey, Louie, Looie, or Louy?* They all looked wrong.

I said, "Let's ask Leslie."

Suddenly, Shane dropped his notebook and bolted for the door. "Gotta catch Andy! Be right back."

Just like that, door slamming, he was gone. Seconds later, Leslie came in full of smiles. "What's going on?"

"Shane's tryin' to catch Andy."

"Why?"

I cleared my throat and smiled. "Truth is, we were getting set to ask you something and snap, Shane took off."

"Why is he chasing Andy?"

"Beats me." I held up my notebook. "Which spelling is correct?"

She quickly pointed to *Louie*.

Without warning, commotion hammered the door and in burst the retrievers who happily jumped on Leslie. Shane was next, followed by a confused Andy. Leslie settled the dogs. Andy, puffing, leaned against the pool table while Shane sprinted toward his bedroom.

I looked at my frazzled friend. "What did Shane tell you?"

Andy threw up his hands. "All I know is he comes flying up behind me, almost tackles me, spins me around and says I gotta get back here as fast as I can. So, here I am."

Leslie gave the dogs one last scratch, said goodbye to us and headed for the door. Just as she turned the knob, Shane again blasted through and sent Leslie flying. Luckily, Andy caught and steadied her. Shane muttered a quick apology: Too late. Leslie collected herself, straightened her hair, glared and left.

Out of breath, Shane pointed to the yearbook. "Look at the last page again. I got an idea."

Andy turned, set the book on the table and opened to the last page. I moved to get a better view. Shane began examining the fountain-pen drawing through his magnifying glass. He was quiet and I saw nothing of interest. I caught Andy's eye. He shrugged and gave me the big eyes.

After a minute or so, Shane banged the table with his off hand, whispered "Yes" and pointed. Andy and I leaned in and there it was nestled among the flowers: a small but distinct little sign attached to a pole in the ground. It's tiny message was in perfect script: H.I.P.S. + W.A.S.

We looked twice as hard at the rest of the drawing. Moments later, Shane again struck gold: Third story window on the northeast corner of the mansion, a tiny flagpole bracketed to the outside wall. In the magnifying glass, centered in the tiny flag, sat a coiled snake with the inscription, "Don't Tread on Me."

We looked at each other.

Andy said what we were thinking. "Here we go again. More information that gets us nowhere."

I hesitated. "Maybe not. Go back to that picture in the student government section, the one where Scotty is sitting at a table in the faculty dining room."

I grabbed some paper, studied the photo and scribbled a note. I turned quickly to the football section, scribbled another note and took one more look at Clarice's drawing. Something was coming into focus.

I said, "Look at this. Scotty signs his nickname "Hips" which stands for his quarterback skills, crazy legs an' all that. But, in the student government picture he signs H.I.P.S. just like Clarice." I paused. "Boys, the capital letters are not a nickname, they are a code and I know the code."

Andy had fireworks in his eyes. "So, what is it?"

Shane was studying my notes. "Don't tell me! I can get it."

I was grinning from ear to ear. I felt like Charlie Chan. "Think back to the Diner but, don't think Daisy, think Pete as in Decker. On the day we read the letters, what did he tell us?"

Andy flashed. "I remember. He pissed me off. I think I called him a liar."

I laughed. "Yeah, you sure did."

Andy was mad all over again. "He said that Scotty had a secret girlfriend and a secret place and that he couldn't find out anything else."

Shane added. "Crazy Jesse thought he was gonna kick Decker's ass."

We laughed.

Now I had the fireworks. "Boys, Decker told us two other things that day:

For Decker to get to the secret place Scotty would have to carry him and that the secret place was 'in plain sight.'

"Those were Scotty's words. That's what Decker said. It didn't make any sense. How could a secret place be 'in plain sight?' But, I can tell you this much, H.I.P.S means Hide In Plain Sight." Means that for Clarice, too. If I'm lyin', I'm dyin'.'"

Shane grabbed his magnifying glass and began examining the Senior Class Council picture.

He waved us over. "Look!"

The magnifying glass pulled up an image reflected in the stainless steel buffet counter. The image was a civil defense poster on the wall behind Scotty, just outside the direct camera angle.

The poster read: 'In Case of Nuclear Attack, Report to the Gym.'

Now Shane's eyes had the fireworks. He flipped the glass over and told us to look through the higher powered lens in the corner. Under the official directions, we saw an uneven student scrawl: *If it's there.*

Shane was pointing. "Look at his signature – 'H.I.P.S/SJ.' He thinks it's a joke! He writes, 'HA HA' and then he adds, 'My dad likes it too.'"

Suddenly, I saw it all. There it was in plain sight. "I got it, I got it. The poster is a bomb warning, 'get to the gym.' What a joke. The gym? Sure, pal, if it's there, as in don't count on it." I stared at my wide-eyed friends. "Now, why would Scotty's dad like this picture? Only one reason: He knows hidin' in the gym is a joke. Remember, 'Duck and Cover' under our desks? Stupid, right? Well, Scotty's dad isn't stupid. He's as tricky as his kid is on a football field."

Andy snapped his fingers and nearly yelled, "He built a bomb shelter right in front of everybody! When he was remodeling the house. There's a bomb shelter under the Jefferson place. That's it!"

I yelled, "Bingo!"

Shane was conducting with his magnifying glass baton. "The W.A.S. means We Aren't Stupid. You know H.I.P.S. + W.A.S."

Energy was flying around the room.

I said, "Or something like, We Are Safe. Works either way."

Andy laughed. "Well, it probably don''t mean Weenies Are Super."

I suddenly remembered one more piece. "Hey, remember, 'The problem is below, the answer is above'? Well, the problem is in that shelter below the Jefferson place."

Andy's eyes sparkled. "That's why they want us to 'Let the dead bury the dead.'"

We looked at each other. Suddenly, there was no air in the room and there was also no doubt.

We were all thinking the same thing.

We gotta find that bomb shelter …

Chapter 30
Richard and Rocket

WE DECIDED TO hang on to the yearbook a bit longer. The mind-boggling bomb shelter made a lot of sense and so did a few other things. Clarice was not Scotty's secret girlfriend. We never did buy the secret girlfriend idea and weren't buying it now. It might have been one big goof on everyone.

But, Clarice's note made her an open admirer not a secret girlfriend. As for H.I.P.S., Clarice might have known about the shelter and her drawing might simply mean she was in on the joke.

We struggled with the tiny "Don't Tread on Me" flag for five minutes or so and Shane made a large sketch to take to the library. His dad came by looking for lost keys and noticed the sketch.

He whistled. "Long time since I've seen that old flag."

An ex-RAF fighter pilot, Shane's dad was active in veteran's organizations and always ready to talk. The flag, he explained, had served many purposes over the years but was best known as the original emblem of the U.S. Marines.

Andy took the bull by the horns. "Sir, is there any reason this flag might have been around the Jefferson house?"

He thought for a moment. "Mr. Jefferson was a Marine Corps sharpshooter, good with any number of weapons: rifles, hand-guns, machine guns, all types."

We nodded.

"Any reason you boys are interested in this right now?"

"Nope."

"No reason."

"Not really."

I asked the question we were all thinking. "Uh, sir, do you think, I mean, was Mr. Jefferson good with a bow?"

He was measured. "Anything I might say would be speculation. You know the word 'speculation'? Are you asking me to speculate, son?"

I nodded. "Yes sir, I know the word."

The graying, 6'4" ex-flyer folded himself on to the couch.

"In that case, my best guess would be that he was an excellent marksman with a bow, a sling shot, spitting watermelon seeds or anything else."

Shane turned the conversation. "Dad, did he build a bomb shelter?"

"Why would you ask?"

"No real reason. A military guy might do that, I guess."

"I'm a military guy, I'm just not a shooter. Did I build one?"

"No sir, you didn't."

"Well," he sighed. "Truth is, I wanted to, just never got to it."

He stood and leaned against the pool table. The retrievers were up, planning on leaving with him.

"The answer is yes, he built one. He was a couple of years ahead of everybody. Built it around the time they lost Scotty. I got a tour of the thing the day he finished."

We were glued to his every word. The retrievers settled.

He said, "I took notes. The place was amazing. But, why not? Look at what he did with the house." Suddenly, his memory was firing blanks. "I wish I knew where those notes were." After a minute or so, he apologized and took one last look at the flag sketch. "Good drawing."

Shane said, "Dad, I bet you saved those notes somewhere special."

The residential security expert and company owner looked at his son. "Usually, I put 'em in my desk. But, for some reason, I put 'em someplace else." He looked off into space. "I didn't put 'em in my desk 'cause I didn't want to lose 'em if the house burned down."

We stared at the floor and crossed our fingers. He walked to the utility area off the garage, opened a false cupboard above the washer and dryer, spun a combination lock and grabbed a fist full of papers.

He returned to the couch and for the next thirty minutes we got a crash course on the Jefferson fallout shelter:

1. Several feet underground: Double-entry hatches.

2. Eighteen inch Walls: Concrete, bricks, earth and sand.

3. Entrance: Sharp right turn reduces radiation.

4. Double ventilation system: Electric generator backed by a hand-cranked blower. Pipe to a filter, vents attached to the floor.

5. Supplies: Canned food, bottled water, Civil Defense carbohydrate candies, medical supplies, radio, Geiger counter,

chemical toilet. Cots, blankets, pillows, Monopoly game, cards, books, magazines, diaries.

6. Pocket Dosimeter: Radiation detection device (pen-like tube worn on clothing.)

He looked up. "I'd forgotten about all this. It was something."

Shane asked, "Where is the shelter? I mean, at the Jefferson house."

"Behind the house, next to a clump of trees, hidden by Oleander bushes. Of course, everything looks different today."

He set his notes down and began lifting pillows, shoes, shirts, notebooks and clumps of sock-basketballs.

Suddenly, he turned and grumbled, "Boys, find my keys!"

Instantly, we were all frantic, including the retrievers.

Shane searched the pool table: Glasses, plates, silverware, chips and wrappers.

Then he yelled, "There they are!" and fished a handful out of a corner pocket.

The dad took his keys and carefully studied the sketch one more time. "Boys, why did you ask about the old flag and the Jefferson place?"

I answered quickly, "We saw a tiny drawing of the flag in a bigger drawing and the bigger drawing made us think of Scotty's house."

He adjusted his cap and said, "Listen, I know why you're interested in that old place, the rumors and all. But, it's falling apart and it's dangerous. I don't want you boys around there for any reason. Do you all understand me?"

We answered immediately.

"Yes, sir."

"Yes."

"Uh huh."

He lined up his shirt buttons and zipper and centered his belt buckle. "Good, glad we agree. I don't want anybody getting hurt."

We were quiet. The serious tone had also discouraged the retrievers.

"Boys, clean this place up before you go anywhere."

Eyes on the floor, we gave unanimous compliance. But, the door no sooner closed than we forged our own pact. Shane tossed a sock-ball and caught it as it bounced off the ceiling.

He spoke for all of us, "We gotta find that thing and get into it!"

Our plan was never in doubt. We would it lay out as soon as the garage "police action" was complete. Fifteen minutes later we sat in a circle on the floor.

Andy stated the obvious. "We gotta do this right more than ever. Get caught now and we're really dead."

Shane heaved a sigh. "It's 4:30. Let's go by the Jefferson place around the back. Stay across the street and see if we can see that clump of trees."

Andy grabbed a notebook and scribbled. He drew a rectangle with doors opening from the middle. "The hatch entrance probably looks something like this: Steel with a big padlock. Even if we find it, I dunno how we get in."

I waved for Shane to pull me up. "One thing at a time. Find it first."

We stepped outside, late afternoon: gray, wet and cold, retrievers in tow. Two short blocks later, we stood beneath the antique lamppost on the corner looking across at the spooky old Jefferson place. We crossed the street, turned right and studied the backyard from a safe distance.

Suddenly, Rocket began streaking toward the clump of trees near the Jefferson's kitchen door. Renfro loped behind. In seconds, they were sniffing and circling energetically amidst the dead trees. We screamed and followed. Andy and Shane close, me a distant third. In the foggy distance, I saw a frenzied Ring around the Rosie.

Then, I heard it rip passed.

The bumble bee with the jet engine stinger!

I dove, hit the ground and heard a deep-throated, non-human scream. In the mist, I saw a retriever spinning and collapsing in the dead trees.

Everyone screaming, one dog was down, the other frantic and shivering. I looked in all directions: Nothing.

Andy tore off his jacket, covered one animal and comforted the other.

After what seemed like forever, I reached Andy. Rocket was lying on his side, eyes closed, breathing labored, an arrow lodged in his right rear flank. I looked for blood. It was too dark but the arrow was familiar. Renfro was shivering and whining. I got on my knees and hugged him to my side.

Andy whispered, "We're lucky that the son of a bitch only likes one shot at a time."

I whispered, "Where's Shane?"

"Gone for help."

"What the hell is going on?"

Andy moved the jacket a bit.

His hands were shaking. "What kinda perv shoots a dog?!"

"How bad is it?"

Andy wiped sweat from his face and tried to clear dried spittle from the corners of his mouth. "Not much blood, arrow kinda plugs the hole. Looks like it went in at an angle. Missed the bone maybe. Every once in a while he wants to move. Gotta keep 'im still."

Suddenly, I was sweating, my own breathing shallow. I turned away and wretched violently. Renfro nosed the back of my neck and pushed closer. Andy began gently clearing debris from underneath Rocket whose breathing was now shallow and uneven.

In couple of minutes, Shane arrived. He was out of breath. "Called from the Spencer's. Doc Collins and Jelly are less than five minutes away."

The lights of The Vet Van sliced through the darkness and slid to a stop. Doc and Jelly placed Rocket on a stretcher, stuffed us in, ran three stop lights and fishtailed into the parking lot. Office staff lifted Rocket from the van and hit the ground running.

Doc gave orders for Operating Room # 4 and hustled inside to scrub.

Jelly escorted us to the Waiting Room and offered water. Doc's assistant for the last six years, twenty-one year old Gillian (aka 'Jelly') was entering vet school in the fall. Short dark hair, fine features, slight build, boyish figure, she was quick and fearless. Her nickname was courtesy of her three year old brother who couldn't say, "Gilly." It stuck because her father thought it was 'sweet.' She was three when her mother died giving birth to her brother.

She was hurried but focused. "Be back as soon as I settle Renfro and call his owners. Then, we'll get you home. You guys OK?"

We reassured her. She slipped a leash on Renfro and walked him to the kennel area behind the office. We could hear locks clicking, doors opening and closing and the hum of flood lights. We sat alone: wet, cold and dirty. It wasn't safe to talk. We followed Shane to the restroom and took turns filling the sink with muddy water and the waste basket with paper towels. My crutch tips slipped on wet tile and Shane caught me.

We decided to play dumb about the arrow. Only a few hours ago we'd been warned, so we agreed: Bringing up more bad stuff now was suicidal. Our plan was to focus on the dogs and let time pass.

Andy made a good point. "Look, we don't volunteer anything about the house or anything else. But, if they ask anything dead on we tell the truth."

Shane said, "Don't make up stuff and don't say anything we don't all know. If my dad thinks something isn't right, he'll ask each of us about the whole thing. An' then he'll do it again and again."

We retook our seats in the waiting room and studied the animal paintings. It was 6:00 PM when Jelly returned. Carrying a clipboard, she pulled a chair and began filling out an "Incident Report." She said it was required by the police "any time an animal is harmed, mistreated or killed."

The word "killed" belted me in the stomach.

I gasped. "Is Rocket dead?"

Jelly put up a hand. "No. He's in surgery."

"Is he gonna be OK?"

She shrugged. "Right now, it's anybody's guess. But, Doc Collins is very good at his stuff."

She explained the surgery would take two more hours, that the rest of the night would be the key to his recovery and that he had youth and strength going for him.

She completed the form, sifting clarity out of chaos and comforted us that she would be sitting with Rocket all night. She called our parents and painted us as heroes. She said she would bring us home soon.

My mom opened our front door at 6:30 PM, sent me directly to the shower and talked with Jelly for a few minutes. After showering, I ate dinner with my parents and answered question after question after question. I was surprised that talking made me feel better and tired at the same time. As soon as I finished eating, I asked to be excused and went to bed about 8:00 PM.

As I lay in bed (transistor radio near) I followed Jelly's advice for helping Rocket. She said remembering good times with him and running them in my head like a movie would be like praying for his healing. As I listened to the Wolfman, I remembered a special summer night with Rocket, less than a year ago.

The images walked into my memory wearing a big smile.

****

Under a full moon, I stood alone, poised at the top of a meandering dusty slope about 50 yards from our Fort. The field was empty except for some rusted ghosts, a few thousand memories, the garbage of a lifetime and all those things that go bump in the night.

One hour earlier, I could not take my eyes off Disney's dashing secret hero, Zorro. As soon as the screen credits rolled, I broke through my mom's feeble defenses and headed out.

I remembered the poem as if I had written it.

> The wind was a torrent of darkness
> upon the gusty trees,
> The moon was a ghostly galleon
> tossed upon cloudy seas,
> The road was a ribbon of moonlight
> looping the purple moor,
> And the highwayman came riding, riding, riding
> The highwayman came riding
> up to the old inn door.

At that moment, I was Zorro. Riding my sleek dark stallion, Tornado, down from the mountains, I would single-handedly save the town.

I studied the moonlit shadows and began my descent. The soft thick dirt gave good support and a cloud of dust churned behind me. As I made the first easy turn, my right cane suddenly exploded from my hand and sent me flying. I settled roughly, drowning in dust. I had hit a gopher hole, plain and simple. One cane whacked my hip and wedged underneath me, the other was nowhere in sight.

I panicked.

If they have to come looking for me I am dead.

The dust was choking and blinding.

Suddenly, I saw a big black dog. He had my cane in his mouth, thrashing it around, trying to break its neck. I blinked and looked again and in the glow of a distant streetlight I saw his true deep red-gold color.

I yelled through the dust. "Renfro, bring it"…

He did not react.

I whispered, "Hey, Renfro. Good boy! Bring it."

I was less than dead to him. He didn't move a muscle.

I waited a moment or two and tried the other red dog. "Hey, Rocket."

Immediately, he stopped thrashing, dropped my cane and looked right at me.

I whispered, "Rocket! Bring it."

Again, he stared at me, flopped and began gnawing my cane.

This is a party to him! He's got his 'candy cane'. He couldn't care less about me.

I tried to sound happy and excited, "Hey! Rocky! Come on buddy!"

He scooted a bit closer and kept gnawing.

I grinned.

Hey, that's it! Candy!

I dug out a ragged pack of cherry lifesavers, popped one in my mouth and looked at Rocky. I was lying on my left side, propped up on my forearm. He stopped licking the cane and stared at me for a third time. I waved the lifesavers slowly and made slurping sounds. He sniffed, whined and began an army crawl.

I coaxed. "Come here boy." I held out two lifesavers. "Come on! They're red, just like you."

He did not move.

I whispered hard, "Rocket, come!"

Suddenly, he stood, dragged the cane slowly, dropped it on my knee, gently took the candy and crunched a couple of times.

I petted his head and smiled. "Good boy!"

I scratched his neck and ears and he leaned his face into mine. I kissed him right between the eyes.

In a flash, he pushed me down and laid on my chest. I hugged him hard and tried to push him away. Like a wrestler, he re-positioned himself on my chest and tried to pin my arms with his front paws. I grunted and laughed. I brought my hand to my mouth, worked a lifesaver loose with my teeth and got it between my thumb and index finger. Rocky's nose was right there. I tossed the lifesaver two feet to my right and his eyes followed.

I whispered fiercely, "Go get it! Go."

He quickly stepped away, sniffed out the lifesaver and crunched it down. I grabbed my canes, got to my knees, pushed myself up and dusted off.

"You are very welcome. No, I have no more."

He wagged his tail and gave me a little slurp. I petted him for a minute or so and walked me home. He waited ten minutes on my front porch and I had to say goodbye two more times.

Thanks Rocket, you saved me.

I went to sleep with that memory but I struggled through a long dream about a never-ending surgery.

****

I woke early. My bed looked like I'd lost the wrestling match. I dressed, washed my face, brushed my teeth, wrote my mom a note, stuck a carrot in my mouth and an apple in my pocket and hit the front door quietly.

Andy was sitting on the porch.

He put his finger to his lips and whispered, "Write a note. We're goin' to Doc Collins an' check on Rocket."

"Already did. How long you been here?"

He shrugged. "Maybe fifteen minutes."

I took the last bite of carrot and took a deep breath of wet air. Everything was dripping and nobody was out, not even cats. It was a ten block walk to the vet. We walked mostly in the street, staying far enough away from houses to avoid triggering barking explosions. The middle of the street was also safer for me: none of that gritty, slick roadside mess that kills crutch tips.

As we passed Mrs. Theissen's devil-eyed goat, Purdy, she was trying to eat her way through a chain link fence. A mangy looking thing, somebody said the Theissen's actually got milk from her. Maybe so, but I couldn't imagine drinking it.

Andy sped up and then waited for me. "I hate that damn thing! Those eyes! She looks evil."

I was breathing hard when I caught up, so we stood for a minute. "I know. She does. But, when she was little she was cute."

Andy pulled his cap down. "Sure, why not? Everything's cute when it's little. Bet Satan was even cute when he was little."

I laughed. "Baby Satan? I don't think so."

Father Phillip says Satan was an angel, the most beautiful one. He says angels aren't born, they're created. They don't need to grow. Only people get to be God's children and the only children God will ever have are the ones who come from people.

We continued passed the fire station: three guys washing Engine Number Five. Denim shirts, (sleeves rolled) and breath like horses. The pale sun was breaking through the day's dreary start.

They waved and yelled and we yelled back. They wanted to know about Rocket. We said we were on the way and we'd stop by on the way back.

Andy shook his head. "Everybody knows, whadaya bet?"

I agreed. "The magic of party lines."

We covered the last three blocks easily. Andy threw a rock at a squirrel going up a palm tree and missed by a whisker. We yelled and laughed. Crossing the intersection and entering the parking lot settled us.

Andy checked his watch: 7:00 AM. We entered the glass doors to the waiting room, pushed the red light button on the counter and took a seat. Shortly, Jelly came through the inside door. She looked tired but she looked happy.

She gave us a big grin. "Rocket made it through the night! Doc was here twenty minutes ago and said everything looks fine. We rigged up something so he can't chew on the bandages. We gotta keep him here for a good while, but so far he's good."

We took one huge collective breath, exhaled and exchanged victory handshakes.

Andy glanced around the room. "How bad was the wound and what did the arrow look like?"

Jelly clasped her hands in her lap. "It wasn't nearly as bad as I thought. Doc says the arrow had spent most of its force by the time it hit. And it hit at an angle in the fleshy part of the rear quarter. No permanent damage and not much blood loss. Doc did shave away quite a bit of silky hair but it was only a few stitches. Biggest thing now is him messing with it or an infection."

Andy asked, "What about the arrow?"

Jelly jumped up. "I'll get it. Like I said, Doc is pretty good at this stuff." She returned. "He checked for poison and there was none."

Our eyes widened. The arrow on the tray was like the one in the tree only it was no more than four inches long. The tree arrow measured twelve.

We thanked Jelly, said 'Hooray' once more for Rocket and left.

We barely cleared the door when Andy whispered, "Under perfect conditions, that arrow has a max range of fifty yards. That shot was stupid. Hittin' the dog was a mistake. I was wrong. Whoever's shootin' at us don't know what the hell they're doin'." He lit up like a Christmas tree and hammered me in the chest. "Let's go by those trees again, right now!"

I started shaking my head. "No!"

He grabbed my jacket. "Nobody'll be expectin' it! We'll find those hatch doors!" He was already moving. "Hurry up, butthead! Before everybody gets up."

I protested. "People are already up. This is a very bad idea."

"So, a few people are up. But, nobody expects us to go there now. I know 'arrow boy' don't."

"Who says it's a boy? And slow down! I try to go too fast, I'll fall."

He waited, face screwed up. "Okay, I know 'arrow girl' ain't around either. Look, want me to do it alone?"

274

I caught up. "No, the curiosity will kill me."

We passed the guys at the fire station and yelled that Rocket was okay. They waved and yelled back, everybody wearing big smiles. By the time we reached my house it was almost 8:30 and I was tired. I wanted to rest but Andy again threatened to go the last five blocks without me.

We reached the intersection across from the Jefferson place at about ten minutes 'til 9:00.

Andy was beside himself. "Let's do like we did last night. Go on passed a block, double back an' then cross over into the back yard by the Oleander bushes.

I mocked. "Why not? Worked real good last night."

Andy took off and in seconds he was half a block ahead of me. I put my head down and hurried. By the time I reached the bushes, I was a sweaty mess. Andy was kicking and using a broken branch to scrape at the ground near the trees. The ground was wet, cluttered and overgrown. Massive Oleanders lined the back of the house and gave good cover.

I was looking at the ground and half-listening for that bumble bee sound.

We need tools and help.

I studied the layout. "We gotta get a system and we need tools and help."

Andy was not buying it. "We don't need tools. The hatch is right on the surface. We find it and then we need tools."

I suggested we space ourselves three feet apart, start from the house side of the bushes and move outward toward the trees. Andy used the branch and his shoes and I used my cane. We kept moving to our left toward the street and checking up to the tree line. Once the house to the trees was covered, we could try other directions.

We followed our system for twenty minutes. I was about to call for a break when Andy yelped in pain. He was hopping around on one leg and cursing a dead tree root. I looked closer and started pounding the tree root with my cane.

I paused and wiped my forehead. Suddenly, out of the corner of my eye, I saw light flash off a front bumper. Ray's patrol car was turning the corner about a block away.

I yelled and headed toward the Oleanders.

Thank God for bushes.

I got close to the house, threw my canes down and dove underneath the bushes, snugging my back against the house. Andy was thrashing around at the other end of the bushes and settling against the house as well. I found a line of sight and waited.

It took forever for Ray to muddle his way up the street. He approached the Jefferson lot, slowed and stopped at the curb parallel to the house, directly across from us and dead in my sights. My spot was cozy: He'd never see me in a million years, even if he knew where to look.

He stared at the lot for a while, cut the engine, stepped out of his car, closed the door and walked into the yard. Despite the pale morning sun, he used his flashlight as he circled the lot. He walked like he drove. He covered the three sides of the house furthest from his car first.

I used the time to crawl further in, not even a shoe showing. Cozy was turning steamy and itchy—and there were bugs, big ones!

Ray came around the corner singing, "There's No Business Like Show Business." He stopped in front of the Oleanders, squatted and began examining the scrapings on the ground. He stopped singing. He gave the trees a few flashlight stabs and a bit of the same to the Oleanders.

He re-clipped his flashlight, returned to the curb, scraped his shoes and re-entered his car. He took a small notebook from his shirt pocket, scribbled, said something into his radio and drove away.

We stayed put. Ray liked to wait a few minutes and return. Sure enough, in about five minutes he came flying around the corner, made a noisy stop at the curb and gave everything the eagle-eye once over. Five minutes later, he left again.

Again, we stayed put for ten minutes. Suddenly, Andy was scrambling, backing out of the bushes. He shook, slapped and scraped everything he could reach and then came and grabbed my legs and pulled me out. He helped me up and repeated the slapping and scraping and I got the parts of his back he couldn't reach.

He warned. "We gotta get outta here."

I shook my head. "Not yet."

I moved to the offending dead root and scraped around it. A pinch of metal flashed. Andy dropped and dug with his fingers, partially uncovering the ring of a lock.

We gave each other the big eyes, covered the lock and spent a minute or two disguising our search. We crossed the street quickly and cut through two back yards before we sat on the curb.

Andy spoke first. "We need bolt cutters, a crow-bar and a shovel."

276

I knew a good source. "Decker's got every tool in the world and he goes to the GAD every day between 11:00 and noon. We go there now, wait outside on the bench and ask him."

Our plan was simple: Meet with Decker right now, get lunch at Andy's, grab Shane and meet Father Phillip at St. Luke's at 2:00.

****

Out of nowhere, Ray's cruiser pulled parallel to the curb and stopped next to us. He got out, sat on the front quarter panel, removed his hat and smoothed his hair.

Chapter 31
The Policeman, the Priest and Pinocchio

RAY SET HIS hat on the hood and fussed with the fourth button on his shirt. It would not hold. He pulled a handkerchief from his pocket, took a moment to shine his shoes, refolded the cloth and cleared his throat.

He was friendly. "What are you boys up to this mornin'?"

"Nothin'."

"Yeah, nothin'."

He carefully wiped a bit of mud off Andy's jacket. "Diggin' in the dirt today?"

Andy was quick and easy. "Yes sir, we have. We did a flower bed at Randy's house, had a 'dirt war' an' then checked on Rocket."

Ray looked at me. "This is a funny way to come."

I held eye contact. "We stopped by the fire station to let 'em know Rocket was okay and I was gettin' tired so we stopped here."

"Where are you going now?

"We gotta meet somebody in front of the GAD an' then we're going to Andy's for lunch."

He tried the button two more times and covered it with his tie. "I read the Incident Report from Doc Collins' office and checked out the scene at the Jefferson place, so I'll just close the loop here."

He grabbed his notebook and flipped to an open page. We quickly recited what Jelly had coaxed us through the night before. Ray scribbled, closed his book, and slipped off his car. He took two steps and turned back to us.

"Last time at the Jefferson place. Last night, correct?"

We nodded.

He cleared his throat for the third time. "Both of you look me in the eye right now and tell me you were not at the Jefferson place today."

From our curb seats, we answered.

"No, sir."

"Not today. If I'm lyin', I'm dyin'."

He laughed. "That's good. I'm lyin,' I'm dyin,' I like it."

In seconds, he was in his cruiser and gone. Ray's questions scared us and ricocheted in a million directions:

1. Why was he so worried about us bein' at the Jefferson place?

2. He might ask Jelly about our clothes. What then?

3. Why did he study the dirt where we searched?

4. Why did he think we were lying?

5. Is he really as dumb as dirt?

Questions aside, we decided to use the Chevron restroom on our way to The Great American Diner. We arrived in good shape, surveyed the parking lot for Decker's beautiful two-toned '55 Chevy convertible and took up our posts on the bench.

Fifteen minutes later, we were surprised to see Decker roll out and down the ramp. He slid his wheelchair to within an inch of our knees, laughed and slapped each of us on the thigh, hard.

Andy yelped, "Cut it out."

"Well, well, if it ain't White Fang and Black Tooth! Ain't you guys eatin' lunch with Soupy today? Get it?"

"I rolled my eyes. "We get it, Decker. 'Lunch with Soupy,' very funny."

He pulled back a bit and said he was sorry if he'd smacked us too hard. He was just so happy to see us that he didn't know his own strength.

He rubbed his pale, puffy hands together, grinned and whispered, "Couldn't find my car, eh? On the other side of the building, rising in value as we speak."

I sighed. "Decker, we need to borrow a few tools."

He smiled. "How can I be of assistance to the great Holmes and Watson?"

"We need a crowbar, a shovel, an iron rake and some bolt cutters."

Decker frowned. "Ruth and Gehrig, you gonna rob a bank or what?"

I laughed. "Maybe. You shouda said Sacco and Vanzetti"

His eyes sparkled. "Now, we're talkin'! When and where you want this stuff?"

I said, "Next day or two. We"ll let you know."

Decker nodded and extended a self-satisfied hand.

I had my own fears.

Look at those guns! He's gonna crush me.

He asked, "Need anything else? Gloves, heavy-duty flash lights?"

We shook hands, solid.

No crush! Thank you, God.

"Yeah," I smiled. "We can use all that stuff!"

Decker spun and rolled across the parking lot.

Andy grumbled. "I never liked that guy an' I never will."

I shrugged. "He was cute when he was little."

Andy groaned. "Uh-uh. No baby Satan means no baby Decker, either."

I couldn't argue. Decker's convertible blew by, top down even in the gray mist. He blasted the horn, waved and burned rubber. Andy almost yelled.

I put an arm around his shoulder. "Hey, easy. He's got the stuff and he's gonna deliver it to the Jefferson place when the time is right."

****

It was nearing noon as we headed toward Andy's house, a promise of baloney and cheese, chips and juice and maybe a candy bar. The sun flickered and the sky looked dismal in all directions. On days like this, clocks keep time but Mother Nature loses her place.

It was a hard forty-five minutes and twelve long blocks to Andy's front door. We took a few minutes to clean up and pound the now-dried dirt from our clothes. Andy had to sweep the porch. We looked better than we should have.

We started lunch. In between bites, we admitted we had no idea of where this might end.

Andy drained his drink. "Shoulda got Shane this morning."

I opened my Snickers bar, chomped half of it and talked through the chocolate. "Get 'im now. Let's go."

We cleared the table. I thanked Andy's mom and we slipped out.

****

The pale sun found its brilliance, but remained weak. Everything held its breath against the cold: trees, yards, fences, houses, streets and sidewalks. People held themselves tight, exhaling fog as they moved. We arrived at Shane's door and he stepped out before we had a chance to knock.

He had a big smile: braces, wavy hair and all. "Rocket's gonna be okay. I called earlier and again just a few minutes ago."

We took one more victory lap for our retriever friend, checked our Father Phillip questions, filled Shane in on the morning adventures with Ray, including the silver latch, our escape and Decker's promise to help. He was impressed with the hatch find and as shaky about Ray as we were.

His smile faded. "Ray seems kinda stupid but every once in a while he gets stuff. Since Rocket's OK, he might drop it."

It was quiet. Nobody thought Ray would drop things. He'd studied the ground too seriously, checked back twice and smacked us around with questions. Shane wanted to know the plan for getting into the Jefferson stronghold. We laughed.

Andy jammed fists into his pockets. "As soon as you give us one, we got one."

We started to St. Luke's and Shane changed the subject. "My dad chewed me out pretty good last night about the Jefferson place. I got out of it. Told him we were on the other side of the street and a block passed it and the dogs took off for the clump of trees."

I said, "Your dad bought that?"

Shane's ears turned red. "'Bout like Ray bought your crap. My dad didn't even buy Jelly's hero stuff." He stopped walking. "Listen, Ray's like a drunk sheep dog but my dad is like an old lion with a tooth ache."

Andy pulled his fists out and flexed his fingers. "That's right. Better not piss your dad off."

We were half a block from St. Luke's. It was looming in the mist like a movie set. Fifteen minutes early, we sat on the steps fronting the archway entrance and Shane dropped his bomb.

"You won't believe what my dad told me last night." We leaned in and he spoke a touch above a whisper, "On his Jefferson shelter notes, he saw H.I.P.S. in the corner."

We inhaled. "What?"

He put up a hand. "On the way into the shelter that first day Jefferson said, 'Ask me about H.I.P.S. when we finish. You'll never believe what I got.' My dad said he scribbled the letters but by the time they went through all the other stuff he forgot to ask."

Andy thumped Shane's shoulder. "Wha'd you say?"

"He asked me if I knew anything about H.I.P.S. an' I played dumb."

Andy lifted his cap. "I thought the bomb shelter was the H.I.P.S."

****

Father Phillip appeared from around the corner, a bit of a surprise in his clerical clothing. I am not sure what we expected but he reacted. "Don't worry, it's just me. I look a little different in this stuff but, think of it as a uniform required for work. You know, Shane, like your dad's security guys."

We nodded and stood. Andy and Shane each grabbed an arm and lifted me. He led us down a long tiled walkway, passed colorful stained-glass windows, passed a number of small rooms with exterior doors, to an interior courtyard with picturesque Administrative and Chapel buildings. The tile walkways were clean but slick and the plant beds were also clean as well as rich and dark. Everything in the courtyard seemed aware of us and welcoming.

As we approached the door to the Administrative Building, Father Phillip paused and pointed ninety degrees to our right, highlighting a small adobe red-tiled residence flanked by the larger structures. It rested comfortably behind a shiny black wrought iron fence.

"That," he said, as he opened the office door, "is where I live."

We entered the admin building, met two smiling secretaries (one pretty, one plain) and followed the young priest with the movie star looks to his small but pleasant office. Adobe walls, dark polished desk, floor-to-ceiling bookcases, soft tan carpet, dark leather couch and chair in a corner seating area: All worked to make the space safe, interesting and timeless. There was no clock and there were no wall decorations except for the incredible stained glass window on the west side.

Father Phillip closed the door, ushered us to the corner couch and sat in its matching chair. Feet on the floor, hands on his knees, he welcomed us.

"Fellas, I'm glad you're here today. Can we get you something to drink? Soda, water, tea? Don't suppose you want coffee, eh?" He smiled.

We looked at each other and shook our heads.

I suddenly realized we were stuck.

Maybe this wasn't such a good idea. Do we even really care about this stuff? Scotty's dead. The Father is a nice guy but let's get this over and get outta here.

He turned to Shane. "I think you're the guy with the questions. Is that right?"

Shane took a paper from his shirt pocket. "Well, we all got these questions about Scotty and other stuff. I just wrote 'em down. We only got three questions now. At first, we had 'bout twenty. Wanna hear 'em?"

The handsome young priest nodded. "Fire away. Read all of them once and then we'll take them one at a time. By the way, you're probably wondering what you've gotten yourselves into here. Maybe a little doubt about the whole thing. Let me just say, we'll go quick, we won't beat any dead horses and I think you'll be glad you came."

We smiled and nodded.

Shane cleared his throat and read:

1. If you commit suicide, do you go to hell?

2. If God has all the power, why does he let bad stuff happen?

3. Why do bad people get away with stuff?

Father Phillip stood. "Excuse me, guys but I can tell I'm gonna get thirsty. So, I'm gonna get a soda. Sure I can't get you guys something?"

This time we gave our choices quickly.

"Okay," the priest smiled. "Two Cokes, plus mine, plus one Nehi Strawberry. Uh, Dr. Pepper if I can't find Nehi?"

A quick nod from Shane and the priest was gone.

Andy spoke, "You think he went out to try an' figure out the answers? I do. Why ask to hear all the questions first an' then leave? He's probly got some book somewhere or he's checking with his boss."

Shane and I laughed.

I blurted, "Are you nuts? He's a priest..."

Andy shrugged.

We were quiet for a few moments.

I changed the subject. "Think about Shane's dad's notes. There must be another H.I.P.S. and it must be slick 'cause Jefferson says, 'You'll never believe it.' What's down there, a body, a skeleton?"

Andy jumped in. "Whatever it is, it's gonna be almost impossible to find. When he says, 'you'll never believe it,' I think he means you'll never believe how good the place is hidden."

Shane stood and tucked his shirt. "You might both be right. There might be somethin' weird down there and it might be real hard to find. But, there's another thing we gotta think about. This is Tuesday. We gotta do Louie's letters and get 'em to his mom by tomorrow afternoon and we go back to school next Monday."

Andy's voice crackled, "We gotta do this now! School starts, they tear that place down. We gotta get in there tomorrow."

I threw water on his fire. "No, no, no. We gotta cool it for a day. We can't have any more crap right now. We need a normal boring day."

Suddenly, it was hot. We took off our jackets. Suddenly, we were glad cold drinks were on the way. Andy grabbed all three jackets, hung them on the cherry wood coat rack in the corner and returned.

Shane signed in. "I say we wait a day and go Thursday late night or early Friday. But, we get the stuff from Decker tomorrow and we ask our parents tomorrow about a sleep over in my garage on Thursday night. Askin' a day ahead, it's like candy."

I could see a plan. "We go by Decker's house after here an' we tell 'im bring the stuff to Shane's garage Thursday afternoon."

We banged knuckles together.

Suddenly, something bumped the door. Shane jumped and helped Father Phillip deliver the drinks. A quick drink or two and everyone settled in.

Father Phillip took his seat and looked in Andy's direction. "You'll all be glad to know that I checked all my answers in that big answer book I have in the next room and then I ran everything by my boss."

He paused a moment, to let his words sink in, then winked and said, "Gotcha!"

We laughed like crazy, Andy too. But, his ears were red. Everybody felt better after laughing, Father Phillip included.

We settled and he read the first question aloud. "If you commit suicide, do you go to hell?"

"The short, hard answer to your question is yes but it's more complicated. We do not know all the things God knows. We don't what's in someone's heart and all of the difficulties of his or her life. We don't know if someone was sick or simply made a mistake.

"But we do know some things about God. We know that God loves people beyond imagining. He knows the number of hairs on your head, has your name tattooed on the palm of his hand, knows your thoughts and feelings. He created and personally designed you.

"We know that God will be fair with people and do the right thing by them. God will do the right thing by Scotty."

Shane shifted his weight. "So, is he in hell or not?"

"If, in his heart, what Scotty wanted and chose was to take his life and separate from God forever then, yes, he's in hell. See, God believes in us, believes in our freedom to choose even if what we choose breaks His heart."

"So, he might be but he might not be?"

"Right. See, we know all the rules. We know the deal about suicide. What we don't know about is Scotty and what he was really doing. But,

God knows all that stuff. Bottom line, Scotty will get a fair deal. Like the Bible says in Genesis 18: 25: 'Shall not the judge of all the earth, do right?' In other words, won't God, the judge of everything, do the right thing? And, of course, we know He will."

Andy almost came out of his seat. "But, God is supposed to love people not send 'em to hell. There was a lot of stuff wrong with Scotty. That girl dumping him like that. But why would God send him to hell for falling in love with a married woman?"

The young priest held his ground. "I don't think that's what happened. God doesn't send anyone to hell: They all ask to go. They sign up. They get on the bus. And, if Scotty's there, that's what he did."

Andy looked like his head was about to explode. "What? Excuse me, Father but that makes no sense. Why would people choose hell? Nobody wants to burn forever."

The room was getting hot, prickly sweat on the back of my neck. Father Phillip stood, took a little walk around his chair, took a deep breath and jumped back in.

"I agree with you completely. It makes no sense. But, it's what people do. God says, 'Here are the rules, break them and you'll get hurt.' People do it anyway."

Andy wasn't done. "Why doesn't God just stop 'em? He could right? Like, if you were gonna get hurt and I could stop you, I should, right?"

"He could," said Father Phillip, "but, what's the point? Everybody's just a baby or a puppet. Then we aren't responsible for anything. Nothing's real. Everything's a play with all the parts written."

My jaw was tight and I had trouble making my legs relax and stay in place. "But, God does set things up. I didn't choose to be crippled and I don't think it's fair."

Father Phillip was sweating.

I was studying the floor.

They aren't paying this guy enough.

He said, "Well, we're kind of sliding into your next question so let's go there."

He carefully read question # 2 aloud. "If God has all the power, why does he let bad stuff happen?"

"Again, there is a short answer but it's complicated. Yes, God has all of the power, including the power to give some of His power away. And that's what He did. He gave us the power to make our own choices in a real world and see what happens, good or bad." He paused. "Now, you're right, God didn't give us complete freedom. He didn't give us all of the power— just enough to make us real. It's our little bit of freedom that makes us most real. So, it isn't that God lets bad stuff happen, it's that people choose to do bad stuff."

Shane took up my cause. "But, Randy didn't choose to be crippled. He didn't do anything wrong."

Father Phillip took a quick breath and finished with a bit of a forced smile. He was wiping his palms on his pants. "Let's back up a minute. I'll come back to Randy, if that's okay."

He made eye contact with me. "If you don't want to be in the spotlight here, I understand. Maybe you want to talk with me by yourself or with your friends or not at all. I just want you to be comfortable."

Before I could answer, Andy grabbed the space. "Hey, Father if he don't wanna talk, can we come in an' talk about him? 'Cause, sometimes he drives us crazy with this crap an' we got nothin'."

Father Phillip erupted into laughter, almost fell out of his chair. So, we laughed too. As if on cue, I got slugged from both sides. It felt good and sweet but I still complained.

Once the emotional landscape was replanted, the young priest (getting older by the moment) continued. "Boys, one of my rules is we don't talk about folks who aren't here to give their side of things. If you want to come in and talk about your feelings, that's fair."

It was my turn. "I might talk to you and I might bring these guys. But, I'll tell ya right now, anything these jokers tell you about me when I'm not here, forget it."

He held up his hands in self-defense. "We are getting to the end of our time here so let me touch on a few things about your last two questions."

We all took a drink.

How does he know our time is about up? I see no watch.

"So, here's the deal. People get some freedom and so they are responsible for their choices. If we never get to choose, we never really live. Think about the story of Pinocchio: He's a wooden puppet who comes to life because his father Geppetto loves him so much and wishes for it. Now, the little puppet wants more than simple animation. He wants to be a real boy. Do you guys remember how Pinocchio becomes a real boy?"

Shane answered. "He got mixed up with the wild boys, did bad stuff an' got donkey ears. Uh, I think he turned into a donkey an' ended up trapped in a whale with his father an' then he saved everybody."

The young priest grinned. "That's good but what makes the little puppet a real boy?"

Now I grabbed the floor. "I got it. He gets a conscience about his lying an' cares more about his father than himself."

Father Phillip clapped his hands. "Right! And if Geppetto never lets Pinocchio make real choices and get banged around a bit, he never learns right from wrong and just stays little pieces of wood that move. Geppetto didn't let bad stuff happen. He gave Pinocchio freedom."

Father Phillip took one more swing at the piñata of human suffering. "Randy, let me ask you a question."

I nodded. "OK."

"Okay, here's the situation. You are playing tackle football and you are on defense, linebacker. The play starts. What are you supposed to do?"

"There are certain people I watch."

"Exactly, now suppose you see guards pulling and the whole world coming around left end with the ball carrier in there somewhere. What are you supposed to do?"

"Get to that corner as fast as I can."

"And do what?"

"Stop the whole world."

The priest paused and cleared his throat. "Now, let me just say, your answers are perfect so far. But, how do you stop the whole world?"

"When I get to the corner, I lay out. I dive into the path of that mob and create a pile."

"What if the ball carrier gets through?"

"Not my problem, other people behind me better do their jobs."

"What if you get hurt?"

"So what? This is what's fun! It's what you wait for. Like breaking Bobby Blazer's nose. You know what we say, Father, 'if you're scared you better bring a dog.'"

Father Phillip leaned forward. "Don't you want your mommy to save you? Don't you want your coach to stop you from getting hurt? Don't you want God to stop this? Why are you even being allowed to do something that might hurt you? Aren't you already hurt enough?"

Suddenly, my face and ears were on fire and I was having trouble finding my voice.

Father Phillip waited and nobody breathed. I could feel my heart pounding. I looked around. Shane and Andy were looking away. Father Phillip did not release his gaze.

I whispered, "No."

The young priest whispered, "No, what?"

"No, I don't want to be kept safe. I want to be a real boy."

Andy said, "Me too."

Shane said, "And me."

Father Phillip leaped from his chair and hugged each of us and shook our hands.

He had tears in his eyes. "Just a couple of quick things. The kindest thing that God can do for people who want nothing to do with Him or his rules is to respect their wishes and their choices. That is, let them go to hell. It would be much worse to force them to be in the presence of the most powerful being the universe if they are not on His team. The point is people are real and their choices matter."

Shane raised his hand. "But, God does forgive people, right?"

Father Phillip smiled. "He does. But forgiveness doesn't change the world, it only changes people."

Shane was lost.

The Father added a bit. "Shane, if you get drunk and cut off your arm with a chainsaw and you get to the hospital and you survive, God will love you and forgive you, if you ask. But, he will not give you a new arm. You are a real boy and you must live with your choices in a real world."

Shane nodded. "I think I get it."

Andy said, "Don't worry, Randy and I got it."

Father Phillip smiled again. "And, as for your last question, Shane, about people getting away with bad stuff, let me just say, forever is a long time. God catches up with everybody: Now or in the afterlife. Nobody gets away."

We all chimed in. That made sense. Andy got our jackets and we stood to leave.

Father Phillip looked older and I wondered if we did.

He asked, "Do you guys know why I hugged you?"

Andy was quick. "'Cause we understand why God doesn't save us from every hard thing or…"

"That's it," he beamed.

As we started to leave, he offered to walk us to the Admin doors. He also said that he knew he still had a lot of explaining to do about why bad things happen to people who don't deserve it.

We agreed to meet again soon. Father Phillip said we should let him know.

****

We stepped out into the cold and sloppy afternoon, left the inside courtyard and followed the tiled walkway to the front of St. Luke's. We reviewed our plan: letters for Louie, tools from Decker and Thursday night sleep over at Shane's. I said I thought Decker was going to be a problem unless we could find a way to get him in on things.

Shane was skeptical and Andy was a dead "No way." We agreed to go home and write a letter to Louie and talk tomorrow. We walked together as far as we could and then went our separate ways.

I surprised my mother by coming in the front door at 4:15, alone. She was in the kitchen, chopping something. She asked about Rocket and I gave her the good report. She was very pleased to hear that we had been at St. Luke's in the afternoon for a talk with the new priest.

"I heard about him," she smiled. "They say he looks just like Troy Donahue, that movie star."

"Uh huh, he does."

"What did you talk about?"

"About Pinocchio and bein' a real boy, not a puppet."

She raised her eyebrows but went right along with her chopping. She gave me permission to watch TV but I told her I had to write a letter to Louie. As soon as I said the word "letter," she stopped her chopping, wiped her hands and handed me an envelope.

She was very interested. "Somebody must have just stuck it in the box. There's no stamp or return address. I bet it's a love letter from some cute girl."

I wasn't so sure.

"Well, aren't you going to open it?"

"First, I gotta write Louie."

My mom shook her head. "Boys."

I went to my room, opened the letter and read. There was no greeting, date or signature. The paper and envelope were cheap and plain.

It was printed by a thick, felt pen.

Leave the Jefferson place alone. I can hit what I want. I want the dog dead and the dog is dead. None of this concerns you or your friends. All you are going to do is get yourself or your friends hurt. Don't show this letter to anyone.

I was shaking. I tried to fold the letter and get it back in the envelope.
I had no idea of what to do.

Chapter 32
The Good Old Days

It took some minutes for my brain, hands and breathing to team up again and suddenly my eyes and ears left the reservation. Everything fuzzy, ears chugging like a freight train. My thoughts were pistol shots ricocheting in a box canyon.

Tell my mom? Call Ray? Talk to Father Phillip? Call Andy and Shane?

I pulled my jig-sawed self together, hid the letter in my math book (Nobody looks in math books.) and headed toward the living room telephone. Halfway down the hall, a hard thump hit the front door followed by a stringy doorbell. I stopped in my tracks. My mom answered and Andy and Shane stepped inside. One shared look and I suggested the big tree out front.

It was nearing five o'clock, sun closing up shop. We sat on the bricks lining the flower bed and stared at the big tree. It was quiet. Looking at us, the old tree saw three shaken faces matching three identically scary letters.

Andy began pacing, fists in pockets. "This is big trouble. This is a direct threat."

I chuckled. "It's a 'die-rect' threat alright."

Andy grimaced. "Very funny but I ain't laughin'."

Shane had a different idea. "Suppose this is just some crap from somebody?"

Andy continued pacing. "We gotta think this through."

For the next ten minutes, we squeezed out as many questions as we could and tried to reach an agreement about what to do.

1. Is this a Decker joke?

2. Is this Blazer or somebody else from that bunch?

3. Is this Ray?

4. Is this the mysterious stranger from Scotty's bedroom?

5. Is this Scotty's dad?

6. Is this somebody we don't know?

7. Is this from those telephone voices?

8. What if we drop everything?

9. Should we report the letter?

10. What is hidden at the Jefferson place?

The idea that the letter was a Decker or Blazer joke was possible but not likely. Each was dumb enough or mean enough but making written threats didn't fit either of them.

Every other suspect slapped us with the same question. Why?

Suddenly, Andy snapped his fingers. "Are the McKinleys back? They'd do this crap in a New York minute."

Shane skipped a rock across the street. "They'd hurt the dog but they can barely write their names. Besides, both are still in jail."

Andy tried again. "What about their old man? We made his kids look bad."

Shane asked, "Who says, 'New York minute?'"

I sighed. "Uncle Billy."

Andy rolled his eyes. "You guys don't buy old man McKinley?"

I said, "They've always been bad, why would the old man care now? I don't think he could shoot a bow if you paid him and the printing on the letters is way too good for him."

Shane asked, "Could the guy you saw in Scotty's room be old man McKinley?"

Andy shrugged. "Why would he be up there?"

Shane smiled. "Maybe there's some ugly secret about the McKinleys and Scotty."

I scratched my head. "That makes no sense. Scotty killed himself over a woman. How could those fools be involved?"

Without warning, Shane took us in another direction. "Could the mysterious stranger in Scotty's room be the guy who met with him at the diner, the one who showed him pictures?"

Andy sat next to me. "Gotta talk to Daisy and compare."

I asked, "What if you draw a picture?"

Andy grinned. "Who knows? I might win a contest."

We beat on these questions like a tar baby and came to a few ragged conclusions:

1. No matter the threat, we had to finish this.

2. The truth was somewhere in that bomb shelter.

Our more immediate problem was Pete Decker, and I had a solution.

"Let him in on everything and ask him to play two parts: lookout and getaway driver."

Andy was fussing with his cap. "Won't be enough. He'll want to go down there."

Shane said, We tell him everything, he'll blackmail us. He'll be out of control."

Andy grimaced. "We all know he's a bully."

I tried again. "You guys are right, Decker's a jerk. But, I think we're stuck."

My backside was hurting. Andy pulled me up fast. I caught myself and steadied up. Everything was stiff and cold.

Suddenly, I had an idea.

There might be a way through this.

I cleared my throat and put more push in my voice. "I know Decker can be a butt. He pisses me off, too. But, I don't think the guy wants to be a bully. I think he wants to be a hero."

Andy dug in. "Decker wants to be a muscle-bound jerk. Why do you think he can't get along with anybody? We said it all before. He's always alone and there's a reason."

Shane piled on. "His head is as paralyzed as his legs. You should get that."

I took a deep breath and talked into the dark. "The guy who wanted to be a priest, wanted it so bad he still hates 'em today. I say, we let him help us. Something quick where he gets to be strong, be a hero."

Andy's eyes narrowed. "What strong, hero thing?"

I talked fast. "He uses the bolt cutters, breaks the lock, helps lift the hatch and closes it once we're inside and helps lift it when we leave. He's fast and the ground won't bother him."

From the front door, my mom yelled, "Dinner."

We agreed to stay quiet about the letter, ask for a Thursday night sleepover and meet at Shane's tomorrow morning.

Shane yelled, "Louie letters" as he disappeared into the dark.

I walked to the front door, fresh out of ideas. In the warm cheerful kitchen, the scary letter seemed more like noise from Old Man Crotch.

Maybe this time next year the Jefferson mystery will seem simple. Old Crotch, what a—

My mother jolted me. "Don't sit! Wash your hands."

Scrubbing dirt from my fingers, I laughed out loud.

****

The images came up easy: The neighborhood at its crazy best. It was one of those endless, numbered summer days and I was bored: My cue to hit the front yard. I could almost taste the heat. Mid July, late afternoon, 112 degrees and at least 100 under the massive Modesto Ash parked near our curb. Gracefully shading the bigger parts of our yard and the street, it was fifty feet tall.

Stationed at the tree's base, I waited in ambush for the yellow jackets, their stingers no match for my fully-loaded garden hose and spray-gun. The wasps knew my range but I knew their attention span. I turned my sights on two unsuspecting enemies.

It was dripping hot.

I took aim and squeezed the nozzle.

Instantly, an explosion rocked the block—a deafening boom that knocked both me and the yellow jackets off course.

I looked in all directions.

Left over 4th of July?

My ears were ringing and it was raining glass on the lawn, the flowerbed, the driveway and the street. I dropped the hose and it wriggled across the lawn like a green cobra with a silver head. I looked for blood but I seemed to be okay.

In a few seconds, Old Man Crotch burst onto his driveway and exploded.

He looked at me, pointed at the crystallized, jagged hole that used to be the rear window of his old car and screamed, "Boy, you done played hell, now ain'tcha? Wait 'til your daddy gets home an' finds out you done broke the windows outta my car! Throwin' your damn rocks! He'll wear you out boy! Bust your ass good! Where's all your friends now? Runaway, I spose."

I didn't say a word.

He's gonna stroke out!

He was scraping through glass, almost stalking. But he never left his driveway.

I walked to the edge of the flower bed. I could see that every window in his old Ford was blown out, including the windshield. Apparently, Old Crotch's clunker couldn't take one more second of July heat.

He kept pacing.

I thought.

You shoulda stayed in your old house down by the cul-de-sac. Down there your car was in the shade. I liked the Robinsons. I wish they still lived next door. Aaron was retarded but at least he was sweet.

He was wiping his skinny face and neck with a handkerchief, breathing hard, coughing and spitting. His 32 caliber pistol was nowhere in sight. Eyes bloodshot, speech clear for a drunk, he was standing strong.

He smiled, wild-eyed, dried spittle crusting the corners of his mouth. "Your daddy gonna whip your ass with a razor strap, boy! You can't go 'round raisin' all this hell, destroyin' an' think you'll get away with it just 'cause your crippled!"

He kept wiping his face and mouth.

Finally, I defended myself. "I'm sorry, Mr. Kellen, but I didn't break your windows and I never threw rocks."

He cleared his throat, coughed hard and spat again. "The hell you didn't! Broke every Goddamn window in my car!"

I said, "Rocks didn't break your windows."

His eyes became hard. He studied the glass confetti. I stayed quiet. Neighbors were spilling into the street asking questions. I told them what I could. As soon as old Crotch saw them, he shuffled into his house.

A look or two and the evidence spoke for itself. Satisfied, the crowd disappeared as quickly as it had appeared. My mom missed the commotion and spent a few minutes getting the story from Mrs. Shirley next door. On her way inside, she gave her standard "I don't care what he says, you leave that old man alone, don't back talk and don't torment him" speech.

I looked down, except for when I was supposed to look up. This was not a conversation.

Suddenly, I was alone with the yellow-jackets, the hose and the heat. I carefully picked a spot, dropped to my knees, propped myself up with my left cane and began slowly picking glass from the lawn and tossing it to Old Crotch's driveway. I had to clear the lawn and flower bed. I knew my dad.

I reached for a big chunk of glass and heard a loud thump behind me.

I glanced over my shoulder. The white-haired albino, Bobby Blazer, hit the ground, rolled and stood. Jean shorts, no shoes and white tee shirt, he looked like a cross between a vampire and a newly-hatched, alien chicken.

Watery, blue-veined skin, beady eyes, beak nose, thin mouth and baby teeth, he gave me the creeps.

His voice was weak. "Hey, Randy," he cackled, "Just thought I'd drop by. Just flew in from about twenty-five feet."

"You jumped from twenty-five feet?"

"Naw, I was up there about twenty-five feet before all the explodin' started an' I just now climbed down an' dropped the last ten feet."

"Whada you want?"

"Me? Nothin'. I was just thinkin' what an old crap-faced crank Kellen is."

I stood, moved about five feet toward the flowerbed, turned and faced Bobby. Standing under the tree, he was my height, but spindly, like a puppet.

"Uh huh," I said, "he's a crank alright."

His eyes narrowed. "I'm gonna finish the job on that old clunker. Let air outta them tires an' bang on his door 'til he'll comes out again."

He reached in his pocket and held up a small screwdriver in a fake toast.

His eyes were dancing. "Here's to Kellen's ole clunker, R.I.P."

I took a baseball stance and shifted my weight to be able to swing with speed and force. I studied him for a moment and for the first time I saw something girlish and fragile. I had seen his cowardice before but this was a surprise.

I laughed.

He brought the screwdriver down to his waist. "You think it's funny, right? I mean, the tires and messin' with the old man? I heard about the shit he give you that day. Man that was outta line."

Our eyes locked. I wiped my palm and the handle of my cane on my shirttail. "You're the one who's funny."

His whole body went slack, hands at his sides. He grinned, turned away, started to take a step, let out a big sigh and turned back. He tried to look fierce: Tough assignment for a vampire-skinned, chicken-faced loser.

He spat. "Eat shit crippled boy. Gonna cane me to death?"

I grinned like it was Christmas. "Albino asshole."

Bobby looked around. His situation was complicated. To get to the old car, he had to run through a glass-spiked lawn, past me trying to whack him silly, through a glass-filled flower bed and across a glass-covered driveway, without shoes. After that, he had to carefully let the air out of each tire while I stood by just out of his range and caned him to death.

I gave him some friendly advice. "This would be a good time for you to scrape up a few IQ points in a bag and figure something out. You might push me down but I will hit you at least once with this cane and I promise you, I will hit you as hard as I can."

He made a big deal out of spitting. "Shit! I'll just pick up some glass and start throwin'."

I wiped my face on my shirt and belly-laughed. "Go ahead! Pick up glass in your bare hands throw it while you're running away. That what you want? Everybody knowing you ran away from me? You throw once and I'll be close enough to hit or tackle you. And, I swear, I will hurt you."

Bobby leaned against the tree and laughed, his greasy white hair dripping. "You're all talk, crippled boy. We should get Decker over here. Neighborhood Crippled Olympics."

I was getting tired of standing in the sun. "Do something, Bobby! One of us needs to shut up."

He was quiet. So I pushed. "Difference between you and me is that you don't wanna get hurt. Me, I don't mind gettin' hurt. I don't care."

Bobby threw his hands in the air, slapped his thighs and grimaced. "Come on. You don't even like the old man! Whada you care about his tires? I'm just gonna have a little fun."

I yelled each word slowly. "I—like—his—tires."

Before Bobby could answer, I heard a familiar voice behind me. "Can anybody get in this game?"

Andy walked passed me. He was adjusting his cap. Shane stopped just to my right.

The albino raised his hands and squawked. "This ain't fair! You guys know that."

Shane smiled and jerked his thumb in my direction. "Uh, we're here to make sure he don't kill you. We know how he can be."

Andy continued walking, stood next to Bobby and patted him on the back. "Go ahead, take care of business Bobby. Don't let us bother you. Go on, knock him out. Kick his butt. We'll make sure it's fair. We won't let him run away."

Bobby laughed and put the tiny screwdriver in his pocket. "Shit, I ain't gonna fight nobody. I'm a lover, not a fighter. Everybody knows that. Besides, I gotta be gettin' home."

He laughed: thin and high-pitched.

I taunted. "This is a big day for vampire-skinned, chicken-faced boy. After gettin' me and old Kellen, he's goin' over to the elementary school and wreck the little kids' toys."

Andy's laughter exploded. 'Vampire-skinned, chicken-faced boy!' Is that what you said?"

Shane's grin now showed all his braces.

I tipped my imaginary cap. "I try to please."

Suddenly, Andy delivered a hard, two-handed shove to Bobby's chest. The little puppet folded like an accordion and cowered on the ground. Andy grabbed an arm, jerked him to his feet, spun him around and shoved him into the street. Bobby cursed a blue streak, hopped around on the 112 degree asphalt and took off.

We huddled up under the tree. Andy apologized for butting in. Said he hated the albino so much he couldn't help himself.

I asked, "How'd you get here?"

Shane said, "We heard the big blast."

Andy added, "He was scared crapless like he always is."

I grabbed the hose and blasted the bees. "He couldn't get around me and get to those tires. Glass everywhere. Jerk had no shoes!"

Shane wiped his forehead. "You mighta hurt him with that cane."

Andy laughed. "Unless you hit his head! I dunno how it can be that hard when it's that empty."

I laughed. "His head's not empty, it's full of crap."

We decided to get a rake, a shovel, a bucket and a broom and take care of the glass. Shane took the broom, knocked on Kellen's door and told him we were going to clean up his driveway. He nodded and closed his door. Later, Shane came by, a pile of glass in tow. He was sure that the old man had heard him.

For the record, the old man never reported to my father and never repaired the car.

****

I was drying my hands when my mother's voice jolted me back into Tuesday night and a current mystery more complicated than a double steal with a suicide squeeze.

I walked down the hallway toward the kitchen.

Bobby Blazer will never be a real boy. No wonder it was such fun to break his nose.

I returned to the table more concerned about what to say to Louie than any scary letter. My mother asked about Louie's father and I said I thought Mrs. Kerensky was alone. My mom called her "a poor thing," said she was proud of us for writing letters to Louie and asked me if I thought Mrs. K. was rich.

Mouth full, I shrugged.

My mother shook her head. "How can you not notice? You notice everything."

I shrugged again.

My mother began clearing the table and setting aside a plate for my dad. "I just don't see how she can make it alone. Maybe her parents are helping."

I finished my mashed potatoes and handed over my plate and silverware. "I think I heard Louie say that he was adopted and when his mom was asking us to write letters, she said something about how she wanted Louie even if nobody else did."

My mom began wiping the table, pointed me toward the sink and raked table scraps into her left hand. "All the more amazing! My hat's off to her. You be sure and write that letter."

I began rinsing dishes. "It's Tuesday. Can I watch 'Dobie Gillis' and then write the letter?"

"Finish these dishes first."

My mom left the kitchen and I moved through the dishes. My hands were busy and my mind floated toward Bobby and another kid.

Sometimes it is fun to hurt people, even people who don't deserve it. Bobby deserves it each and every time... But, that kid Timmy. The kid with the thing that makes your head too big... Hydro something. He wasn't a bad kid, just quiet and soft. I picked on him, talked mean. Even slugged him in the back once for no reason.

That's not true. I had a reason... I hated his weakness: his soft voice, his thin bones, his cartoon forehead and slender fingers and his sad eyes. And I hated that he walked so carefully, like a giant-headed balloon in a Thanksgiving Day parade. I hated that he gave grown up answers in a little boy's voice.

When I first hurt him, I felt good and strong. But later, I felt sorry and even more now. I wish I could take it back. The day I hurt him, Timmy was the hero, the real boy, not me. I was wrong. I was worse than Bobby. I have thought and thought and thought. I do not know why it felt good to hurt Timmy, to shame him, but it did.

I tried to watch Dobie, but I couldn't. Same old stupid story. He wants her, she wants money.

Which one of them is more stupid? Easy. He is. It's wrong to fool others, but it's always worse to fool yourself. Dobie's problem is always the same. No matter how bad Thalia is, she is always a bit more beautiful than he is smart. Dobie's never gonna be a real boy, either.

****

Writing to Louie should have been easy but it wasn't. Suddenly, I wasn't at all sure he could read. He didn't read any Scotty letters at the diner. It bothered me just enough, like a stiff label inside the collar of a new shirt.

I didn't trust my words coming to Louie through someone else's eyes. So, I wrote a phony letter, a letter that could have been from anyone to no one. I could see the puppet strings between the lines.

My mom read it and said it was fine. She said I was a good friend to Louie. But, I knew better. I knew that good friends write real things. So I shredded the phony letter and wrote a real one.

I read it over and the hair on the back of my neck tingled.

Dear Louie,

I hope you don't die. I hope you get to come home soon. I miss you. It was great when you made us laugh in the parade. You looked perfect in your Uncle Sam stuff. I laughed so hard. I loved it when you won the game of War and told Jim he didn't have to get in the bag. That made you a real good guy, buddy. Also, I will never forget what you said to me at the Diner. You are the reason I got my first real kiss. Remember Daisy?

If you do die, I hope you go to heaven. Father Phillip says God is fair to people. If He is, you got no worries. You never acted like a baby or a jerk. Please get well Louie. Nobody can take your place.

You're friend,

Randy

PS. You got a real nice mom. She loves you.

My mom asked to read the second letter before I put it in an envelope. She got tears in her eyes and said she hoped the other letters were half as good as mine and if they were Louie would be well in no time.

I did not understand.

If letters can get people well, why don't we just write a million of 'em?

I asked her how that could be. She just rolled her eyes. "You know what I mean."

I told her again that I didn't understand how writing a nice letter could help Louie get well. She fussed a bit and told me that I would understand it better when I was older and that if I wanted to understand it sooner I should think about it more.

So, I did.

If it works, why doesn't my mom just write a letter for me? Pretty sure you can't write for yourself... Maybe I should try it... No, really stupid. Dobie Gillis stupid.

I got ready for bed and asked my mother about a sleepover at Shane's on Thursday. She hesitated but agreed. She was so happy with my letter to Louie. I asked her again how the letter could help him get well. She said part of getting well is wanting to and my letter might make him want to. That made some sense but not enough.

I went to bed with a radio full of fantasy, a head full of questions and a heart full of dreams.

Why does everything seem to work just a little but not all the way and not all the time? Try hard every time, on every pitch. Some work, some don't. Pray for stuff, mostly doesn't work. But it worked for Rocket. What is praying? Is it super-wanting? Being nice only works sometimes. Why not every time? Scotty was nice...

Softly, my Cherokee grandfather, Grandpa Starr (my mother's father) stepped into my thoughts. Jet black hair, bright blue eyes, copper-red skin, high cheek bones and hawk-like nose, he left the Indian reservation in Oklahoma at age 19, refused to register with the Bureau of Indian Affairs and married my grandmother, a white woman with a French background.

I went with him on his job once, irrigating crops. I sat at the beginning of a row while he used a long iron rod to turn on water and walked the row to check the flow. We did this row after row all day. To me, my grandfather was a big man. In fact, he was a tiny 5'4".

We ate lunch in the shade of his old truck, parked on the dirt road separating the fields. I asked him about praying and if Indians prayed.

He walked to the head of a row, grabbed a fist full of mud, walked back, sat on the running board and held both hands open, palms up.

I will never forget what he said. "Stuff one hand with mud and the other with wishes and see which one fills first."

He walked back to the bubbler at the head of the row, rinsed his hands, dried them on his khaki pants and asked if I understood what he meant.

I hesitated and nodded. He smiled, pushed his false teeth out and popped them back in.

He showed me both of his empty hands. "Prayers," he said, "are wishes. They fly in the smoke of a fire and they ride in the dust of horses."

He told me not to say any of this to my grandmother or my parents.

I went to sleep with Drifters beautiful, "Please Come Home for Christmas." The Wolfman howled and then whispered in his Hall of Fame voice, "Ladies and Gentlemen, the fantastic Drifters. Keepin' Christmas goin' 'til New Years. Here on the Wolfman Jack Show."

I wondered about Scotty and Louie and Decker. I wondered about Timmy.

I wondered what was in Scotty Jefferson's secret place.

But, most of all, I wondered if God really was fair.

Chapter 33
The Best Laid Plans

WEDNESDAY WAS SUPPOSED to be a "lay low" day, a slow everything down, stay out of trouble, deliver letters to Louie's mom and make plans for Thursday night's attack, day. I opened my eyes, glanced at the desk, saw Mickey's hands sneaking up on 7:00 AM and tried to make sense out of bits and pieces of last night's messy sleep.

****

I was at a carnival or a county fair: Dust-filled walkways marked by hay bales, a midway stuffed with early evening lights, colors, smells and sounds. But, something wasn't right, like the kink in an elbow that needs to be popped. For one thing, I wasn't walking. I was floating about ten feet off the ground, a giant balloon in a Macy's Parade. For another, the folks below me seemed to be moving normally but getting nowhere.

I was thinking.

This should feel creepy but I feel nothing.

To my right, Scotty's voice was waving people into a tent to see "D.G. the Bearded Lady."

Surrounded by life-sized posters of Delores in a sheer body suit and fake beard, Scotty was dressed in white pants, stripped jacket, white shirt, red bow tie, straw hat and plaster-thick white make up.

His blood-red lips moved but his voice was a second or so late. He paid no attention to me.

I could not control my floating and the night swallowed my voice. A dark-blue Keystone Cop, Ray stood at one side of the tent entrance. A silver and pale-blue ballerina, Daisy stood on the other side, taking tickets. As the scene faded, I saw Bobby Blazer, the jester, (in stunning red and blue velvet) stroll by carrying his head under his left arm.

****

I shook these images, dressed, ate breakfast, told my mom I was delivering my letter to Louie and hit the front door headed to Shane's. It was another dirty misty day of gray changeless drizzle. I passed Purdy, the devil-eyed goat and smacked her chain-link fence as hard as I could. I wanted to give her a bloody nose. Though she never turned her head, her spooky eyes followed me.

I passed the fire station.

Nobody out this morning.

I cut between the Chambliss and Dover houses and came out on Shane's street. I smiled every time I passed the Dover place.

I could not resist and it never got old.

She's gotta name her next kid, Ben.

I arrived at Shane's and knocked on the door. We went down the hall and into the garage. He took one couch, I took the other. I handed over my letter.

He put it with a stack of others on the pool table. "I got everybody's, except Andy. Louie's mom's comin' by to pick 'em up after 2:00 today."

I said I hoped the letters would help. We talked about whether or not Louie could read. We weren't sure. But, we agreed that we had to write him a good letter no matter what.

Shane asked, "How do you know your letter is good?"

I shifted on the couch. "Stuff happens. Hair goes up on the back of my neck."

Shane nodded. "Mine made my mom cry."

"Yeah, mine too."

A quick knock on the side door and Andy entered. He tossed his letter on the pile, added one more "mom crying about Louie" story and then asked the big question of the morning.

"What about Decker?" He answered his own question. "I thought and thought and there ain't nobody else to ask about it. I just don't know. I'm beat, boys."

Shane stacked and rubber-banded the letters and started for the door. "Give these to my mom 'case we aren't here when Mrs. K. comes by." He stopped in his tracks. "What about Father Phillip? He's cool and since he's a priest everything we say stays private. It's the law."

We stared.

Shane shrugged. "Be right back."

Andy kept pacing. "This is gettin' too messed up… Dogs hurt… threats…" He pointed a finger at me and his eyes lit up. "And, what's even worse, we been warned. Ray, Shane's dad, take your pick."

I sighed. "I know. We got warned and things are messed up. But, do I really think Decker's gonna let us off the hook?" I shook my head. "He's gonna think we're lyin'. He'll think we're gettin' stuff from somebody else an' tellin' him to buzz off. An' then, he'll go there by himself."

Andy said, "He does, it's on him."

I raised my voice, "You know what he'd call you if he was here right now? A candy-ass flake."

Andy sat on the arm of the other couch. "I couldn't care less."

At that moment, Shane returned, grabbed both my arms and pulled me up. "Your mom's on the phone."

We looked at each other. Mothers never call for good. You're getting a call, you're in trouble. Better start thinking of excuses or a few good lies.

I started toward the hall, Shane and Andy in tow. "Where you guys goin'?"

Andy said, "We might be able to help."

Shane was nodding. "Yeah, brothers... you know."

I looked at the ceiling. "Dip sticks! You can't help me on the phone. That only works in person."

Andy did not give up. "We'll be right there, just hold the phone out so we can hear."

Shane pulled my sleeve. "Whatever you do, don't lie."

We reached the kitchen. Shane's mom handed the receiver to me, herded everybody out and left to put clothes in the wash.

My mom was worried. Daisy had called and relayed a message from Reggie. "Have Randy stop by this afternoon for a short talk."

My mom wanted to know "right now, young man," exactly what trouble I had caused. She was convinced something was wrong. I told her things were fine, Reggie was always nice and he probably just wanted my opinion on a contest or something. She threatened me with "something worse than death" if I wasn't telling the truth. I told her not to worry. If anything was wrong, Reggie would've called her and banned me from the diner for life. I didn't know anything else to say.

She sighed, told me to be polite and to come straight home after. When I returned to the garage, the talk was still on Decker.

Andy was pacing. "We're screwed. Better get a plan and get over to Decker's. I don't even remember how he got in on this."

I groaned. "My fault. He was the first guy I thought of when I thought about tools."

Andy sat on the edge of the pool table. "Shoulda used Jim or Tim. They can get tools easy." Suddenly, he shifted. "Hey, wha'd your mom say? Big trouble?"

I paused, "Uh, I don't think so, not really."

I explained about Daisy's call and the meeting with Reggie and we agreed that we should all go. We spun the Reggie deal like a top, but no matter how we turned it, we hit a dead end. We did agree on one thing: We would drink water and even then, only if offered.

That decided, we were back to Decker.

Shane reached under the pool table and grabbed his notebook. "Doesn't matter how we got Decker. We got no time. Gotta get a plan."

Andy nodded. "So, start. What should we do?"

Shane pointed to me. "Decker as a hero will work."

Andy was rubbing his forehead like he had a headache. "Get in, get out, okay. But, no getaway. We mostly need him as a lookout."

Shane wanted to make a list of tools and other supplies.

I disagreed. "First, let's decide who's goin'. We need more than Decker."

We haggled a long time and decided we needed everybody except Jesse. He was too hard to control.

Shane left to call everybody about the sleepover while Andy and I worked on the details of getting into the Jefferson shelter.

Folded neatly inside his notebook, Shane had his father's notes. As Andy turned the page, they fell out. We began reviewing them. A few things jumped out to us:

1. Buried underground. Double-entry hatches.

2. Eighteen inch thick walls.

3. Entrance—sharp turn.

H.I.P.S. You'll never believe what I got.'

Andy scribbled on a new page and folded and replaced Shane's dad's notes.

Shane returned with good news. "Everybody will be here tomorrow. Called Jelly. Rocket is good an' we should come by an' visit him."

I stuck my hand up. "Gotta do this stuff first and then Rocket."

Andy nodded toward the notebook and pointed to the inside pocket. "How'd you get the notes?"

Shane grinned and whispered, "I know the safe combination."

Andy dug inside the notebook and handed them over. "Already copied everything we need."

Shane was up in a flash and returned breathing easier.

Andy repeated his earlier warning. "Better not piss off your dad. We do, we're dead, Fred."

I barked. "We better not get caught!"

We laughed and got down to business.

Shane picked up his notebook. "I thought out a basic plan. Leave at 2:00 AM, walk to the shelter. Decker is waiting with tools in his trunk, helps lift hatch. In and out in twenty minutes and back home."

He finished, paused and looked up. "Whadaya think?"

We gave him a thumbs up. But, we wrestled with the details. Counting Decker, we had a team of eight: four inside searching and four outside doing lookout. We finished main and back-up plans and stared at the page.

Shane spoke for all of us. "Feels weird. Like we aren't really gonna do it."

I mumbled, "Lots of stuff goin' on and we been warned."

Andy was still thinking about the plans. "If you guys are scared, we don't have to do this. Shane, you tell the guys what this was about?"

Shane shook his head. "I only told Jim because we need masks for going inside. But nobody else knows anything."

Andy paced in front of the pool table. "So, if we want, we can quit this thing anytime all through tomorrow. Nobody ever knows the difference." He snapped his fingers. "Twenty minutes! We barely get in there. Make it thirty. Somebody can give the hatch a tap and we're outta there. And, if there's an' emergency let's have Decker fake a bad horn, like it won't turn off. No cop or passer-by can ignore that."

I declared, "I don't know how many steps are in there, but I'm goin' in if I have to crawl."

Shane said he didn't think there were more than five or six and Andy said there was a good chance for handrails.

He patted my shoulder. "Either way, we'll get you in and out."

Shane shrugged. "We could leave him out there with Decker..."

I threw a cane at Shane and missed. We started to make a list of tools/ supplies and something popped into my head. "We need two or three feather dusters and a can or two of bug spray."

Shane scribbled and we had a complete list in no time. Andy left to call Decker and we went over what to do in an emergency. We wondered if guys would follow the plan or just break and run. It was exciting to think of guys being chased by Ray. Secretly, we almost wanted it to happen.

The final plans were simple.

PLAN A

1. Post lookout at corner with whistle.

2. Find and clear hatch doors.

3. Decker cuts lock.

4. WD 40 on hatches.

5. Rope through hatch handles and lift.

6. Inside team thirty minutes. (Hatch closed)

7. Inside team comes out. (Hatch open)

8. Close hatch, cover up, collect tools go home.

PLAN B (Emergency)

1. Whistle warning.

2. Decker parked at corner/draws attention.

3. Inside team stays, outside team covers hatch and hides.

A few minutes later Andy bounced in. Decker was waiting for us 'with questions' and we better get a move on. But, he took one look at the plans and asked us a question.

"One big thing wrong with all of this. You guys see it?"

Shane and I looked at each other.

He teased us. "It's as plain as the noses on your faces."

We studied the page.

Suddenly, I shouted, "We need another step! After the inside team comes out, they switch and let the outside team go in! The whole point is to see inside the shelter."

Andy screamed, "Bingo! Those guys would be so pissed they'd go in anyway."

****

It was eleven blocks to Decker's. I wanted to go by and whack old Purdy in the nose, but I got overruled. We decided that the only way to have a chance with Decker was to tell him everything.

He lived with his parents on the top of a tiny hill on a small lot in a shaky old two-story mess. It leaned left as if fighting an imaginary fifty mile an hour wind. More than "personality," it seemed alive in a cartoon way, like Casper the Friendly Ghost's house. Scrubby, straggling trees lined the looping concrete driveway leading to an open carport, near the front door. Every growing thing was struggling and it wasn't a simple winter sleep. Here, things struggled year round. Empty, abandoned lots everywhere: rats, stray dogs, drunks-in-cardboard-boxes. All things ruined twisted or rotting— welcome.

We trudged up the curving concrete: Air wet, dirty and still. More than bad, it smelled weak. Our eyes reached the top first. There sat Decker in the carport, in the convertible (top down, facing us) smoking a cigar and reading. He made a show of putting down his magazine and splashing a glimpse of beautiful naked girls.

He smiled, blew a few smoke rings. "Hey, Huntley and Brinkley! Brought a cub reporter with you, eh? Good." His eyes twinkled. "Nice day for reading."

Shane and I grinned. Andy did not. Decker pointed to three folding chairs propped against the house and motioned to Andy and Shane. They set up a half circle near his car door. I quickly laid out the story, telling Decker enough to explain our interest in the shelter and let him understand his role. He was surprised to know that there might be more to Scotty's death and that someone (or ones) might be worried enough to hurt us.

He growled, chewed his cigar, spat over the passenger door and cleared his throat. "I wanna kill you guys, that's one thing but nobody else touches your pointy little heads unless I say. Anyway, Daisy likes you guys."

We smiled and made it clear she was our favorite also. I moved on to the details of our main and back-up plans. The more I shared, the more he nodded and the more his eyes sparkled. He liked everything, strong man, horn of distraction, all of it.

He showed us the stuff in his trunk: Everything we could ever need or want and more, including two sets of walkie-talkie radios with a two mile range and miner's hardhats with lights. Our eyes bugged out of our heads. We screamed and yelled and we pounded Decker. He grinned and covered up but he let it all in. I gave him a copy of the plans. We shook hands all around and agreed to meet at the Jefferson kitchen door at 2:00 AM Friday morning.

We floated down the driveway. Andy couldn't stop talking about the walkie-talkies and the headlight hats. Shane winked at me and I nodded.

Andy skipped in front and walked backwards. "We hugged him! We pounded him an' he didn't kill us! This is gonna be great! Best thing we ever did, I swear."

We grinned and sped up. Next stop, Reggie's Great American Diner.

****

By mid-afternoon, the diner was filled but not crowded. We entered, found our home booth and wrapped ourselves in the familiar colors, sounds and smells. We settled in and looked for Daisy.

She soon appeared and slid in next to me. She whispered that there would be no meeting with Reggie, that she was the one who wanted to talk. Before I could say a word, she glanced over her shoulder, saw Reggie returning and pretended to take our order. We told her we had no money. She smiled and kept scribbling.

She slipped out of the booth and read from her order book. "That's three cheeseburgers, three fries and three cokes. We'll have that right out."

She whispered again, "I get a break in ten minutes. The order is on me. I'm glad you came."

Just like that she was gone.

No one spoke but I felt the pressure to whisper. We traded weak guesses about what all of this might mean, but decided to wait for Daisy. Suddenly, Bobby Darin's "Dream Lover" was all over us. We laughed and quietly argued. It was a tie. We hated it as much as we liked it. Soon, Daisy returned, three plates on her left arm, drink tray balanced in her right hand. Once the table was set, she checked her watch and signaled Reggie.

She began by telling us to eat while she talked and she requested that we not ask her any questions until she was finished. So, we ate and Daisy talked.

She spoke just above a whisper, "Last night, a little after midnight, I walked to my car in the northeast corner of the parking lot, my regular spot. Reggie usually walks me out because we leave together after he locks up. But, last night, I left without him. He had some paperwork. I thought about askin' him to walk me out but it seemed silly so out I go, on my own. Turns out that was a mistake."

We stopped eating and Daisy motioned, so we started again.

"As I reached for my car key, I heard a voice behind me, telling me not to turn around or make a sound. I felt something hard in the middle of my back and I froze. No use to try and turn around anyway, no lights in that corner. So, I stayed still. Reg always says, 'Better a live coward than a dead hero.' That saying came to me at that moment.

"Then I heard paper rustling and a black glove stuffed a note into my jacket. Then the voice said, 'Tell those boys to butt out of the Jefferson's business.' The voice then said he was going to leave and that I would be hurt. No wait, that I would be sorry if I moved or called any attention to myself for the next five minutes. He also said it would be a bad idea to tell anyone else about this."

She paused and took a sip of water. Again, we stopped eating.

Again, she whispered, "Eat... eat..." She wiped her glass with a napkin. "So, I stood there for what seemed like a long time. But when I unlocked my car and looked at my watch, it was only 12:15. I don't think the voice talked more than a minute. Of course, when I did look around, no one was there."

The table was quiet. Daisy opened and smoothed a folded scrap of paper and read.

Tell the boys to leave the Jefferson house alone. Last time dogs, next time...?

When she finished, her hands were shaking. She did not look up. She put the paper away and excused herself saying she would be right back. At first, we were upset. Things were getting more complicated and more out of control. But, it soon came down to a very simple decision: Either we do this thing Friday morning or we drop it right now.

The beauty of the decision was clear. Either way, our friend Daisy was off the hook. No reason to give her any more information and risk getting her more upset. On the other hand, asking her a few questions might help us. We created a quick plan and waited.

When Daisy returned, we were finishing our fries. She slipped into her spot and asked us if we knew what the note and the voice were about. Andy explained that lots of kids were jealous that we were pretend-treasure-hunting in the old Jefferson house and they were trying to throw a scare into us with a few pranks.

Daisy sat up straight and looked us in the eye. "So, you think the other night in the parking lot was a prank?"

Shane was quick. "Probably, yes. The only difference is that by gettin'
you involved, they might be able to get us in trouble and scare us too.
Hitting us twice with one punch. If it works, it's real smart."

I took a quick drink and jumped in. "The thing that makes the other
night such a good prank is that everybody knows we lo… Uh, excuse me.
What I meant to say is that you are one of our favorite people."

Daisy leaned in and smiled. "Look at you, blushing. How sweet."

Andy saved me. "I was wondering, how'd you know the glove was
black?"

Now, it was Daisy's turn to blush. "Actually, I don't. I never really saw
it. I guess I just thought it was black because it was dark and that's probably
the color most criminals use."

Blush gone, I chased the other part of Daisy's story. "Did the voice
sound like a kid or an adult?"

Daisy grimaced. "Could be either one or somebody disguising."

"Did the voice seem to come from a space at, above or below you?"

"At"

I had one last, big question. "Did you recognize the voice? Have you
heard it before?"

Daisy smiled. "That's just one question?" She took a drink and paused.
"At first, no. But in the restroom, I remembered. I think the voice sounds
like the mysterious guy who met with Scotty in the diner, the guy who
showed him pictures."

Chapter 34
Bombshells Everywhere

THE IDEA THAT Daisy might recognize the voice was a bombshell. We played things down and stuck to our plan. The "voice" was nothing more than a jealous prank. But Daisy could not shake the note and she was more than worried. She was rattled, like a pitcher whose confidence is shot.

She asked, "What does 'last time dogs' mean?"

We looked at each other like infielders deciding who should catch the pop fly.

I grabbed this one. "A few days ago, we followed Rocket and Renfro, the Christenson's retrievers, into the Jefferson's backyard. And while we were in that mess of trees someone shot Rocket with an arrow."

Daisy sat bolt upright. "Who was it? How bad was the dog hurt?"

I shrugged. "It was too dark. Seemed bad at the time but he's gonna be okay."

She frowned. "Wait a minute. I did hear something. Was there a story in the paper?"

Andy and I looked at each other.

As soon as he saw us draw blanks, Shane took over. "I found the vet in time, Rocket's gonna be fine. But, we had to talk to Ray."

Daisy leaned forward. "He find anything?"

Andy took this one. "If he did, we never heard."

Daisy leaned back and signaled Trudy, her older and wider co-worker. Built like a refrigerator, she carried herself like Daisy's twin. She arrived a bit out of breath and wearing a big smile.

Daisy flashed us a quick glance. "You boys like some dessert?"

We hesitated. Daisy turned to Trudy. "Three berry pies and three Cokes and coffee for me, please."

Trudy smiled and scribbled. "Coming right up."

Daisy leaned in again, resting her elbows on the table. "Why all the interest in the Jefferson place? You found some letters and a locket, right?"

I said, "Yeah. It was Linda in the locket."

She drummed her glossy fingernails on the table. "I remember the letter and the locket. But, why would anybody get crazy about that?"

We admitted we were stumped.

She sat back, pulling softly on her right ear. "Unless there is something else in that house, something really good or really bad. And somebody's afraid you're gonna find it."

We were quiet. Trudy delivered dessert and drinks all around. She slipped the check to Daisy, smiled and left. Daisy gave her coffee a blast of sugar, buried it in cream, stirred and took a sip.

She frowned. "What else did you find?"

I glanced at Andy and Shane. We had a plan, but no hard and fast idea of how much information was too much.

So, mouthful of pie or not, I answered. "Mostly junk from the attic, memory stuff."

Daisy took another long sip. "I suppose the question mark at the end of the note means next time people?"

We nodded.

She added more cream and caught Trudy for a warm up. "You guys been around the Jefferson place a lot?"

Andy answered. "Only a few times, maybe three. But we walk by there all the time and always on the other side of the street. We were on the other side of the street when the dogs took us into the backyard."

I added. "It's really spooky. You can see the room where Scotty shot himself."

Daisy nodded and sipped. "Glad nobody's been hurt, so far. I mean, people. But, this note seems serious. The more I think about it, I better turn this over to Ray. I need to talk to Reg, too. They might ask you guys about everything, too."

We told her she needed to report as soon as possible and that we'd tell everything we knew.

Suddenly, she grimaced and took another sip. "I just realized, Reg's gonna go crazy. You guys know how he is."

We groaned. We knew Reggie's temper, if only in legend. Daisy fortified herself with one more big slurp and signaled Trudy for another refill.

She was now talking more to herself. "He's gonna watch me like a hawk. Jesus, he already does. Now, it'll be armed-guard escorts to and from my car."

The refill arrived and was again properly disguised. Daisy gulped, winced and shrugged. "Can't stop Reg. He'll have to get this out of his system." She leaned back and dropped another bombshell. "He was an Army Ranger, Special Forces, a sniper. So, Reg gets really upset, it's not good, not good at all."

Our mouths fell open, our eyes bugged out. No matter. Daisy, lost in her thoughts, never noticed. Or if she did, she didn't care.

She quickly finished her cup and started to leave. "Your parents know about all this stuff?"

Andy gathered himself. "Yes, they do. They know all about Rocket bein' shot."

She smiled. "Good. I know they want you safe and so do I. I'm glad you came, glad we talked."

Suddenly, I was hot.

Daisy asked, "Are you okay?"

I felt hotter. "I was wondering why you called my mom but never told her about the voice or the note."

She whispered, "The note and the voice scared me. I had to treat it like it was real and keep it quiet until I could talk to you fellas."

Can I ask you one more thing?"

"Sure."

"Why did you say Reggie wanted to talk to me?"

Daisy smiled again. "I thought it might cause a commotion if I were calling for myself. Calling for Reggie makes it a guy thing."

I nodded.

She picked up the ticket. "Thanks fellas. Like I said, you are gentlemen."

We thanked her for everything. But, "everything" mostly meant for treating us like grown-ups. Also, we were happy for Daisy to tell Ray and Reggie everything. When she stepped away earlier, we realized it would look suspicious if we pushed her to drop everything. With Daisy reporting, we looked okay. We were only a small part of the story, not even close to the spotlight. Ray might talk to us but we could handle him. What was there to say? It was Daisy's story. Same thing with Reggie, just dummy up.

Outside the diner, we sat on the bench and tried to settle up. Reggie, a shooter? What next, Renfro the Secret Attack Dog? We debated strolling by the Jefferson place again but gave it up. No reason to call attention to the place or ourselves. Instead, we made our way to the vet to visit Rocket.

315

Andy wanted to mosey through the park and look for Blazer and the Nickname Bunch.

I knew what it was really about.

He admitted. "I'm gettin' real edgy. I wanna thump somebody."

I laughed and bellowed, "Now leaving, Gate 5 for The Retarded Zone and all points west…"

Shane broke up.

I reminded. "Worst thing right now would be getting in some stupid fight."

Andy slammed his cap on the ground, kicked it in the air, caught it and put it back on.

Shane looked left, to the basketball courts. "Hey, Jim and Father Phillip."

By the time we reached the courts, the priest and Jim were standing side by side, bent at the waist, hands on knees scrambling for air: Shiny faces, wet yellow hair, all smiles and steam. Father Phillip pointed to a courtside bench and everybody sat.

Jim was trying to use his wet tee shirt as a towel. The young priest reached under the bench, slid out a leather bag, pulled two hand towels and dropped one around Jim's neck.

Andy picked up the ball, stepped on the court and banked a twenty footer.

Jim jumped up and waved off the basket. "Didn't call 'bank.'"

Andy grabbed the ball, took one dribble, yelled 'Swish' and hit another twenty footer. We yelled and put our arms in the air.

Andy retrieved the ball, tucked it under one arm and asked the young priest, "Hey Father, who won?"

Jim and Father Phillip looked at each other.

Andy turned, took one dribble, shouted 'The bank is open!" and sunk a third twenty footer, this one off the backboard. He ran to the ball and yelled, "Hey Father, did you guys do that stupid, 'Don't keep score' deal?"

Father Phillip chuckled, "Well, we didn't keep score, if that's what you mean."

Andy caught himself. "Sorry Father, my mistake."

Jim waved his towel from the bench. "He killed me 20 to 10."

The priest smiled. "I think maybe you took it easy on me."

Jim smiled and Andy took a seat. Talk turned to the end of vacation, our upcoming sleepover, favorite baseball players, how to do a crossover dribble and Rocket's recovery. Father Phillip had heard about Rocket's injury but no details. As we described the events of that night, St. Luke's newest employee kept shaking his head and smiling.

When the part came up about Jelly calling us heroes, Father Phillip shook our hands, congratulated us and called it "one of those adventures that helps you become real boys, not imitations." He asked if any of us had ever read, *The Hobbit*. We said we had, thanks to the Book Mobile Lady. He said he had pulled it from his bookshelf a few days ago and when he came across the part about "ordinary magic" he thought of us.

We were all a bit lost.

I said, "I don't remember any ordinary magic."

He nodded and warmed to his subject. "Early on, the narrator says, 'Hobbits have no special magic, just the ordinary magic that allows them to disappear when big folks come along.' " I nodded and he continued. "Well, I've been thinking a lot about our conversation in my office and I think growing up is like God's ordinary magic."

He leaned in closer and so did we, like ghost story time at a campfire.

He spoke softly, "Ordinary magic fools folks. It's neither dazzling nor death-defying. It's just the simple ability to disappear when big people are around."

We were still lost.

The priest sparkled. We could feel his energy. "Growing up happens under the radar of most grownups. They don't even see what's going on. Suddenly, the kid is gone and there stands a new grown up! Seems like magic!"

Andy said, "They can't see the inside changes."

Father Phillip beamed. "That's it! It's 'ordinary' because it happens to everyone. So we kind of think of it as nothing special."

It was quiet.

I could not believe my ears.

Hidden in plain sight! Wow.

The young priest stood. "I'll shut up now, but I just wanted you guys to know that God's doing His part in your lives—even if it seems like nothing special is happening."

I said, "Worked for Bilbo, why not us?"

It was time to go our separate ways: Jim and Father Phillip heading home, the rest of us to Doc Collins.'

After a step or two, our new Catholic friend dropped his own bombshell. "Hey! You guys hear? The Jefferson place was condemned today. It's all fenced off, warnings posted everywhere."

We straggled back to the bench. For a long time, there was nothing to say. It felt like that day Old Crotch went off in center field: Wooden puppets staring at the ground again.

Real boys? Feels more like the belly of the whale...

Andy slumped. "We are screwed."

I stared at my shoes until I couldn't see them.

Shane tried. "You know, it isn't so bad. I mean, it isn't like we lost anything real. We can always have another adventure."

Shane made sense. He was logical but he was wrong. Dead wrong. As wrong as Scotty Jefferson.

I wondered.

Is this some of that ordinary magic?

I said, "Long time ago, our dog was killed. Run over in the street after midnight. An Akita/Lab mix, best dog ever. Lots of fire: loyal and smart.

"My mother said I could get a new dog. I said, 'I don't want a new dog. I want my dog.' It doesn't matter if you get a hundred new dogs and all of 'em are great. It's never okay that you lost your dog—not in a million years."

It was cold.

I mumbled, "Never did get another dog."

Nobody talked for a long time. Suddenly, Decker came to a screaming to a halt thirty yards away. He was waving, honking and yelling. We got to him in no time.

He rammed his right thumb. "Get in! We got trouble, buckaroos."

Shane and Andy threw me in the front seat and jumped into the back. Before the doors closed, Decker was laying rubber, leaving a smoke trail as nasty as any formula one dragster. We stopped eleven blocks later across from the Jefferson place. What we saw was nothing short of staggering: An eight foot high chain link fence. Behind the fence, the old house was crumbling under the weight of new yellow and black "No Trespassing" signs.

We stared for a while.

Without warning, Decker opened his glove compartment and tossed around Moon Pies.

He tore the cellophane with his teeth and ripped the marshmallow cookie free. "Guaranteed to break the chain link curse or your money back!"

He smiled big but our toast was less than half-hearted. Decker finished his cookie, fired up, took one slow cruise around the block and stopped. He asked if the plan was still on. We struggled and admitted that we were out of ideas.

He laughed, gave us some jazz about being quitters, put up the top, rolled up the windows and whispered, "I gotta new plan."

He waited, for effect.

We waited, for energy.

Decker's voice and eyes intensified. He asked us if something other than the fence was bothering us. We shook our heads and mumbled. He told us to be patient. He then drove slowly and stopped at the backside of the Jefferson lot.

He kept his voice low. "See that?" He pointed to the padlocked gate. We nodded.

"Notice anything special about it?"

We were stumped.

He waited. "Look where it is."

We might as well have been asleep. We saw a fence and a gate, nothing more.

He urged us. "It's here, way in the back. Busy streets are clear on the other side."

Decker's eyes and voice were pushing. "Look at the padlock. It's nothin' special. Not serious at all. Nothin' here to protect anyway. No tools or any of that. This lock is here just so nobody goes in there and gets hurt or killed before they knock everything down. There's no lights out here either."

We all saw it at the same time.

Andy shouted, "No new plan, don't need one!"

Decker laughed. "Moon Pie breaks the curse every time."

Suddenly, everything was better. But as I took a closer look, I saw a problem: The padlock was too high for Decker.

When I mentioned this, he said, "I got this."

He would wear his braces, stand and lock his knees in place. We would then hold him steady (like spotters in the weight room) as he used the bolt cutters.

"Not much to it," he smiled, "unless something goes wrong."

Decker took one more look and said something that made us feel even better.

"The fence is actually a good thing. It catches attention. People come by and they see what they expect. They do not see other things. The fence is a shield. If we are out there at night with no fence and Ray comes around the corner, lights blasting, we stand out like a three-headed dog. This way, we got double protection, the fence and the dark."

Suddenly, everything was double better.

Then, Shane piped up. "It's still early. What if, later tonight, they put a guard dog out here?"

Decker was ready. "They're not gonna do that. There's nothin' to protect. And, if they're gonna go as far as a dog, they probably just drag a trailer out here with a watchman, too."

Andy came back to the dog. "If they do stick a dog out here, what do we do?"

Decker rubbed his hands together, eyes jumping, big smile. "Use a big chunk of raw meat to distract 'im and (if we need it) my secret weapon." He flashed. "Don't ask me for details." He leaned forward, still smiling. "I'll just say this much—it starts with cayenne pepper."

I smiled.

Back in business! What a day! One bombshell after another! Like to see that cayenne pepper thing.

We returned to the park and went over our plans one more time. We concentrated on the emergency plan. According to Decker, the key was creating a big enough distraction which he said he'd do—or die trying. Given enough time, we would never be found. He also suggested that we pre-assign hiding places so that everybody not end up behind the same bush.

We closed our office in Decker's car, wished him luck and set out for the vet. Decker smiled, waved and headed in the opposite direction.

We had walked about five steps in the grey drizzle when Shane pointed us back to the park. He said it didn't matter if we hustled to see Rocket; right now we had to talk. It was important that we get ourselves straight about all the stuff. We decided we were happy with the way Decker had come through and that we were right to lay low about Daisy. We also knew Friday morning should finish this mystery one way or the other. The shelter would tell the tale.

But, when it came to Reggie as a sniper, our brains were as sticky as honey. We turned ourselves inside out. Daisy was our friend. She wouldn't mess with us. Maybe there was other stuff she didn't know. Did Reggie have some connections to Scotty or Richard Jefferson? Or to the disappearing Linda? Shane mentioned that his dad was in a couple of groups of ex-fighter pilots, one American, one British. Scotty's dad and Reggie were both snipers. Were they members of an ex-sniper club?

No matter how tangled we got, it always came down to this: All we knew about Reggie was that he owned and ran a great diner, cared a lot about Daisy, was a sniper in the war and would never shoot a dog, threaten kids or scare his most popular waitress. We had to leave it there.

We assigned the inside and outside teams, diagrammed hiding places on the Jefferson lot and still had enough time to see Rocket.

Afterward, Shane and Andy came home with me to help explain our "Reggie talk." We practiced our answers for my mom, Ray and Reggie.

We talked about hiding some guys inside the Jefferson house. Ray, for one, would never go in at night. But, none of our guys would either.

We stood to leave and turned to see Jim sliding around a corner, steaming full speed at us and out of control. I felt like a pin in a bowling alley and I got ready to be blasted. There was no time to move but knowing a hit is coming helps.

Suddenly, Jim's eyes looked big and wild. Everybody was screaming. I turned to the side, hoping to go with the hit and avoid being slammed into a bench or tree. At about the ten foot mark, I thought I was a goner.

At that moment, Andy and Shane gang-tackled Jim, grabbed his arms, spun him away. It looked like two tall guys giving a shorter, chunkier guy an "airplane" ride.

I started laughing. But, in a few seconds, there was nothing to laugh about. Jim was heaving. Even in the cold, he was sweating.

He shook his head. "Rocket's gone! Somebody stole him!"

Chapter 35
A New Ally, an Old Friend
and an Old Enemy

SUDDENLY, MY INSIDES were a rollercoaster.

This is the worst thing ever.

Andy slumped. "This is worse than if he was dead."

I tried to stay calm like Frank Hardy. "Jim, is Jelly sure somebody took him? She's sure he didn't just get out?"

"Yeah," he nodded, "she's sure. Ray was there takin' the report and Rocket's place out back was all torn up." Shane started to say something but Jim stopped him. "One more thing: You know that plastic thing they put on Rocket so he wouldn't mess with his stitches… That whole deal is in pieces all over the place an' there's blood on the concrete."

Shane's voice was cracking. "What did Ray say?"

Jim shrugged. "Just keep an eye out, I guess. But, Jelly already got his picture on a flyer. She's gonna put 'em up everywhere."

Andy flinched. "Yeah but this isn't a missin' dog. This dog's missin' 'cause somebody wants him missin'. Flyers won't do much."

****

Andy was right, but we were glad for something to do. We arrived at the parking lot just as Jelly was putting two rolls of masking tape in the front seat of the Vet Van next to two stacks of yellow flyers. She was grateful for our help. I sat in the front seat next to Jelly, everybody else in the back. Her plan was simple: Cover as many areas as possible in the next two hours and worry about tomorrow, tomorrow. Start with the three blocks near the office, then neighborhood stores, shopping centers, the post office and the police department.

I still wanted to be smart like Frank Hardy. "We should put an ad in Lost and Found."

Jelly agreed. "I think we can make the evening paper."

Delivering the flyers, she would stop the van at one end of a street and Shane and Andy would each take a side. While Jim taped flyers to street lamps and telephone poles, Shane would stuff mail boxes. After the first stop, it became a contest about who could get back to the van first. We were done with everything in no time, including the police station and newspaper.

Jelly thanked us for helping and asked, "What about a quick Coke at Stan's?"

We could not resist. Stan's Drive In was a concrete island in a sea of asphalt, an art deco flying saucer, marked not only by food and fun but by beautiful girls in short skirts and roller skates. In no time, out came beautiful Kate: red hair, green eyes, dazzling figure. She took our order and slipped away. Slowly, we put our eyes back in.

Jelly smiled. "She's a very pretty girl."

We looked at each other.

Andy talked. 'You'll get no argument from us."

Jim's whisper was hoarse, "She's a traffic-stopper."

Shane mumbled, "Wonder if she's as nice as she is pretty."

Jelly looked at him. "That's a very perceptive question."

Shane was lost.

I rescued. "College word. Means smart or insightful."

Jelly nodded and congratulated me for knowing such a fancy word. Jim claimed that he knew it too only I said it faster.

Shane thumped Jim's nose. "Pinocchio."

Everybody grinned, including Jelly, and Jim turned red.

When the drinks arrived, Jelly told us the official story of Rocket's disappearance: She refilled Rocket's water at 2:00 PM, checked on a couple of cats and a parrot, hosed down the inside courtyard. Everything was fine. An hour later, Rocket's pen was open and empty, the lock destroyed, blood and plastic all around. Beside Rocket being gone, something else bothered Jelly. She could not figure out why the staff had heard nothing.

Andy asked a question which seemed to hit Jelly, like a shot to the ribs. "Did you find a letter around Rocket's pen or the office?"

"No, I don't think so. What kind of letter?"

"A threat, somethin' like that."

She shook her head. "No, nothing like that."

Suddenly, Jelly was in a hurry to return to the office. Within minutes, we were pulling into the parking lot. She thanked us again and sent us on our way.

We began the ten blocks to my house without much talk. I mentioned that we needed to clue everybody in to wear dark clothes, tough shoes and long pants tomorrow. Shane volunteered to make those calls.

I stopped to rest for a moment. "Jelly was bugged by the question about the letter. You guys see it?"

Andy nodded. "She was in a real hurry to get back."

Shane added. "There's a letter alright. Must be."

I said, "Only one reason she wouldn't tell us."

Andy kicked an empty can about twenty feet. It banged off old man Bremerton's garage door.

He grinned. "Wish that had been ole Purdy's ugly mug." He walked over, picked up the can and tossed it in Bremerton's garbage can. "It's a trick they use all the time in the movies. Keep some of the evidence secret, stuff only the bad guy would know. Later on, some joker knows stuff he shouldn't know and bam, you got 'im."

I knew immediately. "This is Ray's idea not Jelly's. And we're the jokers."

We were about four blocks from my house, sticky hot inside our clothes. I stopped one more time, wiped the drizzle off my face, pointed to Andy. "Remember, you wanted to whack somebody and I said 'wrong time?'"

He took off his cap and wiped his forehead. "Yeah, what? Gonna whack me, now?"

I laughed and so did Shane. "No, but I do wanna hit something, right now!"

We turned left for two blocks and parked ourselves opposite that evil-eyed old goat, Purdy. She immediately began head-butting her battered chain-link. Amazingly, the thing was still standing.

We told Purdy, in no uncertain terms, what we thought of her and what she could do with her head-butts. Andy and Shane each picked up a stick and I positioned myself to give the fence a good enough whack to send Purdy's nose into orbit, right next to Sputnik. We did a quick rock, paper, scissors for who would go first.

Andy stepped toward the fence, took a couple of practice swings and asked a question. "Know why they named her 'Purdy?'"

"No."

"Nope."

Andy took a tight powerful quick swing, stepped into it, turned his hips and extended his arms. His stick struck the fence violently, sending shock waves in all directions.

He grunted through clinched teeth. "They're stupid. Can't say, 'pretty'."

His near-perfect swing smacked the fence and old Purdy's nose dead on. But, it merely backed her off a step or two.

Shane said, "Fence saved her."

We waited for her to mosey back, but no dice. After a few minutes, Shane and I gave the fence a good thump anyway.

The last few blocks to my house slipped by, but as soon as we turned the corner, we saw trouble. Parked comfortably across from my house, sat Ray in his patrol car. When he saw us, he got out and leaned against the hood.

As soon as we got close enough, he pointed to the curb. "Have a seat, boys. We gotta talk."

He opened his tiny notebook. "Jelly says you all asked her about a letter being left about Rocket."

We nodded and agreed. Ray pushed his cap back, massaging his eyes and the bridge of his nose. "Boys, why would you do that? Why would you ask about a letter?"

I volunteered. "Seems logical."

"Well," he grimaced. "Here's the problem. Jelly didn't quite tell you the whole truth. On my orders, she was not to say a word about the letter to anyone."

Andy blurted, "You mean there **is** a letter?!"

"Here's the problem. I told Jelly to keep the letter quiet. Nobody on the Doc's staff even knows about it. The doc does, 'cause she took it to him at the very first and later he gave it to me."

It was quiet. We were studying his shiny shoes.

"Boys, I kept it quiet for a reason. Only people involved in the crime know about the letter…"

More silence.

He was rubbing his whole face now as well as the back of his neck. "So, boys, how did you know about the letter?"

Andy began pacing. "We didn't. I mean, I didn't. I'm the one who asked Jelly but I didn't know anything, I swear. You know I'd never hurt Rocket."

Ray was still rubbing his neck. "Yeah, but I gotta ask. Where were you guys this afternoon between 2:00 and 4:00."

Andy exhaled deeply. "At the GAD and at the park. You can check with Daisy and Father Philip."

Ray was scribbling in his notebook. "I'll check. You were together the whole time. Nobody left at any time, right? I mean, nobody even left to use the restroom, correct?"

We answered fast and loud.

"Right."

"Yes."

"Correct."

Andy sat, but my backside was killing me. I looked at Andy and nudged Shane. They stood and pulled me up.

Ray closed his notebook, started to leave and stopped. "One more thing. Son, why would you think of something like a letter out of the blue, like that?"

Andy smiled. "It seemed like a kidnapping to me—only for a dog. And in most kidnappings, they leave a ransom note."

Ray nodded, scribbled some more, thanked us and left. We watched him turn the corner.

Andy fussed with his cap. "He knows we know somethin' more than we're tellin'."

We walked across the street, entered the front door, said hi to my mom and headed to my room. She stopped us and asked about Reggie. We told her, no big deal, just getting our opinion on stuff. She was relieved.

It was good to close the bedroom door. We looked at each other. What next?

****

We picked our spots: Shane on the top bunk, me on the bottom, Andy on the floor. We took another run at the Rocket mystery. The "arrow guy" was behind this, but beyond that we were stuck. Why go after Rocket again? What did the new letter threaten? Is the bad guy trying to save the Jefferson place? Why? The Jefferson place gets condemned, torn down, the lot gets rebuilt, his secrets are safe...

So, why try to keep the old place standing? Isn't this the guy who's worried about somebody finding something? Unless destroying the place might uncover the shelter and tell the world his secrets. Then again, maybe this guy doesn't even know about the shelter, he's just not been able to find what he is looking for in the house. Our heads were spinning. So we left the Rocket mystery right there.

We talked over the shelter break-in one more time. We were ready and excited. Shane left to make calls and Andy headed home for dinner. It was strange to be alone.

Suddenly, I couldn't think of a thing to do.

God, if there's something you can do to help Rocket, please do it. Sure would like to have a dog like him someday... Go everywhere with me. Ray thinks we could hurt Rocket?

I looked around for something to read and settled on "Kidnapped" by Robert Louis Stevenson. Today, it seemed like the perfect choice. Somebody said it was about a boy near my age. I opened it and began...

Chapter 1

I Set Off Upon My Journey to the House of the Shaw's.

I will begin the story of my adventures with a certain morning early in the month of June, the year of grace 1751, when I took the key for the last time out of the door of my father's house.

Mr. Campbell was waiting for me by the garden gate.

"Well, Davie, lad," said he, "I will go with you as far as the ford, to set you on the way." And we began to walk forward in silence.

"Are ye sorry to leave?" said he, after a while.

"Why, sir," said I, "if I knew where I was going, or what was likely to become of me, I would tell you. Since my father and mother are both dead, I shall be no nearer to them here than in the Kingdom of Hungary, and, to speak truth, if I thought I had a chance to better myself where I was going, I would go with a good will."

****

Suddenly, my mom was calling for dinner. My parents were interested in Rocket's disappearance. My dad had never heard of such a war on animals. He figured this person was "some kind of mental case."

My mother shook her head. "He or she needs to find something else to do with their time."

I was surprised my mother suspected a girl but my father said, "Enough crazies out there. It could be a woman." He then said the most interesting thing yet about the bad guy or girl. "Anybody goes after innocent, defenseless animals is weak. Can't stand up to people."

I told my dad he sounded just like Richard Diamond. He grinned and mom rolled her eyes. He finished his steak, winked at her and said he'd rather be the tough guy, private detective Tom Lopaka from "Hawaiian Eye." I laughed. He was right. That show had it all: mysteries, pretty girls and Hawaii.

Mom changed the subject and asked me if I knew anything more about Louie. I told her there was nothing new but Mrs. K. had picked up the letters. We didn't talk about Louie's coming death but I saw it in her face.

Dad said, "Better get a move on if we're gonna watch "'Hawaiian Eye."'

I finished my macaroni and cheese fast. I was hoping Hawaiian Eye might be about kidnapping but it wasn't. Three guys trying to find the same woman: One wanted to help her, one wanted to marry her and one wanted to kill her. The detective stuff was great but my eyes really popped every time I saw Connie Stevens, a Sandra Dee look alike. She played Cricket Blake, a singer at the hotel where the detectives had an office. She was something.

As soon as the show ended, I was off to bed. I pulled up the covers (transistor radio touching my ear) and listened to Wolfman announce The Fleetwoods' "Come Softly to Me."

Another perfect song…

So many beautiful girls… How does God do it? How does He decide which ones get to be pretty? Is it all luck? God created luck, right? The main thing is get a pretty one. But, how?

I better pray about Rocket. God, please help Rocket…

I drifted off quickly. Connie Stevens and Sandra Dee: a dream combination.

****

Eyes open, Thursday morning. 6:30 AM. Big day and then, tonight. Mickey clock on my desk, always perfect and bright, pretty little white-gloved cartoon hands, happy face.

If colors stayed new forever would they still look ordinary after a while? Nobody's gonna sleep tonight… Maybe we should go earlier than 2:00. Hope Rocket's okay… The letter. Why threaten the vet? He can't do anything. This isn't about the vet. This is another warning… for us.

There was a note next to my clock.

Randy,

Clean the garage today. Move everything, get underneath and behind. Refrigerator too. Do it right or you'll do it again.

DAD

I did my sink stuff and dressed fast: old, ragged stuff. At the table, my mom suggested an egg along with my Raisin Bran. She also said I had enough milk in my cereal for two bowls.

I smiled. "I just keep adding cereal 'til the milk's gone."

"Well," she said, "just don't waste food. Children in China are starving. Besides, you're going to need lots of energy to get that garage clean. Everything you need is already there."

I reminded her about the sleepover at Shane's and we had the usual, "Aren't you staying over there too much?" talk. It ended as always. "Well, if it's okay with his mother…" I asked if I could return bottles to get money for stuff to eat at the sleepover. She hesitated and said yes but told me I better stop asking her for things or there would be no sleepover.

I was up and headed to the front door. I opened it and screamed. Lying on the front porch, bloody flank up, Rocket was muddy from here to there, happy tail thumping. My mom grabbed towels, handed me a wet wash cloth and went next door to get Mrs. Shirley.

I began wiping Rocket's face. His gums were bloody and he had tiny scratches on his face and nose. His coat was scuffed with leaves and plant stems like he'd run through a hedge or a rose bush. Except for the mud, his arrow injury looked okay. He also had a plain, red bandana around his neck. When I tried to touch it, he pulled away.

My mom returned with Mrs. Shirley who brought a plastic tarp. After some planning, they slid Rocket on to the tarp and carried him to Mrs. Shirley's car. We all rode to the vet. Rocket lay in the back seat across my lap. I placed my hand lightly on his head. He rested, his breathing steady. Mrs. Shirley and my mom wondered why he had come to our porch.

I knew right away. "The Christensen's both work so he tried us."

As I spoke, we were pulling into the parking lot. I waited with Rocket while my mom and Mrs. Shirley went inside. Soon, two staff members, along with Jelly, were on the spot to carefully move Rocket. Doc Collins was out but Jelly took a quick look and said he seemed "a bit ragged and worn out but otherwise fine." Two strong guys took Rocket to get cleaned up and we all breathed easier.

Jelly took our quick report and said she'd contact the Christensen's. I wondered about her because of the letter thing with Ray but she seemed like her normal, friendly self.

****

Back home, I wanted to call everybody about Rocket, but my mom sent me straight to the garage, "Work first, play later."

I couldn't figure how a phone call was play, but that didn't matter. I put on gloves, settled on my knees, leaned my left shoulder and ear against the freezer, tucked my right hand behind it, took a deep breath and pushed with my left side and pulled with my right arm. The corner of the freezer moved two inches. I pushed and pulled two more times: two inches each time. I moved, reset and did three more pulls until the freezer was at an angle about ten inches from the wall. I was sweating and starting to get ticked off.

Why do I have to hate the stupid freezer to clean behind it? Getting mad gives you energy? Doesn't seem right. My knees really hurt. My ankles doin' their regular lousy job.

I grabbed a whisk broom and began stirring up bug and spider-infested clouds. I held my breath and turned my face away. The junk was two inches thick. Soon, I had a nice pile of ugly stuff. I shoved a ragged, broken-handled mop underneath and pushed gunk out front.

In the middle of these pull-stuff-away-from-the-wall adventures, I was always worried. In a one-on-one showdown with a spider, cockroach or other deadly enemy, I had one huge problem. Unless I could kill him, her or it quickly, I was never going to get away. I knew all about black widows, roaches and rats but lately I'd learned about the brown recluse. Glad they don't live here. But gigantic cockroaches are another matter: bodies as big as a railroad conductor's watch and they fly! No matter where you run, every time you look up they're coming right at you. My solution: Keep moving, keep looking, don't think and be ready.

God created these filthy guys? They eat crap and clean up garbage. I guess somebody's gotta do it.

I knew the other side of the freezer would be tougher. I can't use my weaker left side. So, I leaned my right side on the freezer, reached behind with my right hand and pulled. Everything moved an inch or so. Three or four more pulls and I had enough room to clean behind and shove gunk out. Putting everything back was a straight push, all shoulders and upper body. Muscles screaming and twitching, I couldn't stay on my knees much longer. I used a whisk broom almost violently and cleared a big area around the freezer. Then, I grabbed my right cane, heaved myself to a standing position and stepped away from the dust cloud. I accidently saw my reflection: I was a gray-haired, ticked off, zombie alien.

I grinned.

Rest of the garage? Piece of cake...

It took the rest of the morning to finish. Moving and stacking, straightening, throwing, clearing, sweeping and polishing. I asked my mom to take a look. She reminded me her opinion didn't count. I asked her to look anyway. She pointed out a couple of do-overs, started to pat me on the shoulder, changed her mind, pointed to the double sink and hurried out. I knew what she was about. I leaned against the sink, took off my gloves, sweatshirt and tee. I put the gloves on the shelf, threw the clothes in the basket and turned on the water. In a flash, she was back with shampoo, soap, wash cloth, towel, clean tee shirt and a nearly-new sweatshirt. She set everything on the washer, turned off the water, pointed me to the driveway and told me the sweatshirt was a gift from my cousin, Perry. Outside, she swept and whacked my pants so hard I felt like an old rug hanging on the line. After a while, she sent me back to the garage.

About the time I got my head under the water, Andy slipped in and whispered in my ear. I jumped and nearly knocked myself out. I grabbed the back of my head, expecting to find blood and spout marks. I was wrong on both counts. Andy was trying not to laugh. I asked him if my near death was funny. He shook his head, said he was sorry and burst out laughing.

I shook my aching head, finished washing and drying my hair and pulled on my clean shirts. I told him everything I knew about Rocket's return (which wasn't much.) He'd heard from Shane, who had heard from his mom, who had heard from my mom. As soon as he heard, he went to see Jelly. She said that Doc Collins figured Rocket "was a little scraped up," but OK. Doc thought he'd been tied up and had managed to chew his way through a rope. I was about to ask about the bandana when my mom stepped though the side door and invited Andy to lunch.

We tore into peanut butter and jelly and washed it down with cherry Kool-Aid. Andy quietly mentioned that the bandana was marked in dark felt pen with one word: **ANYTIME**.

We knew what that meant. But, it didn't matter. After tonight, we'd be done with the Jefferson place forever. We cleaned up, thanked my mom and decided to shoot free throws at the park. We got permission, got a ball and set out. We reached the front yard.

Andy took a deep breath. "Somethin' else I gotta tell you an' it ain't good. Didn't wanna bring it up in the house."

"Trouble with Decker?"

Andy squeezed the basketball, slammed it, caught it and spoke slowly. "Waitin' on the bench in front of the GAD today, I wanted to see Decker. His car wasn't in the parking lot but I heard the door open and I thought it might be him like before, but it wasn't."

"Who was it?"

He set the ball down and put his hands in his pockets. "Older guy, face like leather, khaki pants, brown loafers and matching belt, tan turtleneck sweater, navy blue pea coat, blue corduroy cap, white hair stuffed inside."

"Okay, so you're Sherlock Holmes. So what?

"Point is, I saw his eyes an' he saw mine. And I swear, he's the guy I saw in Scotty's bedroom!"

"Did he recognize you?"

"He kept going. But, I think he recognized me all right."

Chapter 36
Now You See Us, Now You Don't

FOR A MOMENT, we were stuck and did the word dance, starting and stopping. Andy described our situation perfectly. We were slamming into the same old wall. No matter what new bomb, no matter how threatening the latest message, it always came down to the same choice: Keep up the adventure or stop. Put like that, we had to keep going.

Suppose the pea coat guy at the GAD really is the guy in Scotty's bedroom, so what? The place is abandoned and the guy is in there. There have been lots of people in and around that old place for a long time, including us. So much for stopping.

But this time, Andy added an interesting twist. "Even if the cops catch us, they ain't gonna do much: complain, give us tickets, warn us... Maybe make our parents pay a fine, that's it. We're all under age."

I shrugged. "Forget about the cops. Our dads will kill us."

So much for the new twist. We went back inside and got permission to take a wagon-load of bottles to Don's Market. Along the way, I asked Andy why he was looking for Decker.

"Gonna tell 'im that if we get into the emergency plan, he should click his walkie-talkie to 'transmit' so we can hear everything."

I nodded. "That's real smart. Later, we can connect up. He'll know if things are safe."

Andy groaned, "Unless we get caught in the shelter."

I laughed. "Or in the bushes or on the street."

As we neared the market, I said, "Gotta remind guys not to splash light around. Keep it low, use flashlights as little as possible. The other thing is, somebody gets caught, do not tell on other guys. Say it was just them."

Andy pulled the wagon inside. Don was happy to see us. He asked about Louie and shook his head. He counted up the bottles, gave us a little over two dollars, called the box boy, Jeff, and told us to park the wagon outside. Jeff got a hand cart and took away the empties. We hit the aisles and took away the goodies.

Outside the market, we made a plan. Andy would pick up me and my sleeping bag later. At dinner, my father was impressed with the garage. I knew this because he said yes to the sleepover. Andy knocked on the front door just as I finished dinner. My parents said to forget about the dishes.

Andy grabbed my bag. Tim and Jim were waiting out front. They didn't want to get stuck in parent talk. We made it to Shane's garage and avoided his parents, too, except for the dad talk about keeping the noise down and not messing around outside.

The twins showed up and everybody claimed a spot. Andy went over both plans, assigned hiding places and named Danny, Davie and Tim to the outside team, along with Decker. He gave final warnings and reminded us that Colin was the guy to look for at night, not Ray. He said the big deal about Colin was that he wanted to be thought of as cool and could be talked out of anything.

"So," he said, "for Colin, lie your butt off. It'll probly work."

Now began the hardest part of the evening: waiting until after midnight. Time seemed to crawl backward. We ran through every available activity, tested each other on what to do if… ate everything in the room and guessed again at what might be in the shelter.

At 11:00 PM, Shane's dad enforced lights out. It was a teeth-grinding, fussy, itchy, thrashing-around-in-the-dark, night. Like being hungry but stuffed.

Eventually, we slept. How long is unclear but Andy woke everyone to a mumbling, grumbling start at 1:30 AM.

We used the side door and slipped outside quickly. I hoped getting back in would be as easy. The wet cold helped sharpen senses, and after a minute or so the darkness softened and it was easier to see. In the dark, sound was bigger and clearer and whispers hit like darts. In weak moonlight, things were still themselves but even ordinary stuff seemed strange or scary.

I suddenly realized something and called a quick huddle. "You're gonna sense the lights of a car before you see it. When that happens, don't wait an' don't turn or look up. An' don't freeze and play 'deer in the headlights.' As soon as you sense light, get down."

We split up, took different routes and met at the far side of the Jefferson lot. Decker was at his spot, out of his car and near the gate. I could see his steel braces sparkle just below the cuff. He was all dark: jeans, sweatshirt and wool knit cap. He had bolt cutters on his lap, a smile on his face and doe-skin gloves on his hands. He made a point of them. We whispered hello and he whispered our names—only our names. We shook hands. Decker handed the bolt cutters to Danny, lifted himself out of his chair, locked his knees and stood. Andy and Shane held him steady from behind, Jim and Tim spotted in front, ducking away from his Popeye arms, crunching themselves against the fence, hands gently on his waist. He waved for the cutters, lifted them over his head, set them in place, grunted and snapped the chain like a child's toy. The lock fell harmlessly to the ground, lost in the dark.

Suddenly, light flashed around the corner, headed toward us. Decker carefully brought the bolt cutters down, tossed them away and whispered, "Go." Everybody stayed put. Decker fussed with his knees, released the locks and lowered himself into his chair. Then, everybody melted into the dark, face down on the ground. I was between Andy and Shane. I had a perfect view of Decker, partly because I knew where to look. As the light grew closer, Decker did something amazing. He disappeared! He was there one second, gone the next. I blinked and rubbed my eyes. Instantly, the car was on us but its light passed harmlessly overhead. We waited, exhaled and went looking for Decker. He was right where we left him, safe and sound and wearing a big smile.

"I ain't much of a boy scout," he said, "but I do try to be prepared."

He held up a big, dark blanket with one fist and jerked it around like he was wringing a chicken's neck. He then swung it overhead like a cowboy doing rope tricks and let it fall right over—covering himself and his chair. Just like that, he was invisible.

We clapped. He pulled the blanket away, hushed us and pointed to the trunk of his car. Once there, he passed out tools and supplies. He gave Andy the walkie-talkie and reminded us to close the gate. He drove to the corner and parked across the street while we headed to the Jefferson's kitchen door. From there, it was easy to find the hatch. But, digging it out and ripping away dead tree roots was going to take some time. The helmet hats worked. It was easy to see. It took a while to find the outline of the entrance. It was about 4'x4' on a side, opening from the middle, sealed by a giant lock at the end nearest the house.

Andy broke out the walkie-talkie. "Decker, I forgot. We need you in here now. Bring the cutters."

"Be right there."

In minutes, Decker's car was across the street and just like that, he was Johnny-on-the-spot with bolt cutters. This giant lock was tougher. It resisted our strong man's first and second tries. It was difficult to wedge the cutters in at the correct angle. After his second try, Decker moved closer, jammed the point of the cutters between the lock and the doors at a 45 degree angle and pushed. As the cutters' handles moved slowly upward, we heard a creaking sound. Decker paused, took a deep breath and continued his push. As the handles neared straight up, there was a sudden crack. Everybody jumped.

Decker spat out one quick word. "Shit!"

He thought he had broken the handles on the cutters and he was right. They were splintered at the base. He never did cut the lock. But, as he yanked the cutters loose, we could not believe our eyes. There, in pieces, lay the twisted, sprung lock. Shane moved like a cat and jangled the crumbling lock from the hatch. Decker's strength had done what the cutters could not. He had twisted the thing until it simply exploded.

He grinned big and wiped his forehead. "I guess I owe myself a pair of bolt cutters."

We hung in the air a moment and then each guy began to move like his hair was on fire. We placed a rope through the abused metal ring on one side of the hatch doors and pulled. It did not budge. Quickly, Decker took the rope and told the twins to stand on the far side of the hatch door facing him and wedge shovels underneath the half door nearest him. Decker was clear: Pull slow and steady, don't jerk—and pull together. I counted to three and the pull started. The hatch groaned and screeched in protest. Meanwhile, the twins prying with all their might as well. Slowly, the half-door began to lift and move in Decker's direction. Then, it stopped.

Jim stepped away from the rope line, returned with WD 40 and drenched the hinges. Now, Decker alone pulled. The heavy steel door resisted and creaked, but our strong man was relentless, every muscle straining and grinding, jaw set, not breathing.

Suddenly, the hinges broke loose and the door crashed to the ground, inches from Decker's feet. For a moment, we were all frozen in a nighttime tableau. Then, instantly, everybody's hair was again on fire. Decker rushed back to his lookout post. The inside team grabbed masks, flashlights, bug spray and brooms and adjusted helmet headlights. The outside crew hid tools and roughed up the area so that it looked normal. They also worked the hatch door and it was surprisingly easy to lift. Opening and closing would not be a problem, at least on that one side.

Our entry plan called for Andy to go first, rope tied around his chest. If he screamed, got hurt, didn't answer or didn't return quickly, guys were to pull him out, right now. He ventured down the first few steps and disappeared. After a minute or so, he was back, covered with dirt and spider webs.

He pulled his mask down, bent at the waist and gulped air. "Not hard. Handrails on both sides, dirt everywhere. Bugs, spiders, lots of webs, garter snakes, mice. Smells bad. Like goin' into the house, only smaller. Let's go."

Tim looked at his watch. "Go. You got thirty minutes. Then, we go."

Andy went first again, I was second, Shane third and Jim last. I had no problems getting inside. Handrails were dirty, but solid.

I refused to wear the rope. "Can't close the lid. Leave it. If we need it somebody will come get it."

That said, as soon as Jim hit the third step and made the sharp left, the hatch closed.

It hit with a thud and I flinched. Andy was wiping away thick spider webs but they were still hitting me in the face. I stopped more than once, wiping and brushing. The air was dead and rottenness belted us in waves. Stomach twitching, I breathed through my mouth. I watched for flying things and wondered about bats.

Thank you, God for the mask.

I was scared about crawling things. Things I might only feel and not see. Things I could neither reach nor escape.

What if they get up my pant leg?

It was cold and wet and I was sweating. I slapped at the sticky web mess on my sleeve and wiped my forehead anyway.

When I grabbed the handrail, my sleeve was muddy.

Thank you, God for gloves.

After six steps, we reached the floor: a concrete room, a cross between a submarine (close and tight) and a cave (messy and dark). The roof was not high enough for us to fully stand and it was five feet across, at best. It was about eight feet long. There were folded cots, three thin mattresses, a few chairs and a card table stacked against one wall, along with sealed drums of water, lanterns, blankets, pillows, a couple of brooms, a rake and a shovel. The other wall was a floor-to-ceiling bookcase stuffed with canned and dry foods, books, games, writing materials and paper plates and cups. The bookcase was no more than five feet long but it was the boss of that room. At the far end, important things: a generator, a 5 gallon "bathroom barrel," two boxes labeled "clothes" and one labeled "personal items." The bathroom barrel was filled with plastic liners, toilet paper, toilet seat and chemicals. Nobody wanted to dig any deeper. If there was something important in there, it would have to stay.

After poking around a while longer, a few things stumped us. Why were the boxes labeled clothes and personal items, empty? And, more importantly, where was the H.I.P.S.? It had to be here.

Jim moved the bathroom barrel, flashed his light and yelled. He stumbled backward and almost fell. Eyes frozen, he pointed to a large pile of dead rats: a bloody, green and pus-white pile, a half-eaten head, matted, wet hair, long ugly tails, a chunk of crawling flies and bugs and a retching stench.

I turned away, holding my breath. I started to lose control and moved toward a garbage can near the foot of the stairs. I hadn't noticed it when we came in, but I was glad for it now. It was empty. Sweat pouring, I settled for trying to keep it out of my eyes. I wasn't the only one struggling. Groans everywhere, making things worse. I stood over the barrel for a while.

Softly, the wave of sickness slipped away, crisis gone for now. I was a shaky mess and I was starting to itch. That's when I saw it or rather, that's when I didn't see it. I looked at the generator at the far end of the shelter and something clicked.

"Hey," I bellowed, "where's the other entrance?"

Everybody jumped.

"What?"

"Huh?"

"What?"

I pointed to Shane. It was hard to talk through the mask. "Your dad's notes on the shelter. Didn't he say double entrances?"

"Yeah! 'Double entry through hatches in the backyard.' How'd you remember?"

I raised my eyebrows. "I came over near the entrance and I thought, 'What if we got stuck down here?' That's when I remembered your dad's notes."

We looked with new eyes and forgot about rats and sweat and spider webs. We studied the floor and the ceilings. We scraped our way behind stacks and into awkward spaces. We examined the bookcase in detail, removing and replacing items. Jim opened a folding chair and sat, shaking his head. I figured our time was about up and Tim would be tapping on the hatch any moment.

Suddenly, a big, ugly something buzzed into Jim's face and all hell broke loose. He gave it the old windmill, whacked himself across the forehead, knocked his helmet off, fell backward and smacked his head on the side of the bookcase. I thought he was out cold. Andy flipped the walkie-talkie to me and moved toward Jim.

Suddenly, an explosion hit the hatch. At that same moment, Decker's horn blasted long and loud.

He screamed into the walkie-talkie. "Get the hell out, now! Cops everywhere! Both directions. Go! Go!"

We were frantic and frozen. One thing was certain. Our outside guys were no longer guarding the hatch. This was it. We were trapped. Everything was over. All that planning and we didn't plan for cops from both directions! Tim and the twins must have headed for the Oleanders.

Decker was screaming through the walkie-talkie again, horn still blasting. "One car at the gate, the other with me."

I panicked. Instantly, everything went silent.

I remembered.

Don't try to transmit.

I was getting ready to try and talk us out of an arrest. Suddenly, hands grabbed my arms, pulling, yanking, dragging me fast. I dropped both canes, hung on to the walkie-talkie and lost my hard hat. Somebody scrapped everything up and we kept moving.

****

Out of nowhere, in the dark, a crackling click and we were back in business. We could hear every word from Decker's car. It took a moment to recognize Colin's voice.

"Decker, whadaya doin' out here? Why you layin' on the horn?"

"Sorry, Colin, horn's messed up. Gotta short. Just started tonight."

"Have you been drinking?"

Decker laughed. "Naw, you know me, Colin. I got enough problems. Just drivin' around tryin' to think things through, the horn shorts out and all of a sudden, it's the 4th of July right when you guys are comin' by. But, tell you what, if I was gonna drink, tonight would be as good as any."

"How's that?"

Decker cleared his throat and whispered, "This just between you and me?"

"Sure."

Decker mumbled, "Off the record?"

We huddled over the tiny speaker even tighter.

Colin whispered, "Sure."

Decker spoke up. "You know about me and Darlene?"

341

"What about you and Darlene?"

The conversation was interrupted: another car stopping, engine running, door opening and closing. Someone was checking in with Colin, a voice we did not recognize.

"Jefferson lot broken into, fence cut. Somebody digging up an old fallout shelter. Kids maybe, maybe a prank, a dare. Who knows? We lifted the hatch. Nothin' down there except filth and a bunch of ruined supplies. Probably dead rats or somethin' in there as well. Smelled like hell. We closed the hatch, but it has no lock. We'll notify the security people about the gate in the morning."

Colin spoke, "Sounds like kids alright. Whole place is goin' down in a few days anyway."

"Need any help here?"

"No. Seems like Mr. Decker here had some personal problems. Driving around thinkin' about a woman and his horn goes off. Short in the wiring."

The other voice laughed. "Well, Mr. Decker, I guarantee you that you aren't the first and you won't be the last to have his 'horn go off' when it comes to a woman, if you know what I mean."

Decker, Colin and the other voice laughed. There was a pause.

Decker answered, "Officer, I am sure you are right."

Colin said, "Thanks Rick."

Door closing, car pulling away.

Decker coughed and cleared his throat. "Colin, you really wanna know about Darlene?"

Colin hesitated. "I don't need details. Just glad you feel good talking with me. I want good relationships with the public. But, I gotta give you this. Notice to Repair. It's not a ticket, just says you have ten days to make repairs or it becomes a fine. Verify the repairs with any officer and you are clear."

"Thanks, Colin."

"No problem. Go on home now Decker, before that horn goes off again."

Silence... Door closing, car pulling away.

Decker fired up his engine and his walkie-talkie clicked. "Where the hell are you guys? How'd they miss you?"

Everybody grinned. Andy answered, "Right here. Hidden in plain sight."

Decker laughed. "I'll be damned. You okay? Can you get out?"

We looked at each other. Andy started, forgot to press transmit, then remembered and pressed. "We can get out easy. Still got some work to do."

"Find anything?"

"Not yet, let you know tomorrow. Thanks for all your help."

"I think Tim and the twins got my stuff outta there while I was talkin' to the cops. I think it's across the alley, next to Bowen's stack of old tires. At least that was the plan."

"Can't help you there."

"Yeah, uh, I'll check the alley. If stuff's not there, I'll come back and you guys can get it from our other spot, the bushes."

"Okay, we don't hear from you, you got the stuff. We do hear from you, we check the bushes."

"Right."

"Hey, Decker, you were great tonight. Strong Man and The Horn of Deception. Thanks man. You're a hero, a pal. Saved our butts."

"Hey, it's good."

"Hey, Decker, who's Darlene?"

The Strong Man pressed transmit and belly laughed. "Ask Randy."

Andy pressed the button.

I cleared my throat. "Ain't no Darlene."

Decker clicked in. "Bingo! Boys, I'm off. Later alligators! Keep your socks up and your batteries dry."

****

The room was a twin. Dirt, bugs, supplies, down to the last detail, including us. Less splashy than Dorothy's ruby slippers, Jim's crack on the head had worked its own magic. His clunk on the side of the bookcase did more than nearly knock him out, more than give him an egg-sized bump. It made the bookcase move. Held in place by strong magnets, the thing turned on a stainless steel base, revealing a hidden doorway. Once inside, a slight push and the whole thing slid smoothly back, clicking softly into place. And there we were: Hidden In Plain Sight. Jefferson's finish carpentry was masterful. The room was invisible.

Reggie always said, better to be lucky than good. Being in a rotten place never felt better. Listening to the cops on the bookcase side cough, sputter and curse, hearing Decker sell Colin the Brooklyn Bridge, knowing that Tim and the twins were safe...

It couldn't get any better.

343

This must be how Huck and Tom felt at their funeral. Maybe this is how God feels when He secretly sees and hears everything.

Suddenly, the walkie-talkie crackled to life. Decker reported that he had rescued his stuff from the alley and was on his way. We made plans to meet at the diner the next afternoon and settle up.

****

We broke the huddle and just like that, everything was different. We all saw it at the same moment. At the far end of our hidden room, stood a once-beautiful stainless steel safe now choked by years of dirt and scum. We stared and it stared back, like a Buckingham Palace guard.

Suddenly, we all knew. This was it. The Jefferson place held a secret and this safe protected it. The letter-writing dog-napper might be looking for the safe or guarding it or hiding something else. But, it didn't matter. We had to get into that safe and we didn't have forever. We grabbed dust-caked towels, shook them out, gagged and started clearing the lock of hard dirt and webs. It was sticky and frustrating, like scrubbing bug-covered brown cement with a dry rag. Jim pulled a spray can of Black Flag from his jacket. (We had decided not to start the Bug Wars. We might lose.) Jim wanted to use it as a cleaner. Smelled lousy but worked great. Jim blasted away. The dial dripped with poison. Soon the black cylinder and its white numbers were as shiny as a Christmas toy.

Now all we needed were the numbers. We used the same old right, left, right pattern that worked for school lockers. This lock looked a lot like those, only bigger and tougher. And the door had a handle. We hoped the numbers were logical. That is, somehow connected to the Jeffersons. If the numbers were random, we were finished.

So, the guessing began. We used address numbers, Scotty's birthday and the date of his death. We tried assigning numbers to lots of things: family initials, holidays, the first three letters of sniper, hidden, marine and son. We tried the numbers for USC. We tried the first three letters of Trojans, football, quarterback, and defense. We tried the numbers for Dream Girl Linda and Linda Dream Girl. We tried numbers for first letters on the phrases – my secret place, hide plain sight, my only son, our only son and U.S. Marine.

My head was pounding.

We need three stupid numbers. What did Mr. Jefferson say? 'Ask me about H.I.P.S. You'll never believe what I got.' So, what did he have? He had a hidden room and a safe. The only other things he cared about were his wife and kid. And, maybe his kid the most…

We took off our masks, shook them out and put them back on. Not much help.

We headed toward the steps.

I guess we should be grateful for not getting arrested. God I sure hope we get back in the garage. Hope Tim and the twins made it. Probably mad they didn't get inside… No matter, still a cool adventure. Decker was amazing.

I reached for the handrail. Suddenly, the numbers hit me like lightning. I saw them, big as a billboard. How did we miss them? I knew immediately, as sure as I'd ever known anything. It was so easy, so right there in our faces, so in plain sight! I grabbed Andy's shoulder, looked everybody in the eye and squeaked, "I got it. I got it."

Groans.

I added some fire. "It's another H.I.P.S. Come on."

I pulled everybody back to the safe, more groans. "Try 12, 15, 23."

Andy spun the numbers and pulled the handle… Like magic… Click!

Nobody moved. Everybody talked at once.

"How'd you know?"

"Where'd you get those numbers?"

"How'd you do it?"

My mask couldn't hide the grin. "Scotty's jersey numbers: 12 in junior high, 15 in high school and the number he woulda had at USC, 23."

Andy grinned too. "From now on, we call you, 'Frank.'"

I smiled big. "'Mr. Hardy', to you."

Andy took a shallow breath, pulled the door wide and we flooded the inside with light.

We were blinking and sputtering, staring holes through what looked like an empty box. I was ready to cuss and I was going to do a good job. But, I never got a chance.

Andy was closest and he saw them first: two large tan envelopes each with a metal clasp and a chunky pink diary with a button snap. At first, I thought I saw an overweight wallet and for a moment I could see cash busting out of it.

But, a stronger look and my fortune faded…

Andy was quick. "Whatever we got, this is it. Too dirty in here. We gotta get out."

He stuffed both envelopes inside his shirt and tossed the diary to Shane who shoved it inside his jacket. Jim closed the safe and we left as we had come.

****

We didn't know the time, but the outside was as we left it: cold, dark, wet and exciting. The original plan was to return Decker's stuff but he was nowhere to be found and the walkie-talkie was out of range. The Oleanders were inside the fence, no help. Destruction here tomorrow.

Suddenly, a car screamed around the corner, headlights on high, tires slamming the curb, scorched rubber in the air.

We froze: Deer in the headlights. The car froze too, twenty feet from us. Nothing moved. Not us. Not the car.

Why don't they get out?

The car was black inside. No bugs in the light beam, only sparkles. The engine shut off but the lights stayed on and still nobody moved.

Why don't they get out?

Andy's shirt pocket crackled and I almost jumped out of my skin. Then, I heard that voice.

"Hey, boys, need a lift?"

Immediately, we were throwing words like rocks.

"Decker, as soon as this is over, I'm gonna kill you!"

"I'll get the gun!"

"I'll buy the bullets!"

We moved toward the car. Decker shut off his lights and giggled. "Now, boys, settle down. We're all on the same team. You know I can't leave you out here with lions and tigers and bears. Never forgive myself if somethin' happened." He winked. "Just came by for my stuff. Looks like perfect timing. Put everything in the trunk, hop in and I'll take you home."

I got in the front seat. "Decker, I should slug you."

He winked and grinned. "I wouldn't do that. Just hurt your hand."

The back seat agreed and so did I. Decker dropped us one block from Shane's and asked if we'd found anything. We mentioned the envelopes, but played them down. We agreed to meet at the GAD tomorrow after the lunch crowd. Decker wanted to talk. That's all he would say.

The biggest surprise? He would pay for lunch.

****

We took two steps into Shane's backyard and lights flashed in his parents' room.

Shane whispered, "Quick, follow me."

He went straight to the flower bed and unzipped his fly. In a minute or so, Shane's dad stepped out, grumbled and reminded us that he had said no going outside.

Shane looked over his shoulder. "We all had to go at once, so we figured outside was better."

His dad nodded, grumbled some more and told us to hurry up. Thank God he couldn't see us clearly. We used the water hose to wash our hands and faces and took time to get as much gunk off our clothes as possible. Not good at all, but better than nothing. Inside our sleeping bags again, it was fun to tell Tim and the twins our story (or most of it) and to hear theirs.

It was just as we thought. When police showed up from two directions, they thought we were goners. Tim slugged the hatch closed with a shovel (like Paul Bunyan chopping a forest in half) and they dove for the bushes. They saw the police go in the shelter, come out and close the hatch.

Back in the garage, our outside guys wanted answers. Andy grinned in the dark, said it was ordinary magic and a secret that must never be told. To our great delight, "must never be told" drove them absolutely nuts.

Andy placed the envelopes and diary in the "Losing Scotty" box. Sleep came quickly.

Chapter 37
Pictures, Reports, Letters and Surprises

MORNING CAME FAST. We dragged our sleeping bags outside, emptied them and broomed each other off. Shane's mom offered toast and eggs, but we went for cold cereal and ate like wolves. She also stuck a letter in Shane's pocket and said he could read it later. Back in the garage, we rolled sleeping bags and put the room in order.

Andy dug out the envelopes and diary. Energy buzzing, we gathered around the pool table. We agreed to look at stuff as a team, take our time, lay everything out and check things one at a time. Shane grabbed his note book. Andy bent the clasp on the first envelope and flooded the table.

Here is Shane's list.

1. Fifteen black and white crime scene photos. Police Report

2. News clippings on suicide

3. Coroner's Report.

4. Obituary (original + newspaper clips)

5. Dr.'s Report on Scotty's mom, Evelyn. (Sections blacked out)

6. Suicide note.

We handled everything carefully. The pictures grabbed us. They had a power. They pulled and pushed and hit. We couldn't look and we couldn't look away: the bloody mess on Scotty's bed, part of the back of his head gone. It was scary and strange. Black and white didn't seem real. The prints were too shiny. Death seemed bigger than life. Everything posed.

But, things also seemed too real. In a few shots, Scotty looked normal: sprawled on the bed (on his back), head turned left, silver chain and key hanging from his neck, suicide note on his desk.

One photo showed Scotty's mom being pulled away from his bed. Covered in what must have been blood, she stared into the camera, eyes open and empty, looking as dead as her son, her hair and make-up untouched.

These images slammed and we reacted. The twins and Tim left. Jim laughed and ran out. Shane glanced and kept writing. Andy narrated. I felt sick.

The first time through the stack, only Andy spoke and only a phrase or two. My throat ached.

The second and third time through, we asked questions. Why was Mr. Jefferson nowhere to be seen? Scotty's shoes were carefully placed next to his dresser, why? Why was a diary lying next to him? Why were his shirt buttons torn? Why was he wearing street clothes, wasn't he just at a practice? Why a bowl of ashes, shreds of lined paper and a used matchbook near his shoes? Why was he clutching a silver St. Joseph medallion in his left hand?

We swarmed the police report. It confirmed, but added little to the neighborhood stories. Mrs. Jefferson reported that Scotty came in from passing drills at the junior college about 4:00 PM and went directly to his room. She heard the front door open and close and heard him hit the stairs. He did not speak to her, but that was not unusual. He had been "having girlfriend troubles" for some weeks. But, in the last week or so, he had "snapped out of it and was acting much more like his old self." It was a very good sign that he had gone to passing practice. 15 or 20 minutes later, she heard two loud bangs, rushed upstairs, found him dead and laid next to him. At approximately 5:15 PM, Mr. Jefferson entered the house, called for his wife and son, found them and immediately called the police.

The officer noted that Mr. Jefferson reported these events and gave background. And, although Mrs. Jefferson spoke to her husband when he found her, once the officers arrived, she was "unresponsive." Paramedics transported her to the mental health floor of the County hospital.

Neighbors confirmed the timeline of Scotty coming home, the loud noise and Mr. Jefferson's arrival. The death appeared to be suicide, a self-inflicted GSW. The apparent murder weapon, a .38 caliber pistol, two shots recently fired, registered to the victim's father. The son, a licensed and experienced hunter, had access to his father's gun cabinet. No signs of a struggle. The first shot, either an accident or practice, lodged a bullet in the bedroom ceiling. Personal effects included a wallet with seven dollars, a current driver's license, a student ID, a couple of pictures of a blonde, some change and a card for Richard Diamond, Private Detective. The victim's keys were recovered from his truck's ignition. Officers will contact Richard Diamond.

We were stopped in our tracks by the signature at the bottom of the report.

Officer, Ray Riley.

****

The doctor's report on Scotty's mom had "CONFIDENTIAL" stamped all over it, huge sections blacked out. Some words were highlighted in yellow.

Depressive disorder... psychotic depression... splitting... dissociative processes... psychic decompensation... danger to self... structured environment... suicidal risk... Electroconvulsive Therapy (ECT)...

This looked like a foreign language. We understood only a few words. *Depressive, danger-to-self* and *suicidal risk,* but they were enough.

****

The news stories, the obituary and the Coroner's Report offered nothing new. In fact, there was no public mention of Linda. Scotty was simply described as "depressed" during the weeks before his death. The Coroner ruled death by suicide, self-inflicted GSW.

Why did the newspapers ignore the Linda part of Scotty's story?

****

The suicide note made us think.

Mom and Dad,

Forgive me. This is not what I wanted. I tried everything and there is nothing left. I will end all of the trouble and pain here. This is no one's fault. What's done cannot be undone. This is my choice. I love you. Please believe me.

Linda, I love you. No matter what they made you do. We will be together again.

Scotty

351

2 Samuel 12:23

We were spinning. Who were 'they' and what did they make Linda do? Did Scotty find her before he died? Why did she leave? Did something happen to her? Did she refuse to return or did 'they' stop her? What else did Scotty try that didn't work? What about 2 Samuel 12:23?

Shane chased down a Bible and read 2 Samuel 12:23.

"But now he is dead, wherefore should I fast? Can I bring him back again? I shall go to him, but he shall not return to me."

Too confusing...

Shane left to call Father Phillip.

We repacked the first envelope and decided to check out the pink diary. It appeared to be the one in the photo. Underneath its button snap rested a small lock. Andy went to the "Losing Scotty" stuff, retrieved the small wooden box we nearly crushed so long ago and fished out a tiny silver key. It looked like a perfect fit. The lock wasn't rusted and the key wasn't bent or chipped. Still, it didn't work. We tried again and again.

Suddenly, Andy grabbed the envelope, fished through the crime scene photos and we compared the key hanging from Scotty's neck to the one in our hands. The key in the photo was the key in front of us. There was still only one problem. It did not fit. No amount of pushing, twisting or re-trying helped. We huffed, put away the little box and key and stuffed the picture in the envelope.

We were talking about breaking the lock when Shane entered waving his notes.

"I got the story from Father Phillip and one other really cool thing."

We dropped the diary for the moment and listened.

"It's about Israel's King David and his newborn son. The baby is sick and the king begs God to save him. The king does everything he can, wears scratchy old rags, rolls in the dirt and gets covered with horse crap. All to show God that he will do anything to save the kid. But, it's too late and the kid dies."

Andy jumped the story.

He was about to eat his hat. "Hey, what's goin' on? Why was it too late?"

Shane waved his arms. "Let me finish."

Andy asked, "Did God bring the baby back to life later?"

Shane shook his head. "No! Let me finish. The king did wrong in the first place. The baby's mother was another man's wife and the king stole her and had the husband killed. So, this stuff ain't right from the start."

"How'd he get the guy killed?"

Shane shrugged. "Hey, how do I know? Do I look like a priest? Just read the stupid story, okay?"

"Okay, just tell the story."

"Well, that's basically it. All the king says is that the kid can't come to him, so someday he will go to the kid."

"You mean, like when he's dead."

"Yeah, that's it. Father Phillip says there's a bunch of other complicated stuff, but that's what it's about."

Andy shook his head. "Seems like a rotten deal for the kid."

I agreed. "Yeah, rotten all around. I mean, how good is it for the kid even if he lives? Everybody knows his father is a murderer and his mother's a cheat. Being king and queen don't matter."

Suddenly, it hit like lightening. We looked at each other.

Andy was now up and pacing. "Holy crap!"

This changed everything. There was new energy in the room. Now we might get some real answers. Andy grabbed the second envelope and began opening the clasp. But, Shane wanted to pull things one at a time, slow down, take our time. I agreed. Andy shrugged, gently pulled the first item and dropped it on the pool table.

A letter addressed to Richard and Evelyn Jefferson, postmarked 6/18/54, two days before Scotty's death. Andy opened it and read.

****

Dear Mom and Dad,

I was the one who took the money. There was no robber. I just made things look like it. I am sorry. I knew it was wrong, but I had to. I knew you'd never go along. I'm sorry. I know how hard you had to work for $1,000.

I hired a private investigator to find Linda. She is innocent in all of this. She never wanted to hurt me. There are things she could not control. She has no part in what I am doing. She knows nothing. I have not seen her or talked to her. But, I know what happened to her.

None of this is your fault. It's mine. Maybe someday you can forgive me. I love you.

Scotty

Shane scratched his head, Andy paced and I read the letter aloud again. If Scotty had not seen Linda or talked to her, he must have learned something from the private eye. But, what? Was it worth $1,000 or did it just take forever to find her?

Another dead end.

I looked at Shane and suddenly remembered. "Hey, when you came in you said you got something 'really cool' from Father Phillip. We were so cranked on the diary and the Bible thing and you never told us."

Shane's eyes sparkled. "I also asked him about St. Joseph. In the pictures, Scotty was wearing that medal."

We nodded. Shane read from his notes. "St. Joseph is the patron saint of fathers, those in doubt, those seeking social justice and children, including the unborn."

Andy took off his hat, wiped his forehead. "I know what we're all thinkin'. But, let's just keep goin' 'til we empty the envelope."

We agreed. Andy fished the bottom of the envelope and pulled out two tangled silver chains. One held a new, antique-silver St. Joseph medal showing a kind man holding a happy child, the other a small silver key. They appeared to be the chains around Scotty's neck in the crime photos.

We went for the diary and tried the small silver key. The tiny lock clicked open. Andy hesitated and handed me the fat, leather-covered book.

"You read it. We'll listen."

I opened the book. A chunk of pages had been ripped from the binding. I began reading the inside cover, dated a little more than a month before Scotty's death. It was written in tiny, near-perfect, print.

5/29/54

Dear Scotty,

If you are reading this, you have met my step-brother, Ralph, Ralph Riley. He is bringing this to you as a favor to me He doesn't know exactly what's in it. I mean, he hasn't read it. As you can tell, this is not a diary.

First, I am sorry. I never meant to hurt you. At first, being with you was fun. I felt young and important. Now, it seems as if I've ruined almost everything in my life. Today, I wouldn't blame you if you hated me.

You deserved better than a disappearance. But, I had no choice. I wanted to protect myself as well as you. I gave you no warning, because I had none. I am writing this because you deserve some explanation.

My husband…

The page ended in mid-sentence. I studied the ragged roots of the torn pages. The next to the last page was blank. It was crooked and stuck to the inside back cover. I carefully lifted the crooked page and continued reading…

My heart is breaking, but there are things bigger than you and me. I have a family and my kids deserve their family, including their father. You have a family and a great life ahead. You and your family deserve that.

My husband knows about us. Not all the details, I'm sure, but enough. Enough to threaten me with divorce and taking away my kids, unless I "get things right." The truth is he's right. I never should have put all of us through this. The other part of the truth is that you deserve better than me. My feelings for you were and are real, but they are not enough. Our happiness can't be built on a broken family. Somewhere in the back of my mind, I think I always knew that. I know that you can't forgive me, but I pray that you can forget me.

There is something I have to do. I have asked my step-brother, Ralph to help us stay away from each other. Please destroy this book. Don't try to contact me. I am never coming back. This is best for everyone.

Linda Riley Robinson

Wow… Another bombshell. Linda and Ralph Riley? Then, Ray must also know about everything. It was quiet for a minute.

Shane said it best, "I bet Ray and Ralph were those guys on the phone, the ones who didn't want us messing around the Jefferson place. But, let's just keep going 'til we've looked at everything."

We agreed and wasted no time. Something else clicked, like another good number on that combination lock.

I just threw my words out there. "The burned and shredded paper in the bowl next to Scotty's shoes is what's left of the pages ripped from the diary."

Andy pulled a thick stack of papers from the envelope under the letterhead:

Richard Diamond
Private Investigations
Los Angeles, California.

A note was attached.

Kid,

It's all here. More details than when we talked. My secretary got it word for word. Listen Kid, these people are evil. And while we can't stop evil, once in a while we can punch it in the mouth, give it a black eye or knock out a few teeth. And, while it's not enough because nothing ever will be, it's still the best we can do in this world.

One more thing. Kid, read this once and destroy it. Walk away from it. If you can't, it'll destroy you. We can't kill evil, Kid but it can kill us.

R. D.

Ps. $100 is going to St. Joseph's Church as you wanted. This is the only file.

The first page in the file was an eye-catcher, a photo stapled to the cover page: A woman wearing a headscarf, dark glasses and a large overcoat leaving through the backdoor of a run-down warehouse. She was making her way through a dump.

$1,000 buys a lot of information. The thing read like a Bogart movie.

The woman in the photo is Linda Riley Robinson. Shortly after it was taken, she fell to the ground, unconscious and bleeding. I carried her to my car and laid her in the back seat. I took her car keys. She was bleeding badly and I had no way to stop it.

I rushed her to a doctor, but she had lost a lot of blood. I thought she might be dead. My cloth seats were soaked. I called Sam, my secretary, and told her to wait three hours, get a girlfriend and come to the hospital. Pick up Linda's keys at the Nurse's Station, go to the address in my note and get Linda's car. In an hour or so, I paid the hospital $100 and left. Linda was critical, but stable.

I went back to the warehouse. I picked the lock, slipped down a dark, narrow hallway into a small dirty room: sink, wooden table, couple of chairs, one naked bulb hanging overhead, walls sweating. The place smelled like boiled vegetables and day old stuff. There was a stainless steel pan on the floor in the far corner. I forced myself to look.

I didn't have long to wait. They returned singing, laughing and drinking: two fat, greasy people. I waited in a dark corner while they seated themselves and took a blast or two from the bottle. They were pretty far gone.

I planned to break up the room, throw a good scare into 'em and get Linda's money back. But, then I saw the pan in the corner. I thought about the blood-soaked seats. These people weren't just pathetic parasites, they were evil. I would give them better than they gave the baby but not much.

I stepped from the shadows and confronted them. They gave slack twisted drunken denials. I doubled him over with a body shot to the gut. As he toppled, I crushed his nose with an overhand right. Blood everywhere. Another straight, short left cracked his eye socket. She screamed and I slapped her, hard. She shut up.

He was trying to get to his knees. I turned and debated, and then delivered a full-force kick to the groin. He was on his knees alright, but he was out. His forehead thumped the concrete, like a nice hollow pumpkin. I mentioned to her that he might need to see a 'specialist.'

I pulled chairs to the table, slammed her into one and sat across from her. We had a friendly talk. She told me that they had charged Linda $100, that she was 14-16 weeks along and that the fetus was a male. She said that Linda cried, called the baby 'Scotty' and left. She claimed that Linda was not bleeding. I told her I wanted the $100 back. She reached for her purse and I motioned for her to hand it over. I emptied it on to the table. A small-caliber pistol and fists-full of money spilled out. My secretary counted it later, $10,000. I slipped the pistol in my pocket.

For the record, I left on poor terms. As I reached the door, she hit me over the head from behind with a chair. The chair blew up. I turned and slugged her once, solid and hard. I hurt my hand, but I broke her jaw and took out a few teeth. She spun and dropped next to her boyfriend. I ripped the phone out of the wall, broke the light bulb and closed the door.

Minus expenses, the remainder of the $10,000 will go to the Catholic Home for Unwed Mothers in Los Angeles.

Also, for the record, I met with you at a diner near your home soon after these events and discussed them with you. This report reflects that conversation. No further information will be provided about these people or their whereabouts.

R.D.

The rest of the pages in the stack included billing records, daily travel notes, interviews with the missing woman's friends and family and a timeline of her activities from the time she left until the day he found her. It seems that Linda's husband, Guy, was also looking for her and Diamond had done some background on him as well.

Lastly, our jaws dropped. Diamond charged his regular hourly rate for time spent "thinking" about a case.

We were glassy-eyed.

How cool is that?

Andy reached into the envelope one last time. Out came one more business envelope sealed and labeled: "To Whom It May Concern."

Andy opened it and read.

To Whom It May Concern:

I am writing to set the record straight. If you are reading this, you have discovered my safe and its combination. Congratulations. I left this house because it went from a dream to a nightmare. In the end, this house stood for death, the death of not only my dreams, but of everyone that mattered to me. My son is dead and in the ground. My wife is dead with her eyes open. I will never see my grandson.

I have learned one thing. I know how to watch things die. Love and hate are no match for death. In the war, I learned to walk away. I am going to walk away now. I will change my name and build another life in a different place.

Richard Jefferson

Andy heaved a monster sigh. Shane and I just sat, not enough energy to move a ladybug. I suggested we pack all the stuff away and get to the GAD. Andy shuffled pictures and Shane straightened papers. I picked up the big envelope and held it open.

Suddenly, a large, color photo flipped out. In a lush, green, sundrenched meadow stood a group of four men and one woman, all smiling. The four men were armed with crossbows and the woman was holding a paper target. There was no date, but names were listed left to right: Scotty, Richard, Linda, Ray and Ralph. "One big happy family." (Evelyn is taking the picture.)

Andy pointed and yelled, "That's him! That's the guy I saw in Scotty's bedroom and the guy I saw comin' out of the diner!"

He was pointing to Ralph Riley, Ray's brother and Linda's step-brother. Things now started to fall in place. The truth was going off like popcorn, answers coming fast and furious.

Shane fired first. Then, it became a free for all. "Ralph was the shooter. It was his job to protect Linda. He knew why she had to go away. Maybe she even told him. He thought there was something on the Jefferson place that would give away her secret. Dumping a guy is one thing, but killing a baby is another. He couldn't let that come out."

Andy was almost running around the room. "The voices on the party line were Ray and Ralph. Ray probably knew as much as his brother, but wasn't as close to Linda. Then again, maybe the secret was just between Ralph and Linda. And, Ralph's not from here and we don't know where he came from."

Shane was also on to Ray and Ralph. "Ray and Ralph were looking for something hidden, something revealing the secret and they were afraid somebody else might find it. That's why Ralph was up in Scotty's room."

I saw another connection. "There were two different guys who met with Scotty in the diner. One was Diamond and the other was Ralph when he delivered the diary. The diner is the safest place to meet. No danger of bumping into parents or troubles with nosey neighbors."

Andy chimed in. "Kinda like another Hide In Plain Sight thing."

Everybody nodded. Things were rolling downhill now. Suddenly, I understood the 'problem below/answer above' stuff.

I took my time. "The problem—the death of the baby—is hidden below, in the safe in the secret room. The answer is above—with God, one way or the other, once you're dead."

Andy's hat was off. "Whadaya mean, 'one way or the other?'"

"I mean, whether ya go to heaven or hell, it's over and God has settled it."

Shane jumped in. "It's complicated, like Father Phillip said. If innocent babies go to God, then you can be with them in heaven. If they don't go to God, if they just die, then you can be with them in death."

Andy hung his head. "So, Scotty blew himself away because of the baby—not because he lost Linda?"

I saw other little pieces. "It's all about the baby. That stuff on the back of the Richard Diamond card was about the baby: 'his name was Scotty.' 'The Ans. Is y.' means the answer is yes. The question was about the baby. Did she get an abortion? 'It is a sin' was about killing the baby. The smudged numbers are the date that Diamond left the card."

I opened the big envelope one more time. We filled it and headed to the diner. We got to the street and decided to take one piece of evidence with us. Andy went back to get it and caught up with us easily.

****

The Great American Diner was better than great. It was perfect and it was American and so were we. Daisy was smiling and shining and the lights were twinkling. The fog and the frosted windows made everything inside even better. Decker was waiting for us with his own big smile. He was sitting in a booth near the window, his chair folded against the wall. He raised his Coke in a salute. I sat next to him on his left, everybody else across.

He put his arm around my shoulder and never stopped smiling. "Hey, Einsteins."

Andy took the bait. "Why Einsteins? You usually hit us with a one, two punch."

Decker waved to Daisy. "Well, today is a day for three not two. So, I considered Pep Boys or Marx Brothers, but today is mostly about you guys bein' smart. So, I came up with Einsteins."

Shane grinned. "I like it better than 'Hey Alberts.'"

We laughed and laughed and laughed. Daisy came and took our order. She said she knew we had stuff to tell and she would catch up in twenty-five minutes. For the next ten minutes, we rained information on Decker but saved the hidden room trick for last. He said it had been driving him crazy.

Once everything was out, Decker grinned from ear to ear, shook his head and offered only one word. "Amazing."

We had to agree. After all, Decker was buying. Daisy delivered our order and squeezed a quick explanation out of us about the picture.

She shook her head and pointed to me. "Save me a spot. I'll be back in 15 minutes and I'll bring dessert."

The fifteen minutes flew and Daisy was back with dessert and sitting next to me. Trudy brought her coffee and we went through everything start to finish. It was a three-cups-of-coffee trip. She was angry that there was no way to punish Ralph for hurting Rocket.

Decker's eyes sparkled. "Like Diamond says, can't stop evil, but once in a while we can punch it in the mouth. After all, the secret Ralph tried to protect is out."

Shane said, "One of the first things we found was Scotty's gold ID bracelet with the initials SJ + LL. Why LL? Who's LL? Did he really have another girlfriend?"

It was quiet.

Decker held up both hands and took charge. "Gentlemen, and lady, allow me. Scotty did not have another girlfriend. This part of the mystery is easy." He held up his glass in a toast. "Here's to Lovely Linda."

Glasses clinked. Suddenly, Daisy grabbed the picture of the shooters and told us to wait. She was at the grill bending Reggie's ear and pointing to the picture. He was nodding, flipping burgers and shaking fry baskets all at once. After a minute or so, he called the other cook over and stepped into his office with Daisy.

She returned, but did not sit. Instead, she grinned. "Before you leave today, we have a contest for you."

Eyes sparkling, she apologized to Decker. He was too old. He smiled graciously and nodded.

"Now," she sparkled, "I'm going to think of a number between 1 and 100. You each get a guess. Think hard. It's a very good gift."

Our faces were barely big enough to hold our smiles.

Shane guessed 12, Andy guessed 15 and I stuck with 23. Daisy reached into her pocket and pulled out three shiny playing cards, each an Ace of Hearts with a detailed color replica of the Great American Diner on the back.

She handed one to each of us. "You are all winners. Reggie is very proud of you."

She explained that our names were stamped on the back of the card along with today's date a year from now. The card entitled us to one free meal per week for one year with a guest. It included a drink and dessert.

Andy asked, "How do we mark it off when we use it for that week?"

Daisy smiled again. "You don't. Reggie said to tell you it's the honor system. He says it's a Warrior Code thing."

We were readying to leave when Decker stopped us. Beaming like a Christmas tree, the foggy windows made him brighter. "Hey Einsteins, hold on there. I wasn't quite truthful earlier. I really did think about another name for you and I've got something for you."

He reached beneath the table and produced three hefty volumes of *The Three Musketeers* by Alexander Dumas. Each book sported a stunning dust cover: three flashing swords, three handsome men in fancy shirts, royal blue cloaks with gold fleur-de-lis, shiny black boots and matching wide-brimmed hats.

He handed each of us a book and announced, "For bravery above and beyond!"

We left the diner as full as we had ever been. Decker stopped as he was pulling out of the parking lot and we told him that we had a nickname for him, "H-Man" and that the "H" stood for "Hero." He smiled and said he'd put an H on his fishing hat.

We walked to the Jefferson place and stood across the street while the big machinery chewed it to the ground. It didn't take long. I wondered if they would bury the shelter.

And I wondered what we would do tomorrow.

Shane was staring at the ugly hole that used to be the Jefferson place. He absentmindedly stuffed his right hand in his jacket pocket and pulled out an envelope. He opened it and read the following note.

Honey,

I have some very sad news. Mrs. Kerensky called from San Francisco late last night to say that Louie died. She flew there a couple of days ago, shortly after she picked up the letters. It was an emergency flight.

She said that Louie was awake and understood every word of every letter and that he asked her to read them to him twice. She said that Louie said, 'I love those guys.' She also said the letters will be read at Louie's funeral and then buried with him at a family place in San Francisco. She said he didn't hurt. He just went to sleep.

I am so sorry that you have lost your friend. You were all so good to him.

Love, Mum

Shane did not speak. He simply handed the letter to me. I read it and gave it to Andy. Nobody spoke.

Suddenly it was very cold. Nobody moved. We kept our eyes on that big hole across the street. Andy folded the note and gave it back to Shane. We stood a while longer.

Shane said, "Louie woulda liked this hole."

Andy agreed. "He woulda liked all that bomb shelter stuff too."

I smiled. "I know somethin' else he'd like. Let's get our butts back to the GAD!"

We got to the diner quicker than is humanly possible, at least from my point of view. We hustled inside and shared the note with Daisy and Reggie. In a few short minutes we were holding another shiny Ace of Hearts with a detailed color replica of the Great American Diner. The tiny script on its face read, "Louie, The K."

Hugs went all around quickly and Reggie tried to get us to eat. Instead, we took off for Shane's house with much lighter hearts. As soon as we showed the card to Shane's mom, she cried and said she would get it in the mail to Mrs. Kerensky immediately.

As I walked home, cold on the outside, warm on the inside, I wondered about heaven and what a perfect dwarf might look like and I knew what we would do tomorrow.

We would be reading *The Three Musketeers*.

Chapter 38
Back to the Future

SUDDENLY MY CELL phone was buzzing, the retriever was pushing my shoulder with his wet black nose and the Diamonds were belting out "Little Darlin, 'castanets and all. I was having a tough time shaking my fifty year old memories to the bottom of my shoes.

All these years later, it was still a shocker that Scotty killed himself over the loss of a baby and that so much effort had gone into concealing an abortion. Of course, everything had driven him to that place; the baby was just the last straw.

The cell phone stopped ringing and a policeman pulled up behind me and parked. He shut off his engine, stepped out and walked up to my door.

He was polite, handsome and young.

They all look young, like all those baby-faced baseball players.

He asked my name and where I lived. He asked to see my license and wanted to know what brought me out to the golf course this time of day. I answered every question perfectly. I lived a few blocks away and stopped under the shade of this tree to eat a hamburger and enjoy the breeze. He mumbled my license plate into his shoulder radio and turned to me.

"We've gotten some calls from folks who say you park here often and they aren't sure what you are up to, that you look suspicious. They think you might be out here trying to pick up children or something like that."

I exploded. I laughed so hard, Cody started moving around like it was time to get out and play.

"Are you kidding," I sputtered, "I am old and crippled and I can barely walk! There is no room in this car for a child! I have been a high school teacher for forty years—a Master Teacher, a Mentor Teacher, a Teacher of the Month and a Teacher of the Year. I have taught smart kids, less smart kids and really less smart kids. I do not need to pick up a child! I've seen enough children for two lifetimes and for the record, I do not look suspicious. I look distinguished. And, this is no place to pick up children, it's an adult golf course not a miniature one."

Cody was very excited. He was not going to calm down until I did.

The young officer laughed and took a step back. "Well sir, that's the best explanation I've ever heard. I think you've got me on most of that. Forgive the interruption. We get calls out here so we come. Lots of the elderly folks in these retirement villages are easily distressed. It might help if you introduced yourself to some of the people on this street."

I grinned. "With all due respect, I'm not too hot on that idea. If these folks call the police on me for eating a hamburger, they might shoot me if I knock on a door or wave. And, unless they've all got senile dementia, I don't see how they can say they don't know me. The car is Corvette-red and I've been parking here for the last five years."

He smiled. "Yeah, I see what you mean. I enjoyed speaking with you. We get any more calls on a suspicious little red convertible over here we'll tell 'em not to worry. You have a good evening now."

"You too."

He pulled away slowly, spoke into his radio and waved. I looked at Cody. He had settled and was looking at me like he'd been cheated out of a trip to the beach.

I told him what I was thinking. "You know, he reminded me of Ray asking questions and warning us about the Jefferson place. Only this guy was smarter, better looking and far more polite."

I took Cody's silence for agreement. I was reaching for my cell to check missed calls and it buzzed. It was Frenchy Cohen. Someone had thrown glass jars of blood against his front door and a couple of bricks through a living room window. No one was hurt, but there was a threatening note wrapped around one of the bricks. A police officer had taken the report and left. Frenchy was delivering a message. His father wanted to know if I could stop by. I said I had to make one call and I would be right over.

I looked at Cody and called home. Suddenly, the golf course looked suspicious. I gave my wife the quick 3x5 card on the Cohens, both incidents and said that I would be home in an hour or so. She expressed sympathy for the Cohens and told me to be careful.

This afternoon's baseball game seemed a world away. I pulled away from the curb and pushed the accelerator.

The engine hiccupped.

I need to get out by the river. Beautiful curves and straightaways. Nobody within shouting distance. Blow this thing out.

The breeze was warm but soft and the sky was cotton candy, what we used to call sky-blue pink. I was worried about the Cohens. Name-calling was stupid but this blood and brick stuff raised the stakes.

The retriever was giving me the big eyes.

I gave 'em right back. "Hey, don't look at me, pal. You ate junk too. You're in just as much trouble as I am. And, when we get home we both better eat like there's no tomorrow!"

We came to a stop sign and I gave Cody a serious look. "Okay, you know what we gotta do? You got the story straight?" (I knew I could trust the retriever to eat.)

He stood, front feet on the console, wagged his tail and slurped my cheek.

"Good boy."

I drove a few miles, singing to the soundtrack of *The Big Chill*. Everybody sounds good in a convertible on a California summer night, especially if you are singing for a red golden retriever.

Besides, even a goldfish can sing *Sweet Home Alabama*.

I turned the corner and my heart jumped: flashing lights and police cruisers everywhere. And yellow tape…

Jesus! Help!

I pulled into the driveway and parked. Before I could open my door, a slender good looking young man, navy blue blazer, white shirt, red tie, grey slacks, black belt and matching loafers, waved me back, flashed his F.B.I. badge and asked me what business I had with the Cohens.

THE END

Author's Note

ONE OF MY favorite opening lines comes from perhaps the greatest American novel ever written, *Huckleberry Finn.* Huck begins with striking insight and honesty.

"YOU don't know about me without you have read a book by the name of *The Adventures of Tom Sawyer;* but that ain't no matter. That book was made by Mr. Mark Twain, and he told the truth, mainly. There was things which he stretched, but mainly he told the truth. That is nothing. I never seen anybody but lied one time or another…"

In *Ordinary Heroes,* I also told the truth, mainly, with some "stretchers" thrown in to make the thing taste better. Today, we call those "stretchers" poetic license. All characters are composites and some are created out of whole cloth. For plot reasons, events have also been compressed.

The narrative is based on a true story and I write with great affection for all of the folks in this story and for the 1950's of America as well. It was a magical time, a time of "ordinary magic" as Bilbo Baggins might say. The magic that allows youngsters to disappear when grown up folks come along and somehow emerge later (right in front of God and everybody) as successful adults. It was a time of fun, innocence, intrigue, excitement, dreams and danger: A time Huckleberry Finn, Tom Sawyer, Frank and Joe Hardy and even Scout Finch would have liked.

Yet, parts of this story's magic are dark and hard and that's not only the way it was, but also the way it ought to have been and always will be. It's easy to grow but growing up is another matter. Growing up is about willful intention. It never just happens and it's always hard.

Ordinary Heroes is about an All-American kid who happens to be crippled, not some crippled entity who happens to be a kid. His friends are All-American kids, too. The only difference is that sometimes their handicaps are harder to see.

As I sit here fifty years later, *Ordinary Heroes* is a salute to the courage, loyalty and goodness of boys in all times and in all places.

Even now, I close my eyes and see Sandy Koufax, Sandra Dee, Elvis, Wolfman Jack, Howdy Doody, Roy Rogers, Soupy Sales and all the guys in the neighborhood.

I also see the spooky old Jefferson house and some equally spooky bad folks.

Best Wishes,
Ron McCraw
Bakersfield, California
April, 2012

PS. You can help make Ordinary Heroes a movie! Go online to Amazon/Books, type Ron McCraw in the search box and add your comment.

Coming Soon!

A New Novel by Ron McCraw

Light Falling Like Water

An epic thriller involving gangsters, kidnapping, murder, magic and mega millions. Whiz kid Erin O' Hara entered Stanford at sixteen with a perfect SAT. She left at twenty-five with a Ph.D. in statistics, a divorce and a new baby. Today, Professor O'Hara lives with her fifteen-year-old son, Troy, deep in California's coastal Redwoods. O'Haras have called #1 Forest Lane home for one hundred and fifty years. Today, it is also home to Troy's closest friend—his beautiful multi-colored domesticated Siberian fox, Reggie.

So, what about the mysterious stranger with a dark suit, a telephoto lens and a Glock 19? Who sent the fuzzy video showing a Troy lookalike in the crosshairs? What do ex-Mafia types want with this single mom and her son? What does she know that they don't? And what is the fox's secret?

Author Biography

A SURVIVOR OF Cerebral Palsy, Ron McCraw is an award-winning retired educator and counselor. He holds a Bachelor's Degree in English, Philosophy and Education and a Master's Degree in Clinical Psychology and Theology.

He is a Nationally Certified Trainer for Self Esteem Seminars and The International Network for Families and Children.

Father of Andy, Julie and Kelsey, he currently lives in California with his wife, Marti, and his dark red golden retriever service dog, Cody.

The Old Jefferson House

Everybody leaned in.

Andy drew the moment out. He spoke slowly. "Last night, it must have been near midnight, I was walkin' home. I wasn't thinkin'. I looked up an' there I was face to face with the old Jefferson house. I froze. I think I stopped breathin.'"

Davie whispered, "What happened?"

"I dunno. I was kinda starin' at the house and then I couldn't see it. It was like it disappeared an' then came back."

"What?"

"You heard me", he snapped. "But that ain't the worst of it. I seen somebody up in that second story window. Somebody had a light on."

Through an avalanche of curses and questions, Andy made it clear that he couldn't make anything clear. He kept going back and forth: He saw something, he didn't see something, he heard a voice, he didn't hear a voice.

Jesse spat. "Shit. Let's go over there an' see. An', let's go right now, unless you ladies are scared."

Jim laughed. "You bet yer sweet ass, I'm scared. I ain't goin'. Send me a post card, pal."

There was grumbled agreement and it got very quiet. From the back corner, on the other side of the log, Tim Bradford, a kid who never said a word, suddenly declared, "I'm goin'."

It got quiet again. The argument shifted from going or not going, to going now or in the morning. Jim spoke for the morning people.

Then Jesse spoke. "Listen, jerk offs. You go ahead an' tell me there's a better damn time to do this than on Hollow-F-ing-ween."

Silence.

He looked around the room. "Shit."

Andy was matter of fact. "If we're goin', we gotta do this right."